Praise for Linda Goodnight

"The second of Goodnight's Honey Ridge novels is an aching, absorbing, yet uplifting read."
—*Booklist* on *The Rain Sparrow*

"Her beautiful storytelling, coupled with a well-crafted, poignant plot, will touch readers' hearts from the first page."
—*RT Book Reviews* on *The Memory House*

"This is a story of painful emotions, loss, grief, love and redemption. It's loaded with angst but it's quiet, smoldering angst, not in-your-face, slap you upside the head angst."
—*Dear Author* on *The Memory House*

"These characters struggle to help themselves and others, and their journeys culminate in a most satisfying resolution."
—*Bookreporter* on *The Memory House*

"This is the final installment in the Redemption River series, a truly inspiring story of overcoming trying circumstances and discovering personal strength."
—*RT Book Reviews* on *The Last Bridge Home*, 4½ stars

"From its sad, touching beginning to an equally moving conclusion, *A Touch of Grace* will keep you riveted."
—*RT Book Reviews*, 4½ stars, Top Pick

"*The Heart of Grace*, by Linda Goodnight, is a wonderfully poignant story with excellent character development."
—*RT Book Reviews*, 4½ stars

The
INNKEEPER'S
Sister

LINDA
GOODNIGHT

ISBN-13: 978-0-373-79947-3

The Innkeeper's Sister

Copyright © 2017 by Linda Goodnight

The Innkeeper's Sister and all of the Honey Ridge novels
are dedicated to the memory of my son, Travis Goodnight,
a young man who made a big difference in his short life.

I will always, always miss you, Trav, but as your brother reminds me,
we are now 827 days closer to seeing you again in Heaven.
Won't that be a glorious day? Love you forever.

Any fool can be happy. It takes a man with real heart to make beauty out of the stuff that makes us weep.

CLIVE BARKER

CHAPTER 1

Present Day. Honey Ridge, Tennessee

Secrets are like boils. They fester and throb, but until the hard core of truth is released, there is no relief.

Valery Carter lived every day with that festered, throbbing boil.

With trowel in hand, she poked at the weeds springing up around headstones tilted and shrunken by time. The Portland family cemetery hadn't been used as burial grounds in a century, but something about its quiet dignity, about the way it had honored the dead for nearly two hundred years, compelled Valery to tend the small space. Hidden to the south of Peach Orchard Inn in a quiet, shady glen, the gravestones had long since faded to either barely visible or impossible to decipher.

Four of the graves haunted her. Baby graves. She couldn't leave them unattended. Charlotte Portland Gadsden, who'd lived through the Civil War clinging with delicate British fingers to this land and the antebellum mansion that now housed Peach Orchard Inn, had lost four children and buried them here, marking their tiny graves with white stones, now gray, and the dates of their births. Only one infant had survived more than a day. Anna Cornelia had breathed five days before the angels carried her away.

Tiny baby, pink and pretty and helpless. Five days wasn't enough for Anna to know how desperately her mother had loved her.

Valery rubbed a gloved hand over Anna's headstone, scraping away the bird droppings and lichens, tracing the name with her fingertip. She dug fresh dirt to bolster the tilting stone and removed every weed that tried to hide the memory of the baby's short life. The knock-out roses she'd planted last year looked dead, but she remained as hopeful as the bluebird flitting through the trees in search of a nesting place. Babies deserved sunny daffodils and sweet pink roses.

She felt a kinship with the lost babies and with the mother who had, no doubt, knelt in this very spot to weep and mourn and wonder why.

Tears blurred Valery's vision. She understood a little about weeping and wondering why, about bearing the unalterable. Perhaps that explained her affinity for the cemetery every bit as much as her need to numb the memory.

She knew she had a problem. What she didn't have was a solution. Julia and Mama frowned their disapproval, but Lord forbid either of them sit down for a long discussion. Mama claimed Valery would be happier if she attended church more often, otherwise feigning ignorance as if she wasn't as much to blame as Valery. Julia simply pretended the problem didn't exist. The elephant in the room loomed large in the Carter family.

The Carter women held their secrets close to the vest, even the ones they didn't know.

A capricious wind rustled the overhead tree branches so that they rubbed together like dry bones. Valery shivered against the chill, though not from superstition or fear. The cemetery was a place of peace and rest for her as much as for the generations of Portlands and a few Civil War soldiers who'd died at Peach Orchard, then a thriving farm. Except for the deep, festering boil that ached continually, Valery was, she sometimes thought, as dead as they were. She'd felt alive once, but she didn't dwell there any longer.

Inside her zippered fleece jacket the cell phone vibrated. She sat back on her heels, pulled off a glove and fished the device from her pocket.

Don't forget, the text read, guests arriving at four.

Playing hostess at the bed-and-breakfast was Valery's responsibility today, but even when Julia was away in Knoxville with her new husband and son, she worried that Valery would let her down.

Sad but true. She'd let them all down in so many ways, most of all herself, but she still clung to her sister's new marital happiness as proof that she *could* do something worthwhile. Hadn't she been the one to exonerate Eli, Julia's husband, and save him from another prison term?

She sighed heavily. None of that mattered. She was who she was.

It was hours yet until four o'clock and the guests' arrival. Julia's vote of no confidence loomed loud and clear.

She texted back. Got it covered.

Shoving the device back inside her jacket, Valery rose, touched each little stone and murmured soft reassurances to the babies before turning toward Peach Orchard Inn—the house where all four had been born and all four had died.

"This place is a disaster."

Grayson Blake cast a doubtful glance toward his brother and then toward the old gristmill, a relic of days gone by—*many* days gone by—on the outskirts of Honey Ridge, Tennessee.

Grass and weeds choked the entrance, the roof sagged, the water wheel was a tangled mess of moss and rust.

And good grief! Was that a snake sunning himself on the rocky walking path?

"I've wanted this place since I was a kid." His brother, Devlin, leaned forward in the seat of the Jeep, every bit as eager as he'd been twenty years ago when they'd spent summers in Honey Ridge with Grandma and Pappy. "It's perfect for a restaurant. It's historic, quaint, magical—"

"Falling down," Grayson muttered.

"A minor inconvenience. Just look at those bones and this incredible setting." Devlin's hands waved in exuberant demonstration. "Right across the road from Peach Orchard Inn, close to the river and to town. People have to eat as well as sleep, don't they? And the feasibility studies looked promising. Envision the possibilities, my skeptical brother."

When Devlin got like this, Grayson knew he should stop arguing and let his brother run until he ran out of gas, but Grayson was the oldest and the most rational. Devlin was a wild man.

"Requires more thought," Grayson said. And his overriding thought was to hit the road, get out while he could, because if he didn't, his brother would suck him into another money pit that gave him ulcers and kept him pushing a pencil all hours of the night.

"Remember the funeral parlor?" Devlin cocked an eyebrow, black as sin's underbelly and every bit as devilish.

Grayson snorted. Devlin knew when to toss out successes like throwing free bubble gum from a parade float. A piece here and there to generate enthusiasm.

"I remember."

"And the jail and the rusty railroad car and the bank with private dining in the former vault."

Grayson held up both hands in a double stop sign. His platinum watch glinted in the sun. Out of long habit, he glanced at the hands. Time was money, and they had already been in the small rural town of Honey Ridge for two hours without accomplishing much.

He sighed. "Must I admit it?"

"A little humility will do you good," Devlin said, crossing his arms over the suit and tie he wore only when Grayson warned him they might have to wrangle with locals who didn't want an influx of strangers into their quiet countryside. Proper image, in Grayson's view, was power.

Grayson released a huff, but his cheeks twitched. "You were right."

All those unlikely, falling down, pathetic venues had been converted by the Blake brothers into successful restaurants. People flocked to the unusual.

"And I'm right about this one, too. You'll see."

Their brotherly business partnership had coalesced during their college days when they'd flipped houses to pay tuition and buy the occasional beer and pizza. Creating restaurants had, quite simply, evolved. Grayson and Devlin Blake, the nerd and the adventurer. Like peanut butter and jelly, they were as different as could be, but together the brotherly combo worked.

"Want to take a look?" Devlin reached for the door handle.

"I *am* looking."

"Up close. Inside. Come on, let's check it out."

Since Devlin was already out of the Jeep and picking his way through the dead vines and dagger-like weeds, Grayson exited, too. He might as well. Devlin was going in, heedless of danger or the fact that they had no authority to do so.

"We could get arrested," he called to his brother's back.

Dev held up a hand but didn't turn around. "Wouldn't be the first time."

Grayson snorted. "Maybe not for you."

Devlin had been busted the first time right here in Honey Ridge for trespassing at the ripe old age of nine. He'd climbed old lady Pennington's fence to release a pen full of pedigreed dogs.

"I couldn't let those puppies suffer, could I?"

If he'd considered the animals in peril Grayson would have gone along with Devlin's harebrained rescue attempt. "They weren't suffering."

"I thought they were."

True. That was Devlin. If he thought an injustice existed, he was right in the middle of it, usually to his and to Grayson's detriment. In the case of the puppies, Grayson had warned Devlin that no puppy mill existed on the grand estate of Mary-belle Pennington, but his tenderhearted brother had seen an animal rights TV special and could not be deterred. That the boys were nine and eleven could have had something to do with their naïve enthusiasm. Grayson, as Pappy always said, had been born old and wise for the express purpose of look-ing after his impetuous younger brother. Old and wise mean-ing stodgy and serious.

Up ahead, Devlin tromped on, shoving aside low-hanging branches and avoiding a thorny vine. Grayson wasn't so lucky.

The vine slapped his cheek and scraped deep, stinging.

He touched the spot and came away with blood. "I'm wounded. Let's give up the venture."

"Don't wimp out. The end is in sight."

Smiling now, enjoying, as he always did, the brotherly yin and yang that flowed between the two of them and made them who they were.

"Hey!" Devlin came to a sudden stop.

"What?" Grayson trotted to catch up, trying not to consider that he'd probably itch half the night.

"I thought I saw someone in that window."

Grayson peered up at the dirty glass above them on the second floor. "I don't see anyone. Maybe a trick of the light and shadows."

"Maybe." Dev didn't sound convinced. "The woman at the courthouse said the place was haunted." He pointed. "Someone thinks so. There's a bottle tree to capture the haints."

Grayson peered at the strange apparatus, a collection of cobalt blue bottles inverted on the branches of a dying tree. "Superstitions."

"Or someone doesn't want people exploring, and the bottle tree is a kind of no-trespassing warning to scare people off."

"In which case, you and I should not be here."

"Sure we should. Come on." Devlin pushed at a set of tall, heavy, graying doors. They creaked open on rusty hinges to reveal a dark, dank interior. Devlin grinned. "Creepy."

"You love it."

"Absolutely. Remember when we were kids and explored this place? Scared the pants off me."

"That didn't keep you away." Or him, for that matter. Where Devlin went, Grayson felt compelled to follow, and more than once they'd both ended up in hot water.

"I like being scared."

Grayson barked a short laugh. The sound echoed eerily through the dark interior.

"I'm not sure about this, Dev." He bounced a foot gingerly against the floor. "The mill's in a lot worse condition now than it was when we were teens. Could be unsafe."

Devlin, as usual, was full speed ahead and already inside the mill looking around with a rapt expression on his face, the one that said he was seeing the finished product. He had a gift that way, and Grayson had learned to follow his creative lead.

Grayson tapped the walls, smoothed a hand over the ancient lumber. "Aged oak, hard as a rock. We could salvage enough to give the place character and age."

Devlin spun around. "So, you're on board?"

"Let's say I'm softening to the idea."

Devlin's teeth flashed as he pumped his eyebrows. "Want to have a look upstairs and in the basement?"

"If we're going to get arrested, we might as well get our money's worth."

"We won't get arrested. You taking notes?"

Grayson gave his brother a quelling look. He never left home without the high-tech gear of business. The tablet was in the Jeep, but his smartphone would do. "Do you have to ask?"

Wielding a penlight, Devlin jogged lightly up the stairs as if they weren't rickety and two hundred years old. "Get a load of this."

Grayson came up beside him. "Your ghost sleeps in a sleeping bag."

The large open space was mostly empty, whatever milling equipment once used here gone except for a rusted conglomeration of overheard pulleys. On the floor in one corner near the dirt-caked window was a well-used sleeping bag, a hubcap of water, and an assortment of empty plastic containers.

"Squatters?"

"Maybe kids camping out for the scare effect," Grayson said. "We did that once, remember?"

"No, we didn't. I wanted to, but you wussed out. You had a crush on some girl and thought you'd see her if you hung around the Dairy Queen."

Grayson wagged his head. "That was you, Romeo."

"No, no. I remember well. It was the summer before—" Devlin stopped, grimaced "—you know."

"Yeah." Dev knew he didn't like to talk about that time or the difficult year to follow when Devlin had returned to Honey Ridge without him.

"Anyway, I was only eleven and couldn't care less about girls." Devlin smacked his forehead with the heel of his hand. "What was wrong with me!"

Grayson laughed. "When the love hormones finally struck— around thirteen if I remember correctly—you never looked back."

"True. Nothing so wonderful on this planet as the female gender. God knew what He was doing."

"None of which relates to this obvious sleeping place. I tend to think someone has been camping here. Notice how the space has been cleared, as if someone moved things out and swept up?"

"I see what you mean. This room is mostly empty."

"A construction zone is no place for trespassers, kid or otherwise. We'll need signs."

Devlin's face lit up. "So you're on board for the new project?"

"I want to push some numbers first and look at cost versus return."

Devlin shifted on his feet, stuck his hands in his pockets and then took them out. Finally, he went to the filthy window. "Take a look at the view. We can rebuild this upper level as a special venue, cater for parties, rehearsal dinners and such. Maybe a wall of windows here."

The view below encompassed the water wheel and the small falls tumbling into the clear, rocky creek. Woods and nature stretched as far as the eye could see. "The view *does* have potential. People will want to walk down there."

"I like the natural feel, but we'll do some landscaping, add romantic benches and mini gardens."

"We'll have to clear an area for parking."

Grayson started to turn away, eager now to push a pencil on the project and see if a new restaurant on the site was feasible. Something in the brush caught his eye. He squinted. "What's that?"

"Where?"

He put a fingertip against the window. "There in the tangle of kudzu above the creek."

Devlin frowned, peering closely. "I don't see…"

"It's gone now." Grayson pivoted away, his head already filled with schedules and numbers and contractor contacts.

"What was it?"

"Probably a wild animal. A coyote maybe. Or a bear."

"Or our squatter?"

"Possibly." The squatter was the least of Grayson's concerns. Whoever it was would have to find another place to play. He looked at his watch. "Our check-in time is four. We should go."

"The Peach Orchard Inn is across the road, Grayson. We aren't going to be late."

"I don't like to keep people waiting."

Devlin rolled his eyes upward and shook his head. "If you weren't such a genius with your schedules and spreadsheets—"

"Admitting my genius, are you?" Suspicion sprouted in Grayson and grew faster than kudzu. He paused at the top of the stairs to squint at his younger brother. "You only do that when you want something. What gives?"

Devlin stacked his hands on his hips, suit jacket pushed back on the sides. "So what do you think? Won't this make a great Blake Brothers Restaurant?"

"Maybe. After we check in at the B and B, I'll give the owner a call and talk numbers."

"Uh. Grayson. I sort of already did that."

Grayson's eyebrows rose high. "You did?"

"Yeah, yeah, I know, negotiations are your thing, but I got wind of a possible competitor. And I'm sentimental about anything connected to Grandma and Pappy. I want this place. I couldn't let it get away."

Grayson was sentimental about Honey Ridge, too, but business was business. "I don't like the sound of this."

"I knew you'd want the mill eventually. But you sweat the small stuff too much. The early bird gets the worm and all that."

Incredulous, foreknowledge tingling along his nerve endings like electricity, Grayson stared at his brother. "What did you do?"

"*We*. What we did." Devlin grimaced. "We bought it."

CHAPTER 2

Grayson parked the Jeep in the graveled lot at the back of Peach Orchard Inn and exited the vehicle without saying a word to his brother. He was irked. Ticked. Irritated with his impulsive brother, though this wasn't the first time, nor would it be the last.

With long, efficient strides that ate up the tidy lawn, he approached the wraparound porch of the inn. A white two-story with double galleries and tall columns, Peach Orchard Inn was a stunning example of the Greek Revival architecture popular in the early 1800s. His builder's eye was impressed with the careful preservation and restoration of historic detail.

A speckled, shaggy dog—an Australian shepherd, he thought—sprawled on the shady porch under a white wicker table. The animal rose slowly, sniffed Grayson's pant leg, and, wagging his stubby tail, nudged a blue head under the human hand. Grayson rubbed between the dog's ears. "Hello, fella."

Devlin by now had caught up, and the dog turned his attention to the newcomer. "We should get a dog."

"*We* is plural. We don't live together. Thankfully."

"Aw, Gray, get over it. You would have made the deal anyway. I saved you some of your precious time."

There was that, but Grayson wasn't ready to forgive this

clear departure from their established methods of doing business. He was the bean counter, the deal maker. Devlin was the creative genius. "I could have gotten a better deal."

"Maybe." Devlin scrubbed the dog's head. The animal responded by raising a paw to shake, almost-white blue eyes soft and adoring. Like people, dogs adored Dev and tolerated Grayson. He'd never figured that out.

He pushed the doorbell, unsure of the protocol for entering someone else's home even if it was a hotel of sorts.

Devlin didn't share his hesitation. He opened the tall paneled door and stepped into an immaculate foyer and back into a time of carriages and crinolines. Grayson followed, soaking up the architectural details. Over the door, a half-moon window known as a lunette spilled light onto the gleaming oak entry. To one side, a rosewood credenza polished to a sheen held a bouquet of fresh white flowers. Above the credenza, a glass case displayed some sort of artifacts. He saw a leather journal, a pocket watch, coins, and buttons, among other intriguing items. The piece of framed sheet music, tattered and yellow, especially interested him. He moved to the case, hands behind his back, to peruse.

The light scent of peaches, whether real or artificial, whispered on the air. Peach Orchard Inn. Peach fragrance. Nice touch.

Dev, too, had stopped in his tracks to look around with the interested eye of a design master before tilting his head back. "Get a load of that staircase."

With a slight curve of polished banisters, the wide, red-carpeted stairway gracefully rose to the second floor. Overhead hung a small chandelier, glittering in the transom light. The entry was elegant and classy, as befit such a house. A house to explore and study.

However, at present, he wanted a shower more than anything before the ticks and poison ivy could take up residence on his skin.

"They're expecting us, right?" Devlin asked. "I don't see or hear anyone."

"I made the reservation myself with the proprietress, Julia Donovan. We should have knocked and waited outside."

Devlin stepped back to the doorway and thudded his fist against the wood.

They heard a door close and footsteps above them. Grayson looked upward as a terrific pair of legs, followed by a stunning brunette, came into sight. She moved down the staircase with the grace and flounce of a flamenco dancer, her dark hair swinging around her shoulders. In a silky blouse the color of mustard and a slim gray skirt that showed off the perfect amount of curve, she made his mouth go dry.

As she took the last step and moved toward him, a smile on her face, Grayson recognized her...and his stomach dipped with a kind of pleasant dread.

Head tilted slightly, the woman extended a hand, silver bracelets dangling from her wrist but otherwise devoid of jewelry. "I'm Valery Carter. Welcome to Peach Orchard Inn."

Grayson slid his much longer fingers against hers. Her skin was firm and smooth, her nails trimmed but decorated with blaze-red polish. He recognized her, but apparently, she'd forgotten him. No surprise there.

He realized he was staring, and she was waiting. "Grayson Blake. This is my brother, Devlin. We have a reservation."

A tiny frown puckered her brow in thought before her face cleared. "Grayson and Devlin? I know you."

She laughed, tossing her hair so that it made a whispery sound against her shiny blouse. "That's not a come-on."

"Too bad," Devlin, the glib-tongued devil, said, and Valery's smile widened. "As kids we spent every summer here with our grandparents, Evelyn and Jeff Mayfield. They had a farm on the other side of town."

"Yes." She eased her hand from inside Grayson's. "I remember you two. One of you caused a lot of mischief."

Grayson jerked a thumb toward his brother. "That would be Devlin."

She turned her attention to his brother. Hand on her hip, one eyebrow lifted, Valery's expression wasn't a bit businesslike as she teased, "Are you here to save the puppies, the whales or to search for Yeti?"

Grayson groaned. "Maybe you remember us too well."

"The infamous escapades of Devlin Blake and his sidekick? Everyone in Honey Ridge remembers."

Sidekick. Yeah. That would be him.

Devlin turned on his pretty-boy charm. "Yeti? Is he here? Want to join me in the search?"

Valery's laugh sounded, low and warm. "You haven't changed a bit." Her golden gaze focused on Grayson. His insides tightened. The sidekick brother had been an awkward, skinny, nerdy teenager. No doubt she remembered that, too.

"Grayson." She mulled his name with her soft Tennessee voice. Then her eyes danced with humor, and he was certain she remembered too much.

He cleared his throat, checked his watch. "Are we early? I want to get settled and get back to work."

"Such a rush," she mused. "But your rooms are ready. Do you have bags?"

"In the Jeep." Grayson checked his watch again. They still had daylight. "We'll get them later."

"So, what kind of business brings the pair of you back to Honey Ridge?"

"The gristmill across the road. We purchased it."

Her tidy eyebrows arched. "Really? What on earth for?"

Grayson's smile was more of a smirk. He enjoyed the scoffers, the unbelievers who said the Blake brothers couldn't make a design happen. Then, when they did, the surprise and pleasure was so much sweeter.

"You created something beautiful out of this house. We thought we'd do the same with the gristmill."

"Reopen the mill? But why? No one grinds their own grain these days."

"As a restaurant. It's what we do."

Her brow furrowed in thought. "You know, I think I've heard that somewhere. Blake Brothers Restaurants. Isn't there one in Chattanooga?"

"The Depot, with the private dining cars?" Grayson said. "That's us."

"Great steaks. Very posh. Oh." She pointed. "You're bleeding." She opened the credenza and pulled a tissue from a box.

Grayson touched his cheek. "Attacked by a vicious briar."

"Here. Let me." She moved into his space until he smelled exotic perfume, tiptoed up on ballet flats and patted the tissue against his cheek. Up close and personal, her amber eyes were spoked with gold and ringed in black, her lashes thick and long, enhanced with some sort of female magic.

She was like a gypsy enchantress.

Irritated to be attracted and not wanting to be, he took the tissue from her. "I got it. Thanks."

He was no longer an awkward adolescent with time on his hands. Time, he'd learned in the cruelest way, was of the essence. A smart man used it wisely.

"Valery!" a female voice called from somewhere to the left.

Valery's warm smile became brittle. She stepped away from Grayson, slowly turning toward the sound, back straight and stiff.

A mature woman with short dark hair, and trim and tidy in pale slacks and blue sweater, breezed into the foyer.

"Hi, sweetie. I see your new guests have arrived."

"Yes, they have, Mama. I'm getting them settled now." With a pinched expression, Valery said, "Gentlemen, my mother, Connie Carter. Mother, Grayson and Devlin Blake."

Grayson greeted the woman, but refrained from conversation, aware of the tension emanating from Valery. Even Devlin was subdued, his quick eyes taking in the scene. Valery, clearly, was none too pleased to see her mother.

Interesting, but none of his business.

From the pocket of her skirt, the innkeeper withdrew a pair of keys, becoming all business as she handed them to Grayson.

"Guest rooms are upstairs. One of you is in the Mulberry Room and the other is across the hall in the Blueberry Room. Take your pick. They're both open and ready. If you need anything, let me know. Breakfast is between seven and ten, and we serve light refreshments in the front parlor after two until around ten. Coffee and peach tea are available in the kitchen anytime you want them. Help yourself."

Mrs. Carter interjected, "Once you're settled, come back down, and I'll have tea and coffee cake ready." She pointed to the right. "The guest parlor is through those double doors."

"Sounds good." Devlin flashed his winning smile. "We worked up an appetite exploring the mill. Thank you, ma'am."

"You're very welcome. Our guests' comfort is important to us. Feel free to take any of the brochures from the display, walk the grounds and the orchard, sit on either of the verandas with coffee. If you need more towels or toiletries, let us know."

During the recitation, Grayson cast an occasional glance at Valery. Her lips were flat and tight, her expression empty.

Curious, he tipped his head toward his brother, and they

climbed the stairs to easily find the rooms marked with gold plates.

"A little tension down there."

"I noticed." Devlin pushed open the room marked Blueberry, a sunny space in baby-blue that looked out over long rows of peach trees just beginning to turn green. "Wasn't Valery the girl you had a thing for back in the day? The Dairy Queen crush?"

"I had a thing for a lot of girls. Hormonal teenagers do."

"True." Devlin fell back on the plush bed. "But she was flirting."

"Not with me." She was far more Devlin's type. Fun and vivacious.

"I think so, brother. Flashing those big brown eyes at you. Dabbing at your cheek. And the way you held her hand waaay too long, you were definitely into her."

Grayson gave his brother an evil look, spun around, strode across the hall to the Mulberry Room and shut the door. Five seconds later, Devlin shoved it open again. "Want to look at some design ideas?"

"You already have something in mind?"

Devlin shifted, suddenly finding the floor more interesting than his brother's face. "Uh, well, yes. You see—" He cleared his throat, stretched his neck to one side. "I sort of bought the property back in January."

"January! That's months ago."

Devlin spread his hands in a gesture of supplication. "Saving more of your precious time, brother. Permits are done, contractors contacted, and designs in the works."

"Unbelievable." He shot a hand across the top of his head, annoyed and flabbergasted.

"So, what do you say? Want to have a look? See what genius ideas I have for the place?"

Grayson glowered. "Right now, I need a shower."

"You're still miffed about me making the deal without you."

"You think?"

"You'll thank me later." Devlin disappeared out the door, and Grayson could swear his brother was laughing.

Shaking his head, he went into the bathroom and immediately realized his clothing was still in the Jeep. With a beleaguered sigh and ankles already beginning to itch, he started back down the stairs.

Halfway down, he heard voices—contentious voices—and paused.

"What, Mama? You thought I couldn't handle the inn for a whole week? That I'd screw it up without you or Julia here to watch over me?" Valery's voice was furious. Furious and embarrassed.

"Don't be dramatic, Valery. It's just…" A tired sigh. "The inn is full. I thought you'd appreciate a hand with the laundry and cooking."

"That's not why you're here. Did Julia call you? Ask you to drive out and make sure I don't ruin the business while she's in Knoxville?"

"Julia is committed to this inn, Valery."

"And I'm not? Is that what you mean?"

"Are you?"

"You don't trust me."

"Should I? Considering—?" The older woman stopped. Her next words were soft, and all evidence of discord had, curiously, been erased. "Aunt Joanne's asparagus is producing like crazy, and she sent a bunch. Shall we bake some for dinner?"

Silence shimmied up the staircase and hung heavy in the air like stale grease. Grayson debated a retreat, but his ankles itched more every second. He intentionally stepped harder on the next stair, tromping downward with enough noise to give fair warning.

Valery saw him first and flashed a dark, troubled glance at him before pasting on a bright, hostess smile.

"Grayson." She moved his way, giving her mother a sharp, warning look in parting. "Do you need something else for the room?"

"Luggage," he said and exited the house, wondering why Valery's mother couldn't trust her to run the inn alone.

Bourbon. The color of her eyes. Hadn't someone told her that once? A man, no doubt. A forgotten one like so many others.

She listened to the gurgle as the liquor splashed into a glass.

Guests were checked in. All the rooms filled. An older couple who were sweet as cotton candy had arrived last, weary from their long drive and eager to settle in for a nap. She'd made a note to prepare a diabetic snack for the missus.

The newlyweds in the Magnolia suite at the end of the hallway, the only room with a Jacuzzi tub, had come in early, sunburned and glowing, after spending the day floating on the river. They'd been here for three days, sparkling and happy and madly in love. It was both heartwarming and nauseating.

And of course, the Blake brothers. Gorgeous, both of them. Devlin, the pretty charmer, and the quieter Grayson who had definitely come into his own. Tall and lean with light brown hair that would streak blond in summer, he had the kind of piercing blue eyes that seemed to see right through her.

She remembered those eyes. Remembered how smart and fascinating he was. Remembered, too, that he'd ignored her at fifteen no matter how hard she'd tried to get his attention by flirting with other boys. There'd been plenty of others interested.

And look what that got you.

She shook her head to clear the memory of Mama's words all those years ago.

Those days were past. Move on. Don't think about it.

She breathed over the top of the bourbon, inhaling the subtle caramel flavor before sipping. The fire trailed over her tongue and down her throat.

She had placed a moratorium on men after the fiasco with her last boyfriend, Jed, a man who'd turned out to be part abuser, part criminal, and all jerk. If he was the best she could do, she'd prefer to be alone. The social butterfly had clipped her own wings. She hoped they'd stay that way.

She took another sip, breathed deeply and savored the glow spreading through her center. She was still furious with Mama.

Contrary to her mother's opinion of her ineptness, she'd managed the inn for an entire day without upsetting anyone. Refreshments waited in the parlor under glass domes and in silver urns, and the housework was complete. So, who would it hurt if she had a little refreshment of her own before going to the kitchen to set up for breakfast in the morning?

"Asparagus," she muttered, lip curled in derision. As if a green vegetable cured all the evils that stewed between her and Mama like a witch's brew of unspoken needs and un-mentionable secrets.

"For once, speak the truth, Mama. Just once."

But not since she was sixteen, her dancing dreams lost, left in Savannah along with her heart, had Mama ever spoken of this...*thing* between them. Not once after she'd convinced her daughter that she would eventually forget what had happened.

"Your whole future's ahead of you, Valery. Don't look back."

Mocking those long-ago words, Valery tipped up the glass and swallowed.

She looked back every day. Every blessed day, especially since her nephew's abduction.

A child wasn't supposed to disappear, never to be seen again.

She finished the glass in one quick toss, hoping the bourbon would burn away the guilty ache in the center of her chest.

Mama would disapprove if she saw her gulping bourbon. Oh, she wouldn't say anything. That was the trouble. She'd become as silent as the grave, and cast wounded, fuming looks to heap guilt on Valery's head. As if she needed more.

But at least here in her own bedroom inside a benevolent old house that oozed memories and mysteries, Valery had her privacy.

She poured another shot—only a little more to smooth the edges gone ragged from the day and Mama—and tossed it back with a satisfied shudder.

Carefully, she recapped the bottle and slipped it into the shiny pink tote bag in the back of her closet. There were some things Julia didn't need to know.

An easy, pleasant warmth had begun to flow into her veins, and she felt better, steadier, and not so angry. She could smile again.

After a long minty gargle, she sprayed a generous spritz of Chanel in all the right places, breathed in the warm musk and jasmine scent and fluffed her hair.

"There," she said to the mirror as she touched up her lipstick. "Everything is just fine."

Grayson shut his computer, pocketed his reading glasses and rubbed the impressions alongside his nose. "I'm done for the night. My brain is mush. Don't you want food?"

They'd been at it for hours, skipping dinner after several generous helpings of Valery's amazing blueberry coffee cake. Now, his belly gnawed like a mouse at a cardboard box.

Devlin held up a hand, his attention riveted on his laptop screen. "Pizza. Sandwich. Anything."

Knowing his all-in brother, Grayson left his laptop in the room and jogged downstairs. Pizza, if he could locate a place that delivered, worked for him. If not, he'd scrounge more of that coffee cake and make coffee. If he could find the kitchen.

He went through the parlor with its massive white marble fireplace and nineteenth-century decor. The night had cooled, and he had a sudden desire to sit in front of a crackling fire with a good book or a sudoku instead of working. He glanced at his watch. Maybe at some point while he was here, Valery would build a fire, and he'd take a short respite, put his feet up. Maybe. If time permitted.

He stretched his shoulder muscles, aware he'd been hunched over the computer too long.

"Bad habit," he muttered.

"What is?"

He jerked his gaze from the fireplace toward an arched doorway leading to the left. Valery leaned a hand against a glossy white door fame, her head tilted to one side. The innkeeper didn't look the least bit businesslike.

"Talking to myself, for one thing."

Her full mouth, red like her nails, curved. "And the other thing?"

Feeling a little foolish to be caught jabbering to himself, he stroked a hand over the back of his neck. "Poor posture at the computer."

"Very bad for you. Come in the kitchen. Rest that smart brain of yours. We'll catch up while I figure out Julia's recipe for breakfast lasagna."

Grayson's stomach grumbled.

"I was thinking of pizza." He trailed her perfume into an

industrial-sized space done in cream and copper, granite and stainless steel. Nothing nineteenth century here in the kitchen.

"For breakfast?" She turned slightly to show him a lovely profile, her posture as perfect as a dancer's.

He shook his head. "For now. I'm starving. Does any place in Honey Ridge deliver?"

"O'Toole's Pizza and Pasta is great. Need the number?"

"O'Toole's?"

"A fine Italian family." She laughed, and he noticed that her eyes glittered a little too brightly. "Kidding, but even if they're not exactly Italian, O'Toole's makes good pizza. Call them."

He took out his phone. She rattled off a number, and he placed the call. When he finished, she put a cup of coffee in front of him. "Might as well keep me company until the pizza arrives. You need cream or sugar for that?"

"Show me where and I'll get it. We'll be here awhile. Might as well learn the layout."

She pointed, and he opened a cabinet above his head.

"Not that one." She moved across the tiled space and leaned in to open a door to his right. "Real cream in the fridge if you prefer."

Her scent wafted to him, a cover of perfume and mint over another distinctive smell, and he knew why her eyes were a bit glassy. She'd had a drink or two, maybe three, and her beverage of choice hadn't been coffee. Not a big deal. Lots of people had a relaxing drink in the evening, though he was not one of them. He preferred to be in control at all times.

Valery had always been a free spirit, maybe a little on the wild side, although that was the skewed view of a fifteen-year-old adolescent who'd seen her kissing a college boy at the July Fourth fireworks display. He'd been crushed.

He moved to the enormous stainless-steel fridge and found

the cream, poured a dollop and leaned back against the granite counter to sip. "Excellent brew."

"Are you a coffee snob?"

"Not at all. You?"

She shook her head. "My sister is. Only the best for our guests, freshly ground and carefully brewed."

He saluted with the cup. "This guest appreciates it."

She treated him to a smile, soft around the edges. "Catch me up, Grayson. What have you been doing since I saw you last?"

"Nothing special. Went to college. Started a business. And here I am."

She pulled open a cabinet and took out a large oblong casserole dish, then moved to the refrigerator for eggs, milk and ham. "I'm sure there's more to the story than school and business."

A few broken, insignificant relationships and membership in too many business organizations weren't scintillating conversation. "Sadly, no. What about you?"

She lifted a shoulder, focused on the casserole. "The usual small-town tale. Julia and I bought this house and became innkeepers."

She didn't sound all that thrilled about it either.

A memory of her niggled at the back of his brain, but he was too tired and hungry to bring it forward. Maybe later he'd remember what she was leaving out.

"The attention to detail in this renovation is exceptional. Do it yourself or hire it done?"

"Most of it on our own. The property is an ongoing project, but the inn itself is complete. The work was hard and time-consuming, but Julia's better now, and that's what mattered."

Before he could ask what she meant, the blue-speckled dog ambled into the kitchen and looked up at Valery.

"What are you doing in here?" she asked and then to Grayson, "He must have come inside searching for Alex when Mama left. He's lost without his boy."

Grayson tilted his head in question.

"Alex, my sister's stepson. He's seven now and such a little sweetheart. That dog watches him as if he's afraid he'll disappear, too."

"Too?"

She shot him a look, bit her full bottom lip. "Everyone in Honey Ridge knows, so I forget that guests don't. Julia's son was abducted nearly nine years ago and never found. Mikey."

He lowered the coffee mug.

"Seriously? Abducted here in Honey Ridge?" The town where kids hung out in the park, rode bikes all over town and chased lightning bugs long after dark? Or they had when he was a boy.

"Unbelievable, isn't it? We've never given up hope but..." Her voice drifted away, leaving the worst unsaid. Nine years was too long.

Grayson pushed off the counter and moved closer. "I'm really sorry."

"Thank you. It was horrible for all of us, but especially Julia." She slathered butter on a stack of bread slices. "Still is, of course."

"Not something you'd get over."

"No. But she recently remarried and is finally happy again. Eli's a good man."

He sipped, held the cup close to his lips and watched her over the rim. "What about you? You're still a Carter, and I don't see a ring."

She placed the bread into the pan in perfect rows, the way his grandmother had laid out quilting blocks. "Single and not looking."

"I hear that."

Her hands paused, her face turned toward him. "You, too, huh?"

"Too busy."

She turned back to the food preparation, but her laugh was brittle. "Yeah. That's my excuse, too."

The doorbell chimed, and Grayson went to get his pizza. Valery was gorgeous, outgoing and smart. In high school, all the boys had wanted to date her, so why were her words more self-mocking than truth?

CHAPTER 3

Grayson woke before dawn, before his alarm sounded, and sat up in the unfamiliar room. The cushy bed felt good enough to sleep another few hours, but he had to get moving. The faster this project went up, the sooner he could move on to another and then another.

He fumbled in the graying light for his watch and slipped it on. Pressing the button, he checked the time and then dressed and made his way quietly down the stairs. Devlin, a night owl, rarely rose this early, so Grayson let him sleep.

They'd stayed up late, chowing on the pizza and sipping Valery's excellent coffee while they argued over designs until his brain had grown foggy. If he knew his brother, and he did, Dev had been up hours longer pouring creative energy all over his sketchbooks and computer. When Devlin was inspired, he was magic, and Grayson was smart enough to indulge a creative gift he didn't have.

So this morning, he went in search of coffee, last night's conversation with Valery lingering at the back of his brain.

The house was silent, so he did his best to maintain the peace, padding quietly into the kitchen where a light gleamed. Although the kitchen was empty, fragrant coffee awaited in a silver carafe, and a fresh fruit bowl sat next to an iced container of individual yogurts.

As he helped himself to coffee, Valery came into the kitchen. "Good morning. You're up early."

"Eager to get started." He gave a slight shrug, dispensing with chitchat. "The mill was once a part of this property, wasn't it?"

With practiced efficiency, she moved around the space. He enjoyed watching her hands, graceful and light as a hula dancer. "It was. Why?"

"During your restoration, did you come across any photos of the original or any information about it that we might find useful?"

"I can look when I have time if you'd like."

"If you don't mind."

"Not a bit." She pushed buttons on the double oven, setting the temperature with a series of beeps. "Actually, I'm thrilled that you're going to restore the mill. It would be a shame to lose all that history."

"We'll lose some, maybe a lot. Our intent is to repurpose more than to restore."

Her head whipped toward him, brown eyes wide. "You aren't going to restore?"

He shook his head. "I'm not a historian, Valery. I'm a businessman. Restoring isn't cost-effective."

"Does everything have to be about the expense?"

It did to him. "If someone had wanted to make a museum out of the place, they should have bought the property long ago, before so much was damaged."

"History lost is gone forever."

He pinched the bridge of his nose, squinting at her. "Are you one of those?"

"One of what?"

"One of those save-the-spotted-owl people?"

"Not exactly, but history is important."

"No argument there."

"If we don't preserve our history, we're doomed to repeat it, and Lord knows, no one wants another Civil War."

"Which has nothing to do with the gristmill."

"Of course it does."

She surprised him. He'd not expected her, of all people, to care anything about history. From his memory, she was not the serious type. All she'd cared about was fun.

"You're not going to march on my construction site waving a sign, are you?"

Her full lips twitched. "Don't put ideas in my head. I *am* a member of the Honey Ridge Historical Preservation Trust."

He held back a groan.

"Don't get me wrong," he said. "I appreciate history and I love old stuff." Including the classic car in his garage that he never had time to work on. "That's why we repurpose. Blake Brothers gives new life and new usefulness to something that's rotting away."

"Julia and I restored this run-down old house to the beautiful home it once was, and we maintained the historical detail. We're doing the same with the carriage house. The process is slow, but we'll get there. Why not do the same with the mill?"

"The mill has been abandoned too long. Without us, that building won't stand another twenty years. Maybe less. It's not on a historical register, so another buyer would simply bring in a bulldozer and start fresh."

When she looked surprised, he added, "Dev checked. A true restoration of a building in that kind of poor condition requires enormous time and money that I'm not willing to spend. Apparently, no one else was either."

"So time and money are more important than preserving history for future generations?"

He really didn't want to argue about this. "You know what? I think I'll grab a banana and head on over. Thanks for the coffee."

"Grayson—" But he was already headed out the door.

By the time he arrived at the mill, the first glimmers of daylight showed through the trees, casting tall tree shadows over the proud old structure. Quiet, broken only by the early songbirds and creek babble, was peaceful and alluring. After the annoying little chat with Valery, peace was welcome.

She made him feel like a vandal, a pillager.

He had a fleeting thought of sitting on the creek bank for a few minutes to soak up the country morning and settle his blood pressure. He brushed it aside, as always. Wasting time wasn't on the agenda.

With his camera in hand, he walked around the exterior snapping photos and taking more mental notes. The foundation, long sunken in the moist earth, would require excavation, maybe replacing. He walked along the edge, observed the old mortar, cracked and crumbling. A clear reason why Valery's idea was absurd.

Still, she had a point. Once he razed the place, no one could turn back the clock.

He studied the building from several angles, mulling. Complete restoration was impossible, but as always they would retain some of the old while creating a modern, upscale restaurant in a picturesque setting. That was what he'd been trying to tell Valery, but she seemed to think that wasn't enough.

Leaning back, he aimed the camera at the waterwheel, the single most important piece to retain. Anything else was disposable. If there was a way to make the wheel functional, he would make it happen. Diners would come for the ambience of water splashing over the paddles as the big wheel rotated.

He snapped a dozen photos from various angles and then aimed the camera at the edifice. The windows, amazingly, were unbroken, and he wondered if they'd been replaced at some point. A reglazing perhaps would save money and keep the history intact. Valery should appreciate that.

The oddest feeling crept over him. And it wasn't chiggers.

Was someone else here? Watching him?

Gooseflesh prickled the back of his neck.

A shadow passed in front of the upper window, and he spun around to see if a tree limb or a cloud could have caused it. Nothing.

Used to Nashville's city noises, the peace and quiet must be getting to him. He cast a glance at the bottle tree, then snorted at his own silliness. He was not superstitious.

Shaking off the jitters, Grayson moved to the front door to snap more photos, pleased that the massive double doors, though timeworn, were solid wood and, with care, could be used to give the restaurant character.

He stopped inside the entry to adjust to the dim confines. Sunlight now peeked through the windows and cracks, shooting pale yellow beams across the bare wood. Dust motes spun like tiny fairies.

A thud sounded overhead. He looked up.

"Hello? Anybody there?"

With a frown, he bounded up the stairs, heedless to their less than sturdy condition. Rounding into the room he and Dev had dubbed the campout room, he saw no one. The space was exactly as they'd found it yesterday.

If someone had been in here, they'd made a quick and tidy exit.

He gazed about, trying to determine exactly where someone would go in a hurry.

Nothing.

"Must have been a squirrel. Or rats."

The building creaked. He jumped, then scoffed at his jitters. He didn't know what his problem was this morning. Old buildings creaked. They made noises. They were often infested with wild animals. And bottle tree or not, he didn't believe in ghosts.

After a few more photos and measurements, he headed back to the inn and Valery's breakfast casserole.

As he left the building and started down the brushy trail, the unsettled feeling came again. As if unseen eyes stared dark holes through his shirt.

He refused to look back.

Valery slid the ham and egg lasagna onto the dining room walnut sideboard, a reproduction piece they freely used. What was the point of beautiful furniture if you couldn't use it? The elderly Steinbergs, early risers, had already left, taking a to-go breakfast of yogurt and fruit. The newlyweds sat at one of the linen-covered tables gazing at each other in adoration.

She shouldn't have argued with Grayson. The guests were always right. With a sniff, she tossed her hair. Even though *he* was wrong.

While she quietly disturbed the newlyweds with the news that breakfast was served, Grayson came in and, without looking her way, helped himself to the food.

An unhappy guest was bad for business.

When he settled at a table, she put a coffee carafe in front of him and smiled her best hostess smile. Eating crow was the pits. "I think I owe you an apology."

He shook out his napkin. "Don't worry about it."

"Will Devlin be joining you?"

He glanced at his watch but not at her. "Doubtful."

"I'll put a plate aside for him."

Finally, those piercing blue eyes looked up at her. "He'd like that. Thanks."

"I really am sorry if I made you mad."

"Let me be clear about something. Blake Brothers is a business, but we aren't the bad guys. We're doing more with that derelict building than anyone has in nearly a century."

"You're right. I shouldn't have said anything."

He held her gaze long enough that attraction curled in her belly. She started to turn away. His voice stopped her.

"Penitence doesn't suit you. I like you better when your eyes are flashing."

His statement startled her. The shy, brainy teenager had changed.

He pushed at a chair. "Sit with me a minute, will you? I have some questions you might be able to answer."

Breakfast was under control and the guests were eating, so she sat, curious and certainly not opposed to talking to an attractive man. That was one of her many problems. Men. Especially attractive men who liked her flashing eyes.

CHAPTER 4

The town was abuzz with excitement, as well as opinions, about the old mill restaurant project. In fact, Grayson couldn't go into Honey Ridge for lunch or gasoline without encountering curious and friendly townsfolk. So it was no surprise when he and Devlin arrived on the construction site one morning to a small gathering.

"We have company."

Grayson stopped the Jeep behind a trail of pickups parked at angles along the edge of a road leading into the mill. Grabbing his tablet and a clipboard, he hopped out.

Devlin handed him a hard hat and grabbed another for himself. "Our very own welcoming committee."

"Or a lot of supervisors."

Devlin laughed. "They do have opinions in this town."

That they did. From the first time he'd eaten lunch at the Miniature Golf Café, he'd gotten an earful of advice from the group Valery called the good old boys, an ever-evolving hodgepodge of five or six men who didn't seem to do much of anything except sit around and talk. Only one, thankfully, shared Valery's opinion that he should restore the building to a working mill.

"I guess they've come to watch the show."

"Big boys like big toys."

They trod the gravel path, more of a trail than a road at this point, toward the noise of heavy equipment and the group of people standing above the falls.

He glanced up at the window, but he'd had no repeat of that first, creepy morning when he'd thought he was being watched. Their intruder must have been a kid, gone now that work had begun. The bottle tree, however, remained intact, blue bottles hanging upside down, according to superstition, to capture the evil spirits from the mill.

The backhoe, like a long-necked dinosaur, chomped its steel teeth into the earth around the mortar and stone footing of the two-hundred-year-old foundation. A pair of men with shovels worked down inside the resulting ditch. So far, only a few areas of the stone required repointing, a testament to strong construction.

Valery would be pleased to hear that. And the way Grayson looked at it, construction saved was money saved. The less they had to replace, the better. There was plenty to do as it was.

Work to shore up the basement was also underway inside the mill, and Grayson felt the old itch to get his hands on some tools and get involved. He and Dev could both swing a hammer or a pickax or anything else the job required, but a team of contractors could work faster, so for now he let them. He would have plenty of opportunity to get his hands dirty.

"Good morning." He spoke to the gathered crowd, a few of whom he recognized from town.

Poker Ringwald, co-owner of the Miniature Golf Café, sipped at his portable camo coffee cup and nodded his greeting. A pack of playing cards poked out of his shirt pocket. "Me and Mr. B. thought we'd take a run out and size up the competition."

Grayson smiled. "We're a long way from opening for business, Poker."

"And even when we do," Devlin grinned his amiable grin, "we'll never match your wife's biscuits and gravy."

Poker laughed and toasted the air with his mug. "Ain't that the truth? Don't be trying to steal her away when you get this shindig up and running."

"You better raise her salary," Dev joked. "Grayson goes after the best cooks."

Mr. B., the local mortician with an unpronounceable last name, wagged his jowls back and forth, expression sorrowful. The man was legend, Grayson had learned, for pessimistic comments. He braced himself not to laugh. Mr. B. was not one to joke around.

Suddenly, a workman appeared in the open doorway and interrupted the conversation. Squat and strong and built like a wall with his clothes covered in dirt and damp with sweat, the man's face was white as plaster. "Mr. Blake?"

Simultaneously, Grayson and Devlin answered. "Yes?"

Grayson stepped away from the onlookers, already frowning. "What is it, Billy? A problem?"

Devlin moved up beside him, sotto voce. "Problems are part of the business, Gray. Don't get antsy."

The workman took off his hard hat and rubbed a forearm over a sweaty head. "I think you better come in here and see for yourself. Both of you."

The odd request ratcheted up his concern. "Is someone hurt?"

Billy tilted his head to one side, mouth twisted. He was still whiter than wall plaster. "I guess that's a matter of opinion."

The crowd hanging around the falls surged closer, listening. Grayson didn't ask any more questions. He'd worked with Billy before. He trusted the man. He'd never gone pale on a job site. Injuries happened, but Blake Brothers was highly safety conscious and had never suffered anything serious. From Billy's expression, their good luck may have run out.

Alarmed, he and Devlin, with their usual synchronicity, exchanged glances and then strode into the building to follow Billy down the steps into the dim basement area. Portable shop lights that dangled from overhead bracing barely dispelled the gloom, and nothing could dispel the dank smell.

The wood flooring, disintegrated badly from time and moisture, had been cleared away along with a fifteen-hundred-pound millstone. Moist dirt, evidence of digging by hand and machine, was piled in the center of the large open space.

Hands on his hips, Billy stood at the precipice of a long trench dug along the interior walls. "Over here."

Grayson stepped up next to the workman.

He heard Devlin's sharp inhale. "Is that what I think it is?"

Grayson went to a crouch, reaching into the ditch to brush away more dirt. He glanced up at his brother, and as their gazes collided, he nodded grimly.

"Bones," he murmured. "And I think they're human."

CHAPTER 5

Between today and tomorrow are graves, and
between promising and fulfilling are chasms.

AUTHOR UNKNOWN

1875. Peach Orchard Farm

So this was how it felt. The age of majority. Benjamin Jefferson Portland was officially a man.

"I don't feel a bit different," he said to the cheval mirror and the image of a tall, sturdy man who had yet to grow anything more than peach fuzz on his upper lip.

Ben grinned at himself as he straightened the edges of his new vest. Silk embroidery over cotton it was, and where his mother had gotten silk thread for such an elegant gift, he couldn't know. Prices were inflated, goods in short supply.

As if the war had not stolen enough from Tennessee, the depression of 1873 pressed down on her with more force than the great grinding stones in the family's gristmill.

He felt the weight every time he looked into his mother's concerned blue eyes or heard his stepfather lament the price of corn. The Chattanooga Railroad was bankrupt. Cotton prices had fallen to less than half while debts rose, and the Negroes so recently emancipated now struggled to exist.

His jaw clenched. Negroes like Tandy.

But worry and regret were for another day. The smell of Lizzy's baking drifted up the stairs and into his bedroom. A spice cake, he'd wager if he had an extra dime, with his favorite caramel icing.

Smoothing the pale hair that matched his mother's one last time, he yanked at fresh cuffs and bounded down the wooden staircase, whistling a tune.

As he crossed the parlor, Ben averted his attention from the wide splotch of dark red stains still visible near the fireplace. Perhaps they always would be. Though the Portland women had scrubbed their knuckles raw, the house could not forget the savagery of war and death that had occurred within her noble walls.

She'd taken in the broken and wounded, every single one, just as she had in the days hence. The house, by strength of his saintly mother, who was neither Union nor Confederate but a British abolitionist, had succored dying soldiers and fractured slaves, held the farm and family together with prayer and hard work, and had been a haven of rest for vanquished Rebs stumbling their way home, broken and near-starved after Lee's surrender at Appomattox.

Ben's steps slowed, the whistle dying on his lips. Peach Orchard Farm had seen no more nor less than any other Tennessee home, but the grief of the years past lingered in Benjamin's memory. Though he'd been but a lad of nine, he could never forget the year his whole world collapsed and he'd come to despise Edgar Portland. His father.

He was a man now. A man with promises to keep. But where did a man go when he had no direction?

A door opened to his left, and his mother exited the parlor, her face beaming with love. He could never remember a time when the normally reserved Charlotte Portland Gadsden hadn't greeted him with this same glowing exultation, as though her sun didn't rise until she'd seen his face.

"Benjamin!" Her skirts whispered against the wood floors

as she came to lay a hand on his chest, smoothing an imaginary thread. "The vest fits you well."

"It's a handsome vest, Mother. Thank you."

"A vest befitting such an august occasion. Happy birthday."

His mother patted his chest, tiptoeing up to kiss his cheek. Her British accent, though faded with time and an effort to fit into a society that looked on foreigners with suspicion, especially after she'd married a Yankee captain, was particularly crisp today.

He embraced her, drew in the lemony scent he would always associate with his mother. He towered over her now, though her perfect posture and the golden hair that matched his own had not diminished with time.

When she stepped away, her eyes gleamed bright with unshed tears.

"Aw, now, Mama, no tears. I have a birthday every year."

"Tears of joy," she claimed with a lifted chin, resting her hands serenely at her waist, tender gaze embracing him. "You've grown into the man I knew you'd be. I'm proud of you, my Ben, and I know your Papa would be, too."

Ben held his smile in place. "It is your pride and pleasure I seek. Yours and Captain Will's."

His stepfather had taught him everything he needed to know to be a man of honor. He couldn't say the same for his father.

"You have always had that from both of us, my son." She patted his chest and turned. "Supper in an hour."

"I smell cake. You don't suppose I could snitch a piece before supper?"

"And risk losing a limb?" Her lips curved. "Lizzy's cake is worth the wait."

He laughed as she exited the room, leaving him to his own devices.

The rare leisure time allowed him this hour to search his father's papers. He'd looked before to no avail, but today he had a right. He was the heir, after all. No one could chase him out of the study with a warning to let sleeping dogs lie.

On this day the farm was legally his, though he had no desire to take control of his father's property, the properties his mother and Captain Will had fought to preserve while he grew to be a man. Not now. Not yet. Not until he'd done everything in his power to right the grievous wrong Edgar Portland had done to them all. And if providence favored him on his birthday, if the prayers he'd prayed for nearly a decade were answered, perhaps he would, at last, find a clue to Tandy's whereabouts.

He made his way down the long hallway that divided the house into two sides and to a room he'd once been forbidden to enter. Papa hadn't liked to be disturbed, especially by noisy boys like him and Tandy.

Tandy. His childhood friend, though some would say a slave could not be a friend. At only nine years old, and lonely for another child, Ben had not understood what he knew now—he was master and Tandy his property. But even now, years after the fact, Benjamin flinched at owning human flesh. Tandy had been his companion, his playmate, and yes, his friend, though Aunt Josie had often scolded him for saying as much. Mama was of a differing opinion, and that was all that mattered to him.

He slipped a hand into his trouser pocket and withdrew the single blue marble he still carried like a talisman. Did Tandy still carry his? Did he, like Benjamin, remember their childhood promise?

Inside the study, he went through the same papers and ledgers he'd perused many times. Older ledgers lined the bookshelves, all meticulously labeled by Logan's tidy hand. Logan, a double above-the-knee amputee from Ohio who'd remained after the war, had become their bookkeeper and an indispensable part of the Portland household. He'd made coming into the study more palatable, though Ben could still envision Edgar Portland's frown of disapproval and roar of anger. No one, not even his wife, had been allowed to touch the ledgers.

As a boy, he'd thought nothing of Edgar's secrecy. He was the father, the man, the landowner. But now, Benjamin wondered.

Ben ran a finger along the bindings until he came to 1865. Taking the book, he turned to January and a time he'd never forget. As he'd done many times, he perused page after page, but nowhere could he find an entry for Tandy's sale. Frustrated, he returned the book to the case and pondered. If his father had entered the sale at all, he'd done so somewhere else. On a whim, Benjamin removed the three ledgers prior to 1865, to a time before his mother and Logan took charge of the books, and he began to work backward from the final months of 1864.

His mother had been locked away in her room, punished by his father in the last weeks of that year. Ben sickened to remember such cruelty to a woman who would never have violated a vow before God, certainly not a marriage vow, and yet Edgar had believed she had.

Ben hadn't understood then. He'd been too young to understand. He'd only known his mother was forbidden to leave her room, and he was forbidden to enter, so he had stretched out on the cold wood floor outside her door and whispered beneath the crack, heartsick and scared. She'd prayed with him and for him, as well as for the captain and for his father, and he'd known she was innocent of whatever evil his father accused her of.

Edgar Portland had been a harsh, vengeful man. They'd all suffered for it. Tandy most of all.

Ben rubbed a hand over his forehead, his happy mood seeping away in the memories. He could always feel his father's angry presence in this room, just as he felt the guilt and loathing and the desperate need for Edgar's approval that plagued him still. Perhaps he could forgive, and God could forgive him, if he found Tandy.

He scoured his father's dark, heavy handwriting, turning more pages. Along with records of farm equipment and food stuffs, he read the list of slaves bought and sold like sacks of sugar and cans of lard. Like his mother, Ben had despised slavery, and yet, they had both been trapped in the practice by an iron-fisted Edgar and a society that thrived on forced labor.

"Martin, thirty-two-year-old field hand, sold to Joe Swartz. Inez, fifteen, housemaid, sold to Jack Plummer."

"But no record of Tandy." Discouraged, he started to return the book when a loose page fluttered to the floor. Not a typical filled page but one with few entries.

As he bent to retrieve it, his breath caught in his chest.

Tandy's name jumped out at him, the last on the page. As if someone had made that final, terrible entry and then intentionally ripped out the page and concealed it inside the wrong ledger, as he was certain his father had. Cruel and vengeful to the end.

With trembling fingers and disbelief, his heart thudding in his ears, he read the entry. "Tandy, twelve-year-old male, to Robert Wellston of Hartford, Connecticut."

His breath froze in his throat. Tandy. At last.

After all this time, Benjamin had a name and a city. Carefully, he folded the sheet and slid it inside his vest next to his racing heart. Blood roared in his ears, flooded his face to a fever.

He'd found him. At last, at last, he knew where to look for redemption.

★ ★ ★

All through supper, Benjamin could think of little except the paper lying close to his heart. It seemed as if Tandy's name burned through his shirt, demanding recompense. Ben barely tasted his birthday supper of fried chicken and buttery biscuits and offered little to the conversation flowing around him in celebration like a bubbling spring.

They were all here, all his loved ones. Even Aunt Josie and Uncle Thad had driven over with their two young ones to celebrate his birthday. He was blessed with so much love. He couldn't help wondering how many birthdays Tandy had spent alone, missing his mama, missing his best friend, missing his home at Peach Orchard Farm.

The bite of biscuit lodged in his throat. He reached for his glass to wash it down.

Aunt Patience, sitting on his right, touched his hand with her long pianist's fingers. "Benjamin, you've hardly touched your dinner and you look flushed. Are you certain you're well?"

Sweet and simple Patience, with her heart of gold and hair of flax, stared at him with worry. She, like his mother, came as close to sainthood as anyone he'd ever met. Patience, with an ethereal musical ability to transport the heartsick to a happier time and the charitable heart to give tirelessly of herself without complaint, was an angel to him. He often wondered why no man had ever won her hand. Though still beautiful, Patience was considered a spinster now, near thirty, and still living at Peach Orchard.

"Aw, Patience, he's hearty as a mule," Aunt Josie teased with a toss of her fire-red hair. "He's dreaming about Emma Tremble and the kiss she will give him for his birthday."

Benjamin managed a feeble grin. He'd not thought of pretty Emma once since finding the ledger entry.

He pushed his plate away. "Supper was delicious, Mama." He raised his voice, "Supper was delicious, Lizzy. Where's my cake?"

A coffee-colored face with snapping black eyes peeked around the corner from the kitchen. "You quit that hollering at the table, Benjamin Portland, or you'll get not a bite of cake from me. Birthday or not."

She tsked loudly and disappeared back into the kitchen, but he could hear her muttering, "Hollering like that at his mama's table. I swan to Goshen."

This time his grin was real. Lizzy, his other mama and his mother's lady maid who'd stayed after the war to work for wages and for love of the remaining family, ruled the kitchen with a sharp look, an iron hand and a lioness's heart.

Ben raised his voice again. "You're to blame. Smelling that cake's got me overexcited. Patience says I'm plum flushed."

Lizzy reappeared with the cake and a shake of her finger, but amusement played around her lips. He could never remember Tandy's mother ever being angry with either of them, even when they'd tromped mud or snitched a biscuit. She'd loved Tandy every bit as much as his mama loved him.

And to punish Lizzy and Mama, Papa had sold a twelve-year-old boy, Lizzy's boy, to some stranger clear up in Connecticut.

Lizzy should hate everything Portland.

He'd always known when this day came what he would do. What he *must* do. For Lizzy as much as for himself and Tandy.

As the cake was sliced, emitting a spicy sweet scent that made his mouth water, Benjamin decided to tell them tonight.

He gazed around the long, familiar table, the wood scarred by war and time, at the beloved faces. Josie wiped gravy from little Sarah's chin as the child protested. Patience whispered something to Thaddeus junior that made him gurgle his throaty toddler's laugh. Will touched the back of Mama's hand, and they smiled at each other, the secret smile of husband and wife. Benjamin's chest expanded with a love too big to hold.

How would they react when he told them his plans? What would they think? Most of all, how would he manage without seeing their dear faces every day?

Mama, he feared, would cry, and her tears would tear at him worse than anger ever could.

But what kind of man would he be if his solemn vow, made with spit and a blue marble, held no veracity?

He finished his cake, chased it with cold milk from the spring, and sat back, restless. Happy, much loved voices chattered around him.

He tapped a spoon against his empty glass. Seven faces turned his direction with expectant expressions.

"Mama. Will. Everyone." He cleared his throat. Sweat erupted on the back of his neck. "I found something today."

Lizzy started to leave the dining room, but he nabbed her slender wrist. She looked at him with surprise and reproach. He loosened his grip and gently said, "You need to hear this, too. Please."

Her black eyes remained wide, but she nodded.

"What is it, Ben?" Mama's normally serene expression grew suddenly wary. "What did you find?"

Licking dry lips, he pulled the folded paper from inside his vest, from the spot next to his galloping heart. "A record of Tandy's sale to a man named Robert Wellston…"

Lizzy's hand shot to her mouth, "Oh, sweet Jesus."

"And," he finished before the questions could begin, "I'm going to Connecticut to find him."

CHAPTER 6

Present Day. Honey Ridge

A skeleton in Honey Ridge was big news. Big, terrifying news.

Valery wiped disinfectant across the dining room tables as Grayson related the discovery. He did not look happy, but he couldn't know the turmoil bubbling in her head.

"A skeleton? At the mill? What kind of skeleton?" She tried to keep the panic from her tone.

"Human, apparently, though we only scratched the surface of the bones before we stopped digging."

Human bones. Dear God. Valery shivered.

"How can you be sure? Do you know who it—" She paused, hand to her throat as her mind tumbled with the horrible possibility. Nine years of deep, unspoken fear rose up to choke her.

Grayson lifted a calming hand and softened his tone. He must have seen her anxiety. "Too early to know, but we shut everything down the minute we realized we'd struck bone. That's the law."

"You've already called authorities?"

"Immediately. Trey Riley from the Honey Ridge Police Department was on-site when I left, stringing yellow police tape all over the place." Grayson didn't look too happy about that. "The coroner should arrive sometime this afternoon to give his assessment. The bones will be exhumed and examined, and after all that, we should have some better answers."

Valery carried the disinfectant into the kitchen. She had no heart for cleaning at the moment, but then she never did.

Forehead furrowed, Grayson followed. He was troubled by this unexpected turn of events, though he wouldn't know how much more frightening the news would be to her. And Julia.

"Trey's a good friend. I'm glad he's there." Glad and terrified. Trey's thoughts would match hers. He'd suspect the worst.

Heart beating erratically, she washed her hands and ran a glass of water. Her throat had gone drier than talcum powder. "How long before they know something solid?"

"No idea. Days. Weeks. Trey couldn't say." Grayson didn't look happy about that either. She understood, though probably for different reasons. The waiting was the hardest part. Waiting and not knowing.

Eyebrows lifted in question, she offered him the tumbler. He took it with a nod of thanks.

Before she could reach for another glass, a car door slammed out back. Valery's heart slammed into her rib cage.

"Oh, my goodness." She rushed to the window, thirst forgotten, to press her fingers against the pane. "I hope she hasn't heard."

"Valery? Are you okay? Is something wrong?"

She turned and saw the worry in his expression. Worry and bewilderment.

"Julia will be upset if she's heard about the—the...bones." The word "body" was too hard to say, too human, too fresh on the minds of everyone in her family.

No body was ever found. Honey Ridge boy still missing.

So many headlines and news reports that had gradually faded away, revisited only on that awful anniversary.

The grief and heartache her sister had endured back then was unbearable. Not that she ever forgot, not even for a second, but Julia had learned to keep moving and had at last found some measure of peace and pleasure with Eli. Now, once again, Julia would be reminded of the abduction and the fact that Mikey had never been found.

"Julia. Mikey. She'll think—" Valery left her guest standing next to the refrigerator and rushed outside, letting the screen door slap shut behind her.

From her expression, her sister had already heard, and Valery was too late to ease the shock. As Julia exited the car, her face was as white as the marble angel hovering over Mikey's Garden.

In her haste to reach her sister Valery's flats slipped on the loose gravel. She slowed, drawing a breath to calm her jitters. Julia needed support, not hysteria from her. She could be shaken on her own time.

"Is it true?" Julia asked.

"What did you hear? Who told you?" She wanted to throttle the big mouth, whoever it was.

"We stopped at the store. The Sweat twins were there. They said a body was found." Julia's hand clutched at the neck of her blouse, a blue silk that made her eyes as clear as summer. At the moment, those eyes were clouded with a grief so deep only another who'd lost a child could understand.

Valery didn't let herself go there. She was here to bolster and reassure, not wallow in her own guilt.

"No." She put a reassuring hand on her sister's arm. That her hand trembled was beside the point. "That's wrong. Not a body. Bones. They aren't even positive the bones are human."

Maybe the last was a fudge on her part, but Grayson wasn't a forensic expert. He couldn't know for sure.

Eli, darkly handsome in a white shirt and a green tie that matched his eyes, slid an arm around his wife's waist. With his quiet strength to bolster her, Valery's sister seemed to relax a little.

"But the bones could be—human. It could be Mikey."

Tenderly, Eli drew Julia against his sturdy chest, murmuring sweet reassurances that left a lump in Valery's throat. Thank God, Eli and Julia had found each other. Thank God, Eli was here.

Julia pressed her face into the crook of his neck for several long moments. Valery could hear her drawing in slow, deep breaths. Then she lifted her blonde head with quiet dignity and gave one hard head bob. "I'm fine. I'm okay."

Her bravado was more painful to watch than if she'd gotten hysterical.

"Let's go inside. Grayson Blake is in the kitchen. He was there. He can tell you more."

As they approached the back door, Grayson pushed it open and stood aside to let them in. Nice guy. Concerned about others. So rare.

"Is she all right?" he asked quietly.

"She will be. She's strong." But Julia hadn't always been strong, and the memory of her shattered, depressed sister worried Valery. She might not survive a setback.

"I didn't realize. Didn't think." Grayson followed them into the dining room where he quickly pulled out a chair for Julia. "I'm sorry."

Julia offered him a quavering smile as she sat. "What can you tell us, Mr. Blake?"

"Grayson. Please."

Valery didn't want to hear the story again. Bodies under the mill. Bones. Dead people.

Not Mikey. Please, God, not Mikey.

"I'll get you some tea." She rushed out of the dining room, feeling stupid for offering tea when her sister's worst nightmare might be coming true.

They'd always believed Mikey was alive somewhere. At least, they'd tried to believe. Julia clung to hope as tenacious as the mysterious antique marbles they found around the inn. But Valery didn't believe in benevolent angels as Julia did. Since meeting Eli, Julia had found her faith again. She had hope. She believed. Valery feared she never would.

The worst had likely befallen her nephew, and guilt was like a cancer gnawing away at Valery's insides.

"Tea. How stupid." She gave the refrigerator door a vicious yank. The contents rattled.

As she poured golden peach tea over a tall glass of ice she wanted a shot of bourbon so desperately her hand shook. She even considered adding a jigger to her tea but resisted. Julia was upset enough. Smelling alcohol on Valery during business hours would send her over the edge.

She stalled as long as she could while Eli's quiet voice reassured his wife, and Grayson added his knowledge of the unexpected grave site.

She didn't want to go back in there and face her sister, knowing what she did. Neither could she allow Julia to fall back into the depression that had almost taken her life. Buying and restoring the inn had saved her sister's sanity and probably her life, whether a benevolent angel hovered over the rooms or not.

Valery Carter was her sister's keeper. She owed her that much.

She took a shaky drink of Julia's tea and guzzled the pretend Jack Daniel's.

Leaning against the brown granite counter, she drew in deep breaths to steady herself. Then she poured a second glass of the sweet beverage, put on her sister-will-take-care-of-you face and returned to the dining room.

"The police are there now, Mrs. Donovan," Grayson was saying. "But from what they tell me, identification may take some time. DNA is a slow process."

Julia nodded, arms tight across her waist. "You'll let me know."

"As soon as I hear anything."

Eli patted his wife's back, adding his quiet strength and love as he stood next to her chair. "Why don't you go lie down awhile, honey?"

"I'm fine, Eli."

Valery set both tea tumblers on the table. "Listen to Eli, Julia. You've had a shock. A rest will do you good. I'll make chamomile tea instead of this and bring it up."

As if a stupid cup of tea would take away the fear that someone had buried her eight-year-old son within walking distance of the inn.

"What if he's been out there all this time? What if—"

"Stop it." Valery made her voice strong and brisk. "Do not let your thoughts go there."

Julia nodded, lips pressed together in a line. "You're right. You're right."

Valery stroked a lock of her sister's hair behind one ear, tender and encouraging. "Go on, sis. Take a break. Take all the time you need. I got this."

Julia blinked her thanks and stood, shaky but quickly regaining her inner grit. To Grayson, she said, "I apologize, Grayson. You've caught me at my worst."

Grayson touched two fingers to his heart. "No apology needed, Mrs. Donovan. If I can do anything…"

He let the offer dwindle as Eli gave a man-to-man nod of gratitude, put his arm around his wife and walked with her out of the room.

Grayson blew out a breath. "I'm really sorry. I never considered what news of an unearthed skeleton would mean to her." His disturbingly blue gaze settled on Valery. "To both of you. You're nearly as pale as she is."

Pale with guilt, with a secret Julia would hate her for. If the whole truth was known, Julia would most certainly hate her because Valery hated herself. How could she expect anyone to understand what she'd done when her sister would give anything in the world to have her child safe at home?

"Sit, and we'll talk about something else." Grayson motioned toward Julia's vacated chair. "Allow me to make up for my colossal blunder."

Valery shook her head. "I have to make tea."

"I'll put the kettle on." Grayson already moved toward the opening into the kitchen, long, lanky legs eating up the distance. "You sit for a few minutes while it heats."

He moved with an unexpected grace for all his lean length. As if her mind couldn't settle, she wondered if he danced, and the thought brought a pang so sharp she pressed a fist over her breastbone.

Moistening lips as dry as those dead bones at the gristmill, she collapsed onto the chair.

Elbow on the table, she propped her forehead in her hand.

Thoughts of the past kaleidoscoped inside her head, of her teen years, of the horrible time in Savannah, and the worst day of all when Mikey didn't come home from school.

Valery had had a choice. Julia hadn't.

Would she be forever haunted? Would they all?

In less than a minute Grayson returned and joined her. She

pushed the extra glass of peach tea at him. "My sister's recipe. It's amazing."

He nodded and sipped. "You're right. It is." He set the glass aside. "Want to talk about him? Or something else?"

"Mikey?"

"Yes."

"Oh, I don't know. Talking is—" She waved a hand around.

"Sometimes good for you."

"You're a pretty smart guy, you know that?" Of course, he knew. He'd always been smarter than the rest of them. Intimidatingly smart.

His smile was soft. "So, talk. What was he like?"

"He was eight and all boy." Eight years old. A baby. An innocent without a care in the world. She stared at the condensation forming on the glasses as if the air knew and wept. "A sweet, witty little guy who loved Cardinals baseball and Star Wars and all the usual things a second-grader enjoys. He was such a good boy. We adored him. He was the center of our family."

"The only grandchild?"

She bit her bottom lip, her breath stuck in her throat.

The teakettle whistled. "Julia's tea."

Relieved to end the conversation, she jumped up and hurried into the kitchen.

Two days later, Grayson pushed back from his desk and closed the laptop. His mind was not on business. Since the painful day he'd discovered the skeleton and upset the Carter sisters, he'd thought of little else. Particularly of the innkeeper's brunette sister.

Valery Carter fascinated him.

There. He'd admitted it.

The girl who'd bewitched him as an awkward teenager

hadn't lost her power. As an adult, she was still the flirty, popular beauty who had boys lined up like ants to a honey biscuit. Now, though, he noticed something more. Something deeper that surprised him, though, given the loss of her nephew, perhaps it shouldn't have. The free-spirited, carefree teenager who'd tossed boys and friends aside with a laugh now cared deeply, especially about her sister.

Deeper or not, Valery was no less flirtatious than she'd been at fifteen, and if the number of times her cell phone chimed were any indicator, men still lined up like ants.

Him included, he thought with self-deprecation as the episode in the dining room swirled in his memory. He'd had the bewildering need to console Valery the way Eli had comforted Julia.

He'd sat with her until the color returned to her cheeks and she'd found her balance enough to respond to his lame efforts at distracting conversation. After he'd made her smile with a story about him and Devlin being treed by a mama pig on Pappy's farm, she'd started to laugh and tease again, and he'd almost asked her out to dinner. Fortunately, his cell had chirped, and he'd excused himself to take a call from headquarters in Nashville. He didn't have time for involvement, especially with a woman like Valery.

As a teenager he'd been too tongue-tied to talk to her. Now, he was smart enough to know that he was too stodgy and serious for a woman like Valery Carter. She'd die of boredom if she spent too much time in his company.

As restless as a windshield wiper, he locked the Mulberry Room and went in search of activity. Today, he had to get something moving at the job site. He had to do something. *Anything.*

Hand on the stair railing, he bounded down the staircase. One of the steps creaked, reminding him of the age of Peach

Orchard Inn and of the many feet that had trod this way. According to Julia, the house had been a Civil War hospital and even now they sometimes sensed the presence of the family who had lived here first. The house was, she told him, slowly revealing its secrets.

He didn't know about all that, but thanks to his grandfather, history fascinated him almost as much as the brunette innkeeper.

Clearly, the old gristmill held secrets, too. Painful, ugly secrets if a buried body was any indicator.

"Hey." Devlin glanced up from his computer as Grayson's feet thudded at the bottom and made the turn into the airy and elegant parlor.

The younger brother was tucked back against a Victorian divan, feet propped on the coffee table as if he owned the place. Grayson could never feel that relaxed in someone else's house.

"Hey yourself."

"Have you blown a gasket yet?"

Grayson glanced at his watch. "Not yet."

Devlin knew how he was about delays. They drove him over the narrow time ledge he walked like a tightrope. He was antsy, already pushing a pencil in hopes of maneuvering other projects and contractors. Today, he'd make inquiry calls to the local authorities and put on a bit of pressure.

"I was at the scene earlier," Grayson told his brother.

"Earlier than *now*?" The night owl looked horrified. According to Devlin's droopy eyelids and the full cup of high octane next to his feet, he hadn't been up long.

Not bothering to grace the question with an obvious answer, Grayson paced to the fireplace and studied an oval photograph of a pretty blonde woman and a Union officer—a captain if he remembered his history about the crossed bars on the man's cap. He'd have to ask Valery about the pair.

Valery again. He huffed out an irritated sound. She was in his head too much.

"Crime scene tape all over the place and it's crawling with authorities."

Even the TBI—Tennessee Bureau of Investigation—forensic people had been called in to investigate.

"And the unerringly curious, too, I suppose." Dev's voice was lazy, slightly amused, as if he got some kick out of watching Grayson's blood pressure rise.

He put his back to the cold fireplace. "The good old boys barely go home to eat. I wouldn't be surprised if they started bringing a picnic lunch."

Devlin made a face and reached for his coffee. "Ghoulish."

"A bit, maybe, but they're more worried than anything, I think."

"Julia's lost son?" Devlin cast his glance toward the kitchen and then upward, not wanting to be overheard by either Julia or Valery. The sisters zipped around the inn, ever busy. Grayson knew because his radar went on high alert every time Valery danced past. Sometimes with a load of towels, and sometimes with snacks or tea or a vacuum cleaner. Always with a smile that made him feel like a silly peacock.

She reminded him of a butterfly, flitting here and there. A toss of dark hair. The slash of smiling red lips. The flirty slant of long, amber eyes.

Ten o'clock in the morning meant one or both of the sisters were in the kitchen or upstairs cleaning rooms for the next round of guests.

They shouldn't be able to hear the conversation, but to be sure, Grayson lowered his voice. "Everybody on-site and in town is talking about him."

"Assuming the worst?"

"Speculating." He huffed a long, frustrated sigh. "I want them all gone. Today would be good. Yesterday even better."

"Pinching your schedule, aren't they?"

"Killing it." He grimaced. "Bad choice of words."

Devlin swung his boots to the floor. "The mill has been there for nearly two hundred years. I tend to think the bones are much older than an eight- or ten-year-old boy."

"I hope you're right. Regardless of who he is or how long he or she has been buried there, our construction site is frozen until the investigation is complete. And heaven help us if we've dug into something prehistoric."

"We'd have to walk away from the project." Devlin suddenly turned serious. His mouth tipped down in thought, and he pulled at his upper lip. "Remember that builder—Josephson, I think it was—who unearthed an ancient Indian burial ground?"

Grayson tilted his head back and studied the ornate crown molding. As if he needed a reminder of what they might be in for. "He lost everything."

"A boatload of everything. Last I heard, he declared bankruptcy and the company was dissolved. Josephson was working handyman jobs."

Grayson hooked his hands behind his back and fidgeted. "Don't buy trouble. For now, we're dealing with some poor soul who can be exhumed and reburied elsewhere, so we can continue our work. Today, however, is shot. Any hope of making progress is a wash. I've sent the crews home."

It set his teeth on edge and poked holes in the budget, but such was the construction business.

"Which means we might as well head back to Nashville." Devlin slowly closed his laptop. For all his positive energy, he wasn't any happier than Grayson.

"You go. I'm staying here as long as needed. Someone has to nag authorities and hurry things along."

Devlin stood up, his face alight with the particular mischief Grayson knew too well. He braced for it.

"Don't think you can fool me. You're staying because of that feisty brunette."

Ah, Valery. Grayson feigned ignorance. "Where did that come from?"

"I got eyes, and so do you. Every time she whips through here with that big smile, yours nearly come out of your head."

Grayson scoffed, though his brother was half right. "Don't be stupid. She's your type, not mine. Fun and flirty. No substance."

He didn't know why he'd added that last part. He didn't know Valery well, and he was rarely so judgmental. But Dev was pushing his buttons this morning.

"I think not, big brother. And don't sound so old. You're not confined to a rocking chair yet."

With a lazy, boneless grace Devlin stretched his arms up over his head. "Do I smell bacon?"

Grayson offered him a scalding glance. "If there's any left for stragglers."

"No worries." Devlin grinned that charmer's grin. As if he thought Grayson would fall for his wiles the way women did. "Julia said she'd save me a plate. I knew I'd be up late." He pointed a finger, still grinning. "And by the way, that pretty brunette of yours was up late, too."

Up late? Doing what? Grayson bristled, a silly reaction to a simple statement. He was, after all, the geek who kept normal hours. Valery's life was her business. "Told you she was more your speed."

"Nope. She didn't stay up late for my benefit. I worked right here until about four. She stopped in to offer coffee around one, and then she went out."

"Out. As in with a date? At that hour?"

Devlin lifted a shoulder. "Don't know. Didn't hear a car. Not my business."

"Nor mine." He spun toward the foyer. "I have work to do."

Devlin laughed. "No, you don't."

Grayson groaned. Devlin was right. The stalled construction made him grumpy, and his brother's needling made him worse.

He spun back. "Go eat, and then go home. I'll call when I know something."

With a salute, Devlin started toward the kitchen as Valery entered the parlor. Regardless of how late she'd stayed up last night, she looked as fresh as the daffodils popping up in the gardens around the inn. Fresh and beautiful in a flippy red skirt that kissed her knees and a white top that hugged all the right places.

His ornery brother looked over his shoulder and pumped his eyebrows at Grayson in a *hubba-hubba* expression. "Don't implode while I'm gone."

Valery gave Devlin a warm smile and then shot Grayson a quizzical look. "Are we imploding? This early in the morning?"

The businessman looked harried, all right, and she felt a little sorry for him. Sorry, and attracted to his perfectly groomed, buttoned-up appearance. Did he have any idea how good he looked in immaculately pressed gray slacks and a turquoise shirt that turned his eyes to aquamarine?

"Delays."

"Make you crazy." She'd once had that same drive, that same perfectionism, and recognized it in him.

He hiked an eyebrow. "Am I that obvious?"

She laughed. "The fact that you looked at your watch when you asked is a dead giveaway."

His grin was sheepish. "We have so much to do, and contractors are already scheduled. This delay could take days or weeks and cost us months, not to mention the money. With our tight schedules…"

"Schedules made by you." She'd seen the spreadsheets and neatly penciled pages on his desk. Being the cleaning lady gave her insight. She hadn't looked on purpose. They were simply there.

On second thought, maybe she had looked on purpose.

"A tight schedule keeps construction on track, keeps things moving along. Time, as they say, is money, and it waits for no one."

"But there's nothing you can do about a skeleton buried on your job site."

"Right." He breathed out a long, frustrated sigh.

"Then why not relax?" He was tight as a fiddle string. "You're in a beautiful setting with miles of woods and creeks to explore. You're a short drive from the river and loads of activities. Fishing, rafting, you name it. Have you even walked the grounds or driven up on Honey Ridge?"

He shook his head. "Not my thing."

"No? Then what is your thing?" She curled a lock of hair around her index finger and tilted her head, instantly aware that she was coming on to him. She stopped, dropped her hand to her side.

"Business."

"Ah, come on. There has to be more to life than work. Any hobbies? Anything you do for fun?"

"I mostly don't have time for frivolous time wasters." He

stuck a hand in his pants pocket and jingled the coins there as if releasing pent-up energy.

"But if you had the extra time, what would you do?" She moved closer, tilted her head again and touched his arm. As hostess, helping him relax was her job. At least, that was her excuse.

"What did you like as a kid?"

A little smile edged up the corners of his mouth. A nice mouth, sexy and male and firm-looking. Actually, all of him looked good, from his tidy brown hair to the way he filled out a shirt.

A tingle radiated up the back of her neck. She, who had sworn off men forever. Again.

She didn't know what was wrong with her. She knew the trouble men could be. The trouble *she* could be.

But Grayson seemed like a good guy, not her usual loser type. Exactly the reason he would never be seriously interested in someone like her. Like the men she dated, she was a loser, a woman who'd thrown away the greatest gift in life.

The fact that she was even thinking about Grayson in this way disturbed her. It was ridiculous.

But what was the harm in having a conversation?

She moistened her lips and ignored the nagging voice in her head that said a good man, especially one as smart and steady and controlled as Grayson Blake, was out of her league. She'd been out of control since she was fifteen.

"I see that smile," she said. "Tell me."

"Oh, nothing important. For some reason, I thought of the band Devlin and I used to have back in high school."

"You were in a band?" She'd always had a thing for musicians.

"Three of us. Dev, me and our best friend, Gil. We thought we were the Backstreet Boys with instruments and destined for the big-time." He chuckled. "Didn't happen, of course, but we played some gigs and made a little money."

"And the girls went wild." She knew about that, too. She'd followed her share of boy bands.

"Devlin was the star, witty and outgoing with loads of charisma. I was the stuffed shirt at the keyboard."

She waved a dismissing hand. "Keyboard players are hot."

He looked amused. "And you know this, how?"

She wagged a finger at him. "Never mind."

He laughed, and then exactly when her negative imps went silent and she started to enjoy yourself, Grayson looked at that blasted watch.

"I should head back to the mill. Maybe they've learned something."

Before she could change his mind, he left her standing in the foyer, wishing her company had been enough to keep him here.

CHAPTER 7

The next morning as dawn grayed the sky and intense quiet hummed in the spring-scented air, Grayson drove the Jeep the scant distance between the inn and the gristmill as the radio played oldies from the nineties.

He didn't know why he'd told Valery about the band. She probably thought he was an idiot, but those were some good times. He and Dev and Gil and the music. Music was medicine for the soul, and his had been in rough shape back then.

Funny how he seldom touched a piano these days when he'd grown to love it as a teenager, even though the skill had originally been forced upon him by scared parents to keep him away from sports and anything rigorous that might compromise his shaky hold on life.

Mom and Dad must understand a bit of what Julia Donovan felt. Not to that extent, of course. Their child hadn't disappeared, but they'd been afraid of losing him just the same.

He'd been terrified, too. Death wasn't something a thirteen-year-old was supposed to face. But, by God's mercy, he'd faced the Grim Reaper and come out the victor. For now.

Time was a clock winding down, a river flowing through his fingers.

The road leading into the construction site was bumpy and

rough. He jostled along, making a mental note about repairs if he ever got his property back from the state of Tennessee.

He was starting to wish Devlin hadn't gotten him into this. Again.

He parked along the back side of the mill near the waterfall. One of the reasons he came out early each day was to breathe in the fresh air and listen to the creek dance over the small rocky falls. He did his thinking here and could answer emails and make notes in his phone in a peaceful, beautiful setting before the crowds arrived.

Valery was right. Honey Ridge was a hidden jewel of nature and history. If he could find the time to explore, he would. Maybe she was right about that, too.

As his boots crunched fine gravel outside the mill and broke the quiet, movement caught his attention. He stopped, squinted.

Down on the creek bank sat a man and a dog. Of all the people who'd swarmed the mill in the last few days, this one was new, though new wasn't quite the correct term for the rumpled old trespasser.

"Hello." Grayson raised a hand.

The man nodded in reply as if he'd been expecting the company.

Grayson skirted the rocky bank of kudzu and followed the narrow trodden path down to the water's edge to the pair. The dog, some sort of spaniel cross with long curly-haired ears and brown speckles, thumped its tail on the packed earth.

He noticed a fishing pole stuck between two rocks and a red bobber lolling on the water a few feet out.

Trespasser. Poacher.

"Catch anything?"

"Not yet." The old man motioned toward the rock next to him. "Sit a spell."

The old man's invitation surprised him enough to smile.

"This is my property." The words were mild. He didn't mind the trespassers, at least not yet.

"I know it." The stranger chuckled softly. "But I'll let you sit a spell anyway. Oats and I have been waiting for you."

Intrigued and amused, Grayson didn't sit "a spell" but propped his hands on his hips. "Oats?"

The dog perked up and moved closer, shiny brown gaze friendly, tail swishing the air. Grayson offered a hand for the dog to smell.

"She's a good girl. She won't bite."

"Good to know." He took the liberty of stroking the long, silky ears as he studied the newcomer.

The old man's eyes matched his bristly mustache and hair, an iron gray that made him appear to be all one shade except for the sun-darkened, time-wrinkled flesh that furrowed his brow like plowed rows of rich earth. He had apple cheeks, a tattered gray bill cap, and the palest blue eyes imaginable.

"I'm Grayson Blake."

"I know who you are. You and your brother refurbishing the old mill is a good thing, even if you're putting me out of a campsite."

"So you're the one?"

"Uh-huh. Thought you had a ghost, didn't you?"

"No." Grayson squatted. He hadn't intended to. He didn't have time, but something about the old man intrigued him.

A cigarette stub with ash as long as Grayson's thumb dangled from dark, yellowed fingers. The old man didn't bother to flick, and the ash grew heavy and fell to the rocks.

"You know me, but who are you?"

His uninvited guest ground the cigarette out and put the butt in his shirt pocket. "Lem Tolly's the name. You've met

Oats." At her name, she started the tail thumping again. "Quite a fuss about the bones you found."

"Too much fuss for my tastes."

"Got your business in a twitch, don't it?"

Grayson laughed, though he wasn't at all amused. "You could say that."

"Well, let me tell you a thing or two, son. This mill here is history. Full of ghosts and stories. Some of them true and some of them we'll never know. But they're here anyway."

"You believe in ghosts?"

The old man's mustache twitched. "I believe the past talks. Take those bones you found. They've got a story that's been hid for a while, but now they'll do some talking, and we'll know."

"Know what?"

The man's laugh was rusty and produced a cough. "That's what we're going to find out, now, isn't it? What we don't know."

Grayson huffed softly, amused and maybe annoyed at the non-answer.

"I hope it's soon, whatever it is. I have a business to run."

"Tsk. Tsk. You look at that fancy watch of yours again, you're gonna get whiplash."

"Restaurants don't build themselves."

"What do you know about this place, son? Besides the prospects for a profitable eating joint?"

"Not much. What about you? Are you acquainted with its history?"

"Well, that depends on your definition of acquainted. And that's where it gets sketchy." Lem offered a cryptic lift of bushy gray eyebrows. "Now, that skeleton of yours. Right interesting to find a man buried beneath a gristmill, don't you think?"

Grayson leaned in closer. Did the old fella know more than he was saying? "What makes you think the skeleton is a man?"

"Did I say man? Hmm. Funny how that happened."

"I don't suppose you put him there." The statement was mild and off the cuff, but he was dead serious.

Lem chuckled before turning his attention to the red bobber floating on the clear-as-glass water. "No, sir, I did not. But somebody did."

That went without saying.

Grayson swatted at a dive-bombing honeybee as his cell phone buzzed against his hip. He fished out the device and read the messages. He was behind already. Tension pulled at the back of his neck. He reached back, massaged.

Oats went on alert and pointed her nose toward the trees and a road that wasn't visible from the mill. The sound of a vehicle engine grew louder.

A coroner's van pulled close to the big double doors.

And the day's fascination with the gristmill skeleton was about to begin.

CHAPTER 8

The cause is hidden; the effect is visible to all.

OVID

1875. Peach Orchard Farm

Lest her hand shake and give away her terror at the mention of Tandy, the slave boy sold so long ago, Patience Portland carefully laid her fork on the long, family-crowded table. The utensil was one of the precious silver pieces that had been buried during the long, painful war, but, she thought with a shiver, not the only thing hidden from malicious eyes.

Following Ben's announcement that he planned a trip up north to distant Connecticut to find Lizzy's son, those at the supper table sat in stunned silence, almost comical in their frozen state.

They would convince him that the trip was folly. They would stop him, she thought, as her stomach sickened.

Sound erupted suddenly as everyone talked at once, fortissimo voices rising in noisy protest like angry children pounding the piano keys. Lizzy stood at the end of the table next to Ben, black eyes wide and hand at her throat, saying nothing beyond her initial outcry of shocked joy.

With a scrape of chair legs against wooden floor, Benjamin slowly stood to his feet, his cheeks heated by two pinpoints of vivid color. Patience clasped her fingers together in her lap, squeezing hard to quiet the anguish of her soul. Dear, wonderful Benjamin, the joy of the family, the heir to all things Portland. He must not undertake this foolish errand. He simply could not.

He raised a palm to quiet the outcry. "Please. Everyone. Please, hear me."

Slowly the noise subsided, and everyone's attention pinned to the tall, strapping young man who bore his mother's coloring and his father's air of command, though where Edgar had been harsh and unforgiving, Benjamin was thoughtful and kind.

"I've prayed for this day for nine years, and now that I know where Tandy was taken, I aim to find him and bring him home."

The cold wind of fear, like the reaper's frigid fingers, prickled the hair at Patience's nape. Tandy could not come home. And she must voice her protest, though she dared not reveal the reasons.

Be sure your sin will find you out.

She fought for composure, long practiced with the empty stare of the not-too-bright and the blessing of guileless eyes. No one ever suspected, and it must remain that way forever.

God forgive her.

"But, darling." Charlotte's hands moved in restless anxiety on the table's edge, her only outward sign of disquiet. But Patience knew her sister-in-law well. Charlotte had borne many children, including precious Anna last summer, but only this one special boy had survived to adulthood. Like the Shunammite woman in the Bible, Charlotte would do anything to protect her son of promise.

"You've no idea if Tandy remains in Hartford or even how to commence finding him. Emancipation may have taken him far away from his owner, as it did so many of our people."

"Connecticut was a free state, wasn't it?" Josie turned her red head from her northern husband to Benjamin. "Why buy a slave and take him there?"

"I do not know," Ben replied, "but I will find his buyer, and perhaps he'll have information as to Tandy's whereabouts. That should not be so difficult."

"Travel is fraught with danger." This from Thaddeus Eriksson, a northern transplant who understood better than most the dark cloud of tension hovering over the still-fractured country. "Outlaws and robbers abound. Rails are uncertain. Supplies are short."

"I can take care of myself."

Patience avoided Lizzy's face. What wild hope the freedwoman must be feeling! To find her only son. And yet, if her hopes were fulfilled—

"Some things are better left alone, Benjamin."

There. She'd spoken and cared little if her voice shook. Let them believe she worried for Benjamin's safety. Indeed, she did, even though other more selfish reasons caused the quiver. "Perhaps Tandy has changed and wants no part of this place where he was born a slave."

Benjamin removed a marble from his pocket, a rich cobalt blue from the set sent to him during the war by the captain. Sunlight streamed through the open windows, and he held the little marble in the light for all to see. "Tandy will want to see me. I am sure of that and I cannot rest until I find him."

"But you were his master. He, the slave." A good argument, she thought with pride. "Will he view you as friend or foe?"

Ben glanced aside, the bright cheeks brighter still. Patience held her breath. Did she dare hope that her point had struck its target?

"Patience may be right, Benjamin." Charlotte's expression

was anguished as she looked at Lizzy. "But perhaps we can send someone else to search."

The two mothers held gazes for a long moment before Lizzy nodded, her eyes moist.

"No." Ben's chin lifted with the stubborn set of his father. "I'm the one who must go."

Captain William Gadsden, head of the table as well as the house since the war's end, wiped his mouth with a coarse muslin napkin, neatly pressed by Patience's own hand. But all the hot irons in the South could not hide the fact that elegant linens no longer existed in the Portland home. Every last one had been used in this very room as bandages for the bleeding soldiers.

Patience cast a quick glance toward the window where so many had bled under the surgeon's knife. The bloodstains never faded, especially from her memory. Even now she could smell the hot, coppery scent of blood, the lingering odor that rose in the heat of the day like a ghost, reminding them all of the violence, the evil of war.

Dread pulled down inside her belly. The fried chicken she'd eaten was heavy as an anvil. She began to play a soothing nocturne on her thighs, her fingers tapping the imaginary keys. Were it not for prayer and her music, she would have lost her mind long ago. Even now, she itched to leave this room and take up her bench in the parlor where the music would erase the memories, the stench, the evil secrets to which she never should have been a part.

Before the mental music could soothe away her shame, Captain Will's voice intruded. Even a sunny melody could not erase some things, especially now that Ben had discovered Tandy's whereabouts—or at least his buyer's home city.

"As of this day, Peach Orchard Farm and Portland Mill

belong to you, Benjamin, to do with as you see fit. You have responsibilities here."

"The farm and mill belong to you and Mama, too, no matter what a piece of paper says. You are the pair who saved it from destruction and from being bought up by greedy carpetbaggers for pennies on the dollar."

The captain frowned, black eyebrows dipping low. "Those days may not be over. Times are hard. The economy flounders, and that affects everyone at this table as well as our financial holdings. We need you here. Your mother needs you here."

Benjamin swallowed. "Yes, sir. Understood. I'll return as soon as I can, but I leave knowing all our interests are in the best hands possible."

"But, son—"

Benjamin aimed his tender gaze toward Charlotte, his voice gentle as the nocturne in Patience's head. "I made a promise, Mother, and I aim to keep it."

"A child's promise. You were only nine."

"Did you not teach me that a vow is a sacred thing, both to man and God? And never to make one lightly?"

"Yes, but—" The bright shine of unshed tears darkened Charlotte's blue eyes. Patience could scarce prevent her own tears, though they were of shame and guilt. Two mothers, perhaps even three, suffered because of her.

"Promising to find Tandy was not a child's vow. As a man I renew it now. I will find him. And if he's willing, I will bring him home."

Later, after the protests quieted and Benjamin had made his plans perfectly clear, the family returned to a semblance of festivity over his birthday. The effort was strained, and soon the party broke up. Thad and Josie drove away in the wagon, the two children settled in the back. Johnny and Logan retired to their rooms over the carriage house, and Will and Mama took up their places in the parlor. Even now, with the smell of spice cake lingering in the house as a reminder that today was a celebration, Patience sat at the piano, playing a tune he didn't recognize, probably something she'd written herself. For a simple woman, she was a gifted composer and pianist.

Ben knew he'd upset the family and understood his mother feared for his well-being, but for nine years he'd planned this day, hoping and praying it would come. That it had come on his birthday was pure providence. Though loath to have any part in making his mother sad, he was a man now, with a man's accountability. A man was nothing if he did not keep his word.

With the sweet flavor of caramel on his tongue, Ben entered the kitchen where Lizzy finished drying the last of the pots and pans. Ben took up a towel to help. She swatted his hand. "Get out of my kitchen."

Ben grinned at her and went right on drying a heavy cast-iron skillet. "Dinner was delicious, Lizzy. Thank you."

She sniffed. "You barely touched it."

"Excitement." He hung the skillet on the hook next to the black stove.

"Mmm-hmm."

"You didn't say much in there."

"Not my place."

"Tandy is your son."

A pained expression flashed across her face. "He'd be a grown man now. I wouldn't know him."

"You're against me, too?" He peered at her closely, surprised. "You don't want me to find him?"

She moved a rag round and round on a serving platter. "More than anything, I want to see him again. You got to find my child, Benjamin. It's right."

"Yes, ma'am, it is."

"You *got* to find him. Your daddy knew. He knew."

Ben's jaw tightened. "I hated him for selling Tandy."

"So did I, but you must not. He's your pappy. Nothing gonna change that. But you can fix what he broke. Yes, sir, you can fix it."

"Captain Will speaks of responsibility here on the farm, but making up for Father's wrong is also my responsibility. I'm the seed of Edgar Portland, his only living offspring. He did this evil thing. Now finding Tandy is up to me."

Her stare pierced him for a moment, as though she saw deep, deep into his soul. She opened her mouth and then clamped it tight and turned away to put the platter in the cupboard. He was certain she'd wanted to say something but had thought better of it. Now a mood pulsed in the room that Ben couldn't quite put his finger on. When Lizzy turned back toward him, her eyes blazed as fiery as a smithy's forge.

"You loved my boy, didn't you, Mr. Ben?"

"Yes, ma'am. Like a brother."

A tiny hiss moved between her lips. She nodded once. "I got something you need to know. Something I ain't never told another living soul. Not even your mama." She looked to the side and whispered, "Especially not your mama."

Unease prickled his skin. "Yes, ma'am?"

"What I say ain't to leave this kitchen, ya hear?"

He swallowed, a little afraid now. Lizzy had that power. Always had. "Yes, ma'am."

Satisfied that he told the truth, she leaned back, her slight shoulders pulling taut, and drew in a long, slow draft of kitchen air. Benjamin held his breath and waited.

For a fleeting moment the housekeeper seemed to reconsider, but then stiffened and tipped her chin up, eyes blazing into him as if to leave a mark.

"You got to find my boy. You got to, Mr. Ben." She looked

around to be sure no one else could hear but lowered her voice anyway. "You ain't your father's only living offspring."

Ben jerked, stunned and confused. "Are you saying…"

In a voice as dark as midnight, she answered. "You know what I'm sayin'."

Then, she yanked off her apron and walked out, head high, shutting the back door with a final snap.

CHAPTER 9

Present Day. Peach Orchard Inn

Grayson thought he heard music—piano music.

Curious as to who played the haunting melody when he hadn't noticed a piano anywhere in the mansion, he closed his laptop, pocketed his reading glasses, and followed the sound down the stairs and into the guest parlor.

After hours of fiddling with Devlin's designs and running through spreadsheets, he needed a break anyway.

Still, the music played, lilting, sad, and lovely.

There wasn't a soul in the parlor unless he counted the pair in the photo overlooking the fireplace. He stood still, listening hard, trying to ascertain location or at least a direction.

Valery appeared in the archway. The music stopped.

"You look puzzled." After flashing him a smile, she went to the fireplace where she stretched up on ballet flats, giving him a pleasant view of her lithe, curvy profile as she set a bouquet of fresh pink and purple tulips on the mantel.

"I thought I heard someone playing the piano, but I don't remember seeing one."

She scooted the fluted vase—a porcelain Edwardian, unless he missed his guess—an inch to one side before turning toward him. "There's a baby grand in the family parlor."

"So I wasn't hearing things?"

Eyebrows lifted above dancing eyes, Valery tilted her head in a charmer's pose. "Then again, maybe you were."

He huffed softly, ruffled to find himself more attracted to her every time they met. "You sound like the old man I met this morning at the mill."

He told her about Lem Tolly and their odd conversation, a conversation that left him wondering if Lem knew something about the bones buried beneath the mill.

"I know who you mean. I've seen him around. He's… different."

Grayson laughed. "You can say that again."

"He's different."

Then they both laughed, each holding the other's gaze until Grayson's neck grew warm, and he glanced away.

He wasn't without female companionship, especially on his own time schedule, but there was something about this particular woman… He knew for a fact, a free spirit like Valery would never adhere to his regimented, organized lifestyle. Maybe that was why she rattled him. She was outside his comfort zone.

He'd have to think about that. About her. As if he didn't already.

While he pondered, she looped an arm through his elbow.

"Come on, Gray," she said, surprising him with the shortened, familiar form of his name. "I'll show you the piano. It's in the family living quarters on the other end of the house."

Through his long sleeves, he felt the heat of her skin and smelled the lush, musky scent she wore. No fruity peach for this siren, she was all heat and exotic mystery.

He definitely felt her heat.

Before he could remind her that he had things to do—even though he didn't—she led him out of the parlor, down the hall and into the foyer. "I want to show you something else first. I think you'll be interested."

"What is it?"

Valery laughed, a throaty music that stirred his blood. The sound gave him thoughts he couldn't fit into his schedule.

"You'll see."

He didn't object to the gentle tug of her arm on his. In fact, he liked it. Though there was nothing sensual about her intent; her sensuality was as much a part of her as breathing. He liked touching her, having her touch him as long as he remembered that Valery was an accomplished charmer, and flirting with any man—not only him—was as natural to her as breathing.

A skinny, sickly Grayson had fallen hard for her at fifteen. The adult Grayson might not be skinny or sickly, but he was still a geek who loved spreadsheets and the perfect order of predictable numbers.

Valery was not predictable.

She drew him into the foyer to the credenza and the display case of artifacts. She inched closer until her side brushed his, barely, but he felt every place they connected.

"Have you looked at these?" She tilted that pretty face up toward his.

He cleared his throat.

The display of antique artifacts had interested him from the moment he'd first walked in the house. "My crews have found artifacts during construction, too—especially Civil War era buttons and coins and mine balls. I never thought of displaying them."

"You have an office, don't you?"

"In Nashville."

"There you go, then."

She was right. A shadow box filled with history would please him as well as his clients. He wondered what had become of the items they'd discovered over the years.

She turned back to the display and tapped a finger against the glass-framed sheet music. "Have you noticed the sheet music?"

He'd expected her fingernails to be long and vampish. Instead, they were short and serviceable but every bit as cardinal-red as her lipstick.

"I have. Each time I walk through the front door. There's something about it…"

Her head whipped toward him. "You feel it, too? I've never told anyone because, Lord knows, they already think I'm loony."

He smiled down at her, lightly teasing, eager to prolong the moments in her quicksilver company. "And why is that, Miss Carter? What insane thing have you done to set the tongues wagging?"

Her smile faltered and she broke eye contact. "Oh, honey child, you don't even want to go there."

Then she gave a brittle laugh and gently slapped at his forearm. "Do you want to play this music for me or not? I've been dying for a pianist to come along so I can hear it."

"You don't play?" There was something very musical about the way she moved.

"Regretfully, no. None of us do, though Mama took lessons as a girl, and she made Julia and I do the same. When it became obvious I had no talent for piano, she enrolled me in… Well, that's not important. How did you become a piano man?"

Memories of that time flashed in his head. "I got sick. My parents were afraid for me to play sports, so they forced me into piano to keep me occupied."

"You must have been very sick. What happened?"

He rarely discussed the terrifying time, but for some reason he told her. "I was diagnosed with Hodgkin's lymphoma."

"Hodgkin's as in cancer?" Her lips rounded in sympathy and surprise. "When?"

"I was thirteen. Right before school was out for summer vacation. Devlin and I were eager to come here for a few weeks with Grandma and Pappy." His gaze drifted to the Victorian credenza, but his mind was far away. "Devlin came that summer and the next. I stayed in Nashville."

"And had treatments."

"Yeah."

"I'm sorry you had to go through that. Your parents must have been terrified."

"They were. So was I. Teenage boys aren't supposed to get cancer and die." He glanced at his watch. He'd been running out of time.

"How incredibly brave."

"I never thought of myself as brave, Valery. A person does what he has to do, even if he's only thirteen. We don't always have choices."

"Nor do we always make the right ones." She studied him in quiet sympathy. "Are you okay now?"

"The docs run tests every year, but so far, I'm good." He didn't like thinking of the alternative, but the danger was always there on the edge of his mind.

"Thank God. I'm so glad. The world would be a worse place without Grayson Blake."

The sweet sentiment caught him off guard. "I could return the compliment."

"Don't. It wouldn't be true."

Where had that come from? "You're a beautiful, kind woman. It's a shame you don't realize that."

Her expression was stricken. "You don't know me that well."

No, but he wanted to. "Maybe we should remedy that problem."

Something flickered in her expression, and her lips curved, not a lot but enough. "Maybe we should."

A little hum of interest and energy stirred the peach air around them. Grayson shifted but not due to discomfort. He was sorely tempted to kiss her, but this was not the time or place, and as she said, he didn't even know her that well.

But he would. Yes, he would.

"Now you know why I learned piano instead of football."

"A forced activity."

"And one I'm thankful for. I would have gone crazy without music as a focus. Mom and Dad wouldn't let me do anything vigorous for a long time. And to tell the truth, I didn't feel like doing anything else. Chemo knocked me out. Music became my hobby, my solace, everything for a while."

"Well, then, Piano Man, will you play for me? Show me your stuff?"

Suddenly Grayson very much wanted to get his hands on a piano and figure out what it was about the sheet music that prickled the hair on the back of his neck.

"The paper must be very fragile. I'm not sure it could survive much handling."

"Fear not, oh wise and sensible one, we made copies when we first discovered Patience Portland's portfolio." She was making gentle fun of his perfectionist tendency, but he was accustomed to the teasing. Devlin did it all the time.

He blinked down at her. "You have more than this one piece?"

"An entire notebook. Patience was, apparently, a prolific composer and accomplished pianist. Most of the pieces are by other people with her notations on the pages, but a good selection is her own work."

"Amazing." He was oddly excited by the news.

"Isn't it?" Her eyelashes fluttered. "Come on, then. Play. You know you want to."

He suppressed a grin. "I'm not getting any work done anyway."

"And the delay is making you very antsy."

"Idle hands are the devil's workshop." He wiggled his fingers at her. "My skills may be a bit rusty, but I'd like to give it a try."

"Oh, I bet your skills are top-notch." She laughed her throaty laugh.

He didn't miss the innuendo, but dismissed it and joked in kind. "Who knows, if the Gristmill Restaurant project goes down the drain, I'll be tuned up for a job in a piano bar."

"I promise to come listen every Friday night and put money in your jar."

"Will you lean on the piano and give me inspiration?"

She leaned in vamp-like and playfully batted her eyelashes, her voice dropping low. "Maybe. If you're really, really nice and play all my favorites."

She tapped a finger against her top lip. Full, red and tilted at the corners in a perpetual smile. He was male. She was beautiful. If his mind wandered off to kissing, he couldn't help it. He, who was usually so controlled and focused, was losing focus today.

"Must be the delays," he mumbled.

"What?"

He shook his head. "Nothing. Thinking out loud. Show me the piano and let's see if I still have it."

She laughed again, and feeling both attractive and attracted, he followed her toward the back of house.

★ ★ ★

He still had it, all right.

All of it. Most of which had nothing to do with his musical abilities.

Valery stood at the corner of the piano facing Grayson as his skilled fingers trickled over the keys of the baby grand to find a rhythm. He smiled up at her, his hands moving as if they didn't need his brain. But with a brain as big as his, he could probably do ten things at once and never break a sweat.

Such, she was learning, was his charisma. His was not the exuberant extroverted flare of his brother, but a quieter, solid confidence that said he knew exactly what he was doing and where he was going.

Valery had never met anyone quite like Grayson Blake. He didn't fit her perception of men in general. The difference fascinated her.

She'd done something out of the ordinary by bringing him into a part of the house few guests ever saw. Here, the family relaxed, invited friends. Guests remained in the public sections of the inn.

But here they were, in the family parlor.

The cozy room, dominated by ornate floral patterns in the muted pinks and greens favored by the early nineteenth century, looked out upon the south side of the house toward the old cemetery and the woods. A white marble fireplace added character to one wall, and an Aubusson-style rug Mama had found in Chattanooga covered the reclaimed heart pine floor. With the heavy Victorian drapes tied back over lace sheers, a weak sun penetrated the room. She was glad they'd gone to the trouble of restoring rather than modernizing the space.

"Name that tune." Grayson's music drew her focus as he played a few bars.

"Easy." She waved a dismissing hand. "'Walking in Memphis.' If you don't know that one, you can't live in Tennessee."

"Dev says the same thing."

"The two of you are really close, aren't you?"

"Like you and Julia, I suppose."

Too close, then. So close that if one bled, the other suffered. And the main reason Julia could never, ever learn what her sister had done.

A tricky line of thinking she should not follow.

She tossed her hair back, feeling a little wild and wishing she were free the way she'd been before bad choices had stolen too much and left her guilt-ridden and yearning for do-overs.

But life didn't work that way. There were no second chances. Only regret and penitence. The only time she felt wild and free was when she'd had enough booze to numb the memories.

"Hey. Earth to Valery."

"Sorry." She tossed her hair back again and laughed to prove she was still a fun girl, both to herself and him. "Play. I'm all ears."

Grayson modulated into a feisty rhythm she recognized immediately. "Brown Eyed Girl." She'd played the Van Morrison CD until some guy borrowed it and never returned it. Guys. Who sang the song in her ear and made promises they never kept.

She wondered if Grayson was that kind. Instinct said he wasn't. If he made a promise, he'd probably write it in his planner, type it into an app with an alarm, and make it happen. He was anchored, sure, and dependable, all the things she wasn't.

She was a wind sock in a hurricane.

But the thought of Grayson singing in her ear tickled her fancy, made her sassy.

She flicked her fingers through the air and teased. "Sorry. Don't know that one."

"Yes, you do. Even a blue-eyed woman would recognize 'Brown Eyed Girl.'"

"You prefer blue?"

He gazed at her, serious for a moment, and she suffered a pleasant flutter. "Brown eyes are beautiful, like warm, sweet caramel."

"Why, Mr. Blake. I do declare." She batted her eyelashes again, one hand to her chest in imitation of every Southern belle the movies ever offered, and was rewarded by his laugh.

The first day he'd arrived, he'd seemed driven and professional and uptight, but today she saw a different side of him. Relaxed, he was witty and warm. The combination was killer attractive.

He stopped playing and spun his knees toward the end of the bench. "You didn't come to hear me play oldies. The portfolio?"

"Oh." She'd been enjoying *him* so much she didn't give a rip about Patience Portland's antique music. Men were a weakness she couldn't seem to resist, no matter how many times she swore to stay away. "In the bench."

He retrieved the book and opened the pages on the piano.

"I thought it was a waste of money," she said, and when his gaze was quizzical, she clarified. "Buying the piano."

He ran an appreciative hand over the gleaming black lacquered finish. "Not original, then."

"No. The original was in the guest parlor. From what we've pieced together from letters, old newspapers, and other documents, Patience Portland taught piano in that room."

"And wrote music."

"Makes you wonder, doesn't it, when you know some of the history of this house? Did she play when the Union army occupied the house? Did her music comfort the wounded? Did she write for her true love?"

"Those kinds of questions are why we repurpose old construction. The thought of those who've gone before, who built lives and buildings, who loved and hated, who made this country what it is, fascinates me." Grayson pointed a finger. "Don't start with the spotted owl thing."

"I wasn't going to, but since you brought it up, why don't you attend a Historical Preservation meeting with me?" She could pretend the invitation was for the project but couldn't deny a thrill at the idea of showing up on his arm. "The Sweat twins might be able to tell you more about the mill. You've met Miss Vida Jean and Miss Willa Dean, haven't you?"

"Oh, yeah," he said wryly. "At the mill, at the café, on the street. I even found them standing over the open grave down in the basement, pressed against the police caution tape, debating how poor Mr. Bones met his demise. Those ladies are everywhere and full of advice and stories."

"I'll admit they're eccentric in their matching outfits and daffodil hair, but if anyone knows Honey Ridge, they do. They've lived through much of its history or know someone who did." She tilted toward him. "So, what do you say? There's a meeting next Wednesday night. Someone always brings home-baked refreshments, so we can linger and argue about the spotted owl."

She flashed him a smile to let him know she was joking. No one would attack him about the restoration. The town was thrilled that someone of the Blake brothers' reputation had taken an interest. As he'd reminded her that first day, the gristmill would decay and disappear entirely if not for them.

"Refreshments are always good." The corners of his eyes crinkled. "But everything depends on where we are on the mill project. Hopefully, we'll be up and going by then, making up for lost time."

Time. Now that she knew about his teenage brush with death she understood his drive a little better. The clock was ticking for them all. Grayson felt that pressure more than most.

He turned his attention to the sheet music and began to tentatively locate the notes to Patience's melody.

After a trial run-through, he played in earnest, smoothly, easily, as she'd expected of him. Grayson would do nothing halfway.

The music began with a dreamlike quality as pure and innocent as a spring day.

"Beautiful," Valery murmured. "She was very gifted."

So was he.

Grayson nodded and continued to play, his long, powerful fingers flowing effortlessly and a surprising passion in his expression. Given his passion for work, she should have known he'd be passionate about other things.

She closed her eyes and let the music swell over her, warm and sweet and sweeping her away like a current running toward the ocean.

Valery retreated to her dream world, swaying to the music, recalling the pure joy of those times when she was lost in the music and movement. Her body remembered what her mind tried to forget.

Suddenly, the music stopped.

Her eyes flew open. Her pulse beat strangely in her throat. Of joy and beauty and freedom.

"What?" She sounded breathless.

"You're a dancer."

Anxiety trickled through her, more acid than sweetly flowing current. "Not anymore."

Dance had been her whole life, her love, the tool her mother had used to control her. She'd chosen dance and thrown away the best of herself.

Memories of Savannah flashed through her head, a Technicolor movie screen. She mentally slapped at the images as if the consequences of her decision could be that easily eradicated.

"I remember now how dedicated you were and the way you danced to everything. Even at the Dairy Queen."

And in the parking lot and at bonfires and football games and parades. Anywhere there was space she danced whether formally or for fun. Dance was her life, her love, her everything.

She didn't dance anymore.

"Teenage stuff." She forced a smile.

"Come on. I remember a lot more than that. You were a serious student, a real talent. Grandma even predicted you'd end up dancing on Broadway or in the movies."

"Every girl dreams of becoming a singer or dancer. Every boy is convinced he'll be a pro athlete. Reality is a whole different ball game."

"True, Dev and I were going to be rock stars." His eyes twinkled. "But you were better than most. I can't believe I didn't recall until now. You did some music videos up in Nashville, didn't you? And you were the talk of Honey Ridge that summer."

Please, don't remember anything else. Please.

"Didn't you go to New York one year to train with some big-time dance teacher?"

He remembered.

CHAPTER 10

Much later, after the house quieted and the night stole the sun, leaving only gentle moonlight in exchange, Grayson couldn't settle down. The music and Valery played on his mind. So did the project. Too much to think about.

He couldn't believe he'd told her about the Hodgkin's. Discussing cancer wasn't exactly casual conversation. But he didn't regret it. He'd learned something about her, too. She wasn't all fluff and flash, after all. She'd been compassionate and thoughtful.

Something had troubled her when the conversation had turned to dancing. For some odd reason, she didn't want to talk about it, and shortly thereafter, she'd made an excuse to leave, leaving him to explore the old sheet music alone. What was it about the topic that shook her so much she'd hurried away?

Playing wasn't nearly as much fun without her.

After a while, he had closed the baby grand and had gone back to work, where he'd called every official dealing with the skeleton crime scene. He had gotten nowhere. The project was officially stalled.

Heartburn tormented him like a hot balloon beneath his breastbone.

He paced from one side of the Mulberry Room to the other, looked out the window, came back to the desk and searched for a book. He wasn't in the mood to read or even to update social media. And he sure wasn't in the mood for time-wasting chats with friends.

Time. Wasted. He glanced at his watch, scrolled through his calendar, tried to find ways to manipulate the schedule to be doing something on the project during the delays.

He wanted to work, to get on with business before it was too late.

His cell phone vibrated against the rolltop desk where he'd set the device to charge. A glance at caller ID revealed his brother's face grinning from beneath a Santa hat. The photo always made Grayson smile. Devlin had worn the ugliest sweater known to man to last year's office Christmas party. Nobody out-partied Devlin.

"Hey."

"I knew you'd still be up prowling. How's the ulcer?"

Grayson touched his chest with two fingers. "Burning."

Devlin knew how delays and skewed schedules ate at his gut.

"Go downstairs and ask the pretty brunette for some milk."

"Milk never works." But he would probably take the advice anyway. "What's up in Nashville?"

"The manager at Blake Brothers Nashville quit."

"What? Why?" Acid pooled in his belly and burned a brand-new hole. "I thought Lacy loved us. We pay her well."

"Sony Records paid her more."

Grayson let out a groan but couldn't begrudge the woman her dream. "Good for Lacy."

"Yeah. She's been working a long time for this break. I told her to go be a star and bring all her rich friends to the restaurant."

"How fast can you hire someone to take her place?"

"That's your gig, Gray." Grayson had figured he'd say that. "I don't do schedules and human resources, but I can manage the operation for a few days until you come up with a plan. Lacy gave me a stack of applicants."

"Great. Email them to me, and I'll get the interviews set up ASAP." Driving up to Nashville for a few days for the interviews would take his mind off the mill debacle. He was glad for an excuse to *do something* besides hassle officials, listen to the good old boys speculate on Mr. Bones's identity, and wonder if he was getting a thing for a woman who would break his heart.

There was a hum on the other end of the phone before Devlin spoke again, quieter now. "One of the applicants is Faith Madison."

Ah. So that's why Dev had called.

"Do you want me to hire her?"

"I don't know."

"We can dump her application in the garbage. You don't owe her anything."

"She doesn't owe us anything either. The breakup was mutual."

So he said. Grayson had never quite believed that. Faith was the only woman who'd ever turned Devlin's head so far around only the girl in *The Exorcist* could have swiveled farther.

"Tell me what you want me to do."

"Let me think about it overnight."

"It's your call."

"Right." Devlin let out an exasperated huff. "On a better note, how are things progressing with the brunette?"

He ignored the question. If Devlin didn't want to talk about Faith, Grayson sure didn't want to discuss Valery. He couldn't honestly answer anyway. He was still mulling.

"Did you know they have a piano at the inn?"

"Did you impress her with your repertoire?"

"A Steinway baby grand. Black lacquer. Perfect pitch. Getting back into the music felt good." He hadn't played since—what?—Christmas, maybe?

Devlin groaned. "You're waxing poetic about a musical instrument when you have Valery Carter to look at? She must *really* be getting under your skin."

She was. "She's an enigma."

"Big word. Speak down to me, egghead."

"I don't understand what makes her tick."

Devlin's laugh rang in his ear. He held the cell phone a few inches away.

"Since when does any man understand what makes any woman tick? Enjoy her company and stop trying to analyze everything. A woman, especially a woman like Valery Carter, will never fit into one of your mathematical paradigms."

Tell him something he hadn't already figured out. "She used to be a dancer. Did you recall that?"

"Can't say I did, but at the time you were mooning over her, I was more interested in Shaelynn."

"And Bridget and Marly and Feather Ann."

"Oh, man, I hadn't thought of Feather Ann in years. I wonder if she's still around Honey Ridge?"

Grayson chuckled. "I'll be sure and ask the good old boys."

"You do that. Hey, I gotta go. Someone's at the door."

"Okay. Let me know about Faith. Talk to you tomorrow."

As he started to hang up, Grayson heard his brother say, "Go drink some milk…and try not to combust."

Tossing the cell phone back onto the desk, Grayson decided to give the milk a try and trotted downstairs. He passed a pair of guests on the red carpeted stairs going up as he came down and nodded, politely standing to the side to let the couple pass.

The Donovan family had, apparently, retired to their part of their house, and the downstairs was quiet and dim. He wouldn't mind playing the baby grand again, but he wouldn't intrude on their space.

One small light glowed from the parlor, a night-light of sorts and another even smaller one from the foyer to guide late returners to their rooms. He rounded through the dining room into the industrial-sized kitchen and opened the big silver side-by-side. The bright light blinded him as he reached for the milk.

The aged Australian shepherd ambled slowly in, tail wagging as he sniffed Grayson's shoe.

"What are you doing in here, boy?" Normally, the dog disappeared with Alex, Eli's quiet little boy.

Grayson set the milk carton on the granite counter to pet the dog. The affable canine ambled to the back door and looked over his shoulder, his graying muzzle visible.

"You need out?" Grayson didn't know the protocol. Did the family allow the old fella out at night? Would he be in danger from coyotes or black bears?

While he was debating, the dog raised a paw, scratched at the wood with insistence and whined.

From outside, a slurred voice responded, "I'm coming. I'm coming. Keep your pants on."

The back door opened. Valery stood to one side of the old-fashioned screen door, swaying slightly as Bingo trotted past and into the darkness.

When she spotted Grayson, Valery offered a slow, lazy, sensual smile. Her body language loose and relaxed, her eyelids drooped the slightest bit. "Well, look who's here. The handsome piano player. Jus' the man I wanna see."

Grayson's heart sunk. She'd been drinking. A lot.

"Valery? Are you all right?"

A stupid question. Anyone who drank alone in the dark wasn't all right.

"Join me? I am all by my little lonesome." She tried for a saucy toss of her head but swayed off balance and grabbed for Grayson's arm.

He caught hold of her and stepped out onto the porch, hoping to spare her the embarrassment of having another guest see her this inebriated.

She leaned into him, face tilted up. Her mascara was smeared as if she'd been crying. The smell of hard liquor emanated from her, and her lipstick had faded to nothing but a line around her mouth.

Grayson touched her damp cheek. He hadn't intended to touch her, but he felt sorry for her. He was also confused. Valery was beautiful, smart, personable. Why was she so sad?

"Why were you crying? What's wrong?"

"Not a thing, handsome, now that you're here." She ran both hands up the front of his shirt and draped limp arms over his shoulders, her upper body pressing into his for support.

"Did something happen?" He had the surprising need to find the culprit and throw a punch. "Is it anything I can help with?"

Something clicked inside his ever-analyzing brain. She'd been fine, happy, energized until he'd brought up her love of dance. Had *he* inadvertently caused this episode?

Or was this a delayed reaction to the skeleton in his mill? Had the worry over her nephew festered and grown until she'd sought escape? Again, his fault. He'd handled the announcement badly.

She exhaled a long sigh, bathing him in alcohol breath. Her voice dipped low and sultry. "You like me. I can tell. I always know when a man wants me."

Her words saddened rather than titillated him. He wanted

her, all right, but not like this. He wanted the saucy, laughing Valery, who danced and preserved history for future generations, the Valery who ran a bed-and-breakfast with thoughtfulness and grace, the Valery he'd seen playing with Alex and the dog and placing cheerful flowers in a woman's room after her boyfriend had stormed out of the inn and left her.

"My piano man. So strong and smart under all that control. Sexy." She tiptoed up, lips even with his, close enough that he felt the warmth from her mouth. "You want to kiss me, hmm? Do you?"

Heaviness, like a lead pipe, replaced the burning in his belly. As much as he'd like to kiss Valery, he wasn't the kind of man who took advantage of an inebriated woman. What pleasure was there in that?

The big question remained. Why did she feel the need to get drunk all alone and come on to him? Did she do this with other guests?

Somehow he didn't think so. He knew how to read people. In his business the skill was crucial. He'd sparked something this afternoon that had set her on this destructive course. This was his fault, but he didn't know why.

Something was wrong in Valery's world tonight, and he was so far out of his element, he didn't know what else to do. So he pulled her into a protective, aching embrace, listened to her ramble, and wondered what haunted this beautiful woman he couldn't get out of his head—or his heart.

The next morning Grayson's alarm woke him before dawn. He dressed, grabbed a banana from the fruit bowl, made a thermos of coffee, and headed for the mill. Breakfast would wait.

Later this morning, Devlin would email the manager applications, and tomorrow he'd make a run to Nashville. Today, he'd wrap up everything he could here...which wasn't much.

He was hoping the old man and his dog would be at the creek again. Lem Tolly had seemed intently interested in the skeleton, and the more he thought about their strange conversation, the more Grayson wanted to know why. If Lem knew something, he intended to find out.

The man also reminded him a little of his grandfather, and he missed Pappy with a pang strong enough to make his eyes water.

Pappy, who'd taught him to love old things, though they'd never had the time to finish the classic '57 Chevy they'd been rebuilding together.

He rubbed the back of a hand across his face, his heart suddenly heavy.

He hadn't worked on the green-and-white Bel Air since Pappy's death three years ago. A moving company had loaded the car onto a trailer and brought it to Nashville to live in Grayson's garage. Someday he'd finish Pappy's—and his—dream car. Someday. When he had the time.

Pappy would have been ecstatic about the mill project.

"Make the old new again. Appreciate history." He could practically hear his grandfather's voice.

Grayson tossed the banana on the Jeep seat, appetite gone and fatigue a factor this early morning.

He'd slept little last night, his thoughts filled with Valery. He was a problem solver, a man who analyzed and studied until the solution became clear. If she'd let him, he'd help, but he didn't know if she wanted or even needed help. Maybe this had been a one-time incident. Because of the issues at work, perhaps he was seeing a problem where there wasn't one. His gut instinct said there was. More troubling still, he cared.

He wondered how Valery would feel this morning when she awakened to remember last night. Part of him wanted to text her, to tell her... He didn't know what.

He parked the oversized vehicle on the dirt and gravel trail leading into the mill and considered scheduling this road to be widened and resurfaced right away. Every bit as quickly he changed his mind. If the entire project ended up scratched, he'd lose too much money and time.

The mill was silent. No TBI or forensic people had yet arrived. The single security guard keeping watch beside the double doors waved a greeting which Grayson returned.

Until forensics finished, TBI insisted on a round-the-clock guard. Even in this out-of-the-way spot, treasure seekers and the curious could damage crucial evidence.

Eager for a few minutes alone, he started around the building and down the incline toward the peaceful creek.

The alarm on his watch sounded. After a quick glance, he shut it off.

"How many alarms you got on that thing, son?"

Grayson looked down, squinting in the direction of the voice.

Lem Tolly sat in the same spot as before on a rock across from the waterwheel, a spot where the foam began to settle and form a clear, quiet creek. Silvery shad darted beneath the glassy surface.

"What are you doing up so early, Lem?"

"Waiting on you. Enjoying the Master's handiwork. Breathing fresh air. Sun will shoot through those trees in a minute, and I don't want to miss that." He chuckled softly. "I'm a busy man. Almost as busy as you."

The notion made them both grin. Sitting around watching the sunrise didn't accomplish a thing to Grayson's way of thinking, and he had a feeling Lem could discern his opinion.

A leaf shivered loose from a willow, like a graceful lady shedding a glove which she dropped daintily to the silver, mirrored swirls. The leaf circled, then twirled in a pretty ballet before racing downstream. The leaf reminded him of Valery being swept along by some inner torment, the music inside her dancing and swirling and pleading for release.

Was that it? She no longer danced but wanted to? But why would she give up dance when she'd been talented and successful at such a young age?

"Got a smoke?" Lem asked.

"No." Grayson stuffed his hands in his pockets and gazed around. Keys jangled impatiently against his fingertips. "Where's your dog?"

"Visiting the squirrels." Lem pointed a finger toward the woods. "See that goldfinch and his bride?"

Grayson squinted. "Where?"

"You got to focus, son. A man who moves at the speed of light misses the little magic." Lem Tolly motioned to the ground. "Sit."

"I'm expecting a conference call soon."

"Sit. I suspect your watch will remind you."

He was right about that. Grayson dusted off a rock, tugged at his pant leg and perched.

"Listen. You hear that?"

Grayson stilled, straining to hear. "What?"

"You tell me."

Annoyance quivered through him, but out of respect for his elders, Grayson focused on the sounds around him.

"A breeze in the trees," he said to humor the old guy. "Birds tweeting."

"And?"

He bit back a sigh. Who had time for this nonsense? "Water. That's it."

"That young cottonwood yonder?" Yellowed brown fingers pointed. "Give a listen. She's celebrating."

Celebrating? A tree? But Grayson did as the man asked, and he heard the most amazing thing. Awe replaced the irritation.

He cast a quick glance at Lem. "Applause. I hear distant applause."

Lem offered a toothy, tobacco-stained smile of pride as if Grayson was his prize pupil and he'd won the spelling bee. *"And the trees of the fields will clap their hands.* Smart fella name of Isaiah knew what he was talking about, eh?"

"I've seen hundreds of cottonwood trees, but I've never heard that sound." Like a thousand tiny, clapping hands.

"All that rushing around you do. Setting alarms. Looking at the phone as if cyberspace holds your future. Pacing this property when there's not a thing you can do to hurry the investigation. You need to slow down, son, and notice the magic. This is where you'll find your answers."

"Easy for someone who's retired, but I can't run a business sitting on the creek bank listening to trees clap."

"Maybe this is your business now. Maybe all your questions can be answered right here."

"What questions?"

"That's for you to decide."

Grayson barked a soft, frustrated laugh. Lem Tolly talked in riddles half the time, and this was no exception.

"That woman of yours. She comes down here sometimes."

Probably with a bottle of Southern Comfort and some other guy. "I don't have a woman."

"Huh. Denial. I know a little psychobabble." Lem poked a stick at the grass. "She's been coming down here by herself, usually late at night, ever since that little nephew of hers went missing."

Grayson cut him a sharp glance. "What do you know about that?"

"Sad. That's what I know, and Miss Julia nearly losing her mind over it."

"Who wouldn't?"

"She never quit looking, you know. A woman is strong like that. She didn't give up." Lem's gaze grew distant and lost, his mustache drooping. "All those years, and she never did forget about her boy."

"Are we still discussing Julia?"

The old man blinked and focus slowly returned. Grayson wondered if he was senile.

"Yes, yes. Julia." Lem smacked his lips. "A strong woman. Miss Valery, she's a different kind of strong. Nobody sees it."

"But you do?"

"Uh-huh. Did she tell you how she came to be at Peach Orchard Inn?"

"I have a feeling you're going to."

"Smart." Lem chuckled. The brown speckled dog broke through the trees and trotted to the creek for a slurpy drink. "The inn was Valery's idea, but not for herself. For her sister. The whole town was worried about Julia. That husband of hers left her."

Grayson blinked in surprise. "Eli?"

"No, no. Mikey's dad. The lawyer. They fell apart without their son. Julia became a ghost in her own house, dead inside, too depressed to keep on living. If not for that pretty woman of yours, she might not have."

"You're saying Valery bought the inn for her sister?"

"Bought into it. Pushed Julia to restore and open the house as a bed-and-breakfast. The way I see things, Valery single-handedly pulled her sister back from the edge."

If what Lem said was true, Valery was far deeper than she appeared, though now that he heard, Grayson wasn't surprised.

A shallow party girl wouldn't drink alone to hide her pain. She wouldn't care enough.

"How do you know all this?"

"Honey Ridge isn't that big, son. Folks know everything if they slow down and pay attention." He shifted on the rock. "You got a smoke?"

"Same answer as last time."

"I need to quit anyway." He patted the dog whose attention riveted on a downy woodpecker skittering up a tree trunk. "She dances."

"Julia?"

Lem let out a huffy bark. "No, boy, keep up. Your woman. I see her now and then, dancing right over there on the edge of the falls, dancing the ghosts away when she thinks no one is looking."

Grayson cocked his head, squinting at the old man and tempted to tell him about last night. Hadn't he wondered what haunted Valery Carter? "You think she has ghosts?"

"We all got ghosts. You got 'em, too. You and that watch and that fancy tablet thing you're always tapping at."

Grayson shifted his gaze to the water. "I'm a businessman. Time is money."

"Time is more than that to you. I see it. You're running from time while trying to hang on to it. A conundrum." His fathomless eyes stared a hole in Grayson. "What ghost chases *you*, Grayson Blake?"

A mysterious shiver, like a cold shadow, moved over Grayson. He glanced away from the piercing stare. "Only the ghost of the poor soul holding up my construction project."

"Hmm. Old Mr. Bones. Interesting how you're the one who found him. Ever wonder about that? Ever wonder why you? Why now, after all these years?"

Grayson's glance was sharp. Lem had used the same phrase

again. "All these years? Do you know something you haven't told?"

"See? You got questions. Lots and lots of questions."

"That's not an answer."

"Well, sometimes a man's got to dig for himself and seek patience until the past decides to talk."

Lem spoke in riddles, and Grayson couldn't decide if he was a soothsayer or a little crazy. "How long have you lived around Honey Ridge?"

"Oh, off and on forever. Maybe longer. I travel some, visit my forefathers and see what they have to teach me."

"You have roots here? Family?"

"As sure as you do. Maybe surer."

"What does that mean?"

"A metaphor for you. See those little fish down there? Darting, rushing, trying to avoid disaster. You're like them."

"I'm avoiding disaster, all right. Financial disaster if this project goes under." An alarm sounded. Grayson looked at his watch.

Lem chuckled knowingly. "Tick, tock, tick, tock."

Frustrated by the riddles and non-answers, Grayson pushed up from the cool rock. The sun had split the trees and blasted white radiance through the clearing. His belly gnawed at him.

"Have you had breakfast? You're welcome to come back to the inn with me. Or I could drive us to the café."

Lem waved him off and turned back to the water.

Grayson set the thermos of coffee on the rock next to the old man and walked quickly up the incline.

The sound of distant applause followed him all the way back to the inn.

CHAPTER 11

But I have promises to keep,
And miles to go before I sleep...

ROBERT FROST

1875. Peach Orchard Farm

Benjamin adjusted the pack on his horse one final time and turned to bid his family farewell. They circled around him, breaking his heart with their brave smiles, especially his mother, who kept her British composure even though her summer-blue eyes were filled with rain clouds, giving away her despair.

One by one, he said his goodbyes, a lump in his throat. He had no timetable, no way of knowing how long his search would take. He did not, however, inform his family of this troublesome fact.

"You'll wire if you need anything." Will shook his hand with a grip that lingered as though Ben was still the little boy he'd taken under his wing. But respect and confidence mingled with Will's love and concern. He knew, as did Benjamin, that many of his former soldiers had been younger, and yet, they'd faced far more danger than this trip would encounter.

"Yes, sir. Thank you, sir. But have no concern for me. Take care of Mama."

Will smiled, his gaze moving to the woman at his side. He

slid an arm around her waist, not hiding his affection. "'Twill be my greatest pleasure."

Ben gave a nod, satisfied. William Gadsden loved his mother with a devotion that had kept him alive in a Confederate prison and brought him all the way across the country after the war to find her. They took care of each other, unlike the treatment Mama had found at the hands of Edgar Portland. Distaste for his father was sour on his tongue.

"The horse will take me as far as Nashville, and I'll ride the train from there."

None of them mentioned the obvious. The heir to Portland Farm and Mill had never ridden the train. He'd never traveled alone anywhere outside Honey Ridge.

"Clare Marsden is expecting you in Nashville. I wrote to her."

"Thank you, Mama." Clare had moved to Nashville with her husband, only one of many farming families gone under and seeking a livelihood rebuilding a railroad decimated by war.

"She'll feed you well and board the horse." Mama pressed a letter into his hands. "Give her this for me."

He nodded. "I will."

Her hand lingered against his skin too long, and Benjamin had to step away before emotion overtook him. He made the rounds of farmhands and freedmen, noting the absences of Lizzy and Johnny. Lizzy's, he understood. "Where's Johnny?"

Logan leaned on his two wooden crutches, the legless pants, folded in half, swaying with his movements. He pointed his chin toward the orchard. "Yonder."

With long strides, Ben crossed the yard, rounded the columned porch and went to find the former Union soldier. He couldn't leave without saying goodbye to the man who saw more with his sightless eyes than most people saw with perfect vision.

"Johnny," he called.

"Here, Benjamin."

Ben smiled. Johnny knew every voice.

He found the blind man, only ten years older than himself, waiting for him a dozen steps inside the orchard, a stack of fragrant peach limbs at his feet. His wise fingers seemed to know which to prune and which to leave behind.

"Is it time already?" Johnny asked, lifting his face to feel the sun as he felt for the dark glasses stuck in his suspenders. Finding them, he slid the spectacles over his damaged face and adjusted his cap bill lower as he always did in company, though Ben had known him too long to be put off by his disfigurement.

"I want to make Nashville by nightfall."

Johnny stroked strong fingers across his lips, nodding. "You have a care now. Won't be any of us along to drag you out of the creek or help you down from a tree."

Tenderness welled inside Ben until he wondered if he was a man grown at all or still a little boy, tagging along behind Logan and Johnny and Old Hob, though the ancient Hob had passed last year, leaving a hole in Benjamin's heart. He'd loved the old black man and Hob had loved him.

"You help Captain Will look after the womenfolk for me, will you, Johnny?"

"No need in asking when you know the answer."

"Aunt Patience, in particular. She seems especially nervous about this trip." He didn't understand it, but his younger aunt had come to his room first thing this morning, pale and red-eyed. "She begged me not to go."

A softness crossed the sightless face. "Miss Patience, she's a fragile soul. I'll keep a sharp lookout for her. Don't you worry."

Johnny Atkins had loved Patience for as long as he'd known

her. Everyone on the farm seemed to know but her, though Johnny thought he kept his feelings hid, a remarkable belief seeing as how he lingered in the doorway when he heard her voice and rushed to carry baskets and offer a hand even when she didn't need one. The blind soldier was devoted to Benjamin's aunt and had been since she'd nursed him back to life during the war with her gentle care and soothing piano.

"Will you ever tell her?"

Johnny pulled back, his expression never changing. "Tell her what?"

Ben spoke plainly now, knowing from terrible experience that there were no guarantees in this life. He planned to return, but Thaddeus was right. The way was fraught with danger.

"That you love her." His voice was quiet, lest he embarrass the former soldier.

Johnny shook his head. "No man deserves her, but all can admire her. Even a blind fool like me."

He heard what Johnny wasn't saying. The fear that Patience, like the woman he'd left behind in Ohio, would turn away from a blind, disfigured man. Johnny had had his heart broken before.

"Maybe you're only a fool in silence. Patience sees you with her heart."

"I have nothing to give her, Benjamin." Johnny sighed, resigned to his fate. "But I will look after her as long as I have breath, and I will be grateful she calls me friend."

Ben had to be satisfied with that, though he ached for his friend and farmhand. Johnny worked as hard as any of them and never complained about the awful toll the war had taken, but he saw himself as unworthy of love because of his injury and Betsy's rejection.

Johnny loved Patience, and unless Ben missed his guess, Patience loved him. Yet both remained silent.

With a final clap of shoulders, the men parted, Johnny back to clearing the peach orchard and Ben toward the front of the house. As he passed the back porch, Lizzy stepped outside. She hadn't joined the family in the front yard, and Benjamin understood why.

He paused at the bottom step, the memory of her revelation thick inside him and all muddied up. Hurt and confusion and anger tangled with a hundred questions he could never ask.

"Goodbye, Lizzy."

She wiped her hands on her apron. "I know you got questions."

"Don't. I remember my father well enough. Keep your secrets."

She held him with a black, black stare, demanding he understand the unthinkable when he already thought his father was a monster. Now he knew for certain.

"All right, then. You go on. Do what you got to do. I'll see to Charlotte." Lizzy wagged her head, face long and sad. "Your mama be the finest woman I ever know. Always good to me and mine, a rare thing in this world. But don't ask me to regret having Tandy."

Ben had known his father was evil, as he knew Lizzy was so loyal to his mother she'd unintentionally forfeited her only child.

Understanding those two things told him the whole story, and the burden of finding Tandy grew heavier on his shoulders.

Every day except Sunday Patience taught piano to the children of Honey Ridge. Today, after Benjamin had made his departure, she was thankful for the distraction of Nelly Jacobson and her reluctant brother, Everett. With a child on either side of the piano bench, she guided them through the melody. Soon, seven-year-old Nelly would leave her older brother behind and require separate lessons. Not that Everett cared. The boy proclaimed for all who would listen that he'd rather be fishin'.

"Well done, Everett. See the progress you achieve when you practice?"

Everett gave a soulful sigh. "Yes, ma'am. Thank you, Miss Patience."

The parlor door opened, and Patience didn't have to look up to know who stood in the doorway, but she looked anyway, her heart lighter for doing so.

Johnny, his hat against his chest, the dark glasses making it impossible to read his thoughts, said, "Miss Patience."

"Yes, Johnny?"

"The children's father is ready to go."

Everett bolted from the bench as if his pants were on fire while his sister gathered the practice book and waited politely to hear her assignment for the next week.

The children filled a place in Patience that she couldn't explain, perhaps because she had none of her own, but she would teach piano to the little ones even if no one paid. As it was, finances were strained, and she was grateful for the money or the bartered goods that came her way.

Unlike the other family members her prospects were limited. She wasn't smart enough for business, and numbers confused her badly. Papa had blamed her lacking on the difficult birth that had caused her mother's death. When she was small she'd forgotten a lot of things, but Papa had never let her forget that she'd killed her own mother.

She had death in her blood.

Everett almost made it out the door, but Johnny snagged

the rambunctious boy by the collar. In a kind voice, he said, "Now, Everett, you go back and show your manners to Miss Patience. That's how a gentleman behaves."

Chastised, Everett returned, head down. "Please, accept my apology, Miss Patience. Thank you for the music lesson."

She placed her hand on his shoulder, smiling. "You almost left without a cookie."

His head popped up. "Was I good?"

"Good enough for a cookie." She handed both children a gingersnap. "Practice at least one hour a day, and you'll have an extra next week."

"Yes, ma'am." Scattering sugary crumbs, he dipped from one foot to the other.

Taking pity on him, she said, "You may go. Tell your mother hello."

Johnny stepped aside, and the boy shot out the door, thundering across the wooden porch like a stampede. With ladylike dignity Nelly followed, climbed into the wagon with her father and brother, and waved as they drove away.

Standing in the sunshine, hand raised, Patience heard Johnny chuckle.

She looked at him with a smile, knowing he couldn't see her but sure he could hear the humor in her voice. "My most eager student."

"Most eager to leave."

Patience laughed then, and so did he, standing together in the warm sunlight, both of them shattered but, for different reasons, pretending that they were not, and going on with life as best they could.

Johnny. Wonderful, broken Johnny who made the days brighter simply by being in them.

She cared for him, a caring she allowed to stretch only to friendship for reasons that would shock him. Though the war was thankfully past, its legacy lingered, and she felt as responsible for his blindness as if she'd fired the shot that took him down. He was a good man with a giant heart and kind ways, like Charlotte's Will and Josie's Thad. But he could never be her Johnny. Not the way they both wanted.

When the laughter died, Johnny tilted his head, a lock of dark hair falling onto his brow. She admired the fine, curly hair that he kept meticulously combed, though he kept it longer than fashionable to cover some of the scarring. He'd tried to grow facial hair, too, but the damaged skin would not cooperate. How he shaved remained a mystery to her. Perhaps Logan helped him.

She wondered if he knew that neither long hair nor scars could ever hide his handsome soul.

"I'll be getting back to the orchard. Do you need help with anything before I go?"

"Someone needs to eat these other two gingersnaps."

The good side of his mouth lifted, and she remembered the days of spooning broth between his lips and of how his valiant, uncomplaining determination to make the most of a horrid situation had touched her and kept her awake at night, listening for his voice and praying. But that was before the darkness, before her soul was blackened with remorse and secrets too dangerous to share.

"You gonna make me practice the piano first?" he asked, and she was grateful that his teasing voice pulled her back from memory's dark ledge.

She licked lips gone dry and kept her voice light. "Do you want to learn?"

"I like hearing *you* play, Miss Patience. You sure don't want such as me ruining a perfectly good tune."

She touched his elbow lightly, holding out the cookie plate

so that it met his hand. "Try one of these. You might change your mind."

His capable fingers found the gingersnap, and they lingered together on the wide veranda companionably enjoying the sugar and spice while chickens pecked the ground and farm life flowed around them.

For a moment, Patience let her mind wander, pretending that she was an honorable woman with the right to enjoy the company of a good man. She turned to face Johnny and stepped closer, admiring the strength in his arms and the way his shoulders stretched the white cotton shirt. Tidy with the cookie, he caught the crumbs in a hand held below his chin.

He was a talented man who could gentle a horse or mend tack and trim trees that he couldn't see. And he carved little woodland animals, his fingers remembering their beauty. She admired him for that, as well.

"Ben should be getting close to Nashville soon," he said. "He's strong and smart. Don't fret over him much."

The pleasant fantasy evaporated like the steam above a coffee cup. She moved slightly away, reminded.

The chasm between her and Johnny was too wide to cross, and she wasn't brave enough to even try, especially now that Ben was determined to find Tandy.

All she could do was pray that her nephew's quest went unfilled and, God forgive her, that Tandy's whereabouts were never discovered.

CHAPTER 12

Present Day. Honey Ridge

Valery's head was the size of a watermelon, and someone was making it worse by playing the piano. Grayson. Of all the inconsiderate...

Above that unwelcome racket, Julia, or God forbid, Mama, pounded against the bedroom door louder than a jackhammer.

"Keep your pants on," she muttered and stumbled across the room to open the door a crack. The piano music stopped. "What?"

Julia's knowing gaze swept over her. "Oh, Val."

"I'll be right down." Valery shut the door in her sister's pitying, sanctimonious face. The last thing she needed was preaching from the saintly sister who had never done an evil thing in her life. What did Julia know of guilt and regret?

She growled low in her throat, a sound that ground at the back of her eyeballs.

She wasn't being fair and she knew it, but really. Couldn't a girl have a few relaxing drinks after a long, trying day?

The churn in her belly and the taste in her mouth a reminder that she'd had more than the few she'd intended.

Since Mikey's disappearance she was getting worse and couldn't seem to stop.

And she'd come on to Grayson. Come on strong.

With a groan, she held the top of her head on and stumbled to the bathroom for a quick and chilly wake-up shower before dressing for the day. Visine and carefully applied makeup covered a multitude of sins. Surface sins.

If Julia cooked eggs this morning, her stomach would revolt.

Thankful for the natural wave, she ran a brush through her hair and hurried downstairs, pretending nothing was amiss. Julia would play along. Silence was the Carter way.

Inside the dining room, Eli set out plates and folded napkins into pretty shell shapes, her usual job. He was dressed for work in dark pants and tie, though he'd ditched his jacket to take up the slack she'd left by sleeping late.

"Sorry." She blithely offered what she hoped was a dazzling smile. "I overslept. Darn alarm didn't go off."

Eli said nothing but handed over the napkins and went into the kitchen. He was not happy with her. Anything that ruffled Julia's pretty feathers stirred his protective side. Valery appreciated that. Really she did. Julia had learned to be strong again after her tumble into destructive depression, but having Eli's support took a load off both sisters. Valery didn't have to constantly worry about her sister anymore.

Too bad Julia couldn't say the same.

After she finished folding the napkins, Valery streamed back and forth between the kitchen and dining room with the morning's buffet-style breakfast. Thankfully, today's fare was a casserole and French toast, though her stomach still protested the overly sweet smell of warm syrup.

Never again. Not that much booze.

Yeah. Like she hadn't made that vow a few dozen times.

As she battled the nausea, breathing through her mouth as she worked, Grayson entered the dining room.

Her heart squeezed, yearning toward him in the most ridiculous manner.

He'd been kindness itself last night. She hadn't been too drunk to remember every single detail of being held against that broad chest. His heart had beat against her ear, steady, secure, and his strength and compassion had ebbed into her until she'd wanted to stand there forever, safe in his arms, safe from the ugly memories, safe from herself.

"Good morning." His gaze searched hers, and she had to look away from the questions and the sincere concern.

She refused to blush, having learned long ago the art of bluffing her way through bad situations—usually of her own making. Instead, she put on a happy face, her voice chipper as a cheerleader as she pretended no ill effect from nearly a pint of bourbon.

Her belly convulsed at the thought. Today, even the smell of bourbon would take her down.

"Isn't it?" she said. "A gorgeous spring day."

Not that she'd had more than a glance out the window, but she'd heard Julia say as much to one of the other guests. "Have a seat and I'll bring a coffee carafe."

She flounced out of the room, aware he watched her in his thoughtful, analytical way and praying not to humiliate herself by throwing up on his work boots. She flounced back in with a smile pasted on her face.

"Real cream. No sugar. Right?"

"Good memory."

"You must have really enjoyed playing that baby grand yesterday."

"I did. Why?"

"I heard you playing earlier, when I first woke up." *And I wanted to throttle you.*

He frowned. "I wasn't playing."

"No?" That was weird, but weird things sometimes happened in this old house. "Must have been a dream."

He glanced around the room. Only one other table was occupied. In a lowered voice, he said, "Are you okay?"

"Great. Perfect." She pretended complete ignorance. "With this beautiful weather, I think I'll take off this afternoon and—and—and—" she floundered, looking for something that would make her sound full of energy and not the least bit hungover "—go on a picnic."

Wry amusement crinkled the corners of his eyes. "A picnic? You'd waste an entire afternoon on a picnic?"

"Waste? Waste!" She pressed a palm to her chest, feigning complete insult. "What else could be more important to do today?"

He arched an eyebrow, his mouth twisted. "Go stir-crazy?"

"Seriously. Come with me. You need to relax." *And I want to spend time with you, fool that I am. I want to prove to you I'm not that drunk from last night.* "I pack a fabulous picnic lunch. We can drive up on the ridge and I'll show you the valley. It's breathtaking in spring."

He was already shaking his head. "One of our restaurant managers quit. I have applications to go through and interviews to set up."

"That will take all day?"

"Well, no." He looked none too happy about that.

"There you go, then. It's a date. One o'clock."

Before he could argue more or allude to the porch episode, she hurried out of the room, rushed to the nearest bathroom... and promptly lost the remains of last night's dinner.

★ ★ ★

A picnic. Of all the idiotic time wasters.

Grayson circled the small, secluded clearing high over Honey Ridge. He had to admit the area up here was pretty with the town spread far below and the air as sweet and clean as a baby's conscience. But he felt at loose ends, strange to be doing...nothing.

His cell phone vibrated against his hip. He read the text, blew out an airy huff, and shook his head.

He'd parked the Jeep at Valery's direction in the lot of a small park that was basically a turnout point marked by a thick cable run between two massive oak trees. A few scattered benches dotted the wooded space leading to the edge of the ridge. Trash cans perched next to each bench, marring the beautiful landscape but keeping a swarm of honeybees happy.

Hands jammed in his pockets, he jiggled his keys and listened to the bees. From the nearby bait shop–convenience store, the only business he saw on the ridge, a car motor rumbled, though from here, among the foliage he and she were secluded.

Valery stood near an outcropping of kudzu-covered rock, her fingers wrapped around the top of a short metal railing. She looked pretty as usual but more sporty this afternoon in red capris and white tee with red beaded bracelets dangling from one wrist. He liked the look.

"Come to the edge and look down." Turned at an angle, her chestnut hair blew back from her face. Glamorous cheekbones arched beneath dark-lashed, amber eyes.

With a sigh, he joined her. "I should have driven up to Nashville today." His brother had texted a reminder to stop thinking like a nerd and start thinking like a man alone with a beautiful woman.

He was trying. She was definitely beautiful. It was the control freak inside his brain that gave him trouble.

"You said yourself tomorrow works better anyway. So relax. Live in the moment. Smell the roses." Valery's smile flashed white between lush red lips.

Eyebrows arched, Grayson feigned a look around. "Not a rosebush in sight."

"Silly. You won't die if you aren't working."

That was the worry. He'd die before he finished. Logically, he understood that no one died without leaving things unfinished, but the inner pressure remained. Hurry. Time is running out.

He wished he was more like Devlin...

With his hands in his pockets, his shoulders tense and the back of his neck starting to throb, he felt jittery, but admittedly was interested in the ridge and the beautiful, smiling woman a short railing from going over the ledge.

She was like his brother. Living on the edge and trusting that she wouldn't fall.

Except Valery kept stumbling, and Grayson wanted to be there to catch her when she fell.

That's why he'd agreed to this picnic. Valery was a mystery to resolve, a puzzle to decipher. Devlin would mock him for comparing her to one of his endless puzzles.

He peered over the bluff's edge. Below lay the town of Honey Ridge looking as small as an architect's model, but more vibrant and green. The river, like a shiny blue ribbon, wound around the town, shooting creek fingers in all directions. On the distant horizon, dark purple mountain peaks jutted toward the sky. The Great Smokies.

"Admit it." Valery rocked back on her heels, grinning. "I was right."

She was all flirt and flounce today and looked no worse for

last night's episode. Still, he wondered and wanted to ask even though she'd made it clear she would not revisit the topic.

"Right about?"

"The view? The sunshine? The picnic?"

"The jury is still out. The day is young." His smile let her know he was joking. "You were right. Are you happy now?"

She bumped him with her side and laughed softly, a breezy, easy sound that pleased him. For now, last night's trouble was behind her, and she was happy. Or pretending to be.

He thought of what Lem had said about her having ghosts. What ghosts haunted her, drove her to drinking past the point of recreation? Last night, he'd walked her to her bedroom. By then she'd been maudlin and crying, muttering about what a bad person she was. His heart still hurt to remember.

His cell chirped, and he walked away from the ledge to read a second text from Devlin and dash off a reply.

Valery turned to watch, expression contemplative. The air current caught her dark hair and lifted it back from her face again. Luminous eyes flashing and posture as perfect as a ballet dancer, she took his breath. Sucked it right out of his lungs.

"Your interviews are scheduled. You've texted someone twice in the ten minutes we've been here, and you've spoken to Trey Riley at the police station and at least two contractors since we left the inn." She came across the small clearing to pluck at his arm. "Relax, Grayson. Can't you? For a little while?"

Her disappointed expression stabbed at him. He was being impolite, insulting, and so ingrained was his work ethic, he hadn't even realized how his behavior affected others. Her.

This woman had intrigued him since he was a kid, and now she wanted, for whatever reason, to spend time with him. Somehow he had to turn off the ticking clock inside his brain.

"That was rude of me. I apologize."

He stuffed the cell phone in his hip pocket.

"Did you put it on silent?"

He blinked in horror. "You're kidding."

Laughing, she shook her head and went to sit on the blanket she'd fluffed over the green grass. Flipping open the top of a large picnic basket, she began to set things out, including a little vase of artificial sunflowers.

He lifted his eyebrows.

"Mama," she said with a twist of her lips, "insists that the conventions of polite society must not be ignored under any circumstances. People will talk, and Lord forbid if we Carters should allow that to happen."

Something about her tone caught his attention. She wasn't joking, and this wasn't the first time he'd gotten the drift of tension between Valery and her mother.

"The flowers are a nice touch." In two long strides he joined her. "What other magic do you have hidden in there, Houdini?"

The silliness lightened her up again. "Chicken salad on buttery croissants from the bakery in town. Heavenly. Also, roast beef wraps I made myself." She chuckled. "Eat at your own risk. And hot wings with mozzarella sticks, fruit, chips and two different desserts. Brownies and dark chocolate truffles."

Amazed, he said, "Is this a picnic or a week's vacation?"

"I wasn't sure what you liked so—" She arched her shoulders, and he saw her insecurity. Flamboyant Valery was surprisingly vulnerable.

"I'm a guy. I like food. Bring it on." He patted his stomach. "I'm a growing boy who eats his own cooking too often."

The reply must have been what she wanted to hear, because she smiled and piled his plate high.

While they ate, they talked. Of mundane things, of the view and the small town, the mill and the mysterious skeleton.

He chewed the last bite of creamy chicken salad. "Did you know a man walks over a hundred thousand miles in his lifetime?"

Her mouth curved in amusement. "I'm sure you'll beat the record. What do you do back in Nashville for entertainment besides read the encyclopedia?"

"The usual. Watch a little TV, go out with friends or my brother, take in a ball game or a concert. What about you? Any hobbies?"

"I like to grow things, flowers in particular, so Julia gives me the run of the flower beds. And of course, the Historical Preservation Society. And shopping. All girls love to shop. You?" She popped a grape into her mouth.

"Definitely not shopping." He grinned.

"Then what?" She poked a finger at him. "Business does not count."

He thought of the old Chevy in his garage. He hadn't worked on the Bel Air since Pappy's death three years ago.

"I have this old car. A real classic. My grandfather and I were restoring it together as a project. After he died… I don't know. Didn't have the time for it, I guess."

"You should make time for the things you love." She poured him another glass of lemonade. "Like playing music. You're really good. When we get back to the house, will you play again?"

He didn't say the obvious, that she should take her own advice. But more than limited time separated Valery from dance, and since today she was her usual vivacious self, Grayson was reluctant to stir up trouble.

"I'd like that." He'd already wasted a day, not that spending time with Valery was wasted time. "There's something about Patience Portland's compositions that keeps niggling at

the edge of my brain. Something about the chord arrangements in certain places."

"I didn't notice, but I'm not a musician." She reached in
the basket. "Want a grape?"

He held out a hand. "Sure. Thanks."

"Uh-uh." She drew her hand back as if to throw. "Open
wide."

With an eye roll, he opened his mouth. The grape popped
him on the forehead. She squealed and clapped a hand to her
mouth, shoulders shaking with mirth.

Grayson laughed. "Major league material you're not."

"Practice makes perfect. Try again."

She tried four more times, each worse than the last. By the
time the fourth grape whapped him in the eye, they were both
laughing too much for an accurate aim.

"My turn." Grayson grabbed a handful of fruit.

"Don't blacken my eyes. No one would ever believe what
happened."

He took aim and tossed. The grape plopped between her
perfect lips. They both blinked in surprise. "I couldn't do that
again in a million years."

"Try." Like a baby bird, she opened her mouth. Grayson
walked toward her on his knees and dropped the fruit inside,
towering over her as she chewed, her gaze clinging to his.

Desire stirred in him. He wanted to taste the sweet grapes
on her lips. Remembering last night, he resisted, sitting down
beside her instead. Was he ready to get involved with a complicated woman like Valery Carter?

The air pulsed with bees and questions he wasn't ready to
answer.

Yearning and troubled to feel that way, he stretched his
arms high over his head and refocused on the blue, blue sky.
Clouds drifted past, fluffy and lazy.

Sighing, unsure he'd done the right thing by giving into the desire to be with her, he fidgeted, looped his arms over upraised knees and glanced at his watch.

"Are you anxious to escape me?"

Grayson heard the insecurity in her voice.

He gazed at her again, searching her beautiful face while his pulse thrummed like a cricket's dance against his throat. "Not even a little."

Her lips curved and she touched his cheek. "You're a nice man."

"Nice meaning boring?"

"Not even a little." Her words echoed his.

"You're a nice woman."

Her gaze flickered. She swallowed and glanced away.

Before he knew what she was about, Valery was behind him, her hands on his shoulders. "You're tight as an elephant's girdle."

Mind humming with her quicksilver moods, Grayson tried to relax into the massage. He certainly needed one.

Head lolled forward, he gave her access to all the places that habitually spasmed. She found them, kneading gently and then deeper with surprisingly strong fingers. "You know what else you need?"

Yes, he did.

"I'm afraid to answer that question here alone in a secluded place with a beautiful woman."

She made a throaty growling sound that only flashed more scenarios through his head.

"Besides that." She whapped his shoulder with her fist. "Yoga."

Suddenly, she stopped the slobber-inducing massage. "Sit cross-legged and close your eyes. Follow my lead. This stuff is magic."

"I can't follow your lead with my eyes closed." He shot her an ornery grin but copied her posture.

"Good. Now roll your shoulders back and down."

He did, and she took him through some neck rolls and head stretches. Easy. There was nothing to this yoga stuff.

"That was the warm-up. Now, come into your warrior stance."

Like a fierce ninja, she bent one knee while the other leg stretched far behind her. He followed suit, grinning at how ridiculous he felt but how gorgeous and fierce she looked. "Glad no one can see us."

Except him. He liked watching her twist her slim, lithe body into...interesting poses.

"Feel that stretch in your thigh?"

He felt it all right. His thigh was on fire.

"Warrior three position. Straighten your front leg as you lift the back leg straight out behind you. Arms tight at your sides, upper body and left leg parallel to the floor."

Grayson watched in amazement as she perfectly executed the move. "I don't know..."

"Sure you can. Try."

Dubious but game, he imitated her pose...and collapsed in a heap.

Valery burst out laughing and tumbled down beside him. He lay on his back, suitably humiliated but enjoying every ridiculous moment and laughed until his sides ached as much as his thigh muscles.

He rolled toward her. She'd flung her arms above her head, her brown hair spread around her and the sun through the trees dancing on the highlights.

"You were right about the picnic." He leaned up and in. "And if I don't kiss you, I'm going to implode."

She grabbed his shirt collar. "We can't be having that."

With a happy sigh and the little imp in the back of his head shouting a warning, Grayson kissed her.

She tasted like grapes. Really sweet, warm grapes.

He'd kissed her. The hottest, most perfect kiss of her life. Then he'd backed away, trailing his fingers through her hair, touching her face, telling her she was beautiful inside and out and making her believe it.

Sex for the sake of sex she understood. Romance stunned her, confused her. And made her feel like a cherished princess. She hardly knew what to do with the feelings rushing through her.

Who would have imagined Mr. Perfectionist with the schedules and tech gadgets had a tender, romantic side?

She felt like mush.

They capped a perfect afternoon with a walk along the ridge, holding hands like teenagers, talking about nothing and everything before driving back to the house.

She was reluctant to end her time with this man who made her feel like something more than a cheap party doll.

As they entered the inn, the smell of peaches wafted thick and sweet from the kitchen. She paused in the doorway leading inside the kitchen and waved. "Need any help?"

At Julia's surprised look, Valery suffered a pang of guilt. She should have asked that question before taking off for the day.

"Everything's under control. Did you have fun?"

"We did." With Grayson close behind her, Valery felt bolstered. "I've convinced him to play more of Patience Portland's music for me. If that's okay with you."

"Nice to hear someone playing again. You're good."

Valery didn't mention the music she'd heard this morning. Grayson had heard it, too. She was sure he had. Even though no one could have been at the keyboard.

"A bit rusty," Grayson said modestly. "But I'm enjoying the practice. Thank you. The baby grand is something special."

Julia gave Valery an I-told-you-so glance. "I think so, too. Go ahead. Enjoy."

Eager to escape her watchful sister, Valery led the way through the house.

Once inside the family room, Grayson removed the folder of sheet music from the bench and took his place at the piano.

"Play something I know first."

"'Brown Eyed Girl'?" His fingers found the notes and made her smile.

Without an invitation but confident she was welcome, Valery scooted onto the bench next to him. He still smelled good, even after the long afternoon outdoors. Brazen as always, she scooted close to inhale the very faint scent of his skin-heated cologne, to feel his arm and thigh brush hers, and recall the way he kissed.

"I had a good time today. Thank you for going." Her heart danced a little, foolish dreamer that she was.

"I enjoyed it, too. Thanks for asking."

They stared at each other for two beats in which she wished she was a better person, a woman worthy of a man like Grayson.

But she wasn't and the truth hurt. Yet she'd chase after him while he was here like she always did when a man interested her. Men were like bourbon, irresistible and intoxicating.

She sighed and, not wanting to be melancholy, forced a smile.

He kissed the tip of her nose and then turned his attention to Patience Portland's handiwork. He played the haunting melodies that made her want to cry and laugh and dance all at the same time.

When her throat was full—of the music, of him, of the impossible—he stopped.

He couldn't know, thank goodness, the turmoil raging inside her like a hurricane.

"This piece right here." He tapped the notations. "See?"

She saw nothing but musical notes, a few she recognized, but most were a foreign language.

His fingers trilled through a few bars. "Something about the arrangement of chords and certain notes. It almost reminds me of a cryptogram."

Puzzles. The man loved puzzles.

Valery tilted back, surprised. "You mean a secret message?"

He frowned. "I don't know for sure. Without a key, a musical code is hard to decipher, but yes, that's what I keep thinking about when I play this piece."

"A musical code? I didn't know there was such a thing."

"I've read about them."

"Go figure." Grayson's capacity for knowledge impressed her.

His glance was amused. "Some musicians like Bach wrote musical codes for fun. Any music student knows about Bach, and of course, nerd that I am, I wanted to know more. I always thought if I could come up with a musical code, I could send messages to my brother."

"Why?"

"Because we were boys. Didn't you ever write secret messages to your girlfriends?"

She snapped her fingers. "The backward writing thing. I was a master. Nikki Riley and I used to pass notes in boring government class and the teacher could never figure out the message."

"About boys, no doubt."

"With Nikki and me, absolutely!" She laughed, but there

was no real mirth. She, Nikki and Carrie had their share of secrets, but some things were too scary even to write in code.

Suddenly a thought hit her. "Oooh, maybe Patience had a secret lover."

He smirked. "A romantic idea."

She elbowed him. "And altogether possible. Why else would a young single woman write coded messages into her music?"

"Deciphering the key, if there is one, is the only way to find out for sure. Do you mind if I take this sheet up to my room? I'd like to study it."

"We have a printer in the office. I'll make a copy for you."

"Make copies of these, too." He handed off four other pages. "The more I have to compare, the more likely I am to discover repetitions and anomalies."

"*Anomalies.* Big word."

He laughed, and something happy and light bubbled in Valery's chest.

She led the way toward the inn's office, glad for any reason to hang around the tall, handsome Nashvillian.

CHAPTER 13

Valery slipped off her dirty shoes on the back porch and tossed a pair of equally dirty gardening gloves on top. Spring cleanup began this morning, bright and early. Julia tackled the house, thank goodness, while Valery headed for the gardens and the orchard. But no matter how much mulch she laid or how many weeds she extracted, tracking dirt and mud inside the inn was reserved for Alex, Bingo and guests.

Following the noise of industry to the kitchen, she found Julia standing on a step stool, all the sparkling, polished glasses from one cabinet arrayed on the counter before her. Even in jeans and T-shirt with her hair up in a ponytail, Julia managed to look gracious and elegant, the quintessential Southern hostess. Like Mama, perfect in every way.

Even as children, Julia would sit quietly on the porch in her Sunday dress with white patent-leather shoes and perky hair bows absolutely pristine while Valery hung upside down by her knees from the swing set, too antsy to do nothing until Mama was ready for church.

"Ah, the smell of lemon." She sucked in a deep inhale.

Lemon cleaner and polish filled the house, the only time of year any scent other than peach took front and center.

Julia glanced down at her. "You look exhausted."

"So do you. Jobs well done, then." Valery offered a high five. The sound smacked an echo in the kitchen. "All the flower beds are mulched and every weed ripped out by the roots."

"Closets and cabinets cleaned and rearranged. This is my last one." Julia placed a set of stemware on the second shelf.

Every spring, they scrubbed, waxed and polished the inside and landscaped the outside before peach season began. After the fruit came in, preserving, freezing, and jelly-making took second place only to guests. Running an inn with an orchard was nonstop, but Julia reveled in the work. Valery not so much. But what other choice did she have?

"Looks like you have great help." Valery crouched beside the dark-haired boy sprawled on his belly on the tile floor. His short, jean-clad legs were bent at the knee, seesawing in the air. Having a child in the house had made such a difference, and like her sister, Valery had fallen hard for Eli's sweet son.

"Hey, Alex. How was school today?"

"Okay." Alex gave her a shy grin and resumed coloring. "I'm making a new picture for Aunt Opal."

Aunt Opal was the old woman who'd cared for Alex until Eli had come for him. After a debilitating stroke she lived in a senior care center, refusing to move into the inn or "become a burden." That was Opal. Stubborn, outspoken and tough as nails. The old woman loved Alex and Eli as if they were her own. They returned the feelings, and Eli did everything he could to make Opal's life easier.

Her sister had married an honorable man. Just when Valery had become convinced there was no such thing.

With a soft smile, she stroked the little boy's slender back, grateful to have him to love. He had a heart as big as a mountain and was sweet as honey. "That's very thoughtful of you, Alex. You're such a good boy. Aunt Opal will love it, I'm sure."

Julia set the last glass inside the cabinet and stepped off the stool. "When Eli gets home, we're going to the care center to take Aunt Opal out to dinner."

"That's nice." Valery snagged a clean glass, drawing a quick scowl from her sister, and pushed the water lever on the refrigerator. "Where are you taking her?"

"Wherever she wants to go, and then we'll spend some family time together at the center." She rubbed a lemony-smelling sponge over the countertop. "Will you keep an eye on things while I'm gone?"

Valery, in mid-drink, paused and lowered the glass. "Don't I always?"

"Yes, but…" Julia shook her head. "Of course you will. Thank you."

Valery's jaw tightened. She heard what Julia didn't say. She wasn't dependable. Swallowing the anger, she tossed back the rest of the water and put the glass in the dishwasher.

"I picked up fresh flowers for the foyer this morning," Julia said, expression cautious. "Will you arrange them? You know how awful I am at arranging."

An olive branch. Valery accepted it. "You're not that bad."

"Yes, I am. When I stick flowers in a vase, that's all I do. But your arrangements look artistic and professional."

More compliments. A red-letter day.

"Because I like doing it and you don't." Valery took the paper-wrapped flowers from the refrigerator and sniffed the blooms. "These are pretty. The yellow cremones will really pop against the white daisies and dark pink alstroemeria."

She was showing off a bit. The flowers were simply mums, lilies and daisies but the fancy names sounded impressive.

Julia laughed. "See what I mean. To me, they're white, yellow and pink flowers with some greenery. To you, they're people with names."

Complimented, Valery chose a vase from under the sink,

took a pair of scissors and went to work. Neat-freak Julia scooped the clipped ends off the counter.

Her fingers knowing what to do with the flowers, Valery gazed at her sister. "You must have been in the attic."

"I was looking at some of the furniture stored up there. Why?"

"You have a spiderweb—" She didn't get the words out before Julia started an undignified slap and swipe of her entire body.

"Where? Get it off. Hurry!" Shuddering, Julia gyrated and slapped at herself until Valery could no longer keep the grin off her face.

Alex stopped coloring to gaze up in concerned wonder.

"She's fine, Alex. Don't worry." Laying aside the scissors and a long-stemmed mum, Valery went to her sister's rescue. She brushed the faint strands of dusty white silk from Julia's hair. "Got it. You're safe."

Her sister was the bravest person she knew, but mention a spider and she fell apart.

"Stop grinning." A blush flared on Julia's cheeks. "Spiders are evil."

Valery's grin widened. "Straight from the devil."

Alex got up, markers forgotten on the floor, and wrapped his arms around Julia's legs. "I'll kill the spiders for you, Mom. Don't worry."

"My brave boy." Julia hugged him to her, face soft.

Over Alex's head, the sisters exchanged understanding glances. Alex wasn't a replacement for Michael, but he was a warm, loving boy who needed a mother. And Julia needed a child.

Valery's throat clogged, tight with unwanted emotion.

After a long moment, Alex pulled away and smiled his

gentle smile. Then he gathered his coloring pages and exited the room.

Valery watched him go. "Does he still play with Benjamin's marbles?"

"Sometimes. Not like he did in the early days of counseling." In grief over the loss of his mother, Alex had turned inward, latching on to a set of antique clay marbles and playing with an imaginary friend named Ben. Except Benjamin hadn't been imaginary. He was a real boy who had lived in this house over a hundred fifty years ago.

"Does he still talk about Ben?"

"Sometimes. Eli and I have learned to take any mention of the angel boy in stride."

"I remember how it used to freak Eli out."

"Until he realized the house has...something special, a gift of healing, I like to think." Julia spritzed the countertop with cleaner. "It healed me."

If only the inn could heal her as well, but how could it? Her wounds were all of her own making.

"No one has found a marble in a long time. Not since Hayden," Julia went on. "I guess none of our guests have required Ben's special brand of healing."

No one but her. She'd found her share of marbles lately. More than her share, and they offered an odd kind of comfort. For some reason, she didn't want to share that information with her sister.

The marbles seemed to appear at random out of nowhere but only to those struggling with some emotional war. The famous writer, Hayden Winters, had found several in his months at the inn.

She didn't believe in ghosts, and no guest had ever complained of frightening occurrences or things that go bump in the night. Some heard music, as Grayson had. A few heard boys' laughter outside the Blueberry Room but assumed the sound came from Alex. No one was ever afraid at Peach Orchard Inn.

The bed-and-breakfast inn had a benign presence, an angel, she and Julia believed, and Valery liked thinking he watched over them and their guests. And left marbles as a comforting reminder of his gentle, giving presence.

"Neither Grayson nor Devlin have mentioned finding one," she said.

"Healthy souls." Julia glanced up at the ceiling. "I know you're dying to ask. Grayson came in around noon, went upstairs and hasn't been back down."

She had been. "Not for lunch?"

"No, and he didn't order out either."

"He's a workaholic. He forgets to eat."

"Who does that?"

"I know, right?"

Julia glanced at the clock on the cook range. "Eli will be here soon. I need to get showered and dressed and get Alex changed."

Valery poked the last yellow mum into place. "Doesn't this look springy and cheerful?"

"It does. See? So artsy and pretty." Julia bussed her on the cheek. "You're amazing. But you smell sweaty."

"I'll shower in a bit, but you better get crackin' if you want to be ready when Eli gets home. Go on, I'll clean up my messes. Promise." She spun the vase around as an idea took root. "Even the best care facility gets dreary. Why not take this bouquet to Opal, and I'll pick up some others for the foyer tomorrow?"

"Valery. What a sweet, kindhearted thought. Opal will be thrilled."

"I'll leave the vase here on the counter."

Later, after Julia and family had left, Valery went to her room for a shower, plotting what she'd fix for her solitary dinner. She didn't like to eat alone. In fact, she didn't like to *be* alone most of the time. She was a people person with friends scattered all over the state and plenty of them in Honey Ridge. She could invite someone out.

No one came to mind except the workaholic in the Mulberry Room.

She picked up her cell phone twice to send a text but changed her mind. She didn't want to read an impersonal message. She wanted to see him.

Hair fluffed and swinging loose around her shoulders, she trotted up the stairs to the Mulberry Room. Devlin had driven away earlier this morning and had yet to return. She didn't know where. Guests weren't required to ask permission to come and go. Long-term guests had the run of the property and a special entrance key.

She lifted her hand to knock and froze. Inside, she heard the mumble of Grayson's baritone voice. He must be on the phone. Maybe a conference call or a Skype meeting. Though she was tempted to press her ear against the door and listen, she refrained. Never had she invaded her guests' privacy, and she wouldn't start now, not even with a man she'd kissed.

Instead, she turned and went back downstairs to the kitchen, her stomach complaining about the now long disappeared spinach salad she'd eaten for lunch.

As she fried bacon for a sandwich, she thought about Grayson and threw in a few extra strips. He was a pleasant surprise. He hadn't turned into a jerk, and he worked too hard. No surprise there, but a man had to eat.

When the pair of BLTs on toast was ready, she added several kosher dills to the plates and put them on a tray with two glasses of milk. The man hadn't eaten all day. He needed milk.

For good measure, she added a half dozen of Julia's peanut butter cookies.

A broken-stemmed cremone lay forlornly next to the water faucet, discarded in favor of its long-stemmed brothers. Because the bright color made her happy, she placed the flower along the tray's edge and started up the stairs. At the Mulberry Room door, she balanced the tray on one hand, proud that she could, and knocked with the other.

She heard movement and then the door opened. He looked harried and tired, sleeves rolled back, top two buttons open as if he'd wrestled with them. Behind the black-framed reading glasses, his eyes were rimmed in red.

He heaved a weary sigh. "You're the most beautiful thing I've ever seen."

She laughed. "Me or the BLT?"

"Both. Is that for me?" He stepped to one side. "Come in if it is. If it isn't, come in anyway, and I'll talk you out of it."

Suddenly very glad she'd thought of this impromptu room service, Valery entered. Grayson took the tray, pushed the laptop to one side of the desk and set the food in its place.

"A flower. Nice touch."

At the sincere praise, she glowed inside. "Julia said you've been holed up in here all day. I thought we could share a bite."

"A genius as well as beautiful." His gaze lingered on her, taking her in, making her feel important as if he was both glad and a little astonished that she'd thought of him.

"I've never visited in a guest's room before."

Those blue eyes warmed. "That's a good thing."

She laughed, almost giddy to be here with him. When had she ever felt that way about a man?

He handed her one of the plates. "Sit in the armchair. I'll take the desk."

"Because the food's there?" she teased.

His lips curved. He had a wonderful, gentle, friendly smile that warmed her all over. "You caught me. I was hoping you'd think I was being chivalrous."

Valery settled into the mulberry floral chair, plate on her lap, her gaze on this most unlikely male companion. He was so not her type, and she realized, for once, this was a good thing.

"You haven't tasted my cooking yet. Julia's the chef."

"I know perfection when I see it. Nothing better than a warm BLT, and this one looks and smells like paradise. A man and his bacon…" He chowed down, taking a man-sized bite that had him moaning and rolling his eyes in exaggerated appreciation.

Valery laughed, enjoying his pleasure, enjoying him. For a reaction like his, she would take cooking classes. Was a man's stomach really the way to his heart?

For a few quiet moments, they ate, and she had to admit the sandwich tasted delicious, exactly the right amount of salty crisp bacon and fat, juicy tomato.

When Grayson finally slowed down for a drink of milk, more than half the sandwich was gone. He glanced at his watch and then sheepishly at her. She twitched an eyebrow.

"I didn't realize it was getting this late. No wonder I'm starved."

"What are you working on that was so important you'd skip lunch?"

He put his sandwich on the plate. "Want to see?"

"Sure. But finish your BLT first."

He dispatched the remaining sandwich in three bites and tilted back in the desk chair with a relieved *ahhh*. "I'm a new man."

"I like the old one pretty well."

His gaze captured hers. There was heat and lightning in those blue depths and a sincerity she was unused to from men.

"Food and a compliment. Come here, I'll show you what I'm working on."

Valery put her sandwich aside and moved to the laptop he indicated as he shoved the empty tray aside. Rolling the chair to face the desk, he tapped the mouse pad, and the screen came on. A few quick swipes and he opened a graphic mock-up displaying the interior layout of a rustic but classy restaurant.

Valery leaned over his shoulder. He smelled good, manly and clean, the way he always did, and her belly fluttered at the attraction she felt at being this close. Brazen, she placed her hand on his shoulder. Warmth. Strength. Tension.

"Did you do this?"

He looked up, smiled. "I did. What do you think?"

"I think you're incredibly talented."

"Not talented. Simply proficient with software. Any geek could do this."

She squeezed and released the tight muscle in his shoulder. "You had to have the vision first. That's talent."

"Devlin's the designer, but once in a while I get a good idea. The mill restaurant strikes a chord with me. I want it to be perfect." He arched his shoulders upward and rolled his neck. "Didn't realize I was this tense."

"Very tight." Without asking, she began to work the muscles along the top of his shoulders.

"You don't have to do that."

Her hands stilled. "You want me to stop?"

A pause and then, "No."

When she'd danced, keeping the muscles loose was paramount. Constant exercises strained and pulled and caused aches and soreness all over the body. She knew how to make them better.

Muscle memory took over, and she kneaded broad shoulders, the soft cotton of his shirt sliding easily beneath her fingers.

"Your trapezius muscles are the problem. Sitting slumped over the computer has them in a spasm." She slid her thumbs up the sides of his neck, and he shivered. She eased the pressure.

"Does that hurt?"

His head moved slightly. "Feels good."

"You're very tense right here." She followed the hard muscle into his hairline and up the back of his head. The warm scalp under his dark, crisp hair sent sensations up her arms.

"Lay your head on the desk and relax."

"Easy for you to say." But he did as she instructed, forehead on his forearms. "You don't have to do this."

"I know." She wanted to, so she continued the massage, tightening and loosening the muscles, kneading, stroking her thumbs deep into the tissues.

For an athlete, working tight muscles was an act of defense. Here in Grayson's room, the two of them alone and attracted to each other, a massage could easily become a sensual thing.

They were as close as lovers, her body leaning into his back, though a desk chair stood between them. Still, she was aware of how he appealed to her, how physically appealing, masculine and sexy he was.

If she kept this up, she knew where it would end. In a way, she wanted it to happen. Then, she could be done with him. He would be exposed as another in a long line of users. She could despise and resent him and move on. But another part of her desperately yearned for a man to love her, *all* of her, not just her body.

The room was warm, the air heavy with bacon and the undeniable element of desire. Her own. Maybe his.

She dipped forward and placed her lips against the warm

flesh of his neck. And that's when she heard the sound. A long, sighing breath and a gentle snore.

Valery laughed softly, kissed him again and tiptoed out the door.

A first. She'd put the man to sleep.

CHAPTER 14

Hope deferred maketh the heart sick, but
when the desire cometh, it is a tree of life.

PROVERBS 13:12 KJV

1875. Hartford, Connecticut

Two weeks turned into three as Benjamin made his way across
the recovering South and into the North by railroad and once
by riverboat. Today, on a mild afternoon in July, he stepped
down from the railcar while smoke curled around his legs
and the clang and rattle of metal made the Union Depot a
noisy place.

"So this is Hartford."

From the depot, he could see a tall spire rising above the
city. He stopped a uniformed porter toting a steamer trunk
from a Pullman car. "What's that building yonder?"

The man's black face gleamed with sweat, but he didn't re-
linquish the heavy trunk. "The state capitol?"

"Where could a man start if he wanted to find someone?
There?"

The porter's gaze narrowed. "He in trouble with the law?"

"No." Ben frowned. At least he hoped Tandy was living
right. "He lived with my family for a time. We were separated during the war."

Wariness tightened the man's posture. He squinted at Ben
a moment longer before backing away. "I can't rightly say, sir,

but I gots to carry this trunk to the carriage or Mr. Jenson will know the reason why."

Ben watched him go, wondering at his sudden reluctance.

With his satchel in hand, for porters were only for the rich, he strode away from the train, moving onto a busy street. Elegant carriages rattled past. Ladies in fine dresses and veiled hats bobbed in and out of shops. His aunt Josie, with her skilled needle and penchant for beautiful garments, had likely never imagined such finery.

Hartford must be a very wealthy city.

He'd never been north of Nashville until now and felt as if he'd arrived in a foreign country. The size of the city shook him. How would he ever find Tandy in a place of this size?

Agog at the sheer number of businesses and homes, churches and hotels, Ben walked on.

Above everything, smoke curled from tall factories spearing the sky to his right. He turned left onto Asylum Street, a roadway that bustled with business. From here, he smelled the nearby river, a relief to a country boy who already missed the mountains and woods around Honey Ridge.

He passed shops selling everything from writing machines to cough drops and from velocipedes to automatic beds such as he'd never laid eyes on. The sheer volume of goods to a country Southerner was both wonderful and unsettling.

Shoninger Pianos and Organs caught his attention, and a wave of homesickness hit him. A fair-haired woman sat at a piano in the window, her nimble fingers playing "Für Elise." For a fleeting, wistful moment, Ben imagined the woman to be Patience, and he missed her and his mother and his home with a vengeance.

For the first time since leaving Peach Orchard, he began to have doubts. Hartford city was vast. He was a stranger with little money and no knowledge of where to begin.

Would he even recognize Tandy if he found him?

Shaking off the melancholy with a reminder that he had come too far to quit, he hoisted his bag and moved past the lilting melody.

By now his belly was his most immediate concern, seeing how he had taken not a bite since early morning at the last train stop. The warm biscuits had been light and fluffy and the hot gravy satisfying but both were long gone.

His nose led him down the street where a row of eating establishments beckoned. Eager to conserve his funds, he chose the Half Dime Lunchroom which promised a good meal for a small price, though he didn't expect the food to be anywhere near as tasty as Lizzy's fried chicken and spice cake.

He pushed open the door and entered the establishment, hoping to find more here than a meal. He was greeted by the strong smell of coffee and a toothy woman in a green dress and white apron, her forehead fringed like the forelock of a chestnut horse.

"I'm Belle," she said. "Today's special is pot roast, and the coffee comes with."

Her words were clipped and quick, and Ben had to compute the unfamiliar accent before nodding. His mouth pooled at the thought of hearty roast beef, a rarity at home where pork and poultry and wild game made up most meals. "Thank you, ma'am, I'll have that, if you please."

She cocked her head to one side. "You're not from around here, are you, mister?"

"No, ma'am, but I'm looking for someone, a Robert Wellston. Perhaps you know him?"

She twitched a shoulder. "Sorry, no."

In a swish of skirt against the wooden floor, she moved away, leaving Ben to ponder his next move. He gazed around the establishment. Three other men hovered over plates piled with food. At a table near the window, a woman and a man sat together, leaning close in quiet discussion.

The toothy waitress returned with a coffee cup which she filled from a copper pot. The strong smell rose like a beacon, and he sipped carefully at the hot, powerful brew. In minutes she returned with his plate piled high with food.

When she saw his expression, she sniffed. "You looked hungry."

"I am." He smiled, comforted by her kindness. "Thank you, ma'am."

She left him to fill coffee cups at the other tables and greet a trio of rugged newcomers. Benjamin ate with gusto, thinking of his journey and where to go from here.

When the waitress returned to offer apple dumplings, he shook his head. Much as he'd enjoy the dumplings, the roast beef and potatoes had filled him, and he still had money in his pocket.

"Perhaps you could recommend a hotel or boardinghouse?" he asked.

"At the end of this street, you can take your pick. They might be able to help you find your friend, too."

"Can you suggest where else a man might look?"

She gave his questions some consideration, a furrow beneath her thick fringe. "The courthouse, perhaps? And you can place a classified in the *Hartford Courant*."

She gave him directions to both places, and with a hearty thanks, he paid his bill and went back out on the busy streets, more encouraged now that his belly was full and he had some direction.

First, he journeyed to the newspaper office and wrote out a sizable advertisement. By the time he finished, evening was upon him, and the courthouse had closed for the night. Refusing to be discouraged, he found the City Hotel recommended by the waitress and signed the register.

The mustached clerk, skin as pale as Aunt Josie's and not much older than Benjamin, peered at Ben's signature. "Where you hail from, Mr. Portland?"

"Tennessee."

"You've come a long way. What's your business in Hartford?" Like the waitress, he spoke quickly and clipped his words.

"I'm looking for someone who lives here. Or he did nine years ago. His name's Robert Wellston. Perhaps you've heard of him?"

He didn't mention Tandy. A former slave garnered little attention, and to make matters more difficult, freedmen often took names of their owners or made up one of their own. Tandy could be anybody by now.

The clerk smoothed a finger over his mustache as if he was proud to have one. "Something about the name sounds familiar. I'll ask my boss, if you want."

"I do. Thank you, mister."

"John. Just call me John."

The name brought on another bout of homesickness. "Mind if I wait while you ask your boss?"

John chuckled. "You'd be waiting awhile. Boss won't be back until tomorrow. Here's your key. Number seven. Would you be wanting a bath? I can send up hot water."

A hot bath after weeks of travel was luxury, and he responded with a hearty "Yes," before bounding up the stairs.

The hotel room featured a large, high bed, a chair and heavy draperies with a pitcher and bowl stand. Another luxury that did not pass unnoticed or underappreciated.

He tossed his satchel on the bed and flopped, tired and eager for rest, onto the thick, fat pillows. From the bag, he withdrew a pen and paper and scratched off a letter to his mother. He'd made a point to write her every two days and ease her fears that the world would gobble up her only child.

Once he'd written about the grandeur of Hartford and the fine meal and fluffy bed, he rested against the pillows and awaited his hot water. He was far from home, as Tandy had been that winter long ago. Somewhere in this city, his best friend lived.

Ben reached into his pocket and withdrew the blue marble, shiny from constant rubbing. They'd made the promise and traded marbles, though the small glass balls were exactly the same. Still, to him, this one was Tandy's, and he'd waited nine years to return it to its proper owner.

Did Tandy wait, too? With a sigh of confidence borne of friendship, Benjamin believed he did.

Tomorrow, even if he had to walk every street, he would find Tandy. If all went well, this time tomorrow, he'd pen the good news home to Peach Orchard. And the entire family would rejoice.

CHAPTER 15

Present Day. Honey Ridge

"I wanted to tell you first."

Grayson squatted next to the hole in the mill's basement floor. Valery stood at his shoulder.

As soon as he'd heard, he'd called and asked her to come.

For once, the mill was empty, security gone. Lem hadn't appeared this morning to ramble and spread his brand of philosophy, and interest in the empty gravesite had subsided once the bones had all been removed.

The ancient building was eerily quiet, like a graveyard. Which Grayson supposed it was in a manner of speaking.

"The forensic results are in."

Valery gasped, her mouth round, her face going pale in the dim basement. "Is it—"

He tugged her hand into his hand and rose. "It's not your nephew."

Her breath came out in a rush. "Thank God. But who, then?"

"The bones are very old. Male, early thirties. Forensic dated them back to the mid-1800s, probably Civil War period, which coincides with much of the area's history. Many men disappeared during the war, either in battle or as runaways or deserters."

He sounded stiff, like a professor dictating notes. Truth was, he was relieved for Valery and her family as well as for himself. The police tape was finally gone, and he could call in the contractors.

"You'll know best how to tell Julia."

Valery nodded, her long hair falling down around her shoulders.

Over a week had passed since he'd fallen asleep on his desk. When he'd awakened she was gone, but a fragrant note slipped beneath his door teased him for the faux pas.

"You owe me." The words were surrounded by little smiley faces.

The next morning, they'd shared a laugh, though his smile had been sheepish. He must have been half-dead to fall asleep with Valery in his room.

As an apology, he'd attended a meeting of the Historical Preservation Society with her, though he jokingly called it the Hysterical Society. The Sweat sisters and their parrot, Binky, had kept him laughing or shaking his head all evening.

Grayson had also driven to Nashville for a few days and hired Faith Madison at his brother's request as restaurant manager. He was still pondering that interesting turn of events. Devlin insisted she was business only, but Grayson wondered who was kidding whom.

While there, he'd checked on other projects and then spent his spare time studying Patience's musical notation. The more he studied, the more convinced he became that he was looking at a cryptogram.

No puzzle was more demanding than the one they'd found beneath the mill.

"Maybe whoever put the bottle tree outside knew something we didn't," she said.

"What does that mean?"

"Someone knew a body was buried here. Someone afraid of ghosts. The mill has a reputation."

"So I've heard, but I'm a skeptic. Not that I don't believe in God. But ghosts? The jury is out. Have you ever experienced anything supernatural?"

"The inn has an angel." She looked up at him. "Don't call me crazy. You heard the music."

He had. "Had you heard it before?"

"The music is new. At least for me. Julia doesn't tell me everything. She's afraid…" She crossed her arms.

"Afraid of what?"

"Never mind. Let's go outside. That hole is giving me the creeps."

"Afraid I'll push you in?"

"I'd have a heart attack." She hurried to the stairs and trotted up. He followed, wanting to laugh at her, but a dead body, no matter how old, deserved more respect.

When they came out into the cloudy day, he led the way around to the creek bank and regretted not seeing Lem and his dog there.

"Did the coroner indicate how the man may have died? Or why?" Valery asked.

"Yes."

Something in his voice must have forewarned her. She lifted her face, her hand at her throat. "How?"

"He was murdered."

Julia cried. From relief. From the fact that Mikey's whereabouts still remained a mystery. From the sheer stress of wondering about the bones buried at the mill.

Eli, thankfully, was home when Valery returned to the inn. She'd sent Alex up to his room with a pack of gummy fruits and a promise to play video games after dinner. Then she'd called her sister and brother-in-law into the family parlor to break the news.

Valery had cried, too. No amount of kindness or euphemistic phrasing changed the fact that she'd brought up the most painful topic in either of their lives.

"Thank goodness," Julia said, and then her face had crumbled. "Oh, what am I saying? A man was murdered. How terrible am I to be relieved?"

"Don't, honey." Eli sat with an arm around his wife. He kissed the side of her hair, and she buried her face in his neck.

The comforting, loving action moved inside Valery with such power, she wrapped her arms around herself.

The unspoken truth hung between them, fresh and excruciating. Mikey was still missing. She hadn't wanted the bones to belong to her precious little nephew, but at least, if they had, Julia would know. They would finally have closure.

Closure. She needed it, too, but as with her sister, dangling in limbo had become their way of life, and closure couldn't come. Some sins lingered forever.

Seeing the fresh grief return to Julia's face reminded Valery of what she had done. She was the cause of her personal heartache. Julia was not.

Someday she'd have the courage. Someday she'd face Mama with the truth only the two of them shared.

Throat tight enough to cut off her airway, she excused herself and left the couple alone. They didn't need her, and she couldn't bear another minute of Julia's haunted expression.

Needing to be alone, she carried her guilt and shame down the hall into her white-and-black bedroom, her retreat from the Victorian world of the inn. Splashes of red, like blood, broke the stark modern canvas.

A flower catalog had come in today's mail and waited on her bed. She picked it up and flipped through the pages. Pink roses reminded her of Charlotte Portland Gadsden's babies buried in the old family cemetery.

Babies.

Tears slipped down her face. Would Julia ever see hers again? Would she?

Desperate to be numb and to shut off the image rising in her thoughts, she took the pink tote from the back of her closet and quietly left the house…and headed toward the cemetery and all those lost babies.

CHAPTER 16

Present Day. Peach Orchard Inn

Had anyone mourned the dead man all those years ago? Had his family waited and prayed, ultimately passing from this life without ever knowing what happened to their loved one?

Life was uncertain and death was a mystery. Nobody understood that better than a man who had faced his own mortality.

Wearing these somber thoughts like a shroud, Grayson left the gristmill and returned to Peach Orchard Inn.

Devlin would return in the morning. The contractors, except for two, had been rescheduled to begin work at eight. Finally, the Blake brothers could get back on track with this project without losing more time or money.

Had Mr. Bones known he was running out of time that last fateful day? The day someone stabbed him in the back and buried him beneath the gristmill?

Murder.

Grayson couldn't quite seem to shake the eerie thoughts. God, Grandma always said, had a plan for everyone. Was death by murder Mr. Bones's destiny just as life through the fire of Hodgkin's disease had been his? Did cancer still wait around some dark corner to grab him by the throat again, this time to take him all the way to the grave?

He shuddered at the miserable thoughts. It was not death that frightened him. A dying person, even a teenager, took the time to reconcile his life with God and eternity. Death was inevitable, even if he'd prefer to put it off as long as he could. But it was the agony of living through the treatments again and witnessing the fear in his mother and father and brother that scared him.

From the dining room came the voices of other guests as he entered the foyer. The smell of freshly baked cookies filled the house, but none of the family seemed to be downstairs.

He wondered how Julia had taken the news. With strength, he was sure, but with a heart full of loss that remained unresolved.

In passing through to the staircase, he glanced up at the couple over the parlor fireplace. They seemed to offer their approval, of what he didn't know, and the whimsy of his thoughts caught him off guard. He was neither whimsical nor superstitious, but as soon as the thought came, he heard music.

The soft, tinkling sound seemed to come from everywhere and nowhere, an indication that the piano and its player must be in his head.

Like Patience's sheet music. It niggled at the back of his brain, teasing, challenging him to discover…something.

He bounded up the staircase, escaping his melancholy thoughts as eagerness to apply yet another solution overcame him. Computer software. Algorithms. He'd become convinced the music held a secret code of some sort, and when his intellectual curiosity was aroused, he didn't stop until he was satisfied.

He loved a good puzzle. Crossword, cryptogram, sudoku, any puzzle. The music presented a unique challenge, and if figuring out the code brought him in contact with the innkeeper's sister, he wasn't complaining.

Perhaps Valery was correct, and Patience had a forbidden lover.

While his laptop loaded, he took out the sheet music and held it up to the light. Nothing unusual there, but from outside the window directly across from the desk, a flash of color caught his eye.

Sheet music momentarily forgotten, he went to the window. Valery in a shiny blue blouse walked away from the house, her head low, her body language melancholy.

Something swung from her right hand. He squinted. A pink bag?

Contemplating, he breathed in through his nose, hands on his hips.

The conversation with Julia must not have gone well. Valery was distressed. Alone and upset.

Without thinking, he tossed the paper aside and trotted down the blood-red stairs and out the back door. By then, Valery had disappeared through the tree line.

Curious and, if he was honest, concerned, he followed. If Julia was troubled, Valery was troubled. He'd learned that about her. She carried her sister's losses as well as her own.

He instinctively knew she needed someone as much as Julia did. Today, he wanted that someone to be him. Never mind their differences or his fear that a woman like Valery could break his heart. She needed him.

As he crossed the large back lawn and passed through the tree line, the space suddenly cleared into a little cemetery he hadn't known was there. Hidden by the trees and set back among the viney brush, the burial ground was not visible from the house. From the gray and weathered condition of the stones, the graves were old.

On the far side of the cemetery, Valery stood with her back to him, the pink bag on the grass and a bourbon bottle in her hand. One palm rested on a headstone.

Grayson's heart sank to his boot heels. "Valery."

She spun around, holding the bottle behind her back. "Grayson! What are you doing here?"

"I saw you leave the house. Is everything all right?"

"If you mean Julia, she's okay, coping. Eli is with her."

"I was asking about you," he said gently.

"Oh." Her posture eased. "That's nice."

He moved closer, stepping carefully around the stones. "What is this place?"

"The Portland family cemetery." She gestured with her free hand. "No one's been buried here in years."

Yet she came out to a place of the dead. Alone. With a bottle of bourbon. The aloneness worried him. Valery was a woman who needed and enjoyed being with people. She was a gregarious extrovert, the life of the party, the fun girl. Alone was not her personality.

"Someone plants flowers. You?" Neat, well-kept greenery and spring color sprouted all around the small plot.

She inclined her head. "Someone has to."

"Why?"

Her slender shoulder lifted. "I like it here. It's peaceful, and I feel this—don't laugh—this connection."

"Maybe I feel it, too." *Like the affection and pity I feel for you, strong enough to draw me out here. Strong enough to mess with my head and my heart.*

"Do you?" Her words were tremulous.

"Every grave has a story." The solemn comment won an approving blink of whiskey-colored eyes, veiled eyes that hid the truth but couldn't hide the pain.

He didn't add that Mr. Bones had a story, too. No use stirring up that ghost again today.

With the bottle carefully concealed behind her back, an action that sent a pang through Grayson, Valery trailed her fingertips over the top of a headstone.

"She lost her babies. So many babies."

He stepped closer. "Who?"

"Charlotte Portland, the woman in the photo above the parlor fireplace. Eli found that picture, oval frame and all, during the carriage house renovation."

"I've noticed it. Who were they?"

"Charlotte and the Yankee captain she married after the war. William Gadsden. We don't have a photo of her first husband, Edgar, but his family built this house and the gristmill."

"How did Charlotte end up with the captain?" Could she have been the subject of Patience Portland's clandestine musical notes? "Did she leave her husband for a Yankee?"

"Not Charlotte. She was deeply religious, and her captain must have been, too. Her letters show that she loved him but was not willing to break her marriage vows. We also know she was locked away in her room by her husband for writing letters to the captain."

"That wouldn't go well today."

"Edgar was thrown from a horse and died, and sometime after the war ended, Charlotte and her captain found true love right here at Peach Orchard."

"A romantic story."

"But tragic, too. Marrying a Yankee in the post-war South was not popular." She bent toward the headstone, blocking his view, and he was amazed how she smoothly transferred the bourbon bottle to the back of the stone, effectively hiding it from him. "Four babies are buried here, too. Little Anna was the last, the child of Captain Gadsden. How desperately they must have prayed that she would survive. She lived five days."

The sadness in her voice made Grayson's throat ache. She went to her knees before the faded stone and traced a finger over the faint lettering. "I think about her, who she would have grown up to be. Does she dance or sing or plant flowers or have a boyfriend? Babies. Little helpless babies tossed by the wind of fate and choice."

Tugging at his pants legs, Grayson eased to his haunches beside her. "Choice?"

She startled, an odd reaction he thought, as if she'd forgotten his presence. "God chooses when and where we're born. That's what I meant by choices. Today, with modern medicine, all four babies might have lived."

He caught the faintest scent of bourbon. "No way of knowing for sure."

"So much loss." She looked at him with a wounded expression. "Their little angels touch my heart."

"You like kids."

"Don't you?"

"Yes." They were in his life plan. Someday. And when he was with Valery, *someday* seemed to move closer. His computer brain didn't like the algorithm, but his heart paid no attention.

"Have you ever thought about kids of your own? You'd make a great mom."

Her eyelashes fluttered in surprise. "Me?"

"Sure. Look at you. Sympathizing with Charlotte. Mourning her lost children." And Julia's. But he didn't say that. "And you're great with Alex."

She dropped her gaze to the grass. "No, no. Some people aren't meant to have kids. I'm too—"

"Too what?"

"Selfish."

"I don't believe that."

She shook her head and didn't look at him. Grayson floundered to know where to go from here.

Every time he thought they'd made a connection, something changed, and she withdrew.

He stood and walked a short distance away, flummoxed and troubled. The graveyard exuded peace and quiet, much like the inn itself, as if Heaven reached down in mercy and compassion.

He was being whimsical again, but he couldn't deny the gentle, benevolent mood swirling over the cemetery. Over all of Peach Orchard Inn.

Angels lived at Peach Orchard Inn, but no ghosts. The only ghosts were inside Valery Carter.

She came here seeking peace, but what price was peace found in a bourbon bottle?

He slid a hand under her elbow and raised them both to a stand. Turning her to face him, he loosely held her forearms and tugged her to within inches of his chest. Grayson wanted to hold her close and soothe all her hurts and chase away her ghosts, but he listened to his logical brain instead. He was not only walking on hallowed ground, he was playing with fire. Valery could burn him badly.

Gently, he said, "I have to ask you something. I need to know."

She cocked her head to one side.

"What makes you come out here all alone with a bottle of booze?"

Valery pulled back, shame flushing through her body hot and cold and relentless. "I don't know what you mean."

Grayson held firm, his expression calm and rational, as if he was reasoning with a child. She should be angry at him for prying, for sticking his nose where it didn't belong. But she couldn't muster up the energy. Not with Grayson.

He knew. He'd seen. And his opinion mattered more than she'd ever intended. Now he'd never want to see her again.

"It's not so much the alcohol that bothers me, Valery. It's that you feel the need to hide it." He gestured toward the stone where she'd hidden the bottle.

Neither Mama nor Julia would have said a word. They would have seen, but cold silence and troubled glances would have been their response.

Confrontation was impossible in the Carter family. Someday, though, she'd gain her courage. Someday, she'd break the silence.

"What I do is none of your business."

Instead of haughty insult, the words tumbled out in a whimper.

Grayson, as steady as a mountain, held her with a look. "What if I want it to be?"

"Why would you?" After what she'd done, why would any decent man care about her?

"Ah, Valery." He sighed deeply and pulled her into a light hug, a caring embrace that nearly brought her to tears.

She didn't resist. Right now, she had no desire to be anywhere other than in Grayson's arms. Resting her head against his chest, she listened to his steady, solid heartbeat. He was so secure. So safe and confident and solid.

Would he want to touch her if he knew the truth?

The silent graves listened, patient and kind, while overhead in the sweet gum tree a blue jay scolded.

"Lem says you have ghosts," he murmured. "I concur."

Lem, the old vagrant, what could he possibly know?

Her mouth curved against Grayson's cotton-scented shirt. "Do you? If two such great minds concur, it must be true."

He didn't respond in jest. He simply waited, holding her, the question out there. What haunted her? What horrible thing was she trying to numb with bourbon? Though she couldn't tell him, Valery understood the psychology of her brokenness.

Julia's child had been stolen. Valery had thrown hers away. She'd sold her soul for a pair of dancing shoes.

The cruel cosmic joke was on her. She had gotten exactly nothing.

What she didn't know was what to do about it.

"When I was sick—" Grayson's voice rumbled in his chest and tickled her ear "—my parents went through pure hell."

Valery remained silent, listening, intrigued and relieved by his change of subject. The last thing she wanted to address were her reasons for over-imbibing. Silence made her sins invisible.

"We were all scared, but my parents more than me. I made my peace with death. But Mom and Dad were shattered. They felt responsible to make me well and suffered guilt because they couldn't."

"Making you well wasn't in their power," she murmured.

He tilted back, and she felt him look down, felt him touch the top of her hair. Featherlight. Gentle. Tender.

"No. But fact and feelings don't always agree, and their emotional response didn't change. Mom stopped working to take care of me. Finances took a hit. Medical bills piled up. Dad got an ulcer, and Mom couldn't deal at all. She stopped sleeping to sit by my bed, afraid I'd die in my sleep. She lost weight and cried a lot but tried to keep the rest of us, particularly me, from knowing."

"But you knew."

"Oh, yeah. I was there. Her eyes were always red. The house was heavy with worry, and when I was in the hospital, fear was palpable. After a while, the strain took a toll. Mom started drinking."

Valery's stomach dropped. So, that's where he was going with this.

She lifted her face to look at him, solemn and steady. "What happened? Is she okay?"

"Dad saw what was happening, though Mom hid the vodka and denied she was drinking. She became a master at mouthwash, minty gum, and pretending all was well even when her eyes were glassy and her voice slurred."

"I'm sorry."

"Dad and my grandparents intervened and got her treatment, but I felt guilty for a long time. If I hadn't gotten sick, she wouldn't have either."

"You know that's not rational."

"Feelings rarely are." He pushed her back a slight distance to stare into her face. "Your feelings matter, Valery. To me. Mom was afraid of losing a son, afraid she'd failed her family, and because of the fear, she *did* fail us. For a while. Her strength came in learning to deal with fear and stress without the vodka. We both got well."

"Thank God." Valery heard what he was saying and some place deep inside knew he was right.

"I do. Every day."

He stroked a hand down her back, and she thought of the innocent fun and sweet kisses they'd shared that day of the picnic. Now they were here in a quiet cemetery talking of alcoholism and cancer. Grayson Blake was a deep well, a man who would despise her if he knew the real reasons she sometimes drank too much.

"I'm concerned about you, Val."

"Don't be. I'm—" She started to say "fine," but couldn't lie. Not to Grayson. "Life doesn't always turn out the way we plan. I've made some stupid mistakes."

"We all have." His voice was gentle and thick with an understanding that spoke deeply to her spirit.

"Not like mine." The need to share her greatest sin with someone—*anyone*—pushed up inside her like hot lava from an active volcano. She swallowed down the burning impulse, afraid if she allowed the vent to blow, neither of them would survive.

So she cheated.

"When Mikey disappeared..." She let the words dwindle, hoping he'd take the bait and swim away from her sins. The drinking had started then, but Mikey wasn't the only reason.

God forgive her for using her abducted nephew as an excuse.

"Booze won't bring him back."

"I know." She stepped out of his arms, afraid to continue the conversation lest she say too much and have the humiliating experience of watching his concern turn to disgust.

Sooner or later, it would happen. He'd see her for who she was, and he'd drive away in that big Jeep of his.

"I should get back to the house. Dinner soon," she said abruptly, eager to get away, though mostly from herself.

After touching her fingers to Anna's headstone in a silent goodbye, she started out of the cemetery, the ground beneath her feet soft and moist.

"Valery."

She turned back. Grayson held up the pink tote, her secret stash bag, and the pint of Jack.

"Forgetting something?" There was no accusation in the question, nor in his quiet, steady expression.

She stared at him a long moment before saying, "You keep it."

Then she hurried out of the graveyard, chased by the truth she needed to be free.

CHAPTER 17

I have spread my dreams under your feet
Tread softly because you tread on my dreams.

YEATS

1875. Peach Orchard Farm

Johnny Atkins stopped his work in the cornfield to lift his head and listen. Since losing his eyesight, he'd developed the ears of a hunting hound, able to hear the slightest noise.

"Somebody's crying," he said to the freedman working at his side. Captain Will and Miss Charlotte were dedicated to hiring the ex-slaves and they were excellent workers, far better than the likes of him. Jeremiah made up where Johnny lacked.

"I don't hear nothing, Mr. Johnny. You got ears like a jackrabbit."

Johnny could hear the smile in the man's voice. "I better go see. Somebody might be hurt."

"You go on, then. I'll finish out this chopping and see what Miss Charlotte wants done next."

Johnny was already moving toward the sound of weeping. It was a woman's voice, and his heart squeezed with worry. Had something happened?

As he drew closer, his feet moved faster, stumbling now and then in his rush as he recognized Patience's voice, a voice he could separate from a crowd of hundreds.

"Miss Patience," he called. "Is everything all right?"

The crying stopped and so did he, confused now about where to go.

"Where are you? I'm coming to help."

She was silent for another moment or two while he caught his breath and wiped the sweat from the back of his neck with a rag.

"Here," she said in a tremulous voice. "In the cemetery. But I'm all right, Johnny. No need to come any nearer."

Wild horses wouldn't stop him, though he rarely visited the cemetery, which sat a hundred yards east of the house. Too many fellow soldiers lay beneath that soil, unclaimed by the living. Soldiers, like him, who would never return home, though his was by choice and theirs was not.

After making sure his sunglasses and hat were in place to protect the lady's sensibilities, he felt his way with a stick and his free hand to the fence leading inside the graveyard.

Finding the gate, he lifted the latch and stepped inside the quiet resting place. Holy ground, he thought, a place of God and peace. "Where?"

"Go back, Johnny. Don't bother yourself. You have work to do."

The words were enough to guide him and he found her, both by scent and sound. She always smelled like lavender, a flower she grew in the side yard and pressed into sachets and toilet water and gave as gifts. Everyone had a distinctive scent, and he'd know hers, the same as he knew her rainwater and honey voice, anywhere.

"What's wrong, Miss Patience?" He touched her arm, pretending he did so to guide him next to her. Her skin was delicate beneath the thin cotton she wore to protect from the sun. "You ought not to be out here in this heat."

"I've had a...difficult morning and didn't want Charlotte to hear me."

"Why?" He was prying and she'd likely rebuff him, but he cared too much to leave her alone in tears. If someone had upset her tender heart, they would answer to him. "What's wrong?"

"It's Benjamin—" Her voice broke. "Oh, Johnny."

"Benjamin?" He stiffened as fear struck him in the chest like a mine ball. The boy was a little brother to him, though neither a boy nor little any longer. "Is he hurt? Sick?"

"No, no. Nothing like that. He's on his way to Colorado to find Tandy. I'm so afraid for him…"

She began to cry in earnest now, and though Johnny didn't understand why she'd be this upset about an extended trip, his heart ached to hear her cry. Before he could think of all the reasons not to, he took her in his arms and pulled her close to his chest.

She stiffened like a frightened mare, and when he loosened his hold, she relaxed and came back to him, leaning in, resting her forehead against his chest with a sigh.

Johnny's heart soared. He was holding Patience in his arms, something he'd longed to do for years. He kept his hold light, gentle as he would a fragile bird, so scared was he of upsetting her more.

"There now. It can't be that bad," he said softly. "What's happened? I thought Tandy was in Hartford."

If Patience was offended about the embrace, she didn't show it. She remained in the shelter of his arms, a slender, feminine reed made of silk and sunlight. Johnny thought his chest would burst from the pure joy of touching his dearest love.

"Charlotte received a letter today." Her breath waxed warm on his neck. He fought off a shudder, so great was his pleasure.

"Benjamin learned that Tandy's owner, Robert Wellston, was a wealthy hotel owner."

"There, then. Isn't that good news? Ben's found him."

"No, not yet." She shuddered back a sob. "Wellston sold his hotel and moved to Colorado a few years ago. He took Tandy along. Ben cannot go there, Johnny. He mustn't."

Ah, now he understood. She feared for Ben in a strange and wild place like Colorado. The papers were full of frightening stories about the West, of robbers and Indian trouble and disreputable men. He knew because Patience read them to him.

"Ben will be all right," he assured her, purely, he told himself, to keep his promise to Benjamin. "Don't you worry yourself one bit. He's a smart boy, and God will watch over him."

She trembled in his arms until he wondered at her great fear. Patience was not a woman given to hysterics.

"You're a good man, Johnny Atkins. So kind and thoughtful."

She laid her head against his shoulder, and to show her it was all right, he raised his hand to the silken hair falling loose against her back.

"Your hair's like silk," he murmured, forgetting himself. "So soft. Logan says it's the color of corn silks. Beautiful as an angel's."

She stiffened again, and he knew he'd overstepped. Regret filled him as she pulled away. What was wrong with him? He should cut out his tongue for insulting her.

"I better get back to the house." Her rainwater voice had turned curt. "We've pickles to make."

"I'm sorry if I offended. I shouldn't have— I was only concerned—"

"No offense taken, Johnny. I must go."

He heard her move away, her skirt brushing the grass and tombstones, each obstacle sending a different sound into his ears. But the sound he heard the loudest was his own heart, beating for a woman he could never have.

★ ★ ★

Later, after supper when the lightning bugs danced over the fields, Johnny stood in the warm night listening to the music. First, of the cicadas and the distant train, of the night birds and crickets and tree frogs that sang him to sleep, and then of the music drifting from the parlor window. Heaven's music, he was certain, played by an angel sent to earth.

He didn't go inside. Couldn't after his mistake in the cemetery. Instead he stepped silently onto the porch and settled into a rocking chair to listen to Patience play. The melody was unfamiliar, maybe one of her own compositions, but the sad and yearning tune pulled at a place inside him.

He tilted his head against the cool wood, glad for the darkness that covered his ugliness. Here, in the night music, he could pretend to be a man listening to his lady love, and dream of the future he'd never have.

CHAPTER 18

Present Day. Honey Ridge

She'd never heard music as lovely as the baby grand beneath Grayson Blake's long, skilled fingers.

Valery sat on the bench beside him, enjoying an excuse to be close to a man for whom relaxation was a dirty word.

But no one worked at the mill on Sunday afternoons. Even she had gone to church this morning. Her mother had nearly passed out from the shock. Valery had ignored her, choosing to sit in the back pew where she could close her eyes and pray in earnest.

Last night in the cemetery with Grayson had shaken something loose inside her. Half the night, she'd ruminated, seeking answers and finding none. Attending church had been... refreshing. The roof hadn't fallen in. Lightning had not struck.

After the service, she stood outside the white frame church with the Riley women listening to Carrie's wedding plans.

"Carrie asked me to be in her wedding." She didn't realize she'd spoken out loud until Grayson stopped playing to look at her.

"I met her at the mill with her fiancé, the writer," he said. "She seems nice. They both do."

"Carrie's the sweetest."

"Are the two of you good friends?"

"We used to be before—" Before Jim Beam and Jack Daniel's had become her preferred pals. Before partying with user men became more important than a true friend like Carrie. "I don't want to...mess up and spoil her wedding."

What she really meant was, she feared she'd get blitzed on the wedding champagne and make a fool of herself.

Grayson put his hand over hers. "Do you want to be in the wedding or not?"

"Yes. Of course. I adore Carrie. Plus, I love the bridesmaid parties and showers and all the girly things we get to do. Nikki—that's Carrie's sister who runs the boutique in Honey Ridge—has booked a spa weekend for all the women in the wedding party. Facials, massage, spray tans, pedicures." She pressed her hands to her chest in faux excitement. "Girl heaven."

"Can't miss that." His voice was amused. "You and Julia work seven days a week. How often do you take off for a whole weekend?"

"Really?" Valery tossed her hair and laughed. "You, of all people, are asking me that?"

His grin was sheepish. "We're talking about you, not me."

"Oh, so my work issues matter, but yours don't?"

"Absolutely. I'm a guy. Guys are different."

"Thank the good Lord." She fluttered her eyelashes at him and was thrilled when he laughed. Laughter looked good on him. Real good.

"I don't see the problem," he insisted. "Say yes."

"Well." She tapped her bottom lip. "The Mountain Lodge Spa *is* on my bucket list."

"There you go. Problem solved." He made an imaginary

check mark in the air. "One less bucket list item. What else you got on there that I can help you with?"

I want to hold my daughter and tell her I'm sorry. But she didn't say that one out loud. No one could help her with that. "Italy."

"I could treat you to Olive Garden, but I don't think that's what you have in mind."

"No, but their all-you-can-eat pasta bowl is tasty."

He pointed a finger. "Put that on my bucket list."

"You have to do better than that. Tell me your craziest item. The one thing you wanted most as a kid."

"To run with the bulls in Spain."

"Really?" Her hand dropped to her lap. "Me, too! I still do. And you know what else?"

"What?"

"I think it would be super fun to make a guard laugh at Buckingham Palace."

His mouth curved. "And I want to Segway through the Grand Canyon."

"Do they let you do that?"

He lifted both hands. "Why ask?"

They both burst into laughter. Staid and controlled Grayson was surprisingly more fun than he first appeared. Quick-witted, smart, he made her happy in a way she hadn't been in a long time.

She leaned into him, inhaling his woodsy cologne. His hands rubbed up and down her arms, friendly, affectionate.

Valery understood men on an elemental basis. She knew he liked her. A lot. She was afraid he wouldn't if he knew the real Valery.

"I bet you really do have a bucket list," she mused. "Probably typed up in your computer and backed up to a cloud."

"To a cloud *and* a flash drive."

"I knew it. Do you really have all those things on there?"

"Really do, but I haven't looked at it in a long time. I started the list when I was sick and thought I might not live to do any of those things."

"I would say that was sad, except you're alive, and you can do anything you want to."

"Within reason. Most of all, I'd like to finish the car Pappy and I started together."

"What's stopping you?"

He started to look at his wristwatch, and she grabbed for it. "Give me that thing."

"Hey."

In the next instance, they were wrestling over his watch. The bench scraped the floor as he jumped up to escape. She stalked him, darting a hand toward the offending timepiece. He dodged to one side.

"No, you don't."

She leaped at him. He held his hand high over her head. She rose up in a ballet leap she hadn't attempted in years, caught his arm, and quickly slid the watch from his wrist.

Grayson stood with hands on his hips, looking ruffled, annoyed and amused all at the same time.

The band dangling from her first two fingers, Valery ticktocked the watch back and forth. "How much ransom will you pay?"

She danced around him, grinning, teasing, the watch glinting in the sunbeams while he watched her with eyes that had gone predatory. A hum of energy stirred the air. She danced closer, leaning in, preening for him like a bird.

Suddenly, he pounced, and she was body-pressed against the wall faster than a blink. Stunned, thrilled, Valery forgot all about the watch and turned her focus to Grayson. He was full of surprises, her piano man. She liked that about him. A little wild. A little unpredictable. Who knew?

His head lowered, slowly, slowly, and breath coming short both from exertion and emotion, she strained up to meet him.

One hand to the back of her head, gaze holding hers in a hypnotic stare, he touched his lips against her mouth. The moment was electric. Sparks flew—maybe in her imagination but they definitely flew.

She sighed against his mouth and deepened the kiss, basking in the way he made her feel. Worthy, not cheap. Cherished, not used.

Oh my. My, my, my.

When he finally eased away, his expression as stunned as she felt, Valery touched her lips with her fingertips and then touched his.

"Ransom paid," she whispered.

With a slow smile, he raised his hand to eye level.

He'd reclaimed the wristwatch.

CHAPTER 19

The rumble and roar of heavy equipment was the best sound Grayson had heard in weeks. Clipboard in hand, he roamed the construction site, checking off his list, noting safety elements, making calls, texts and plans.

Nothing spelled relief like getting things done, particularly when his brain was overloaded with thoughts of a certain vivacious, fun-loving, kissable brunette who had his head twisted all the way around.

Yesterday afternoon in the family parlor, things had gotten out of hand, out of control. Not that he was complaining. Kissing Valery well and often had officially found a place on his bucket list.

Crazy. Messed up. The control freak residing inside him didn't know what to do with her. One thing for sure, he wasn't leaving Honey Ridge until he figured it out.

At the rate the mill project was moving, he had plenty of time.

One thing he'd learned. Hanging out with Valery relaxed him. She made him laugh and think about other things besides work. Maybe he'd drive home to Nashville next Saturday and work on Pappy's car. The garage was full of boxed car parts waiting for him. Maybe he'd invite Valery to tag along.

Someone called his name. He glanced up and waved toward the backhoe operator to let him know he was getting out of the way. It wouldn't do to be so lost in thoughts of Valery that he got run down by one of his own employees.

Hands on hips, he surveyed the busy scene, relieved to find it so. The more work they did, the more tension eased from his shoulders.

Devlin was back. So was the old man and his dog.

Grayson watched in amused interest as Lem Tolly strode around the outside of the mill, an unlit cigarette butt dangling from his lips. Occasionally, he paused to look up and contemplate the work in progress, the weathered face as brown and wrinkled as tree bark. Oats trotted at his heels, diverting now and then to race with a yip into the woods or into the creek, reemerging with a shake of her fur.

Now that Mr. Bones had been removed to a more appropriate resting place, the other curiosity seekers came in spits and spurts. At least one of the good old boys from the café popped by every day for updates but no longer lingered to share pithy comments and unsolicited advice.

With construction back in force, visitors were not allowed inside the basement. Mr. B., the undertaker, in particular, was disappointed his mortuary had not been asked to handle reinterment of the skeletal remains. That did not, however, keep him from sharing his depressing quotations including the oft-said, "Life is short and full of sorrows."

Fifty yards up trail from the mill, Devlin stood talking to a man and woman. The man was tall and dark and elegant, even in jeans and a pullover shirt. The woman was slim and pretty with short, dark hair tucked behind her ears. Hayden Winters and Carrie Riley. Even from here, he saw the tender looks they gave each other.

Tender, like his heart these days.

Grayson was glad to have his brother back in town, though Dev's teasing about Valery had taken on new meaning.

Grayson was deeply attracted, maybe even falling in love with her, but he also liked to control his world, an impossibility with a free-spirited woman who might have a drinking problem.

Not that he could control his heart any more than he could control Valery Carter.

She hadn't asked for return of the pink tote bag, and in the days since, she'd flirted and laughed with not a whiff of alcohol about her person. She almost convinced him she was happy.

He knew better.

The big question was why.

His text beeped. Glad for the distraction, he read the message and shot back a reply, then walked up the trail to his brother.

Devlin made the introductions. "Grayson, Hayden Winters and his fiancée, Carrie Riley. Carrie's the local librarian and Hayden is—"

"—the novelist." Grayson shook the man's hand, finding it surprisingly strong for a writer. "We've met."

"Hayden's interested in the skeleton you found."

"For one of your thrillers?"

Winters lifted a shoulder. "I never know where I'll find an idea. A skeleton seems a pretty good place to start. Who was he? Why was he killed? Did someone get away with murder?"

"All questions we can't answer."

"That's where imagination kicks in."

"And yours is vivid. I've read your thrillers. I also read your book about the people of Peach Orchard Farm. Valery gave me a copy. Fascinating."

"Thank you."

"Historical fiction is a real departure from your thrillers."

"That's why he used his father's name," Carrie said. "That, and to honor his dad. He had a great dad."

The pair exchanged knowing glances, and Grayson figured there was more to that story. "Reading your book gave me ideas for the restaurant. Your descriptions were astute and accurate."

"Intentionally so. I wanted to do Josie and Thad and the Portland family justice since they owned the mill and the house. Facts we learned from the letters Julia found and from old documents, census, church and courthouse records." Hayden took Carrie's small hand in his. "And my fiancée's meticulous librarian skills."

She beamed up at him, her heart in her dark brown eyes. Love. Such a beautiful thing with the right person.

"I'm especially interested in Josie's sister, Patience. Did you learn anything about her in your research?"

"She wasn't my focus, so, no. Only the few things you read in the book. Why?"

"She left behind a number of piano compositions."

"Which," Devlin interjected, "my brother is endeavoring to play and decode."

A frown appeared between Hayden's green eyes. "Decode?"

"A hunch I have that the notes are saying something in code. Like a cryptogram. Valery thinks Patience had a forbidden lover and sent secret messages to him through her love songs."

"Completely possible, given the times," Hayden said. "Society wasn't forgiving if a woman chose the wrong sort of fellow. But Patience also lived during the Civil War. Lots of espionage going on there, though someone like Patience, given what we know about her, is an unlikely spy."

"A spy? I hadn't considered that angle. Maybe you could give me some pointers on the best means of researching."

Devlin groaned. "Grayson, what difference does it make? It's old sheet music that has nothing to do with the restaurant." To Hayden and Carrie, he said, "My brother's like a dog with a bone when his curiosity is roused."

"Same here," Hayden said with a slight smile. "Give me a call anytime. I'll share what I have."

"Or stop by the library. I'm there most of the time." Carrie's smile was bright as the sun. "Except when I'm out with my sisters shopping for the wedding."

"When's the big day?" The grin Devlin shot toward Grayson was speculative enough to make him roll his eyes.

"Not soon enough," Hayden said.

Carrie laughed and held out her left hand. A diamond sparkled in a circle of blue sapphires. "June 17, but we're tempted to elope now and forget all the fuss."

"I'm all for it." Hayden hooked an elbow around her neck and gave a playful tug. "But your parents would never forgive me."

"Plus, we promised Brody he could be a groomsman." To Grayson she said, "Brody is a young boy we know. He and Hayden have a...connection, I guess you'd say."

"Big wedding, then?"

"It gets bigger every day. If my sister has anything to do with it, she'll invite the whole town."

Devlin scratched at the side of his neck. "All this talk of weddings is making me itch."

Hayden grinned. "Just wait. Your time will come. The right woman will come along, steal your heart right out of your chest, and you'll happily agree to a wear a monkey suit or anything else she wants."

Devlin looked anything but convinced. "I wish you all the best with that, Hayden, my man, but I gotta get back to work before I suffer an asthma attack."

Grayson laughed with the others, but as his carefree brother strode away, he wondered if wearing a monkey suit for a beautiful woman was anywhere in his future.

Valery followed the music down the hall, peach tea glasses in each hand.

She'd heard the melody before, Patience's song, but this time the sound wasn't in her head. She and Julia had given Grayson carte blanche to use the piano anytime he wanted to. Like her, the music seemed to draw him in. Compel him. And he spent every free moment, as scarce as they were, trying to unravel what he saw as a mystery. She was beginning to wonder if they were both wrong, but after last Sunday afternoon, she couldn't stay away if she wanted to. Her desire to be in the family parlor had nothing to do with music or cryptograms.

That was her big problem. If a man interested her, she pursued and got a little wild. Grayson interested her more than anyone ever had. Even when they were awkward teens, she'd found his intellect and dignified reserve mesmerizing. Now, he seemed to return the interest.

Determined, though, to keep herself under control, Valery stepped inside the Victorian room as the handsome piano man paused to make notations above the copied music.

"I brought peach tea." She lofted both glasses.

He glanced up, smiled, and her stomach fluttered. He dazzled with that crinkled corner smile, though she suspected he had no idea how attractive he was.

"Sounds refreshing. Thanks." He took a grateful sip, *ahh*ed appropriately and returned the glass.

She sipped, too, enjoyed the cool, fruity sweetness before setting the two glasses on a side table. "What are you doing?"

"Exchanging notes for letters." He tapped the sheet. "An idea came to me."

"Still trying to figure out if Patience hid messages in her music?"

Grayson nodded. "I'm positive she did, and since each note is named by a letter of the alphabet from A to G, I'm trying to determine if the notes spell out words."

"What about the rest of the letters?" She moved to stand next to him, peering at the notations. "Wouldn't it be hard to write a message without the entire alphabet?"

"That's my problem. I don't know." He leaned back and pinched his bottom lip.

"Does using A to G spell anything?"

He blew out a sigh. "Not yet."

"Maybe we're wrong." She slid onto the bench next to him, glad for an excuse to sit close to this man who had her wishing for the impossible. "Maybe it's only pretty music with no secrets."

"No. There's definitely something here. Call me crazy, but I *feel* it."

He was the least crazy person she knew. Logical, sensible. A regular Mr. Spock except for the emotion in his fingers... and his lips.

She glanced at his mouth and then back to the music. *Keep it under control, Valery.*

"So do I," she said. "Patience's music is...magical, touching."

"Sometimes sad and melancholy. Sometimes happy and innocent." He trilled a few bars, and the music lilted through the room as fresh and sweet as the scent of peaches.

"Pain and relief." She understood more than she could reveal.

"I wonder what pain she needed relief from?"

"Maybe the music will tell us."

"And maybe we'll never know."

"Doubter." She tapped the back of his long, lean, magical hand with the tips of her fingers. "If there's a code, that brain of yours will discover it."

"Your confidence inspires me."

She laughed. "Inspire me with the music. Maybe I'll hear something you've missed." As if that would happen.

He played, and as always, she *was* inspired, though she couldn't pinpoint the reasons.

Valery began to hum the melody he'd played over and over in his search for answers.

She rose from the bench to move around the family room, swaying softly as she hummed. Music and movement went together. She couldn't hear music and remain still.

There lay release and relief. Perhaps Patience had secret heartaches, painful truths she dared not share, and music was her method of coping.

The way dancing had once been Valery's.

But she'd given it up, put it away, ostracized the cause of her greatest regret.

The music stopped.

She twirled toward Grayson. "Play. Please. Don't stop."

If he thought her request odd, she didn't care.

The music commenced, a whispering brook rising to rapids, tumbling through the room, through her.

Valery went to the window and looked out toward the cemetery and the baby graves. She closed her eyes, blocking them out, but the soaring, aching music brought the pain to the surface. A boil to be excised.

No. Not a boil. A beautiful rose nipped too soon by the frost of a selfish heart.

Valery's shoulders and arms began to feel the melody, and she allowed them movement.

Behind her eyelids the vision rose up, a genie in a bottle.

The one she kept tightly capped. The beautiful rose she'd thrown away. The tiny pink bud of humanity. Her baby. Her child. Her daughter.

Music swelled in her ears and through her body. Her chest filled with such heartache she could hardly breathe. Still, she swayed and moved and pictured herself dancing for her baby girl, dancing away the past and the pain and the demons that chased her. Dancing away the need to be numb.

She didn't want to be numb anymore. Not with Grayson. She wanted to feel the emotions rolling inside her, yearning toward a man who was too perfect, too controlled and far too smart for such a woman as her.

The longing to dance again, to become immersed in the art, to feel free and joyous and worthy of love became a soul-deep throb.

Grayson glanced up from the piano and saw Valery standing next to the window, swaying as if in a beautiful dream.

His fingers faltered.

Every time he played, he saw how the music affected her. Eyes closed, full red lips parted, her lithe, graceful body swayed, practically begging to break loose and really dance.

He couldn't understand why she denied herself something she clearly loved. But the subject of dance, he'd discovered, was taboo. Each time he brought it up, she scurried away.

Today he didn't want her to be anywhere but here with him.

Devlin was right. He was getting in over his head.

CHAPTER 20

There is a sacredness in tears. They are not
the mark of weakness but of power. They speak
more eloquently than ten thousand tongues.

WASHINGTON IRVING

1875. Colorado

Colorado was as wild a place as Benjamin had ever seen, and
the trip from Connecticut to Denver even wilder. Though
the railroad promised a connection from east to west, railroad
employees had gone on strike, and violence erupted all along
the rail lines. Even the Pacific rail from Kansas to Denver had
been hit by vandals.

Never one to seek trouble, especially when it was none of
his making, he'd ridden boats, farm wagons, stagecoaches and
even hitched a ride with a family in a covered wagon all the
way into the sunflowered fields of Kansas.

To pay his way, he'd chopped wood, picked beans and
helped a merchant unload a stalled freight car, driving wagons
many miles with the needed supplies. He'd seen teepees and
Indians, sod houses and ramshackle towns perched here and
there across the wide prairies of Kansas and into Colorado.

The journey was an adventure he'd only read about in
books, but like Marco Polo, he was now seeing a different,
rougher, heartier side of humanity. Mama would be worried
sick if she knew, so he wrote letters filled with descriptions

of the beautiful countryside and friendly towns and his confidence that he would find Tandy.

With a sigh, he wondered if his confidence was sorely misplaced. Two days in the bustling town of Denver and he'd learned nothing other than the many ways a man could be parted from his money.

Lively music penetrated the walls of open saloons and gambling houses, and laughing men went inside and came out drunk or fighting mad.

Because his pockets were close to empty, Ben spent nights on the ground, his belongings beneath his head to protect them from theft, the luxury of a hotel room in Hartford but a pleasant memory. The chilly Colorado nights had caught him by surprise, and he'd awakened stiff and cold on that first morning.

Last night, he'd joined himself to a campfire surrounded by tents of men working as miners or cowboys. Sleeping by the campfire had kept him warm enough, and at daybreak he'd shared hardtack and coffee with a buck-toothed gent from Idaho. The hardtack wasn't Lizzy's hot biscuits, but the dried bread had filled his belly, and he'd been grateful for the friendly company.

They'd parted ways, the buck-toothed Emil to the Diamond Lily mine and him to wander the busy streets of the newest state in the union.

The morning sun thankfully warm on his back, he soaked in the sights, as magnificent in their difference as Hartford was from Honey Ridge, and stopped every man along the way to inquire of Robert Wellston.

He knew better than to ask for Tandy. Besides not knowing if Tandy had taken a last name, he figured most white people paid little mind to the freedmen among them. As to him, he stopped every dark face that would speak to him, though none seemed inclined to share information. Fear, he supposed, though he assured them that Tandy was in no trouble.

At noon, he stepped out of a mercantile, once again disappointed to discover nothing but a cordial shopkeeper. He paused beneath the overcast sky to decide his next move while watching a streetcar rumble past. The conveyance was a marvel, an invention such as he'd never witnessed.

While he gawked, a fancy carriage pulled up a few feet from where he stood. A lady in fine dress toting a lace-trimmed parasol stepped down and gave him a once-over. Then she smiled. "New in town, stranger?"

"Yes, ma'am. I'm looking for a friend."

She laughed a low, throaty sound. "You come down to Mattie Silks's place, and you can find lots of friends. I got the prettiest girls in the territory waiting to meet a handsome young fella like you."

Her boldness shocked him as he realized what she meant. Heat rushed up his neck to his beardless cheeks. "The man I seek is Robert Wellston. Perhaps you've heard of him?"

The woman looked him up and down again, this time as if assessing what manner of man he might be. "And if I have?"

"I'd be obliged to know where I could find him."

She pondered while he fidgeted, aware they drew stares and whispers from passersby. Finally, she tilted her head to one side and said, "What's your name?"

"Benjamin Portland. From Tennessee," he added when she continued to take his measure.

"Tennessee? You're a long way from home." She twirled her parasol, dipping it to shade her rouged and powdered face. "And you're a friend, you say, of Robert Wellston?"

"Yes, ma'am, though not exactly. He bought a slave from my father in 1864, and I aim to find him. Tandy's his name."

"This Tandy. Did he steal something?"

"What? Steal?" Ben frowned. "No, no. Nothing like that. I...owe him something."

She hiked an eyebrow in disbelief at the claim. "Begging your pardon, Mister Benjamin Portland of Tennessee, I must be going. Dressmakers don't like to be kept waiting."

With a swish of full, lacy skirts, she turned her back on him and entered a nearby building, leaving him annoyed and bewildered.

That night he wandered back to the smatter of tents along the edge of the city, weary and disappointed at his lack of progress but relieved to discover Emil and his tent had not pulled up stakes.

"Mind if I join you?" Ben asked, holding up a loaf of bread he'd purchased on the streets.

Stirring a pot over a campfire, Emil, his face as dirty as the streets of Denver, lifted tired eyes to Ben. "You're welcome, along with your bread."

Ben tossed his satchel to the ground. "Smells good. What is it?"

"Rabbit. Caught him in a trap out by the claim. I traded half of him for a handful of onions and potatoes to make us a hearty stew."

Ben's belly danced with anticipation. "Should be enough for breakfast too, then."

"Beats hardtack and beans."

"That's the truth."

Both men laughed and settled in. Ben went for more firewood while Emil stirred the pot. Then Emil headed for the creek for water and a wash-up.

When the stew was cooked, the two men sat on the ground with tin bowls full of fragrant rabbit.

"Any luck finding that Wellston feller?" Emil asked as he dripped stew down his whiskered chin.

"No. I'm beginning to wonder if he came here after all. Maybe he intended to when he left Hartford but found a better place and stopped along the way."

"That would be a right shame, after you've come so far. What are you gonna do? Go back to Tennessee?"

Ben swirled a pebble-sized potato around in the tin. What else could he do? The West was vast. "Tandy could be anywhere."

"True enough. A man not afraid of work can make a fortune out here. And if he's like me, with rambling feet," Emil wiggled his sock feet close to the fire and laughed, "he'll go wherever it takes to strike it rich."

He hadn't seen Tandy in so long, Ben had no way of knowing what kind of man he'd grown to be. Maybe he worked the farms in Nebraska or Kansas. Maybe he'd headed to the gold fields of California or the cowboy country in Texas.

Over two months on the road, and he was no closer to finding Robert Wellston and Tandy than he'd been in Honey Ridge.

Above the quiet sounds of a half dozen campfires, someone began to play a fiddle in high, sweet notes that drifted over the hill and made a man feel lonely.

"You're welcome to camp with me and move when I do." Emil dipped a bread chunk into his stew and held it up, dripping. "I heard tell Leadville's the place to be. We could partner up, prospect, and get rich together."

"That's a generous offer, Emil, seeing as how I don't know a thing about mining."

Emil shoved the bread into his mouth and talked while he chewed. Mama and the aunts would have had his hide in a handbasket. "You can work, can't you? Bend your back and ply a shovel and a pick?"

"Sure. Been doing that all my life." Ben's spoon clicked against the tin bowl. "You ever think of going back to Idaho?"

"Nothing for me there. The bank took the farm in '73. That's when my brother and me headed west to try our luck." Emil swallowed, stared into the dancing campfire. "Pete's luck ran out last winter."

Before Ben could offer condolences, a horseman appeared on the ridge and began to pick his way toward the makeshift tent village.

Emil jacked an eyebrow toward his rifle, lying only inches away from his hand. He set aside his bowl and reached for the weapon. "Fine buckskin he's riding."

"Wonder what he wants."

They had their answer in moments when the man in a fringed jacket called out, "Benjamin Portland?"

Easing his rifle from his satchel, Ben rose to a stand, shoulder muscles tense and ready, though he kept the rifle casually at his side. The West was wild. A man couldn't be too careful. "Yes, sir?"

Fringed sleeves waved like willow leaves as the tall stranger stepped from the horse. "I hear you're looking for Robert Wellston."

Ben's shoulders eased as hope nearly gone resurfaced. "I am. Do you know him?"

"You got any coffee in that pot?"

Emil, still on alert, tossed out the remains of his own cup and refilled it for the stranger.

"What's your business with Wellston?"

"He knows, or knew, a friend of mine. I want to find him."

"Why?"

Ben didn't know this cowboy but strongly suspected the stranger knew something or he wouldn't be here. This was the closest he'd come to learning anything. "My father sold him before emancipation. I want to right that wrong."

"He'd be a free man now. Why would it matter?"

"Because I'm a man of my word. The day he left, I told Tandy I'd find him and I aim to do exactly that."

The newcomer rubbed his chin. "Well, sonny, I got some bad news for you. Wellston died a couple of years ago."

"Died?" The hope withered in his chest, squeezing his lungs so hard Ben thought he might choke to death.

"Consumption, they tell me."

"A shame." A rotten, sorry shame.

Despairing, Ben rubbed a hand down his face. Now what? Miles and miles only to discover a dead end?

"Plenty come here for the sanitarium and dry air," the cowboy said. "Most never go home."

"That the case with Wellston?"

"Seems so." The cowboy sipped at the coffee.

"Can you tell me anything about him? What business he was in or if he had a young black man with him?"

The cowboy gave him a long, cool look. "Let me put it this way, partner. There's a Wellston Hotel downtown on Blake Street. You can't miss it."

Ben's heart thundered with the news. Was this Robert Wellston's hotel? And if it was, even with Wellston gone, someone at the hotel could have information about Tandy. "Do you know the place? Have you been there?"

"Too fancy for my pockets, but I've passed it a time or two." Before Ben could pepper him with more questions, the cowboy handed the tin cup back to Emil and mounted his horse. "Good luck to you."

"Much obliged," Ben said.

The man tipped his hat and thundered away, the horse's

hooves pounding the earth while Ben's heart banged against his ribs.

He'd sleep little tonight. Already his brain whirled with endless questions and the giant, galloping feet of hope.

Wellston Hotel. How had he missed seeing it? Why hadn't someone mentioned the place before? Would anyone remember Tandy?

Above the gathering night, the fiddle continued to cry as if mourning the dying day. And Benjamin would lie down on the hard ground, the stars vast and bright above the Rocky Mountains, and pray that tomorrow would bring an end to his nine-year period of mourning.

CHAPTER 21

Present Day. Peach Orchard Inn

"Have you seen my brother?"

Valery stood on a stepladder chasing dust bunnies from the foyer chandelier. She paused, rag in hand, to observe the younger Blake brother. He waited below her, a casual devil-may-care hottie who no doubt understood his masculine charms.

Usually a guy like Devlin sent her hormones into overdrive. But all she saw was Grayson's grinning, puppy-friendly brother. A likable guy, but not Grayson.

"He disappeared at daylight like always." She backed down the ladder and hung the rag over a rung.

"Did he say where he was going?"

"My guess is the mill, but with Grayson, he could also be advising the UN and consulting with NASA while resetting his alarm, talking on his cell and solving the problem of world hunger. All with one hand tied behind his back and half-asleep."

"Sarcasm. I like it." Devlin gave her a fist bump. "What's going on with you and my big, ugly brother?"

Her pulse did a jitterbug. "Nothing like getting straight to the point."

He shrugged, face alight with mischief. "Come on. Give me a tidbit to torture him with. My brother never relaxes, never slows down. But lately, he's spending a lot of time hanging out with a certain innkeeper."

"We're on a mission."

"What kind of mission?"

"You'll have to ask him." She flicked an eyebrow upward. "He's not dating anyone back in Nashville, is he?"

"Not at the moment. Girls get tired of competing with the business."

"Does he always choose the business?"

"So far, but I figure when he meets *the one*—" he jabbed a finger with each word "—he'll prefer her company to a pile of schedules and spreadsheets. Which brings us back to you."

"Your brother and I are having fun together. He needs the R and R, and I like him." Short-term fun. That was all it could be, though her heart ached to think so. She was tumbling down a cliff with a rocky bottom, falling in love with a man who didn't make mistakes. And Lord knew, *she* was a mistake.

Grayson would despise the secret Valery.

"From where I'm standing, it looks like more than fun and games." He shoved a hand in each back pocket and rocked back on his heels, contemplating. "Although, fun and games can be pretty awesome with the right person."

Valery tossed her head and tried for a flip response but came up short. The kind of fun she'd been known to have was killing her. Grayson was different.

"You'll have to ask your brother about that, too."

"I'm asking you." Devlin's expression had darkened from cheerful to serious.

"Nosy, aren't you?"

"Comes with being a sibling. Aren't you and Julia the same?"

Not in everything.

Throat tightening and pressure building in her chest, Valery said, "Usually."

"Sibs look after sibs. He has my back. I have his."

"Right." She got what he was saying. "Are you warning me away?"

"Nah." He chuckled. "I don't mind if you mess with his head. But don't break his heart."

As if she could.

Devlin executed a jaunty salute and disappeared out the door. Valery picked up her rag and started back up the ladder.

Her ringtone sounded. She slid the phone from her pocket. "Hello?"

"Val!" a male voice said. "Where you been, doll?"

She held the phone out to look at the caller ID. Sam Kutcher. Old flame. Sort of. "Same place as always."

"You've been making yourself scarce lately."

She closed her eyes. "The inn keeps me busy."

"Time for a break. We're throwing a big party Friday night. Everyone will be there. You coming?"

She'd been to his parties. All-nighters. Not a soul in the house sober. Lots of extracurricular.

"I don't party anymore." Hoping it was true, she hung up before she could change her mind.

Dusk gathered over the old gristmill as the last pickup truck rumbled down the lane and headed toward the main road. The crew was putting in long hours to make up for lost time.

Grayson glanced at his watch and smiled at the thought, though the smile wasn't amused.

Time lost was lost forever. No one could make it up.

He lifted a hand toward his brother as Devlin tossed a hard hat into a company truck and followed the dust trail. Unlike him, his brother had an active social life. No matter where they worked, he found friends…and usually a new lady to occupy his leisure moments.

There was only one woman on Grayson's schedule. He didn't have to go far to find her.

A single creek frog began an incessant clicking like drumsticks on a woodblock.

He walked around the mill making sure all was secure. As his boots skidded down the rocky incline to the base of the waterwheel, he spotted Lem Tolly taking his leisure on the outcropped rock. The fishing pole, the bright red bobber and a worm type rig rested across his lap.

Grayson hitched his chin in acknowledgment. "Catching anything?"

"Nope." The old man's voice carried up the hill. "Got a smoke?"

Hiding a smile, Grayson shook his head and closed the distance between them. "What are you doing out here this late?"

"I could ask you the same. You got that feisty gal up at the inn waiting. I got nothing else to do."

The dog sidled up for a pat from Grayson. He rubbed the soft curly ears, thinking about Valery and all the feelings he wasn't ready to put into words. "She's not waiting for me."

"You're a fool if you think that. And I am confident you are not a fool, Grayson Blake. But I see how it is. Ghosts are hard to compete with. Even your own." Lem patted his pocket as if searching for the cigarettes he rarely seemed to have. "You figure out what haunts her yet?"

"I think so. At least in part. She used to dance. Was headed toward a big dance career from what I remember." He rolled his shoulders, shrugging off the day's stress. Talking with Lem was like talking with Pappy again, and it felt good. "Now she doesn't dance, and she won't talk about it."

Lem stuck a twig between his lips and wallowed it to one corner. "Figured as much. A woman shouldn't drink alone or with bad men. Some shouldn't drink at all."

Grayson's look was sharp, his eyes narrowed. "You've noticed, too?"

"Uh-huh. A man no one is looking at sees a lot. Big hurt in that sweet woman."

Oats abandoned Grayson to collapse with an *oomph* beside her master. Soon, darkness would come, but here at sunset, bright-colored rays pierced the tree limbs and set the creek on fire.

"How do you know she's sweet?"

"I know. So do you. You see inside her, probably know her better than she knows herself, but right now the view is cloudy. It'll stay that way until she wipes her heart clean of whatever thing she let hurt her so bad."

He'd thought the same. And again Lem reminded him of Pappy and the wisdom that was as much a part of him as breathing.

"She clams up when I ask, but when I play the baby grand for her, she's...different. Happy, but sad, too." He tossed a pebble at a noisy frog. Oats hopped to a stand, alert. "She has this old sheet music. It moves her."

Lem whipped in Grayson's direction, his pale gaze suddenly intent. "From the Portlands? Civil War?"

Grayson frowned. "How did you know?"

How could he possibly know? Grayson certainly hadn't mentioned the music before.

"Old house. Old mill. Old music. Makes sense. This place

has history. Everybody knows. After that skeleton you found, who knows what might turn up? You got to keep alert."

True. But something in Lem's sudden intensity made him wonder. This wasn't the first time the old man had hinted at knowing more about the past than he let on.

"Anything unusual about that music?" Lem said, casual-like but still intense enough for Grayson to notice.

"What makes you ask?"

"Curiosity. I'm a man with deep roots and a bit of history of my own. Humor me. Someday all the secrets will open up like a rose, like your woman's heart."

"What are you getting at?"

"The truth. You'll know when you find it." Lem tapped his heart. "In here, son. In here. Now tell me about this music you and your woman found."

Feeling as if Lem was as much a riddle as the sheet music, he described the irregularities in the chords.

The wizened head bobbed. The twig wallowed from one side of his mouth to the other. "A mystery. A cipher. Uh-huh. Figures."

"What does?"

Lem ignored the question. "You crack the code yet? Figure it out?"

"No. Maybe I'm wrong about a secret message, but I can't seem to stop thinking about it."

"There's a code. Keep looking."

Grayson's alarm beeped, and he checked the time. "I need to go."

Lem put out a hand but didn't touch him. "All this rushing around won't get you nowhere. You got to relax more, son. Slow down. Never can tell what you'll discover. Patience is very important."

Valery had said the same things in her own way. Take his time. Enjoy life. Smell the roses.

In spite of the imp nagging him to hurry, to worry, to get busy and stop wasting time, Grayson stayed where he was, hearing the night move in while he listened to a strange old man who smoked imaginary cigarettes and talked in riddles.

"Do I need to call a doctor? Is my brother actually taking off work early?" Framed in the doorway of the Blueberry Room with Grayson standing in the hall, Devlin looked surprised. And his surprise annoyed Grayson.

"Don't make a big deal of it." Grayson hoped his scowl would make Devlin back off. "The crews can handle things without me. You'll be here and I'm only a phone call away."

Devlin dramatically grabbed his chest. "I'm either hallucinating or having a heart attack. Call 9-1-1."

"Stuff it, Dev."

"But two whole hours, Gray. I've never seen you do that for a woman. The only time I remember you taking off early was when you ran your finger through a table saw." Mischievous blue eyes twinkled. "Valery must be something special."

She was. "I'm driving out to the farm. You didn't want to go, and I wanted company."

Actually, he'd invited her first, though he wasn't sure why except that he wanted time with her away from the inn and the mill.

Footsteps on the stairs drew their attention to the top of the landing. Valery stopped there, hand on the railing.

Grayson's heart skittered.

In fitted black pants and a red blouse with a multicolored scarf tossed around her neck and long brown hair sweeping her shoulders in soft curves, Valery was casually gorgeous.

"I'm ready." Her glance moved from the grinning man to the scowling one. "Am I interrupting something?"

"My brother's being a pain as usual."

She swung her attention to his brother. "Did you want to go with us, Devlin?"

"No, he did not." Taking her elbow, Grayson shot Devlin a warning look before guiding Valery toward the steps. Behind him, Devlin laughed.

"You look amazing."

She flashed him a smile. "Thank you. Am I overdressed?"

"You're perfect."

"Not quite," she answered, but he heard the smile in her voice as she descended the stairs.

He followed, trailing her exotic perfume and enjoying the bounce in her step and the elegant, graceful way she moved as they exited the house and walked toward the parking lot.

Momentarily, her attention swung south toward the hidden cemetery, a reminder of the pink tote she'd left behind. She hadn't returned for it. Early this morning he'd checked and felt no shame in the action. Perhaps he shouldn't stick his nose in her business, but he cared, deeply, and if Valery had been hurt by someone, he wanted to help her heal.

She was messing with his head.

At the Grand Cherokee, he opened the passenger door and then rounded to the driver's side.

"Music?" he asked.

"Sure."

Suddenly, he felt awkward, as if he was a shy, nerdy teenager again.

Valery seemed to have no such compunction, and he thought she'd probably never been uncomfortable with a man in her life. She fiddled with the stereo until lively country music thrummed through the cabin.

"How's the restaurant coming along?" she asked above the voice of Blake Shelton.

"Why don't you come over and see for yourself?"

"Have they removed everything? I mean, all of the…body?"

"There was no body, Valery. Only bones. And, yes, they're all gone. The basement has been excavated to make sure there are no other surprises—"

She stiffened. "You didn't find anything else, did you? Any other signs of graves?"

"Artifacts, tools, buttons and such. That's it. We've shored up the foundation, and now we can start the real fun of renovation." He aimed the Jeep toward Honey Ridge.

"That's a relief. You can take down the bottle tree now, so people will stop saying the mill is haunted."

"My crews like it for some reason, so the tree stays, maybe permanently. Devlin and I thought it would add a nice Southern country flair to the restaurant."

"You could sell them in a gift shop. Really pretty ones of blue glass."

"Maybe." He doubted it. "Or you could sell them from the inn along with Hayden Winters's book and the peach gift baskets."

"That's not a bad idea. You're a smart businessman."

"So you're not mad at me anymore for repurposing instead of restoring?"

She fluttered her eyelashes with feigned innocence. "Did I say that?"

Grayson laughed. "You'll be happy to know we've found a number of things we can preserve. Windows. Lots of lumber, good solid oak. Doors. Even some old latches that will add more authenticity once our guys get them cleaned. We're also repurposing the old grindstones into steps leading to the wishing well."

While they chatted, he drove them through town and headed east until the highway turned to a country lane lined with trees, underbrush, and spring wildflowers. "I've put off coming to the farm."

He hadn't been back since Grandma's funeral two years ago.

"Why?"

"I don't know." He put on his blinker, though there was not a car in sight, and followed an overgrown driveway toward a worn and weathered farmhouse. "No, that's not true. I *do* know. Nothing's the same anymore with Grandma and Pappy gone. Uncle Chuck, Mom's brother, bought the farm, but he doesn't live in the area and he's never done anything with the property. I was afraid of what I'd find."

"Does it make you sad?"

He pulled to a stop on a patch of grass with faint hints of gravel hiding between the blades. Grandma's roses climbed wild and unkempt over a sagging, unpainted picket fence. Weeds surrounded them.

"To see it like this, yes." He opened his door and got out. So did Valery. "To remember the good times, no."

He could almost visualize Grandma in her red Keds and wide-brimmed gardening hat as she poked a trowel into the porch pots. As he'd expected the pots were empty and as weathered as the fence, the flowers long dead.

"We had some great times in that house." Flipping the gate latch, he led the way onto the porch, his footsteps hollow-sounding. "Pappy taught Devlin and me how to do man things, and Grandma spoiled us."

"Man things?" She bumped his side. "What are those?"

"Fix stuff. Fences, cars, tractors, plumbing. Clean fish. Kill chicken snakes."

"Eww. Snakes."

"Grandma was the same. If she spotted the tiniest snake,

she would freeze in place and scream, 'Jeff! Jeff!' until Pappy came running with the hoe." At the warm memory, Grayson rubbed a hand over his chest. "Grandma called him her knight in faded overalls. Good memories."

"Good memories are worth holding on to," Valery said, more solemn than the occasion called for.

He wondered then, as he did so often lately, who or what had dimmed the light inside Valery Carter. "Tell me about your memories." He was prying again, digging into what made her tick. If he'd figured out one thing about Valery Carter, her heart had been crushed and she'd yet to recover.

He suspected a man, a romance gone sour, and with a shockingly jealous vehemence decided the man was a fool.

"My grandparents lived in town like we did. They weren't as exciting as yours." Valery sat down on the top porch step, black sneakers on the second one and elbows on her knees. The bright scarf draped forward.

Grayson settled next to her, saying nothing. He gazed out over the fields once thick with corn, nostalgic for a time past.

Time never slowed down, even for the good souls like his grandparents.

"Those lilacs need pruning." Valery pointed to an overgrowth of dead canes and fresh green sprouts at the corner of the house. "But they still smell amazing."

Grayson trotted to the bush, snapped off a cluster and brought them back to her. "For the lady."

She buried her nose in the tiny purple flowers and watched him with a pleased expression. "I should plant some of these at the inn. They smell like heaven."

"Want me to dig them up?"

"And incur the wrath of your uncle?"

"He wouldn't even notice."

Valery tucked the little bouquet behind one ear. "Have you considered buying the property?"

"Tried. Uncle Chuck won't sell. At least not yet. I keep asking."

"That's too bad. I remember when your grandparents lived here. Mama used to buy eggs from Miss Evelyn, and your granddad plowed our garden every spring when Mama got the itch to raise something."

"Right out there." Grayson pointed. "Grandma's chicken house is behind the garage. Want to see it?"

He rose and offered a hand up. Her soft palm met his calloused one, and they roamed the grounds, peeked in the dusty windows, saw the abandoned hen nests that pinched his heart. They explored the barn where a few bales of hay rotted against one wall, and the cow stall still smelled of milk. Pappy's galvanized milk bucket hung on a post, spiderwebs laced across the top.

"Did you ever milk the cow?" Valery looked like a bright butterfly in the shaft of sunlight streaming in from overhead.

The barn roof needed repair.

He huffed a nostalgic sound and smoothed his fingers over the kickers Pappy kept hanging in the stall to keep Brownie from knocking over the bucket. "I tried. So did Devlin. Milking is harder than it looks. After a few minutes, Brownie got tired of our ineffective efforts and Pappy would take over." Amused, he shook his head. "He would be finished in five minutes flat."

"Poor Brownie."

"She was a patient lady." Grayson held out a hand. "Ready?"

"Where else?"

"Pappy's workshop." He'd saved the converted garage for last. As he expected, when they entered the garage, the presence of his grandfather was as strong as if he'd only gone up to the house for supper and would be back any minute, rubbing his round belly and proclaiming Grandma the world's finest cook.

Grayson paused inside, breathing in the old grease and diesel scent—Pappy smells that slung him back in time.

Peace crept in like warmth on a spring morning.

Patience is important, Lem Tolly had said. Hadn't Pappy taught him the same virtue right here in this building when he'd been too eager to finish a project?

"This is where you worked on the classic car with your granddad, isn't it?" Valery's beautiful face tilted up to him, her expression soft and caring.

"A piece of me lives here." He saw by her eyes that she understood. If he hadn't been falling in love with her before, he was falling now.

Nodding, chest full of her and his memories, he moved to the warped and greasy work bench where he'd learned to take an engine apart and put it back together. A few of Pappy's tools still hung on wall pegs, and a stack of empty buckets laced with dirty cobwebs jammed one corner. Pappy had grown up poor and saved everything. Even bits of string and wire.

"You never know when you'll need it," he'd say, followed by, "When times get hard, we'll be prepared."

Nothing had prepared them for the hard time of Grayson's sickness.

"This is the place I ran to when I found out I might be dying."

"Oh, Grayson." Valery ran a comforting hand up his shoulder. "How awful. You were so young."

"Pappy must have been as scared as I was, but he never let on. He hugged me, let me cry for a while, and then he took me out in his farm truck and let me drive all over the pasture."

He'd asked his granddad a dozen times to teach him to

drive, but the answer had always been no. He was too young. That day age hadn't mattered. Pappy let him drive.

At the sweet memory, Grayson laughed softly.

More than a year would pass before he'd been well enough to come here again. Pappy had let him drive that day, too.

"I wonder why I never heard about your illness."

"Why would you?"

"Honey Ridge talks. Mama always seems to know people's business before it happens."

"I lived in Nashville." He tapped her nose. "And you were a little kid."

"Oh, yes, you're so much older than me."

"Twelve and thirteen are eons apart."

"You mean you didn't notice me when I was twelve and had my braces?"

Maybe not, but he was noticing now. "I had a crush on you when I was fifteen."

"You did?"

"I was too awkward to say anything."

"I wish you had. Maybe then—" She bit her bottom lip and looked away.

"Maybe what?"

"Nothing. Silly teenage stuff." She waved a hand in the air. "I'm getting hungry. Are you ready to head back to town and feed me?"

"Ready when you are." As he led the way to the Jeep, Valery was especially quiet, and he couldn't help wondering why.

Much later, after a leisurely meal at Miss Molly's Café and pleasant conversation with Valery along with frequent interruptions from townspeople asking how the mill project was coming along and if he'd found any more skeletons, Grayson reluctantly started the return drive to Peach Orchard Inn.

Valery had helped him reminisce in a positive manner, and together they'd come up with several more ideas about the mysterious music. He wasn't ready to leave her company, and he suspected she felt the same.

"Do you want to stop by the mill and see our progress?"

The glow of the dash lights set her face in shadows. "It's late."

His mouth curved. "Scared of the bottle ghosts?"

She tossed her head, hair dancing, amused. "I have a knight in a shiny Jeep. Why would I be scared?"

"I don't think I've ever been called that before. I think I like it." He cut a glance toward her. "The mill is beautiful in moonlight."

"Why, Mr. Blake, are you romancing me?"

His tone turned serious. "And if I am? Would you mind?"

She was silent long enough for him to take his attention from the road again and look at her solemn, beautiful profile.

Just as he decided he'd stepped way out of line, she whispered, "Not at all."

CHAPTER 22

Present Day. The Old Gristmill

Valery let herself out of the Jeep, but Grayson met her halfway to slip his hand into hers. Their feet crunched on the new gravel as she marveled at the work his crews had already accomplished.

"You rebuilt the road."

"And added a parking lot." He sounded proud, and she was proud for him. Already the area looked more alive, more cared for than she'd ever seen. "Devlin has a terrific plan for the area below the waterwheel and around the creek. Walking paths, benches, pretty flowers, a wishing well. Maybe even weddings."

She leaned her head against his shoulder. "Can we walk around and look?"

A romantic walk. What harm was there in that?

"Whatever you want."

Oh, how she wished that were true. She wanted so much. So much she couldn't have. She wanted him. She wanted his love and his respect.

How did she ask him to respect her when she hadn't respected herself in sixteen years? But he didn't know those things, and she certainly wouldn't tell him. For now he thought she was someone special, and she wanted to keep him in the dark as long as he was in Honey Ridge.

Walking close, they circled the building, moving slowly, stopping here and there as Grayson pointed out changes or prospective renovations.

A security light illuminated the front of the mill, fading out until the darkness swallowed the glow and left only a half moon to light the creek and waterfalls in silvery shadows.

"It's not spooky at all," she said. "Not like when I was a kid."

"I thought you liked the mill."

"I do. Always have. But you know how kids are. We'd come here on purpose to scare each other. After reading Hayden's book about Josie and Thad, I can imagine what the mill and the inn were like back in the 1800s. Thriving industry. Full of people. Modern for its day."

"They fell in love here. Josie and Thad." He nodded toward the creek. "According to Hayden's book."

"I like to believe it's true."

"Even if it isn't, it makes a great story that will attract customers to the restaurant."

"Always the businessman." She bopped his arm. "Don't you dare look at your watch."

Grayson made a move as if to do exactly that. "Are you going to wrestle me down and steal it again?"

The memory of that afternoon in the family room flashed between them. His gaze lingered on hers. He was remembering, too.

He hadn't kissed her since then. He'd backed away, cautious, and though she didn't like the distance, she'd thought it was for the best.

The night pulsed, as loud and familiar as any Tennessee

night with frogs and katydids and night birds rustling in the trees. A frog plopped into the water, and in the moonlight silver circles moved like radar signals across the shallow creek.

Grayson circled an arm around her waist and, when she thought he might finally kiss her again, said instead, "I'm proud of you."

She hadn't expected that. Proud? Was the man deluded? "Why?"

"The pink tote bag."

She stiffened, unaccustomed to such straight talk, but he drew her close, his embrace light and easy as he gazed down at her with affection.

"You didn't go back for it."

Yes, she had. She'd gone to the cemetery twice since then to plant flowers and, if she was honest, to feel numb. But for reasons she couldn't understand she'd changed her mind and left the tote and its contents right where he'd put them.

"I'm trying to break my bad habits."

"I'd like to help. If you'll let me." He stroked a knuckle across her cheek with exquisite tenderness. She shivered. "You're a special woman, Valery. To me."

Her throat clogged with emotion. She wanted desperately to be as special as he seemed to think. Grayson cared about her. She could tell. Really cared. He was not a party boy who would disappear tomorrow. He was solid, stable, scary as all get out.

"I'm not that special, Grayson. I've made too many mistakes. Shattered too many dreams."

"You're talking about the dance career, aren't you?"

She nodded, needing to tell him, knowing she should. "The dance career I didn't have."

"You were on your way. What happened?"

You do not want to know the answer to that question.

"I loved to dance. Nothing made me happier and more fulfilled than when I was dancing. Everyone, even my teachers and the agent in Nashville, said I had a future in the profession."

"You did the music videos in Nashville. I found a couple on YouTube."

"I've never watched them."

"No? You should. You were incredible. As light and graceful as a butterfly. I couldn't take my eyes off you."

She shook her head. "Why bother? That part of my life is over. Digging up the past is never a good idea."

"If that's true, I'm in the wrong business."

"What you do is different."

"Is it?"

Before she could respond, he began to hum and moved her across the grass in a slow waltz. Her traitorous body knew the way too well and ignored her brain's command to stop.

She shouldn't dance with him. She couldn't. She didn't deserve that kind of pleasure. Yet Grayson continued to sway and carry her along.

He called her special, and here in his strong, decent arms she almost believed him. With him, she felt safe and secure, free of the weight on her soul. With Grayson she felt worthwhile.

He waltzed smoothly, easily, one hand on her waist and the other holding her hand against his heart. She felt the beat against her palm, strong and steady and full of goodness.

Every cell in her body responded to the pure freedom, to him.

She longed to tell him everything, to dump her ugly past and the painful truth at his feet, but fear held her back. Fear of Grayson's reaction. Fear of Mama's.

Her mother would pitch a hissy fit if she knew Valery had even considered airing dirty laundry in public. Never mind that telling Grayson wasn't the same as taking out a full-page ad in the *Honey Ridge Herald*. Carters did not share such shameful secrets. They swept them under the rug, ignored them and, if they tried to break free in other areas, if they drank too much or partied too hard, hushed that up, too.

Valery didn't have a man problem or a drinking problem. She had heart trouble.

What of Grayson? What would he think of her? Would the affection in his touch and in his eyes frost over if he knew? Would he believe as she did that she was an awful person?

But in his arms, gliding across the cool spring grass, his heart beating against her skin, she wanted to believe he'd understand or at least forgive her even if she couldn't forgive herself.

She so desperately wanted to believe again.

"You're humming Patience's song," she whispered, and was rewarded when he tugged her ever nearer to hum softly in her ear. The vibrations shimmied up her neck, lifting the tiny hairs and sending tiny electric charges through her body.

She laced her arms around his neck and rested her head on his shoulder, listening, feeling the rhythm of the music in his movements.

And they danced.

Somewhere in the moonlight and the moment, she put aside the obstacle between his heart and hers, and let herself be happy.

She was falling in love with Grayson Blake.

The dance may have lasted an hour, or it may have lasted a minute. She didn't know, didn't care, and a smug little part of her realized he'd lost track of time, as well. She hadn't needed to steal his watch.

She was vaguely aware of traffic and a baying hound somewhere in the distance, but her time was here and now with the hum of crickets and the whisper of sleepy water sliding over the rocks.

She could stay here all night, waltzing with Grayson.

Too soon, Grayson ended their dance with a dip and a flourish, leaning her back over his arm. She laughed lightly, nearly euphoric. As he brought her back to him, he kissed her once, long and tender, and she rested there, quiet and content in his arms.

When was the last time she'd felt anything near contentment? All the men, the parties, the running hither and yon, had left her soul weary. Tonight, here on Josie and Thad's creek bank, she found rest.

"That was wonderful." She brushed his neck with her lips.

He shivered in pleasure, and his voice deepened, muted and tender. "*You* were wonderful."

She shook her head in denial, but he tilted back, lifting her chin with the tips of his fingers.

"You're fooling yourself if you think you can deny or hide your talent, Valery. You were like an angel in my arms, as light as a butterfly."

"I had a good partner."

"No. I only went along for the ride. You were magical, transported to another plane."

He was right. "That's the way I feel when I dance. Transported. Happy. Free." She hadn't said those words in years.

"There you go, then. It's your passion, and I can't imagine why you'd deny yourself. You were born to dance. It's God's gift, and you were meant to share it."

Valery knew deep in her heart that what he said was true. Hiding her passion made her unhappy, discontent and restless. She'd pursued so many other avenues and not one satisfied.

"I'm too old to start again. The window of career opportunity has long passed."

"Is that true? Or are you afraid of failing? Is that why you gave up your dream? Fear?"

Not fear. Guilt. Penance. But she couldn't tell him that.

When she didn't answer, he pressed. "What about a dance studio? You're so good with Alex. You'd be a great teacher."

The notion rose in her spirit like the phoenix from the ashes. She could teach others to love the art, to express themselves through movement and music. She could dance again.

"I wonder if I could..."

"I know you can. You're a natural."

Hope was a glowing ember in a field of dry grass. Could she? More important, should she? Was it a dream she could pursue?

The idea was so wonderful, her body felt weak with wanting it.

He'd given her much to think about. She placed her palm alongside his strong, handsome jaw, loving the feel of him, absorbing his warmth and sincerity.

"Your encouragement means a lot."

He folded his hand over hers and brought her palm to his lips. "My pleasure."

She knew he meant every word.

An owl hooted and she jumped. Grayson chuckled softly, the sound rumbling in his chest.

"No more ghosts, remember? We've eradicated the last one."

They both turned toward the mill and toward the basement neither could see from here. Mr. Bones was gone now.

Grayson looped his arms over her shoulders and rested his chin in her hair. Valery snuggled close, relieved to switch from her ghosts to the mill's.

"Do you think we'll ever know what happened to him?"

"Doubtful, but stranger things have happened."

"True. Who would have imagined you'd discover a hundred-fifty-year-old grave?"

"Exactly. Someone buried him in secret, but secrets have a way of revealing themselves eventually."

Valery closed her eyes, heard the night music and hoped that he was wrong.

CHAPTER 23

Do not tell secrets to those whose faith and silence you have not already tested.

ELIZABETH I

1875. Colorado

The Wellston Hotel was a grand place, and as Benjamin stepped inside a chandelier overhead caught the light and sent reflections of color onto the walls and registry desk. The desk itself was a semicircular expanse of mahogany bearing a handsome black walnut key rack. Nearby was a contraption such as he'd never laid eyes on. He watched in rapt fascination as the desk clerk pushed a button, sounding a bell.

In seconds, a tall, well-dressed man, the color of creamed coffee, bounded down the stairs. Ben stared up, disbelieving his eyes. He clutched his hat in his hand, mouth dry.

"Tandy?" His gaze soaked in the lost playmate, seeing with adult eyes what a nine-year-old would never have considered. Tandy was as white as he was black, and his eyes were hazel brown, not the rich coffee of his mother's. Ben had no doubt, if he'd ever had, that they were, indeed, half brothers.

Tandy paused, long fingers gripping the polished banister as if he, too, were in shock at what he saw. "Ben? Is it really you? They told me you were in Denver, looking for me, but I couldn't believe—"

Ben moved forward, jubilation building in his chest. "I thought I'd never find you."

Tandy took the remaining steps two at a time, and the pair met at the bottom, grinning like the boys they'd been.

Ben offered a hand which was immediately clasped as they stood staring, each taking the other's measure. Ben was sure, in his travel-worn duds, that he fell short of the handsome dandy before him.

Finally, Tandy spoke. "What brings you to Denver? Gold or silver?"

"Neither. You."

Tandy cocked his head in puzzlement. "Me? You've come this far for me?"

"I said I would, didn't I?"

"I never expected—we were boys. I a slave and you the master."

They were more than that—much more—but now was not the time.

"I came to right my father's wrong." Ben reached into his pocket and withdrew the blue marble. "I got something that belongs to you."

Tandy chuckled, reached into his vest and withdrew the matching ball. "You didn't forget."

"Neither did you."

Light brown fingers rotated the small orb. "This marble means more to me than a game we played."

A lump in his throat, Ben understood. The marble represented family and home, friendship and promises, and the decency of a Yankee captain who only saw two little boys in need, not one black and one white, but one without a father and one with a father who knew nothing of love.

"You have news of my mother?" Tandy pressed on, as eager for news from home as Ben was to tell it.

"She's well." Ben grinned. "Married now."

When Ben told of Abram, the hardworking mill employee who'd married Lizzy, Tandy's face tightened. "Is he good to her?"

"Treats her like a queen."

Full lips curved. "Rightly so or she'll whack him with a skillet."

They both laughed, basking in the shared memories and bridging the years in between.

"You should see her now, Tandy. You must. She's happy and still strong, running the house alongside Mama."

Tandy's face softened. "How does your mother fare? And Miss Patience?"

"Both are well. Mama married Captain Gadsden after Papa died."

Tandy nodded. He'd known, as Ben had, that the captain was a far better man than Edgar Portland and that his heart belonged to Charlotte. "And Miss Patience?"

"Still kind and beautiful, and she teaches piano to the Honey Ridge children."

Tandy's eyes grew cautious. "She never married?"

"No. She never did. And none of us can understand why. There's a man who loves her, and I believe she cares for him, but Johnny won't speak because of his blindness."

"Johnny? The Union soldier? He remained at Peach Orchard?"

"You remember him, then?"

"Of course I do, as I remember how we'd walk around with our eyes closed, pretending to be blind, too. We wanted to be like the soldiers."

Ben shook his head. "Foolishness, though we meant no harm. We hopped around on one leg with stick crutches, and

Logan only laughed and wrapped a bandage on our arms to complete the wounded soldier look."

"Good men, both of them."

"I can't argue that. Without them, we would have lost Portland Farm and Mill after Papa died."

Tandy looked to the side, suddenly pensive, and Ben wondered. Reminiscing about the past and recalling those forced away from him must be hard to hear.

The desk contraption jangled again, and Ben turned to stare at it. "What is that thing?"

"A communication device called an annunciator," Tandy said proudly. "Each button connects to a guest room, the kitchen and dining rooms, the offices."

"Fancier than Josie standing on the back porch hollering her lungs out."

Tandy's chuckle displayed white teeth above his striped black-and-red waistcoat, his melancholy gone. "Mr. Wellston, rest his soul, wouldn't settle for anything but the best. He came here to build a fine hotel and he did."

"You still work here, even though he's passed on?"

"Work. Eat. Sleep." When Ben looked puzzled, Tandy clapped him on the back. "Come into the office. I can see we have much to talk about."

Feeling as if his feet barely touched the ground, Ben followed Tandy down a rug-covered hallway into a small office.

A young black woman entered the room with a coffee tray. "Would you care for anything else, Mr. Wellston?"

"This is all for now, Edna. We'll take lunch soon in the dining room."

"Mrs. Wellston left earlier when you were meeting with the mayor. She asked that I give you this note."

Ben watched with interest, aware that Tandy had changed in more ways than his address. His speech was educated and articulate, his well-made suit a far cry from the homespun britches and shirts of Peach Orchard Farm. And the waitress called him Mr. Wellston.

After pouring each of them a cup, the woman left the tray and exited the room.

Ben lifted the delicate cup, so different from the tin one he'd sipped at daybreak. "Mrs. Wellston?"

Tandy's smile widened until he was all teeth. "Molly. We married last year."

"Congratulations."

"You're still a single man?"

He thought of Emma Tremble and smiled. "For now." He leaned forward, eager to learn how Tandy had gone from a sold slave child to a position in an affluent hotel. "Tell me about your life. Did Wellston treat you well? I prayed for you. Mama, Patience and I."

"Patience, too?" Tandy mused softly, getting that vague distant look again before he blinked and answered Ben's query. "Wellston treated me quite well. From the beginning, when he saw I was industrious and eager to learn, he educated me, taught me how to run a hotel. He worked me hard, but the efforts were worth the result. After Mrs. Wellston passed and he became ill, he turned more and more of the hotel affairs over to me. After emancipation, he allowed me to buy into the business."

"You're part owner?"

"No. Not part. Not anymore." Tandy set the cup on the tray. "Robert had no living children. When he passed, he left his share to me."

"*You're* the Wellston of Wellston Hotel?" Amazed and delighted, Ben gazed around the well-furnished office and then up at the ceiling medallions. The hotel was elegant and beautiful, clearly a successful establishment.

"Hard to believe, but, yes. The West is wide open, and a man of color can do well here." He lifted a resigned shoulder. "Within limits."

The truth pinched inside Ben. Robert Wellston was a good man who'd done right by Tandy, treating him as a son and heir, though he'd purchased him as a slave. Edgar Portland had sold his own child away from everything and everyone he loved. Was it better if Tandy never knew that Edgar's blood ran in his veins?

To cover his consternation, Ben finished off the strong coffee and poured himself another from the pot. He'd have to ponder and pray and keep his mouth shut in the meantime.

Tandy held up a finger. "I'm hungry. Are you?"

"Getting there fast." Emil had shared his rabbit stew, but Ben had been careful to take the lesser share.

"Excuse me a moment." Tandy turned aside to push a button next to his desk.

In seconds, a young liveried boy appeared at the door. "Yes, sir, Mr. Wellston?"

"Tell Trixie to prepare two of her thickest buffalo steaks. My friend and I are hungry."

"Yes, sir."

When the door closed again, Tandy said, "You know my tale. Now let's hear yours. Nine years is a long time to wonder about you and Mama and the family."

So, while anticipating the unfamiliar taste of buffalo, Ben talked of the farm and mill and the depression, of Josie and her family, and the emancipated slaves who had stayed and those who were gone.

When he ran dry of Honey Ridge updates, Ben got to the point of his journey. "Come home, Tandy. We've missed you. Papa's gone. Slavery's gone. You're free to come and go as you please now."

"Free? In the South?" He shook his head. "The law may have changed, but I dare say hearts are not all that different, and there are some things a man can't risk."

Ben frowned. "What do you mean?"

"I run a profitable business. Denver is as accepting as any place of my kind. I would be a fool to leave here."

"Then a visit. Come back with me. Your mama mourns to see your face again."

Tandy's expression, so friendly before, closed up tighter than a widow's drapes.

"No, Ben. No." The answer was short and hard.

"But why?"

Tandy's expression went cold and wary. "I can't return to Honey Ridge. Some things a man can't risk."

"You've said that before. What do you mean?"

"I mean to stay here, Ben. Forever."

While Benjamin struggled to understand the sudden change in his friend, Tandy rose and moved around the desk to the door leading out into the hall.

With a tight smile and a flourish of one arm, he said, "I suspect our steak is near ready. And cherry pie, too. Shall we eat?"

CHAPTER 24

Present Day. Honey Ridge

Music woke Valery, and she sat up, laughing a little as she clutched the sheet to her chest, listening, weaving to the waltz. The music was in her heart. She and Grayson had danced to that tune last night.

Dance is your gift to yourself and others, he'd said. Her gift. A person shouldn't reject a gift.

He was such a wise man.

Tossing back the covers, she hopped out of bed and threw open the curtains.

"It's a glorious day."

During the night, an idea had blossomed in her mind and her heart, one that filled her with such excitement she couldn't wait to get started. Grayson's idea.

Impatiently, she rushed through the morning chores, winning an approving comment from her sister. "You're in a good mood today. Does this have anything to do with your date with our handsome real estate developer?"

"We had a nice time." Her smile, she was sure, gave her away.

"You rarely hum while you're changing linens and scrubbing toilets." Julia's eyes crinkled at the corners. "What happened to make you so smiley?"

"Nothing in particular. I like him." Maybe loved him a little.

Julia smiled. "So I gathered. He likes you, too. Even if you are an odd couple."

Some of her sunshine dimmed. She swung around, Windex in hand. "What does that mean?"

"Opposites attract, I guess. That's all." Julia tossed a pillow at her. "If you're happy, so am I."

Opposites. Yeah, she got that. He was all the good and sensible things she wasn't.

Today she was not letting that fact trouble her. He'd encouraged her, and Grayson was smart. He knew a thing or two and was not given to idle words.

So, sometime between midnight and this morning, she'd formulated a plan. She was going to do better, *be* better, starting today.

When the cleaning was over, she volunteered to do the day's grocery shopping, hopped in her little red Toyota and drove the short distance into Honey Ridge.

Spring popped up everywhere. Red tulips and yellow jonquils, purple iris and early roses colored lawns and porch pots. Honey Ridge's annual spring cleanup was just around the corner, and she was on the committee to plant flowers on Main Street, a labor of love.

Like dance. Even if she'd missed her window of opportunity to dance professionally—and she wasn't positive on that front—Grayson was right about the other. She could teach.

A thousand ideas raced through her mind. Ballroom? Ballet? Jazz? She could dance them all. Maybe classes for adults at night, for kids on Saturdays. She could start small and build an instructional studio while continuing her work at the inn.

Thrilled with the prospect, she cruised up and down the streets, eyeing each empty building.

Abby's antiques had recently closed, and a For Rent sign hung in the window. Valery slowed, contemplating. She'd been inside a number of times to shop for the inn, and if she remembered correctly the building ran lengthwise. One long, empty space.

Excited, pulse jumping, and energy filling every movement, she parked along the curb, got out and executed a happy dance up to the window.

Face pressed against the glass, she cupped her hands to block the glare and visualized the space as a dance studio. The building inside wasn't big, but it would do at first. With mirrors and bars along one wall and perhaps new flooring, the space was workable. Close to perfect.

She knew how to set up a business. She and Julia had waded through the paperwork for Peach Orchard Inn. They still did on a regular basis. If she hit a snag, Grayson would help. She was confident. He wanted her to dance again. He believed in her, believed she deserved to follow her dreams, to share her gift.

A gift. He'd called her dance talent a gift.

He had no way of knowing how much his words meant, or how they inspired her.

Her heart nearly beat out of her chest. She could do it. No one had taught dance in Honey Ridge since Mrs. Findley retired.

"Valery? Honey, what are you doing?"

Valery froze. She knew that voice.

Slowly, stomach sinking, she turned to face her perfectly groomed, always correct mother. Dresden-blue sweater, cream slacks and the pearls Daddy had given her when Julia was born, Connie Carter carried a brown clutch that matched her shoes—no white before Easter, of course, and Easter came late this year.

"Hi, Mama." Valery's excitement seeped away, like life's blood flowing out on the ground. The reasons she'd stopped dancing came rushing back in a tidal wave of regret.

Last night in Grayson's arms, she'd believed anything was possible. Harsh reality knew better.

She was still the same foolish woman today as she'd been for sixteen years.

She couldn't open a dance studio any more than she could dance on Broadway. Nothing had changed. Not one single thing.

Mama had made sure of that.

"Abby shut down the antique store," Mama said. "She's closed for good."

Valery's mouth tightened. She wasn't a child. "I know, Mama."

"Then why are you peeking in the windows?"

The morning sun, so bright and cheerful moments before, disappeared behind a cloud. She glanced up. Rain was coming.

"No reason, Mama," she said with a resigned sigh. "No reason at all."

The structural engineer was driving him crazy.

Grayson removed his reading glasses and pinched the bridge of his nose, neck and shoulders aching with familiar tension. He could use another of Valery's massages, though this time he wouldn't fall asleep. Maybe.

Unable to settle after he'd arrived home from their date, he'd crunched numbers half the night. Then this morning, the engineer had ordered another delay in construction while she examined the waterwheel more closely for defects. Never mind that she'd inspected everything top to bottom during the first delay. She was concerned that the additional excavation required by law enforcement had shifted something.

Trina Grimes was a stickler for safety. That was why he'd hired her, and his head knew she was right to take one more look. He certainly didn't want his new restaurant to collapse with a building full of customers inside.

On the other hand, every delay meant lost money and time. He'd spent hours on the phone—again—with contractors who now threatened to move on to other builders.

Some days he wondered if he should scrap the project, take his losses and move on.

Devlin, as usual, blew off the problem and told him to take a day off.

The scary thing was he'd actually considered doing exactly that. An entire day.

Tossing his glasses on the desk, he tilted back in his chair and thought about the reason he'd considered time off. Valery.

Yesterday and last night had been special. At least to him, and he believed to her, as well.

She'd appreciated the farm and his stories of Grandma and Pappy and had warmed his heart with her memories of them. But the moonlit dance had been the kicker. Holding her, feeling her passion for dance, for life, and maybe for him stirred him deeply. Beyond the smiles and flirtations, Valery was a complicated woman, a puzzle.

Nothing he enjoyed more than a puzzle.

Take the piano music. After a few hours on the internet studying musical cryptography he was more certain than ever that Patience had written a secret message into certain pieces of her music.

He had an idea but no time to pursue it.

The trouble with a big brain was that it never stopped churning even when he wanted it to.

He grabbed his cell phone, scrolled to contacts and pushed the smiling photo Valery had taken of herself when he'd asked her to enter her number. He smiled back at her image.

The phone rang and rang. As he was ready to give up, she answered. "Hi."

"You sound out of breath."

"I'm working in the cemetery."

He couldn't help himself. Heart sinking lower than a snake, his mind went straight to the pink tote. "Need company?"

There was a long pause. "You're busy."

She sounded okay, and he hated that he was suspicious. How did he build a relationship with a woman he couldn't trust?

There was the crux of the matter. He wanted to build something with Valery. Something strong and right.

"Never too busy for you." He couldn't believe he'd said that, but he was telling the truth—and he wanted to be sure she was all right. "The structural engineer is doing yet another inspection today, and I could use a break from the computer."

"Spreadsheet fever getting you down?"

He chuckled. "It is today. I'm juggling schedules again and realigning the budget."

"Sounds exhilarating. Come on out and get a tan with me. Bring your work gloves."

"On my way."

With a jauntiness in his step, he exited the Mulberry Room and bounded down the scarlet staircase.

Earlier Devlin had driven back to the main office in Nashville for the day. The other guests were out and about as well, but from the smell coming from the kitchen, most of them would wander back before long.

Julia was in the kitchen practicing the culinary arts she exercised so well. She managed to look cool and refined even with an apron around her waist and a tea towel over one shoulder. She was a beautiful woman but as different from her sister as he was from Devlin. Julia was the perfect Southern hostess of quiet elegance and sophistication, the kind who would hide any problems from her guests and keep things running smoothly. Valery was a good hostess, but her heart was not in innkeeping or hospitality. She was meant to fly.

He stopped at the arched doorway. "Something smells great."

"Peach cobbler for afternoon refreshment." She peered toward the oven timer. "It's nearly ready if you'd like some now."

"May I take a rain check?"

"Of course. The dish will be on the sidebar until dinner. Coffee and tea, as well."

She turned back to the counter, and he continued toward the back exit.

Bingo, the old Aussie, trotted around the house and followed him past Michael's Garden—a memorial to Julia's son that pinched his heart.

The carriage house beyond the lawn, an ongoing reconstruction project, was unoccupied. He'd seen Eli Donovan and his son out there over the weekend.

The scent of peach blooms filled the April afternoon while the sun dodged in and out of scattered clouds. They'd get rain tonight, and he prayed it didn't delay him further.

With long strides, he reached the tree line, rounded a wheelbarrow and saw Valery on her knees with a trowel.

She glanced up, wearing a somber expression and sunglasses. If she was drinking, he couldn't tell by her eyes. But she didn't smile either, and Valery always smiled.

Again he castigated himself for the suspicions. He had no control over her actions. She was a woman grown. What she did or didn't do was none of his business.

But his heart said otherwise.

He squatted next to her. "Is everything okay?"

"Why wouldn't it be?"

Because I'm afraid you've come here to drown your sorrows, and I don't know what they are to fix them. "You seem…down."

She tossed her head, a gesture he'd come to recognize as an intentional distracter, a way to appear carefree even when she wasn't. "I'm fine. Enjoying the sun. Making the world more beautiful."

She sounded as false as a three-dollar bill.

He sighed. If she wouldn't let him in, all he could do was keep on caring. "What can I do to help?"

"I almost have the hole dug. You can bring me a cup of that compost."

Donning the gloves in his pocket, Grayson did as she asked. "Is this stuff home-grown?"

"Makes sense, don't you think? The inn gives us plenty of discarded foods, peels, and such. Why not use what nature makes?"

"Smart. Organic as well as a money saver."

She sat back on her heels. "You didn't come out here to discuss organic gardening. Why aren't you working? Why another inspection? Did something go wrong?"

"Nothing wrong. The inspector is being cautious because of the extra excavation we had to do because of the skeleton."

She took the cup and dumped the compost into the hole, covering it with loose, moist soil. "I see, and that's wrecking your schedule again."

"Exactly." In spite of himself, he glanced at his watch.

Valery pointed a trowel at him. "If an alarm goes off while we're out here, I may do something terrible."

Sheepishly, he silenced the alarm on his watch. He left the phone alert alone. "Nothing that pressing."

Devlin would break into a happy dance if he heard those words.

From a five-gallon bucket, she took a thorny, bare rosebush. "The one I planted last year died."

"Grandma said roses are persnickety."

"I've lost several, so I'd have to agree. This one is a different cultivar that's supposed to be heartier. We'll see." She set the plant into the prepared hole, holding steady while Grayson covered it with moist soil. "I'm no plant expert, so maybe I'm doing something wrong."

"Looks good to me."

"Said the piano man."

"Hey." He pretended insult. "I've planted a thing or two."

She only smiled while patting the earth around the new bush.

As he knelt beside her, aware that his knees rested on a grave, he glanced at the name on the stone. "Anna Cornelia."

Valery's head came up. She reached out to trace the name with her index finger. Dirt smeared onto the stone, and she peeled the glove away using the wrist piece to wipe off the smudge. "Charlotte's last baby. She was only five days old."

"These babies, they mean something to you." Something more than being a good steward of the past.

Her demeanor had changed, gone quiet, and the air throbbed with unspoken meaning he couldn't decipher.

"Everyone has a soft spot for babies."

"True. Babies bring out a man's protective instincts."

"And our nurturing side."

A woman's perspective, he thought, and marveled at the differences in male and female, differences he certainly appreciated.

Lifting a hand to her cheek, he stroked her hair back, looping the soft silk behind her ear. He wanted to touch her. Needed to.

"I wouldn't mind being a father some day." In fact, the idea grew stronger all the time. "What about you?"

"No interest at all in being a father."

His lips curved. "Smart mouth."

She tried for a smile, but her bottom lip quivered.

Grayson narrowed his eyes, wondering.

"You're an incredible woman. Beautiful. Special. Kind. Warm. And very tenderhearted." *And I'm falling harder and faster every moment.*

Instead of another flippant response, she pressed her cheek deeper into his palm. "Am I?"

His control-freak brain screamed out red alert. She was not his type. She hid secrets he couldn't decipher. If he wasn't careful he was going to get his heart ripped right out of his chest.

For once, he didn't want to be careful or count the costs. Valery had become too important. "You have to know you are."

She bit her bottom lip. "But you don't know me that well."

"I know enough and I hope to learn more."

Valery went silent, pensive, and Grayson wondered if he was setting himself up for rejection.

The awkward teenage boy who'd admired Valery from afar tried to shut him up, but he was a man now who understood relationships. He'd almost been in love once in college, but this was something far different and more powerful.

He didn't know why, but it was, and he wanted to explore every facet of these emotions growing inside.

"I'm not the kind of man who says things I don't mean, so believe me when I say this. Something powerful is happening between us, at least for me, and I want to pursue it. I want to pursue you. If you don't feel the same, tell me now before I make a bigger fool of myself than I already have."

Grayson heard the soft intake of her breath and held his own. Then, in a whisper that sent shivers over his skin, she said, "I shouldn't. But I do."

Joy infused his brain, clouding reason. He ignored the warning shouts and focused on that place inside that had been afraid she'd say no.

Heart thundering, breathing her exotic scent, he leaned in to kiss her. Slowly, he removed her sunglasses.

Her eyes were red and puffy.

"You've been crying." Stunned, he sat back on his heels, romance momentarily put aside.

"No." She jammed the glasses back in place. "Allergies."

"I don't believe you." He reached for the sunglasses again, but she shifted away. "What's wrong? Is it me? Did I say or do something?"

"Grayson, no. Don't think that. You're—"

"Then what's wrong?"

She glanced to the side and back to him. "My mother and I had a—disagreement. I was upset."

That was why she'd come to the cemetery alone. To hide her pain. He didn't even want to consider the pink tote again, but red eyes...

He squinted toward the headstone and then back at her. "What did she say?"

She touched his tight jaw. "You look so fierce."

Did he? He felt fierce and protective as well as frustrated that even now she didn't trust him enough to tell him what hurt her.

Valery had to get away.

She'd barely gotten out of the cemetery without blurting the whole nasty, ugly truth to Grayson. If he hadn't gotten a phone call, she'd have been toast.

She wanted to tell him. She wanted to dump all her garbage at his feet and hope he would forgive her.

But he wouldn't. No one would.

She'd tried before and been rejected, ridiculed, abused. She'd sworn off men forever because of it.

A harsh laugh escaped. Yeah. Right. She'd sworn off men. But she hadn't bargained on Grayson coming along.

Now she paced her room, debating where to go, what to do. Sometimes she thought if she didn't talk to someone, she would implode. Maybe she was imploding already.

She considered the family pastor, but she'd skipped church too often to feel comfortable there.

She couldn't talk to Julia. Her sister would be devastated if she knew the truth, and there was no way Valery would heap more heartache on her.

She considered Carrie. They'd once been such good friends. They'd shared secrets. Nothing of this magnitude, but they'd been close, and Carrie had a dear, understanding way about her.

With renewed vigor, she showered and changed and left the inn. Julia was here. The main work of the day was over. She could deal with the guests.

This afternoon was a physical pain stabbing through her at intervals.

Grayson Blake was too good for her. He wanted more than a good time. He wanted her, to know her, to pursue her. The word, so like him, would have made her laugh at any other man. From Grayson, *pursue* meant something deep and special.

He was too close and too caring. He deserved better. He couldn't fall in love with her. He deserved a good woman who could make him happy, a woman he could be proud of. And oh, sweet Jesus, he wanted babies. But she'd already proven to be a terrible mother, a horrible person.

Grayson's Jeep was gone from the parking lot. The phone call must have been important. For his sake, she hoped no more problems had arisen at the mill.

Dancing there on the mill creek bank flooded through her memory, a night to cherish no matter what the future held for them as a couple.

Driving through town, she turned down a side street toward Carrie's house. Soon, her friend would move to the fancy home Hayden Winters was having built up on the ridge. Carrie, her sparrow-like friend, had found her soul mate in the famous author that few people knew well. He loved Carrie and treated her like a princess. That was good enough for Valery.

No vehicles parked in front of Carrie's small frame home with the bright blue shutters. Valery pulled into the driveway and sat with arms folded over the steering wheel, disappointed.

She should have called first. Carrie was probably with Hayden somewhere falling deeper in love and planning a bright and beautiful future.

Valery didn't want to be jealous. She was happy for her old friend. Really.

With a resigned sigh, she put the car in reverse and left.

Slowly, she drove down the main street of Honey Ridge. Shop owners were locking up. Nikki Riley in a bright blue Mazda RX backed out of the Sassy Sister's Boutique. Valery considered stopping, but she and Nikki had little in common anymore. She drove on, lifting a hand to wave at an occasional passerby.

The town was basically empty with only a few cars heading home for the evening. To supper and family. In Honey Ridge, businesses shut at five or six except for a handful. The grocery store, the lumberyard, the bar.

The craving hit her hard and fast.

She'd give a hundred dollars for a drink.

Automatically, she turned at Second Street. The only bar in town was a shabby joint where customers filled the air with smoke, played pool, and met like-minded souls. Some came for an after-work beer before hurrying home. Others arrived early and stayed late.

She parked in the side lot and killed the engine but didn't get out. A war waged in her head. She'd vowed to do better, to stop degrading herself with booze and men she barely remembered.

But one drink would be enough to soothe the ragged edge of shame, to numb that empty place inside her. She wouldn't let herself get crazy this time.

She made a move for the door handle. Then pulled her hand away.

She should go home. Right now. With a shaky hand, she leaned forward to put the key in the ignition.

A knock on her window made her jump. She swung her head around. A man in a tidy button-down shirt and tan slacks grinned in at her. He was all slicked up for a Friday night on the town.

"Hey, Val, is that you?"

She rolled down her window.

"Are you gonna get out or just sit here and look beautiful?"

"I really need to go home."

He tugged at her door handle. "Have a drink with me first."

"You're married, Mark, or did you forget again?" She'd learned that after the last time she'd had drinks with him. He cheated on his wife, and she didn't want to be the other woman this time.

He held out his ringless left hand. "Divorced. Jackie took the kids and moved to Franklin."

No big surprise there. "That's too bad."

"So, what do you say? Be a pal. Cheer up a lonely guy."

He opened her door and stood there, smiling. Friendly. He wasn't bad-looking.

When she hesitated, he held out a hand. "Come on, doll. I'm buying."

"Well, in that case." She took his hand and let him pull her out of the driver's seat. "One drink. Only one."

And she followed him into the bar.

CHAPTER 25

Things were definitely looking up.

Grayson stood in the open door of his Jeep talking to the structural engineer. He was parked on the new graveled lot outside the mill where he'd been ever since he'd left Valery in the cemetery.

"I can't tell you how much I appreciate the rush you put on this inspection." Grayson gazed down at the short woman in the yellow hard hat. Trina Grimes was a petite, pretty, fluffy redhead who didn't fit the stereotype of a structural engineer, but she was the best in the business.

"We do a lot of projects together, Grayson, and we both want the same outcome—a safe structure for your future customers. Working for someone who won't cut corners is important to me." She flashed him a pair of green eyes that had probably brought more than one guy to his knees. "Putting off a couple of other inspections was the least I could do after the other delays you've had."

"Much appreciated anyway. We're good to go, then?"

She ripped a page from her clipboard and handed it to him.

"Yes, sir. Nothing shifted. In fact, even without the extra bracing you'll add, the old building is quite sturdy for its age.

Your foundation crew did a terrific job of shoring up the old mortar."

"Perfect." He folded the sheet of paper and tossed it onto the car seat. "I'd be glad to buy your dinner as a thank-you."

"Thoughtful of you, but I have plans tonight." Taking out a cell phone, she illuminated the screen. A large digital clock glowed green. "Good timing. I'm out of here. You take care, Grayson."

He lifted a hand and watched her jog to her truck, a high-rise diesel with a hemi engine that rattled the countryside.

Relieved and pleased, he slid into his own vehicle, eager to get back to Valery. After he'd left in such a hurry they had unfinished business.

The creek bank was quiet and empty, a fact that brought on a mild wave of disappointment. Lem hadn't come around in the last couple of days. He hoped the old fella was all right. He missed their talks.

On the way back to the inn, Grayson Bluetoothed the contractors and put them back on the job, promising that this was the last delay. He hoped he was right.

By the time he pulled through the long row of lemon-scented magnolia trees leading into Peach Orchard Inn, he felt back in control. He also felt hungry.

After missing out on Julia's peach cobbler, his belly ran on empty. Intending to ask Valery to dinner, he parked in the lot. Her red Toyota was gone.

The newest wave of disappointment hit a bit harder. Hopefully, she'd be back soon.

He started across the greening back lawn.

Eli Donovan sprawled in an Adirondack chair on the wrap-around back porch, feet propped on the railing, necktie loosened and the top shirt button undone. A glass of Miss Julia's almost famous peach tea was in his hand.

"Evening, Grayson."

"Eli." He paused on the bottom step. "You look relaxed."

"Long day at work. Good, but long." The quiet man ran a nonprofit center for grieving families that was gaining respect all over Tennessee. "Join me. Julia has a fresh pitcher in the fridge."

"I was looking for Valery. Have you seen her?"

"Julia said she took off out of here in a hurry before I came home but didn't say where she was going." Eli sipped at his tea. "That's Valery. She likes her privacy and doesn't get much of it here."

So he'd noticed. "Must be hard, living with strangers all the time."

"Julia was meant to do this. Hospitality runs in her veins. She loves it, loves having guests, loves cooking." Eli hitched his glass. "And I love her."

"What about Valery? Does she love being an innkeeper?"

"Valery is the reason Julia bought the house in the first place."

That much he knew. "Which doesn't necessarily mean she loves it, too."

She'd pushed for the inn's purchase to bring her sister out of depression, not for herself, an admirable act but not necessarily a fulfilling one.

Eli studied him with a long, piercing gaze. "You trying to steal my sister-in-law, Grayson?"

Grayson didn't bat an eye. "Maybe."

Eli chuckled softly. "Good luck with that. Valery's a handful."

Grayson's hackles rose in defense. "A handful of beauty and talent. And she's kindhearted to a fault."

Eli's look was mild. "No argument here."

Grayson relaxed. Eli had meant no disrespect.

His stomach rumbled. He pressed a palm against his shirt. "I was going to ask Valery to dinner, but it looks like pizza may be my best bet. I don't suppose Julia has any cobbler left."

"Sorry. That's a popular dish around here. Alex wanted to lick the pan."

Grayson rubbed the back of his neck, thinking, wondering where she'd gone. She hadn't mentioned any plans for tonight. He could always call her. But as Eli said, she liked her privacy.

Compromising, he shot her a text instead saying simply, Call me.

The sun was low on the horizon, a blast of orange streaks over purple, and long blocks of shade lay over the backyard.

The back of the house, with the memorial garden angel watching over all and the little fountain bubbling peacefully, was pretty. Restful. Relaxing. Didn't Valery say he needed to relax more?

He went inside for the peach tea and returned to sit next to Eli and talk about nothing while he waited for Valery to return his text.

She didn't.

Maybe she was out of range. Cell phones didn't work everywhere in rural Tennessee. He'd been in more than one dead zone since coming to Honey Ridge, and the no-service notices made him crazy.

He was a little crazy now.

He was also starving.

The sound of a car coming up the lane drew his attention. Valery? Leaning forward, he squinted toward the parking lot, eager to see her and continue where they'd left off this afternoon.

Devlin's pickup truck rolled up instead.

With a disheartened sigh, Grayson melted back against the chair and scrolled his phone contacts. "Pizza it is."

★ ★ ★

Over a thick-crust Canadian bacon pizza, easy on the sauce, Grayson and Devlin rehashed the day and set up plans for the rest of the week. Now that they were back on track, there was no time to waste. As the hour grew late, fatigue claimed Devlin, who'd spent most of his day crawling around an abandoned theater that had captured his imagination. Grayson refused to consider an additional project until the mill was finished, and Devlin had retired to his room in an uncharacteristically grumpy mood.

Grayson wasn't tired. He was restless…and lonely.

Work waited on his laptop as always, but he wasn't in the mood. He considered going down to the piano for a while, but little Alex would already be in bed. He didn't want to disturb anyone.

He'd decoded a word on Patience's sheet music today. Anyway, he thought he had, and if he was right about the code key, he'd soon have the rest of the cryptogram figured out.

Valery would be impressed and call him a genius.

He wasn't, but she made him feel smarter than he was, capable of deciphering any puzzle or problem except her.

Restless, and if he'd admit it, wondering why Valery hadn't replied to his text, he walked the hallway to the end where a door led out onto the upper gallery.

Lifting the latch, he stepped outside into the night. He'd not taken time to make the trip before, but the porch view was awe-inspiring. From here, he saw the mill's security light and to the north the lights of Honey Ridge.

Strolling the sturdy wooden flooring of the wraparound gallery, he walked around the house taking in the different views. In the dark country quiet, with lights below and all around, he felt far away from the rest of the world. He thought about the people who'd come before, the builders of this old mansion and the others who had walked these same planks and gazed toward the shadowy bulk of distant mountains and woods, barely visible now in the darkness.

Had Patience Portland stood in this very spot and pined for a forbidden love? Had he been a Yankee like Charlotte's Will? A family rival? A former slave? Had she clung to this railing and concocted the mysterious method of passing notes to him through her musical compositions? Or had she been an unlikely spy for the Confederates during those days when the house had been occupied by Federals?

Perhaps he was completely wrong, and the music held nothing but a heartbreaking melody, but he didn't think so.

His long fingers gripped the railing as he let the night air rest on him. The scent hung heavy with clipped grass and the fresh flowers planted by two women he couldn't get off his mind, one long dead and the other more alive than anyone he'd ever known.

Along this upper porch the innkeepers had placed wicker chairs and small tables for relaxed coffee mornings. With his eyes adjusted to the darkness, Grayson easily found one and sat. He didn't know how long he rested there but he must have dozed. Music wafted on the wind, and he opened his eyes.

"I hear you," he said, and then felt silly but not silly enough to stop. "You want me to know about the messages, don't you?"

The music continued, trilling and happy as if to affirm his statement. Grayson smiled into the night and let Patience have her way with his mind.

"Patience," he said softly in realization. "That's what Lem Tolly meant. *Patience is important.* He wasn't only trying to get me to slow down. He was talking about you."

The old coot knew something about the music, about the mill, about the skeleton. Grayson had suspected before, but now he was certain. The next time Lem showed up, he and Grayson were going to have a heart-to-heart.

He was mulling the new information when car lights swung over the parking area below. His heart jumped. Valery's small Toyota crept slowly down the lane and came to a halt at an angle. She didn't pull into a parking spot. She simply stopped the car on the grass and killed the engine. Car lights spread out over the back lawn, setting the garden angel in alabaster shadow.

Grayson leaned forward, eager to see her, to call out and ask her up. On second thought, he'd go down.

Like an eager boy trying to be quiet in a sleeping house, he tiptoed rapidly down the stairs and out the back. As he stood on the dimly lit back porch, he could no longer see her.

He squinted into the darkness. Had he missed when she'd come inside?

He heard a groan. His heart, light and happy a moment before, stalled. He listened, intent until another sound came. Retching. His eyes fell shut for the briefest of moments before he sprang into action.

Hurrying now, this time with dread and concern, he strode to the parking lot. Valery was on her knees in the gravel, throwing up.

"Valery. Hey!" Rushing to her side, he went to his knees next to her. The gravel dug through his pants leg but he ignored the sharp jabs.

Gently, aching inside, he added his support, one hand bracing her back while the other brushed her hair away from her face. Between bouts of sickness, she moaned and shuddered, panting hard.

The overpowering smell of alcohol nearly made him sick, too.

Heartsick, but filled with a compassion that wouldn't let him walk away, he stayed with her. She was sick, inside and out, and though it drove him crazy not to be able to fix the problem, he couldn't leave her like this.

"Go 'way." With a limp hand she slapped at him, but the motion was too much for her, and she reeled wildly out of balance, nearly toppling over.

He caught her, letting her lean on him. She was drunker than he'd ever seen her. Falling down, stupid drunk.

He held her head until the sickness passed, and she fell against him, weak and breathing hard.

"Better?" he asked, continuing to smooth her hair away from her face.

She nodded.

Disappointment, hurt and pity throbbed in his chest. Why did she do this? Why?

He lifted her to her feet, taking her entire weight against him. She was limp and shaky but not that heavy. It was the weight she put on his heart that was too much of a burden to bear.

"Let's get you in the house."

"Shh. No. Julia gets mad." Her head lolled back. "Are you mad at me?"

He shook his head. He wasn't mad. He was hurt, disgusted and disappointed to the tip of his steel-toed boots.

A helpless, painful love rolled through him. Just when he'd thought they were moving toward something good, she did this again.

"Why?" he whispered, barely aware he spoke the one word he couldn't stop thinking.

Her body wobbled as she attempted to move away from him, but she couldn't stand on her own. "You don't know. You don't know anything."

Grayson didn't loosen his grip. If he did, she'd fall on the gravel. "Then tell me what's going on."

"I can't. Shh. Is a secret." Wobbly as a bobblehead, she lifted a limp finger to his face, missed his lips and hit his cheek. "You'll be mad. You won't like party Val anymore."

"Stop it. You're not party Val. Stop playing this game."

"Game?" She slung his hand from her shoulder and nearly fell again. He made a grab for her, barely catching her before she slammed against a parked car. "You think this is a game?"

Frustrated and bewildered, he said, "I don't know what this is all about, but it doesn't work for me, Valery. I want *you*. I don't want a drunk."

Valery tried for a laugh, but a sob broke from her lips. "Thas all I am." She breathed a heavy, alcohol-scented sigh. "No good for nothing. Go 'way, Grayson."

He wasn't going anywhere. Didn't she get that? Even if his control freak brain knew he was going to get his heart trampled in the mud, he couldn't walk away. Beneath these bizarre episodes of booze and bad behavior, Valery was everything he wanted in a woman. Caring and considerate, smart and talented, warm and fun-loving, the perfect foil to his workaholic ways. He couldn't let her go without a fight.

He pulled her up close, chest to chest, though right now, romance was the last thing on his mind.

"Tell me what's going on, Valery. Give me an explanation of this. This afternoon, I thought—" He broke off, frustrated, and started again. "One day you treat me like a man you care about. Then tonight, this. I want to understand, to help, but you have to give me something to work with."

Intellectually, he understood the futility of reasoning with a drunk person, but the need and pain boiling in his blood was too great to stop.

"Talk to me, Valery. Let me help."

She tilted away, trying but failing to make eye contact. Dark makeup smudged beneath her eyes, and her lipstick was long gone, washed away by hard liquor. He didn't know where she'd been, or with whom, and he wasn't sure he wanted to know. His heart was being ripped from his chest, and all he could think of was the woman in his arms and the mysterious wounds that would do this to her.

He wanted to lash out, at her, at whatever or whoever was the cause. He wanted to punch and kick and eradicate the problem. He was a thinker, a problem solver, a fixer.

He didn't know where to begin.

He braced the back of her head, aware in spite of himself, of her soft, silken hair against his skin. With a groan, he looked up at the inky, glittered sky, seeking aid from Someone somewhere.

"Sorry. So sorry." Her voice trembled in remorse, drawing him back to her. "You're such a good man. Too good." She sighed heavily. "Pretty piano man. Shouldn't like me. Don't deserve—"

Her eyes rolled back, and she slumped, became dead weight, unconscious.

Grayson scooped her into his arms.

Far away a coyote howled. Grayson wanted to throw his head back and do the same. Instead, he carried Valery into the house, taking care to be as quiet as possible. No one else needed to know. No one but him. He wanted to spare her the indignity. Knowing where her room was, Grayson moved silently down the dark family hallway guided only by instinct and good night vision.

Relieved to discover her door unlocked, he managed to find the light switch and flipped it. She hung across his arms and never roused at all.

As he moved toward the bed, he caught quick impressions of the space. The room was completely Valery, dramatic, bold and beautiful. Black-and-white decor found relief in splashes of red wall hangings and pillows and a bright red upholstered chair. A black lacquered fireplace held a bouquet of fresh flowers in a blood-red vase. Most poignant and telling of all was a grouping of black-and-white photos featuring dancers in action.

He laid Valery on a white faux fur comforter and removed her shoes. The shiny silver flats dropped noisily to the hardwood floor.

He'd never invaded her space before, but the only thing in the room that really interested him was her. At the foot of the four-poster bed, she'd neatly folded a red throw. Tenderly, he spread the soft fleece over her inert body, tucking it under her chin as if she were a child. That's the way she made him feel in this moment. As if he was protecting and caring for a child. Though Valery was every bit a woman.

Her dark hair spread out around her on the white pillow, and he smoothed it, hesitant to leave her, wanting to prolong his reasons for being at her side.

Would she be all right? Would she get sick in the night and need him? Would she fall and hurt herself?

His anger had ebbed, giving way to pity and sadness. He ached, weary and heartsick…and incredibly tender.

She was a bruise he couldn't stop pressing on.

For long moments, Grayson stood at Valery's bedside looking down at her. Even smudged with makeup, she was beautiful to him. He saw her as she didn't. Naturally, he saw the physically gorgeous Valery—what man with eyes wouldn't?—but more than that, he saw the beauty inside.

Memories of the teenage Valery came back to him in quick flashes, memories that had disappeared with time and distance. One in particular stood out. Once when some sneering jerk had called him a nerd, she'd jumped to his defense. He'd forgotten about that. She'd called him smart, even then, and accused the boy of jealousy and told him to shut up.

That was the Valery who'd stolen his heart at fifteen and never given it back.

Somewhere between then and now, something had broken her.

Smoothing his fingers over her soft cheeks, Grayson sighed.

He was in love with a woman he couldn't repair the way he repaired old buildings or cars, a woman who was already breaking his heart.

If he was half as smart as he thought he was, he'd cut his losses and back off.

Chest aching hard enough to crack, he kissed her cheek and whispered, "I love you," and then, feet dragging, he left the room and tiptoed down the hallway toward the staircase.

The old house settled around him with a deep, comforting sigh as if it saw and understood heartache, because it had seen so much sorrow in the past.

CHAPTER 26

Patience, that blending of moral courage with
physical timidity.

THOMAS HARDY

1875. Colorado

Ben tossed and turned in the plush feather bed on the third
floor of Tandy's hotel. His mind raced, overwhelmed with the
changes in Tandy as well as with thanks that he'd found his
friend and half brother alive and successful and apparently happy.

Tandy had a wife now, and Ben wanted to meet Molly
Wellston.

Perhaps Patience had been right. Tandy didn't want to return to a place filled with reminders of bondage. He was a
respected businessman, clearly doing well in Denver. This was
his life now. He had no interest in a Tennessee farm where
he'd once been a slave forced to do and go as he was told.

But why so adamantly against a visit? And what of Lizzy?
What of the loving, mourning mother who had searched and
grieved for more than ten years? The mother who had suffered so much for his sake?

Over tasty buffalo steaks and fried potatoes, Tandy had
pressed for details about his mama, laughing as they shared
boyhood stories and reminisced about her with a wistfulness
he didn't try to hide. Tandy missed his mother, too, that was

clear, and longed to see her face and listen to her loving scold. Why was he reluctant to come home for a visit?

He had wrestled and prayed half the night, but suddenly Ben found an answer that would bring Tandy back to Tennessee. Tomorrow, he would once again lay out his request that Tandy and his wife visit Peach Orchard Farm, but this time he would reveal the secret only he and Lizzy knew. Tandy must return because, by all that was just and honorable, Peach Orchard Farm belonged to Tandy every bit as much as it belonged to Benjamin.

Breakfast at the Wellston Hotel was a plate loaded with sausage, eggs and buttery flapjacks as fluffy and light as air.

"You're feeding me well," Ben said to Tandy as the other man sat back in his chair gnawing the tip of an unlit cigar.

"Your mama fed us well—all of us, slave, white, Yankee, Confederate. She made no difference."

"Mama's a true Christian. She believes, as I do, that we are all God's children deserving of grace."

Tandy's lips lifted slightly. "Miss Charlotte lived her faith, though I dare say her opinions were not always well received."

"No. No, they were not, but in her quiet way, she refused to give in."

"And she taught her son to do the same?"

"Indeed. That's why I'm here." Ben put his linen napkin aside and cleared his throat. His birthright could remain his in silence, or he could do the right thing—the God-fearing thing—and share what he knew. "I got something that needs saying."

"Say it." Tandy must have heard the seriousness in his tone. His eyes narrowed and he stilled, intent.

"I never saw you as a slave. Perhaps I was a sheltered, naïve little boy, but I would rather think my mother taught me a better way."

"I know that, Ben, and I'm obliged. As a man who has

seen much I understand now how different things were for me than for most other slave children. Miss Charlotte allowed me much freedom that others did not receive." Tandy's hazel eyes sought his and held on. "Yet I was not free at all. I discovered this uncomfortable truth when your father found me…expendable."

Ben's fist clenched. The metal fork dug into his skin. "Selling you in a fit of vengeance against our mothers was reprehensible. I cannot forget that. Or forgive."

Tandy glanced away, thoughtful but silent. Ben could not help but wonder what memories and horrors he kept hidden behind the quiet face and elegant attire. He had seen more, endured more than Ben could ever comprehend simply because of his skin color.

All the more reason to press on, to reveal the whole truth. Though nothing could rectify or justify his father's actions, the son must try, in some small way, to make amends. "You're more than my best boyhood friend. You were always more, but we were only lads and couldn't understand what must have been clear to Mama. Maybe to everyone."

Tandy's mouth softened as if he might smile. "That we share a father?"

Ben blinked, shocked. "You knew?"

Taking his time to reply, Tandy took out a tiny pair of scissors and nipped the end of the cigar. Once done, he studied the tip but didn't light up.

"I asked Mama once, and she whipped me good and told me never to say such a thing again, but she cried the whole time. Mama was never one for crying. After that I never spoke of it because I understood the cold reality. Being half white didn't matter. Not then. Not now. My other half was black, and I was still a slave."

Ben's appetite waned. He laid his fork aside.

"Papa was a brutal man, taking what he wanted, discarding those who were inconvenient, using others for his evil purposes." Tandy, Lizzy, Mama and so many others had suffered because of him.

Tandy paled, expression taut. "Yes, Edgar Portland was an angry, evil man, and unfortunately, he was not the only one of his kind."

"He and many like him are gone now, suffering the reward of their behavior. The world is changing."

Tandy shook his head, his expression sadly amused. "Not so much as you would like to think."

"But you're a free man now, and a mighty successful one from what I see. You can come and go as you please. Come home."

Tandy sat a long time, studying the backs of his light brown hands. Then he aligned one fine-fingered hand with one of Ben's. They were surprisingly similar. "You have your father's hands."

"So do you."

"I 'spect I do. Are you not ashamed? Repelled?"

"Only because they come from Edgar Portland. Not because of you. You were my brother long before I understood my father's depraved proclivity for the slave quarters, Tandy." He'd despised his father for that obscene proclivity, for the hurt Edgar caused Lizzy and the other slave women he violated. But, like Lizzy, he could never regret Tandy's existence.

He pulled the blue marble from his pocket and handed it across the table. "Then and now I considered you my brother."

"You were a fine and gentle boy. But you're a foolish man."

"Perhaps. Perhaps not." A slight smile pulled at Ben's lips. "I've traveled far to find you, Tandy. Come back with me."

"No. I cannot." Tandy shook his head, the determination in his voice dimming Ben's hopes. "There is more to my parting than you ever knew. Reasons that would put me and others I care about in jeopardy even now."

"What are you trying to say?"

Tandy heaved a chest-deep sigh. "I wouldn't be where I am today had your father not sold me to Robert Wellston. I was not happy then, nor was I for a long time after, but today I am reconciled to and accepting of the benefits of leaving Tennessee."

The memory of that day was sharp in Ben's mind. He recalled his confusion and then the awful grief that swarmed him to learn Tandy was already gone, sold to some unknown buyer. He remembered, too, Lizzy's cries that keened on and on and on.

Through gritted teeth, he proclaimed, "I despise him still."

"As do I, though there are crueler things than being sent away, Benjamin. More wicked, frightful things."

"I don't understand." Ben pushed aside his emptied plate, satisfied in stomach if not in soul. Tandy studied him a long, throbbing moment. Finally, he sighed, and resignation passed over his face.

"I thought it was better if you never knew, but hate will rot your guts. You're too good for that, Ben." He pocketed the cigar and marble and sighed again, heavily, as if he carried a great burden. "Take a ride with me. I have a story you need to hear—a difficult one that I dare not tell here."

A sick foreboding came over Ben as he followed his half brother out the back to a stable where together they hitched a fat bay to the buggy. Tandy's untold story hung between them, as strong as the smell of hay and horse dung.

Ben tried to shake off the uneasy feelings as he listened to his half brother extol the virtues of Denver city, but the unease remained.

Tandy drove the conveyance, tipping a hand to pedestrians as they passed and pointing out various enterprises. He drove next to a clear, rushing creek, slowing as the business district faded into homes and then to countryside. Mountains rose up all around, dark blue in the distance.

When Ben realized Tandy would not speak until he was ready, he broke the quiet. "Colorado's beautiful country."

"Most beautiful place I've ever been." Holding the reins in one hand, Tandy shifted toward Ben. "You could stay. A smart man like you can get rich in the West."

Ben's lips tilted. "Would you give me a job in the hotel?"

Tandy slanted a gaze. "Would you take it?"

"I would."

"Then you're a better man than most. If you noticed, all my employees are colored. White men will sleep in my hotel and allow me and my staff to serve them, but they won't work for me." He pulled the reins up and drew the bay to a stop.

Ben had no answer for this man who'd known far more hardship than he would ever understand. Freedmen still struggled to find their way in a world not far removed from thinking of them as property and lesser beings. It was a dilemma of the soul.

"This creek reminds me of the one that runs by the mill back home. I come here sometimes when I want to remember or to think." Tandy shifted on the buggy seat, facing Ben. "No other living soul, except Miss Patience, knows what I'm about to tell. I am trusting you for my sake but especially for hers, never to breathe a word beyond us three."

"Patience? But—"

Tandy held up a hand. "If you want to know why I can't come home and why Patience has never married, I need your word, Ben."

Fear leaped in Ben's chest. "What does Patience have to do with this?"

"I need your word."

With trepidation, Ben solemnly nodded. "You have it."

And Tandy began to speak.

CHAPTER 27

Present Day. Honey Ridge

Valery woke with a powerful thirst and a hideous taste in her mouth. Somebody was playing the piano again, and she wished they'd stop.

Slowly, her senses cleared, and the music dissipated, a dream. A drunken dream.

Groaning, she rolled to one side as shame slid through her, scorching hot. Her head pounded. She gripped her temples.

"Oh, God," she whispered, licking dry-as-powder lips.

What had she done?

Aware she was fully dressed—a blessing, all things considered—she tried to remember how she'd gotten to bed. The memory evaded her.

The last thing she recalled was a humiliating episode of sickness in front of Grayson.

She moaned again. Why did he have to be the one to find her like that? She'd only meant to have one drink. One! But one became two and two became three. She could handle three with only a head buzz that made her cheerful and fun-loving.

Somewhere after the third shot everything became a blur.

Mark had invited her to his place. She squeezed her eyes tight but opened them every bit as quickly. Pressure banged like hammers against her eyelids.

Had she gone home with Mark? The idea made her sick all over again. She focused, tried to remember, hoped and prayed she hadn't.

He'd accompanied her to his car. She remembered that much, and they'd gotten as far as the parking lot and her red Toyota. Mark claimed she couldn't drive. He was right. But by then she was maudlin and crying, and the only man she'd wanted was Grayson.

She'd wanted to go home.

She'd gotten into the Toyota.

"Thank you," she whispered.

Somehow, by the grace of God, she'd driven home unscathed. Again.

Relief ran like water through her body.

She'd come home to Peach Orchard. She didn't remember the drive and hated herself for that. She knew better than to drive drunk, but she'd been completely toasted before she left the bar.

How had that happened? She hadn't intended to.

One drink. She'd promised. Only one drink.

Then Grayson had found her puking in the parking lot. From there she was blank. No, not blank. Vague snatches, hazy pictures of gravel, car lights and Grayson flickered in her head. They'd argued. He'd wanted an explanation. Had she given him one? Had she told him?

Stupid. Stupid. Stupid.

Gingerly, she swung her feet to the floor. Her stomach rolled. The maniac with the hammer slammed the back of her eyeballs.

This had to stop. She was smart enough to know she was

self-destructing. Something had to give before there was nothing left of her. Or worse, before her driving killed somebody.

The thought made her stomach lurch, and she rushed to the bathroom, sick again.

When the agony passed, she rested her hot cheek against the cool white tile, exhausted and discouraged.

Every time she made a vow, she broke it.

For Grayson this must have been the last straw. Who could blame him? She was out of control, and he was a control freak. The two did not go well together.

She huffed a short, aching laugh.

Understatement of the year.

Why had she ever hoped the two of them could have a relationship?

Easy. "I love him."

Maybe she'd loved him since the time so long ago outside the Dairy Queen when he'd patiently taught her how to solve a Rubik's cube.

But if she loved him, if she wanted him, why was she driving him away?

In hopeless anger, she pounded a fist against the wall tile, and then groaned at the stabbing pain in her head.

Something had to give, starting today.

An hour later, Valery moved around the dining room like a zombie. The sly sideways glances she got from Julia said her sister recognized a hangover when she saw one.

Then, Mama showed up to help clean the woodwork, and the cold silences deepened until Valery wanted to scream at both women. She didn't, of course. Carter women did not raise their voices in an unladylike display. Nor did they discuss the purple elephant in the room. Neither woman even asked if she was all right. They knew the answer, especially

Mama. Mama knew more than anyone, but Lord forbid she mention it.

Valery managed to speak to the four guests having breakfast in the dining room, though Grayson wasn't among them. Thank goodness. She wasn't sure she could face him at all today.

He probably never wanted to see her again.

Rightfully so. She didn't deserve him. He should get as far away from her as possible.

But she didn't want him to go away. She also didn't want him to be angry or hurt. She wanted him to love and admire and respect her the way she did him.

Fat chance of that happening now.

"More coffee?" she asked the middle-aged couple sitting near the window.

With smiling eyes, the matronly woman nodded, and then turned to gaze at the pretty garden outside the double window. "Beautiful lawns."

"Thank you." Usually, a rush of pride filled Valery at such compliments. After all, she'd selected and planted most of the flowers and bushes and helped keep the yard manicured. Today, she was too low to be proud of anything.

She retrieved a freshly filled coffee carafe from the kitchen and then moved around the linen-covered tables, a polite smile plastered on her face, though the clink of silverware drove sharp nails through her brain.

Twice, she stepped into the hallway and took long, deep breaths, fighting nausea. This wasn't her first rodeo. She could do this. Along with Mama and Julia, she could pretend that life was perfect at Peach Orchard Inn.

"Valery, honey."

At her mother's voice, she stilled, pot in hand, schooled her expression and slowly turned. "Yes, Mama?"

"Julia said the eggs are ready if you can serve. She has her hands full with the piecrust."

Prickles of heat bloomed on her neck. Her stomach threatened revolt. Briefly, she closed her eyes before going into the kitchen. Eggs. The worst smell she could think of, so she didn't think at all. Fighting off the gag reflex, she finished serving breakfast as quickly as possible and hurried out onto the thankfully empty back porch.

The fresh air, cool and pleasant, wafted over her too-hot skin. She drew in deep drafts of the spring morning, caught the lemony scent of magnolias blooming down the driveway. Maybe she'd feel like cutting some later to float in goblets on the tables. Out-of-state guests, of which they had three, loved the Southern touch of magnolia blossoms atop crisp white table linens.

Right now, she wanted to escape.

"Valery."

Escape was impossible.

Lips tight, resigned, she didn't turn around as Mama came to stand next to her.

"Busy morning. I'd think you would be inside helping your sister."

Head slowly swiveling, Valery gazed at her mother from beneath aching eyelids. Even on heavy cleaning days, Connie Carter looked perfect and put together. Like Julia. She even wore a single strand of pearls. For housework, no less. Like Grayson, the pair of them had always been perfect. Valery had never measured up.

"I do my share."

"Just because you—" Mama's gaze scraped over her, seeing everything. Valery knew how she looked. Bloodshot eyes, pale face, she looked horrid.

The shame inside Valery nearly killed her.

She was too soul-sick to bristle. Tiredly, she asked, "Because I what, Mama?"

"Never mind."

Never mind. Avoid the topic. Pretend your daughter is not disintegrating before your eyes.

Suddenly, she was tired of her family's polite game of silence. The hangover made her irritable, bold, hateful.

"For once, say what you're thinking." When her mother didn't respond, Valery's irritation elevated. So did her voice.

Through gritted teeth, she demanded, "Say it. Get it out in the open. Blast me. That's what you want to do."

Connie shot a quick over-the-shoulder look toward the closed back door and, in a hissing voice, said, "Stop acting like a shrew. Guests will hear you."

"Oh, will they?" Rage, long hidden, began to bubble in her chest. She raised her voice even more. "I don't care! I'm a drunk! Do you hear me?"

With a sharp gasp, her mother stepped off the porch and walked briskly toward the carriage house. Valery followed, anger growing, burning up her esophagus, flaming in her throat.

"Oh, that's rich, Mama," she yelled toward the blue-clad back. "Walk away. Ignore the problem like you always do."

She was sick, hungover and dying inside. What difference did it make if she said the horrible, ugly words out loud? Half the town knew Valery Carter drank too much and slept around. Silence didn't mean ignorance.

Her mother stopped short of the carriage house and turned around. Far enough, Valery reasoned, that guests could not be privy to her daughter's uncouth behavior.

"I won't argue with you, Valery. It's clear you're having a bad morning."

Valery's laugh was harsh. "A bad morning? Is that what

you call it?" She flung a hand out to the side as if to slash the very air. Mama flinched. "I have a rip-roaring hangover. I was stupid drunk last night. I don't even remember getting in my bed, but I woke up there."

Her mother's face paled. She drew up to her full height, one hand clutching her pearls. "Valery."

"And you know why?"

Mama's hand came up in a stop sign. "Stop this instant. I will not listen to this ill-bred ranting. You should go to your room and get some rest. We can talk when you have yourself under control."

Valery barked another furious laugh. "Talk? You and me? Since when does that happen?"

"We talk every day."

"Oh sure. 'Valery, your sister needs help in the kitchen.' 'Mama, will you fold this load of towels?' That's not talking. That's avoiding the huge, painful issue that isn't going to go away."

"You're clearly overwrought, and I won't discuss this now."

"I'm not overwrought. I'm angry. *Furious.* We have to talk or I'm going to die."

"Drama." Connie's head jerked in a dismissal. "Drama should have been your middle name. From the time you were little, you were spoiled and overdramatic. That's why we put you in dance—where you excelled, by the way. You were going to be something special. But then you were too much of a drama queen to continue. Everything was about you."

Valery couldn't believe her ears. A red rage powerful enough to knock her over flooded into her bloodstream. Her whole body trembled.

In a deadly quiet voice that shook with emotion, she leaned toward her mother. "*You know* why I stopped dancing."

"Yes, I do. To punish me. To punish yourself. To wallow

in self-pity and self-indulgence exactly as you are doing now with this awful drinking."

"Giving up dance wasn't about me. It was about my—"

Connie's hand flew up. "Stop. We will not have this discussion. Let the past rest."

Valery pushed her mother's fingers aside. "Yes, we *will* discuss this. The past can never rest until we get it out in the open. I can never find peace until we do." Her words fell to a whisper. "Please, Mama, it's killing me."

Connie squeezed her eyes shut. When she opened them again, worry filled the blue depths. "I can't bear to think of that awful time. Put the past behind you, honey. Let it go. Stop dwelling on it. You're only making yourself miserable."

"That *awful time* produced a baby." The thought boiling in her brain took root. She'd tried for years to forget she had a child, but she never had. Not for one second. Now, she was desperate enough to give voice to the one thing that might bring her peace. "I want to find her."

Her mother stumbled backward, hand to her heart. Her face grew so pale, Valery feared she was having a heart attack.

She reached out. "Mama. Please. *Please*, don't be angry, but finding her is something I need to do. Nothing is ever going to be right until I try. Searching for my baby is the only way I can ever let her go."

"You can't. Don't even consider such a thing. The child is a teenager now. People would find out. We went to great lengths to preserve your reputation."

Valery tilted her head back and stared at the white clouds passing above. The headache throbbed but not as much as the ache in her heart. Mama had never understood. Valery's concern wasn't about reputation. Maybe she'd cared then, but she sure didn't now.

"Where have you been the last sixteen years? My reputation was shot the first time I got toasted on vodka after you brought me home from Georgia."

She'd been seventeen, devastated and broken, but Mama thought she should instantly forget about the baby she'd birthed in Savannah and return to her former life of dance and friends and teenage pleasures.

Instead, Valery had felt old and used up. She knew things her friends didn't. Things she couldn't tell.

She'd tried to return to the old, fun-loving high school Valery during her senior year. Lord knew she had. She'd been football queen and dated every cute boy Mama had pushed at her, but each night she cried into her pillow for the baby she'd given away. She'd desperately hated herself for choosing dance over a child.

Dance had been the tool, the lure Mama had used to take her baby away. They'd both embraced the promise dancing held for Valery's future. By giving away her child, she could return to her glory and a bright future. At the highly emotional, confusing time, Mama's way seemed best. Neither had reckoned on the aftermath.

So she'd come home to Honey Ridge filled with remorse and shattered in spirit. And she'd refused to dance.

Mama had told everyone her talented daughter was burned out and that the year in New York had not gone as well as she'd hoped.

There had never been a year in New York.

"If you won't consider yourself, think of your family." Mama's words were stern. "We are prominent citizens in this town. We do not need the scandal of your...teenage mistake coming up now, all these years later."

"People are a lot more forgiving than you think. Teenage pregnancies happen in the best of families. What doesn't happen is this." She spread her hands out to her sides. Whether from hangover or fatigue, they shook. "A family that refuses to talk about what happened, that refuses to see that giving up my baby destroyed me."

"Valery Michelle. You're stronger than that. I don't know what's brought up that awful business again, but put it out of your thoughts and focus on today. You have a fine new man in your life. Appreciate him."

Grayson. Part of the reason she yearned for resolution.

"I don't want to hurt or embarrass you or the family, but I can't let this go. I keep remembering that I gave away a baby when Julia would do anything to have hers back again. The guilt is driving me crazy."

A flicker of understanding flashed on Mama's face. Chanel Number Five whispered on the air as she slipped an arm around Valery's waist and snugged her close, the way she'd done when both girls were small. In Mama's arms, safe and secure, trusting that Mama knew best.

"My precious girl, stop this before you make yourself sick."

I'm already sick. Don't you understand?

"When you were little, you were our special one. Everyone noticed you. 'There she is,' they'd say, 'little Valery, the dancer, as beautiful as a movie star. She'll be famous someday.'" Her mother tugged at her again. "Remember? Princess Valery. Queen Valery. You were the belle of the ball, the most popular girl. You had everything."

Valery stared down at the grass, seeing only the dead brown of winter clinging to the new birth of spring.

"Including a baby."

Connie's voice grew soft and compassionate. "When you came home from Savannah, we promised we would never, ever mention that again. Dwelling there hurt too much. Remember?"

Remember? How could she forget? Sick inside, she'd flown

back to Nashville from her pretend year in New York City via a maternity home in Savannah, Georgia. Mama had thrown a welcome home party to celebrate her return. All her friends had come, all except the baby's father, who had, at the first hint he'd gotten her pregnant, rushed back to college never to return.

She'd been sixteen. He was twenty. There could have been all kinds of repercussions about that situation, but preserving the secret had been more important to her family than making him take responsibility.

"You said everything would be fine, and no one would ever know." She pulled away from the warmth and security of her mother's side. Cool air rushed in, chilling her. She rubbed at her upper arms. "But I know, and I can't forget no matter how I tried or how much you want me to. Especially now that Mikey's gone. I have a daughter. Doesn't she matter to you at all?"

"You think you're the only one to suffer over this decision? She was my grandchild."

"*Is*, Mama. She is your grandchild. Your only granddaughter. She's out there somewhere, and I want to search for her."

Her mother's lips flatlined. "Did you ever consider she may not know about you? That she is likely very happy with her life and may not want to reconnect with her birth mother?"

A thousand times, she'd considered exactly that. "What if she does? What if she's searching for me? What if the people who adopted her are too harsh? Maybe she needs me."

"Don't do this to yourself, honey. To your family. To that good man who gets stars in his eyes when you're around. Sixteen years have passed. Why dig it all back up now?"

"A buried past is still there." Like the skeleton unearthed at the mill waiting for the truth to be discovered.

"What if Grayson finds out? You don't want to ruin the one decent relationship you've had in years."

No, she didn't, but she had a feeling she might be too late.

"You stand to lose a great deal and may not gain anything at all. Make the most of this lovely thing you have going with Grayson. Grab him while you can before some other smart woman does. You care for him, don't you?"

"Very much." She bit down on her bottom lip. "But he saw me last night."

"Tell him you were ill." When Valery opened her mouth to protest, Connie went on, a motherly index finger in the air. "It isn't a lie. You *were* ill."

Valery shook her head. A lie of omission was already tearing her apart. She wasn't going to add a white lie to her list of sins. "He's not a fool, and I won't pretend he is. I respect him too much."

Mother's lips thinned. "You're impossible. You won't even let me help you anymore."

"I think you've helped me enough."

"You were barely sixteen. What was I supposed to do?"

"I don't know." That was the crux. She'd never known.

Weary of the discussion that had caused more problems than it had resolved, she left her mother standing there and walked back into the house.

Her relationship with Grayson could never move forward as long as the secret lay between them and as long as she drowned herself in alcohol to hide the truth.

Nor could she ever be truly happy, either by herself or with Grayson, until she resolved the issue of the baby girl she'd given away.

CHAPTER 28

Present Day. Honey Ridge

"You're looking long in the jowls." Lem Tolly sat on the creek bank, fishing pole in hand and line in the water, his dog perched at his side like a furry human.

"Am I?" Grayson stood on a flat rock staring out over the mirrored creek. He was about as down as he allowed himself to get.

"Uh-huh. Pull up a rock. I been waiting on you."

"I could say the same. Where have you been, old man?" he asked affectionately, confident Lem would take no offense.

Yellowed teeth flashed beneath the gray mustache. "Missed me, did you?"

He had. "Missed your dog."

Lem chuckled. "Got a smoke?"

Grayson laughed and shook his head. "Same song, second verse."

Unaffected, Lem gave his fishing reel a twist, bringing the red-and-white bobber a few feet closer to the shore.

"Ever figure out those songs you found?"

"Getting there. I developed a key that seems to fit and deciphered a date." Boots scraping the limestone, he pivoted to spear the old man with a look. "I figured out something else, too. You know more than you're telling."

The gray mustache twitched. "Do I?"

Frustrating old geezer.

"I think you do. So why don't you fill me in and put me out of my misery?"

"Are you miserable?"

"Maybe."

Lem cast a quick look at the noisy construction site. "Business trouble?"

"No."

The project was back on schedule and only a little over budget even with the delays. Grayson always planned ahead for a few surprise expenses here and there, much as he disliked them, though the skeleton had been a first. And hopefully a last.

A half-dozen trucks and large machines dotted the landscape around the old gristmill. Voices rang out in the cloudy afternoon while a team set up and secured scaffolding up one side of the building.

"Heart trouble, then." Lem's grizzled head swiveled toward him. "The flashy brunette?"

"Yeah." With a sigh, Grayson kicked the dirt off his flat rock and sat down. He should be supervising the construction or loading discards in the giant Dumpster like Devlin was doing, but he didn't have the inner energy.

"Dad-blasted perch." Lem reeled in his bobber and dangled an empty hook in front of Grayson's face. "Got my worm."

Dodging the fishy-scented line, Grayson pushed a white foam carton of night crawlers toward the old man and watched as brown fingers skillfully threaded bait onto the hook. One flick of the wrist, and Lem's bobber plopped into the water again.

"How many fish have you caught out of here?"

"Enough. Don't change the subject. You need to get something off your chest. I can see that. What's happened with this gal of yours?"

Last night had been a long one, punctuated with a few hours of sleep and the rest of the night at his computer worrying over the cryptogram in Patience Portland's compositions, a ploy to take his mind off Valery.

His chest had ached so badly for her and for himself, he had chewed half a dozen useless antacids.

One minute he was through trying to understand her, thinking she was still the accomplished flirt and heartbreaker he'd once known. But the assessment wasn't completely fair. The heart she damaged the most was her own.

Just as he needed to understand the secret messages, he wanted to understand Valery.

Maybe he should stop trying.

"Might as well spit it out, son. Like you said, I already know a thing or two."

Grayson's glance was sharp. "You saw her last night?"

"Might have. But she came home to you."

"How can you possibly know these things?"

"I get around. People talk." Lem chuckled. "Except you and that gal of yours. You're full of words and won't let them out."

With a relieved sigh, Grayson told Lem everything, exactly the way he would have told Pappy.

"I don't want her to fall down that rabbit hole like my mother did."

"But you think maybe she already has."

Grayson nodded. The comparisons between Valery and his mother had played around the edges of his thoughts for a while now. Today was the first time he'd faced them head-on.

"Mom nearly wrecked herself and our family." He told the

old man about his illness and the aftermath of his mother's drinking.

"Blamed yourself, did you?"

"Some. Yeah. If I hadn't gotten sick—"

"How was that your fault? Did you want to have Hodgkin's?"

Grayson huffed. Intellectually, he knew better, but the feeling remained. "Of course not."

"Valery's not your fault either."

"I know that, but I care about her. I want to help."

"She won't let you?"

"Not so far. I've tried to talk to her, and I've asked her to tell me what's gnawing at her, but she pushes me away."

"And you're thinking to give up on her."

"Yes. Maybe." Frustrated, he finished, "I don't know."

"Keep trying, the way your father did with your mother."

"What if Valery doesn't want that?"

"She does." Lem fiddled with his reel. The bobber lay on top of the water barely moving in the light current. "I had me a good woman once. She died when we were young."

"You never remarried?"

"Never wanted to. I had the best, and now I have her memory." He tapped his temple. "Ever since then I roam around searching for answers."

"Found any yet?"

"Plenty. One thing for sure, I found you, and I found this mill with a buried skeleton and ghosts of the past. Been looking this way for a while wondering if this old mill holds answers to my questions. Then here's that good woman up there trying to find her way and fighting off some kind of ghost from her past. And here you are doing the same."

"Funny how chance brings things together."

"Chance?" Lem's pale gaze sharpened. "Look out there, lad.

The sun hanging above the universe by nothing. This planet twirlin' around in space so fast we ought to fall off or at least be dizzy. Are you dizzy?"

Grayson laughed. "Not at the moment."

"There you go, then. This world's too big for chance happenings."

Grayson understood what he meant. God was out there somewhere. He'd felt Him during his battle with cancer and had made peace with death. It was life that gave him trouble sometimes.

Suddenly, Lem jerked hard on his fishing pole. "Whoop! Got me one!"

Grayson observed the age-old battle of man and fish while his mind gnawed away at the problem of Valery Carter. Talking about her hadn't helped one little bit.

Valery carefully avoided Grayson for the rest of the day, easy because he left early and didn't return until late. She was too ashamed to face him. What would she say? How could she make up for the harm she'd done?

She couldn't.

But she wanted to.

The next day dawned hot and didn't let up. The fact that she was stuck in the laundry room with a mountain of table linens to iron didn't help. Julia insisted on ironing the napkins and tablecloths to crisp perfection, and today was Valery's turn to do the steamy, hateful job.

She neatly folded a green napkin and pressed a crease along one side. Heat and steam rose from the ironing board in moist waves that curled the ends of her hair and prickled sweat on her upper lip.

She wanted a big, cold drink, and not Julia's peach tea either unless the glass was served with a healthy splash of gin.

Disgusted with the destructive line of thought, she slammed the iron down. Julia poked her head around the door facing. "Everything okay in here?"

"I hate ironing." Mostly, she hated herself.

Julia shot her an amused glance. "You say that every time." And then more seriously, "What did you and Mama fight about yesterday? She was pretty upset all afternoon."

"The usual. She doesn't approve of my lifestyle." True enough.

"Oh." Julia retreated to the kitchen as Valery had known she would. Keep the code of silence. Except Valery hadn't followed the rules. She'd blabbed everything. And in trying to purge her own guilt, she'd hurt the person who loved her most.

No matter how much they differed, Valery believed with all her heart that Mama loved her. Mama wanted what was best for her. But best had meant giving away her tiny, perfect baby. Best meant pretending even now, sixteen years later, that a little girl had never been born.

All of which put Valery right back where she started. Angry, hurt and unresolved.

Some sins were unforgivable.

She needed a drink.

Turning off the iron, she braced the device on its stand and entered the kitchen. The pristine copper and cream room was empty, though something in the oven smelled of cinnamon.

Cinnamon rolls for afternoon refreshment, a favorite of Grayson's.

She poured a glass of peach tea, a pitiful substitute for mind-numbing bourbon, but after the other night, she'd sworn off. Again.

She wandered down a short hall to the inn's office and, finding the room empty, stepped inside and closed the door.

After taking the phone book from the top drawer, she thumbed to the correct page. *Alcoholics Anonymous.*

She stared at the words for long moments. Was she an alcoholic?

Nervous, fingers starting to shake a little, she flipped the page. She found a list of local churches, chose her mama's and tapped the numbers into her cell phone.

As the tone buzzed in her ear, she considered. According to the church directory, the pastor was available for individual counseling and held weekly group meetings. Would he talk to someone who didn't attend regularly? She'd sent the pastor a card when he'd broken his leg last year, and this month alone, she'd attended services twice. Was that enough?

A click sounded and then a masculine voice said, "Church office. Pastor Ramsey speaking."

He sounded kind and friendly as always, but Valery's throat refused to work. She couldn't do it. She couldn't admit the family-embarrassing problem to an outsider. Mama would be mortified.

Sick at heart and discouraged, she pressed End.

Over the next hour, Valery ironed every clean piece of linen she could find. Then she rescrubbed every vacant bathroom and finally went out to the orchard. The pink blooms, even fading as they were now, usually cheered her, and the gentle smell was divine. Today, she barely noticed. She paced the lanes between rows of fertile trees and fought the terrible desire to get drunk and forget everything.

Grayson was finished with her. She'd hurt her mother's feelings. She was miserable and terribly afraid she was losing control of her life. Maybe she already had.

Out of the corner of her eye, she saw a movement from the inn's upper story. She focused there and saw no one. A trick of the sun and shadows. She started to turn away, but music wafted on the wind. Was Grayson playing the baby grand? Had he returned early from work?

Or was the music in her imagination?

Valery closed her eyes and let the music flow over her. Familiar music from Patience Portland's composition book. Grayson played the song beautifully, and she imagined his long, capable fingers against the white keys. Tender fingers that had smoothed her hair away from her face, touched her cheek, and stroked her back in comfort when she'd been so terribly indisposed.

Grayson.

Sighing, she began to move to the melody, swaying and swirling, hands over her heart at first and then out to her sides as piercing sorrow and heartache gave way to pleasure.

The beauty of the music filled her chest, her senses, her mind and her heart. She didn't want the sound to ever stop. She wanted to go on feeling the joy and relief Patience wrote into her compositions.

Patience had known heartache, that much was clear, but she'd known joy, too. The truth flowed from her music. Maybe only another artist or another who'd faced sorrow could hear the message of hope. Valery heard it loud and clear.

Lost in a delicate waltz, Valery pretended she was in Grayson's arms floating over a polished dance floor. Happy. Free. In love.

The music stopped. Peach petals rained down upon her, brushing her skin with their silkiness. Slowly, she came out of her dream world, but the magical fantasy of dancing with Grayson cast a spell over her.

She wanted the dream to be real. To dance. To be with Grayson. To share everything, even the ugly part of her soul.

Valery gazed toward the house. No more shadows. No more secrets.

Suddenly, she could think of nothing but getting to him. She ran out of the peach orchard, her flats threatening to come off in the sprint across the lawn.

A car pulled down the drive. A pair of guests stared through the windshield at the half-crazed woman dashing toward the porch. She waved and, laughing, sped inside the inn and down the hall toward the family room.

She burst inside, breathing hard. "Grayson."

The room was empty, the piano lid closed.

Bewildered, she slowly walked to the baby grand. Patience's compositions were spread along the music rack next to a modern page of Grayson's precise print. She perused the notes. Using different notes and note combinations to form letters, he'd created a key to decipher Patience's secret notes. Above one measure, he had written 1864.

Brilliant. The man was a genius. A genius who might be in love with her.

Curious as to where he'd gone so quickly, she hurried upstairs to knock on his door.

No answer.

She tried Devlin's room. No answer there either.

Julia came out of the end guest room, a pile of linens in hand. "The Hendersons checked out early. Their daughter's having a baby."

A baby. Some of her excitement dimmed. "Need help?"

"I've got it." Julia shifted the load in her arms. "You tackled the ironing. I can handle this. If you're looking for Grayson, I'm guessing he's still at the mill."

"He hasn't been back since breakfast?"

"No."

Valery frowned. "Then who was playing the piano?"

Julia gave her a strange look. "When?"

"A couple of minutes ago. I heard—"

"I didn't hear any music. Are you sure you didn't hear a radio from a passing car?"

"I was in the orchard, so maybe." Not a chance. Patience's melodies were from another time, another world. "If you don't need my help, I'm going to the mill for a minute. I won't be long."

Julia flashed a bright smile, her look speculative. Before her sister could ask, Valery spun toward the stairs and started down. The carpet needed vacuuming. Later.

The urge to talk to Grayson pushed her out the door and into her car. She could have walked through the fields to the mill, but if she had too long to think she might talk herself out of a long, honest conversation.

First of all, she needed to apologize for the other night. She owed him that above everything. She'd put him in an awkward position and hadn't spoken to him since. Her fault entirely.

Then, she would tell him the whole truth once and for all. If he rejected her, she wouldn't feel any worse than she had for days. Years, really.

Grayson was worth the risk of humiliation and rejection. She would share her soul and let him decide if their relationship meant enough to forgive her. This might be the only chance she had to make things right again. She didn't want to lose him. She couldn't lose him without at least trying to set things right.

The old abandoned mill was abandoned no more. Pickup trucks and construction machinery crowded the lane, and noise broke the country quiet. A cement truck beeped and rumbled as concrete poured onto the new parking area. Near one side of the building, a pair of good old boys from the

Miniature Golf Café inspected the scaffolding and talked to a workman in a hard hat. Along with his sidekick, Poker Ringwald, Mr. B. had a morbid interest in the place now that a skeleton had been found. He was hoping for more bones.

Grayson's dream of repurposing the mill into a beautiful restaurant setting would soon be a reality.

She wanted to be part of his dreams. All of them.

Eyes turned away from the newly mortared foundation, a reminder that a man had been buried there all the times she'd come here as a child and again as an adult; Valery searched the area for Grayson.

In work coveralls and hard hat, Devlin appeared from inside the building. He waved. "He's under the waterwheel."

At her alarmed expression, he laughed. "Go on. You'll see him alive and well."

After a jaunty wave, she followed the trodden dirt path around the building and down the incline toward the creek and the bottom of the waterwheel. Water trickled over the falls on the right side of the mill, but the waterwheel on the left remained still and silent.

Grayson and the old vagrant, Lem Tolly, sat on the rocks.

Valery blinked twice, hardly believing her eyes. The workaholic businessman had taken time out of his busy day to sit on the bank and fish?

Her heart squeezed with emotion. The man with the schedule and multiple alarm clocks was learning to relax.

He looked up and saw her but didn't motion for her to join them. Silent and serious, he only stared, a crease between his eyebrows.

Insecurity swamped Valery. Perhaps he didn't want to talk to her. He hadn't sought her out yesterday, a first. Maybe he was ready to move on and forget her. Maybe she'd burned the last bridge, and he was unwilling to build another.

She should go back to the house and forget this nonsense.

But if she did she would be right back where she'd been for over sixteen years. Nowhere.

She searched his face and saw no sign of welcome.

Go, a voice inside her head seemed to insist.

Anxious and uncertain, a knot in her throat, she moved down the incline.

Saying nothing, Grayson watched her, his face unreadable.

She licked dry lips. "Hi."

"Hi."

They held each other's gaze, saying no more.

Valery's heart thundered in her chest. Her knees trembled enough to know she'd lost her nerve. Grayson didn't want her here. She didn't want to be anywhere else.

For an extrovert, she was suddenly tongue-tied, confidence gone. She didn't know what to say.

The grizzled man broke the painful spell. "I'm Lem Tolly."

"Yes, sir. I've seen you around, and Grayson's told me about you."

He chuckled as if he knew Grayson had described him as eccentric and mysterious. "Did you bring your fishing gear?"

She flashed him a nervous smile, grateful for the interruption. "Not today."

Grayson stared out at the glassy pool of water, silent.

"I should probably go—"

"Sit down, child. You didn't come all this way to leave again."

No, she hadn't. Tucking her skirt, she sat.

"What's on your mind, young lady?"

"Nothing really."

"Uh-huh." He spun the handle on his reel. "You wouldn't have a smoke, would you?"

Grayson laughed and shook his head but kept his attention on the water.

"No, sir."

"Figures. The two of you going to sit here and avoid each other or talk about what's eatin' ya?"

When neither of them replied, he sighed. "I reckon the time has come."

Both she and Grayson swiveled toward him. "The time for what?"

"Remember what you said to me, Grayson? That I might know more than I let on?"

"I remember."

"You were right." To Valery he said, "Smart fella, this one."

"A genius." Her eyes flashed to Grayson and quickly away.

"Smart, but not smart enough to know he can't control time."

She jumped to Grayson's defense. "He's getting there. He's a busy man. People need his expertise."

"And you, young lady, are smart, as well."

She snorted. No one ever said that about party Val.

"Laugh if you will, but let me tell you a story. It's a puzzle I've been trying to piece together since I was a boy." He reeled in the line and placed the pole at his side. "I couldn't until I met you. Both of you. You held the missing parts."

Valery blinked. "We did?"

"You and this mill." He rubbed yellowed fingers over a long, silver mustache. "My grandpappy told stories. Most of them were about his daddy and mama back in the late 1800s. Old stories that my mama and me wondered about. Were they true?"

Beneath her palms the rocks felt warm. The sun was hot on the top of her head. "What kind of stories?"

"About this old gristmill, although it wasn't old in my

grandfather's day." He hitched a thumb over his shoulder. "And that house up there. Peach Orchard Farm."

"You mean Peach Orchard Inn?"

"No, ma'am. I'm talking about way back when this place was Peach Orchard Farm and Mill, built by the Portland family."

"Did your grandfather know the Portlands?"

Lem's faded blue eyes held a thousand mysteries as he nodded. "You might say so, child. You might say so."

CHAPTER 29

You go digging in the past you're bound to find some skeletons.

UNKNOWN

1864. Peach Orchard Farm

The weather wasn't too bad for November, and Christmas was coming on fast. Not that twelve-year-old Tandy expected anything from Christmas. Most years, the women fixed a fine meal, and all the hands got the day off. Miss Charlotte and Mr. Edgar handed out new shoes and clothes along with blankets and other fine treasures, including candy and sometimes a toy. Before the war, Tandy had received a jackknife he still carried in his pocket like any sensible farm boy.

When the Union Army and Captain Will left a while back, they'd taken most of the farm's winter supplies. That's why Christmas wouldn't come this year. Anyway, that was what Master Edgar said. He hated Yankees worse than anybody.

Tandy didn't, though. Captain Will had been good to him, even giving him and Ben a set of fancy marbles from his Ohio factory. He sure missed the captain. Ben did, too, and from the stories whispered in the slave quarters, maybe Miss Charlotte missed him more than she was supposed to.

That was why Ben wasn't in any mood to play, and even though the weather wasn't all that cold outside, he wouldn't go hunting or climb trees. Who could blame him? What Mr. Edgar done was wrong. He'd done locked Miss Charlotte in her room. Tandy didn't understand all of the situation, but Ben said her punishment had to do with Captain Will and the fact that he wrote letters to Ben's mama.

Miss Charlotte was a fine, godly woman who doctored the slaves and taught the young ones to read. She wouldn't never do nothing wrong. She was only being kind to Captain Will, the way she'd been kind to every single soldier who had bled on her pretty polished floors.

Master Edgar, though, he could be a mean man when he was in a temper. And he was in a temper most times, so Tandy did his best to stay out of his owner's sight. Even if Edgar was Ben's pappy, Ben was kind of scared of him, too. Especially now, after what he'd done to Miss Charlotte. Weren't right. Not right at all. 'Course Tandy never spoke a word against Master Edgar. A slave child knew better, but he listened and watched.

The house was nervous. That's what Mama said. Like there was gonna be a tornado but nobody knew when or where the storm would hit.

Tandy tried to lay low, helping out where he was told and keeping out of Master Edgar's way. Mostly, he worked with Old Hob or Johnny around the farm, chopped wood, toted water and other chores. Sometimes, like tonight, when the master was in his office and no one else was around, Tandy hid in a dark corner of the big house and listened to Miss Patience play the piano. She didn't mind. Sometimes she gave him a cookie.

He didn't know if Master Edgar would whoop him for being in the house without permission, but he was good at hiding, and he'd do about anything to be near Miss Patience.

Even if he was only twelve, he knew what love was. And he loved Miss Patience. His heart fairly burst out of his chest whenever she talked to him.

Not that he'd ever breathe a word to anyone. Not even Benjamin. He didn't want the master's buggy whip across his back.

Mama was still in the kitchen cleaning up. Who knew where Miss Josie had run off to, and Miss Patience sat at the piano in the parlor. The parlor was a handsome room, even if the army had made a mess of things and all the rugs had been burned because of the blood. The fireplace crackled with wood he'd chopped himself, and the room was much warmer and more cheerful than the cabins in the quarter. So he stayed out of sight behind the heavy drapes and hoped no one would run him off.

Patience scribbled at a piece of sheet music as she often did, occasionally running her gifted fingers over the keys. Then, she'd stop and madly scribble again, writing down music only she could hear.

Tandy was in awe of this magic thing Miss Patience did, just as he was in awe of the woman herself. She was the most beautiful creature on earth. Probably in Heaven, too.

Free with a smile and a word of encouragement, she had sweet ways that made Tandy feel important, like a man. Some said she wasn't smart, but he thought anyone who could work magic on the piano must have a special kind of mind.

Though the garden had been trampled last summer by the Yankee soldiers, Miss Patience still smelled like the pretty lavender flowers. Mama said there were streets of gold up in Heaven and a crystal river and gates of pearl, and Jesus didn't care what color you was. You was free and He loved you. With all that fancy business, Heaven must have a good smell, too. And that smell was Patience Portland.

Sometimes she'd see him hiding in the shadows, smile a secret smile, and invite him to sit with her at the piano. Those were the times he lived for. Even with his worry over Ben and Miss Charlotte, Tandy was in paradise with Patience.

She was older than him, but not too old, and Tandy figured someday he'd catch up with her. When he did, he'd court and marry her. At least in his dreams. They'd run off together some place where no one cared about color or age.

The trill of high piano notes trickled through him the way cool creek water flowed between his toes on a hot day. He sighed, happy as if he wasn't a slave boy who didn't stand a hope of courting a beautiful white woman like Miss Patience.

"What do you think, Tandy?" She turned on the piano bench to inquire of him in the shadows, her pale eyebrows puckered together like Miss Josie's skirt gathers. His heart soared. She'd known he was there the whole time.

Tandy stepped away from the concealing draperies, his chest swelled with pleasure at being singled out. "Prettiest music I ever did hear."

Her eyes, blue as a bluebird's wing, smiled at him. "You always say that."

"'Cause you always write pretty music."

Patience cast a glance at the window where the sky had faded to the dark blue of the Yankee uniforms. When he was older, he might be a Yankee, too, and fight for freedom. He wasn't sure what that meant, but the slave men secretly whispered of emancipation among themselves.

"One more tune and then I must go."

"Go where, Miss Patience?" He shouldn't have asked. Prying wasn't his place. Would she be mad?

She gave him a vague, startled look. "Oh. Nowhere. Up to my room...to finish my mending."

Tandy didn't believe her. Sometimes Miss Patience went for walks at night. He didn't think anyone else noticed, but he knew, and he worried about her out there in the darkness. He'd made up his mind to follow her the next time in case a bear or a mountain lion, or worse, a bushwhacker got after her.

A pretty lady alone at night, in the wild Tennessee country-side when a war was raging, was not safe. No way. No how.

Though his heart broke into a million pieces, he suspected she met a beau somewhere away from the watchful eyes of her brother, who happened to be Master Edgar. Tandy hoped her secret love was Johnny. Since he couldn't marry Miss Patience, Tandy wouldn't mind so much if she married the blind Yankee soldier. He liked Johnny, and he thought Miss Patience liked him, too.

Edgar wouldn't like it one bit, though. He purely hated Yankees and only allowed the handful of wounded soldiers to stay because having them here meant the Federals wouldn't burn Peach Orchard Farm.

To his disappointment, Miss Patience rose from the piano and, taking the sheet music with her, went up the stairs.

Tandy wasn't allowed to go up there unless he was with Benjamin or one of the family, so he meandered into the kitchen to see his mother. She scolded him for lingering in the house, worried Mr. Edgar would see him. Then she hugged him hard, gave him a piece of pone and sent him to their cabin in the quarters.

The moon shone a cold light on the trodden path between the big house and the cluster of small shacks. Tonight the shuttered cabin windows glowed with warm fires. They'd go out by morning and the rooms would be shivery cold. He knew because he lived in one and woke every winter morning in a huddled ball, too cold to get up. But for now the sound of Pierce's harmonica called to him, friendly and warm.

He was almost to his and Mama's cabin when he spotted a lantern flare near the back porch of the big house. Tandy stopped, instantly suspecting the identity of the night traveler, and watched as the light moved across the yard toward the fallow fields between the farm and the gristmill.

The lantern was trimmed low, barely a candle flicker, but Tandy had night owl eyes.

"Miss Patience," he whispered.

His heart dropped to his belly. She was heading toward the mill, even though it was closed for the night and she had no business there.

Unless...

Pone rumbled in his stomach, unsettled.

Unless she was going to meet her beau.

Burning with jealousy and afraid for her even in his hurt, Tandy set his face like flint and followed, hanging back enough that she wouldn't notice him but close enough to keep a watchful eye. He was accustomed to being silent and unseen.

Though Captain Will and his men were gone, soldiers, or worse, deserters, could appear from anywhere at any time. A woman out alone at night in these troubled times was in danger.

What kind of beau asked her to do that? Must be a deserter, a no-account. A good man would come to the big house and speak to the master.

One thing for sure, her man could not be Johnny. Johnny loved her, and he watched over her as much as a blind man could do. He wouldn't put her in danger, and he'd be mad as a bull in a beehive that someone else had.

Whether the man was Yankee or Reb, with a certainty borne of youth and unrequited love Tandy despised Miss Patience's beau.

At the edge of the clearing leading around to the massive front double doors of the mill, Tandy hung back in the weeds. Patience glanced around as if sensing his presence, and he sank lower, holding his breath. She stood for a moment, still and watchful as a doe, before sliding a key inside the big lock. The heavy door groaned open, and the dark inside swallowed her up.

Tandy sprang from his hiding place and raced to the entrance, listening for a moment before creeping inside. The building was as dark as Old Hob's hide, so he stood, waiting for his eyes to adjust.

Where had Miss Patience gone?

"Were you followed?" A male voice spoke quietly into the darkness.

Tandy jerked, heart thundering like a thousand horses.

"No." Miss Patience's answer was soft, sweet, anxious. "But I thought I heard something when I came in."

Silent as death, Tandy slid out of sight behind the stairs leading up to the second level and listened with all that was in him.

"I wager you heard rats, Patience. The mill is full of varmints after the grain. I heard them, too."

"Then we're safe?"

"As safe as we'll be until this bloody war is over."

She sighed, a disheartened sound that drifted on the corn-scented air. "I pray that comes soon."

"As do I, dear lady. As do I. But until then—"

Tandy slid from his hiding place, heart aching but, like a moth to flame, compelled to see with his own eyes the man who had stolen Patience's heart.

He knew the mill well, right down to the smell of powdery meal and grain burnt by the massive grinding wheels. He knew the bins and stacks of corn, the tools on the walls, the augers and separators. Master Edgar sent him here often to load corn or tote finished meal to customers' wagons.

So he quickly located the speakers by sound. Miss Patience and her beau were to his left, near Master Edgar's office.

He eased one eye around the wooden staircase and edged closer until he saw the glow of the lantern. He paused, holding his breath again until he was certain they neither heard nor saw him. Though their figures were shadowy, he could see Miss Patience standing close to a tall, lean man in dark clothes. The lantern glowed at their feet, casting spooky shadows onto the planked floor.

"Here." Patience offered something to the man. "Should anyone ask, I wrote this song for you. I hope you find it... pleasing."

Pleasing? Any man who didn't appreciate the magic created by Miss Patience was a fool who didn't deserve her.

"Everything you've given me is perfect." The man took the music and touched Patience's cheek, caressing her skin. She tilted her head into his hand.

Corn pone rose in Tandy's throat. She loved another. Even the beautiful songs she played were written for him.

"This will all be over soon and then—" The man glanced to one side. Tandy eased deeper into the shadows.

He heard their movements and imagined an embrace, maybe even a kiss, and he was sick to think it. When he could bear no more, he crept outside and waited to follow her safely home.

CHAPTER 30

1864. Peach Orchard Farm

"What you moping around for, boy?" Blind Johnny, as Tandy and Ben secretly called him, tilted his head in Tandy's direction. "You been polishing on that one breast collar half the day and haven't said three words."

"Sorry, Mr. Johnny," Tandy mumbled.

He was moping, all right. Moping, thinking, wishing he hadn't seen what he saw. All the while he worried about Miss Patience. She oughtn't to be meeting a man that way. It wasn't safe. If anyone found out, her reputation would suffer. What kind of man asked her to do that? A coward, that's what. Or a man she ought not to see. A man she was ashamed to know. Master Edgar would have a hissy fit.

"Let me see that collar."

Tandy thought it was funny how Johnny said, "Let me see," as if he could. For certain, his fingers knew things, and he could find a speck of rust on a horse's bit or a worn leather harness faster than Tandy, but Johnny couldn't see a lick.

"I sure am sorry, Mr. Johnny, sir, but I ain't done cleaning it yet."

He didn't want Johnny to get mad at him. He liked Johnny,

and the blind man was patient and friendly. Today, they were cleaning and repairing tack in the carriage house, a winter job. Johnny was teaching him a skill the master insisted he learn, and one he was glad to have. Keeping the tack clean and repaired was better than chopping wood and threshing corn.

"Let me see anyway."

Tandy placed the heavy horse collar in the man's lap, and Johnny ran his hands all over the leather. "Right there, Tandy. See that? A weakness. You got to fix it or the leather won't hold. Bad tack can get somebody hurt."

Tandy's shoulders sagged. He couldn't do nothing right. He felt puffed up, mad and sad, and he guessed he was.

Johnny returned the collar, his head aimed in Tandy's direction. Even if his eyes was covered up with dark glasses, Tandy knew Johnny was staring at him.

"You gonna tell me what's eating on you?"

Tandy considered spilling the beans but, like him, Johnny was sweet on Patience. No use breaking his heart, too.

"I think I got the melancholy, Mr. Johnny, sir. Ben, too."

"A right shame what's going on in that house. Miss Charlotte's a virtuous woman."

Tandy didn't know what virtuous was, but the word sounded good, and Miss Charlotte was all that and more. Even Mama said so, and Mama never missed a lick. They were all worried about Miss Charlotte locked away in her room like a prisoner. Which he supposed she was. A prisoner in her own house. Was she gonna be a slave now, too?

"Ain't there nothing we can do for her?"

"A man's got a right to treat his wife however he chooses, even if it's bad. That's the law."

Didn't seem like a good law to Tandy. But then, a lot of white people's laws didn't seem so good to him.

"If I had a woman as fine as Miss Charlotte—" Johnny

smoothed his hands over the harness, his sightless eyes staring off into the distance "—I'd treat her well, like the lady she is."

Once more, Tandy considered telling Johnny about Patience's secret meetings at the mill. She was a lady, too. Johnny wouldn't let her go roaming late at night where anything might happen.

But in the end Tandy didn't say a word, and he lived to regret his silence.

That night, after a supper of turnips and ham, Patience was fidgety and jumpy. Tandy had seen her moving around the upstairs and in the master's office, but when she'd spotted him watching, she pretended to be hunting for her sewing basket.

Tandy wasn't stupid. He knew where she kept her basket, and it wasn't any of the places he'd seen her. He didn't know what she was up to, but he worried she might sneak off again to see *him,* and jealousy burned in his belly.

Once again as the sunlight faded, she sat at her piano scribbling madly. When he entered the parlor, she startled.

"Tandy, I declare." She pressed a hand to her bodice. "You frightened me half to death."

"Begging your pardon, Miss Patience. Are you all right? Would you be needing anything?"

Two spots of red appeared on her cheeks. She looked all flustered and flummoxed. "Why, I'm fine, silly goose. Why wouldn't I be?"

Her words stabbed Tandy right in the chest. Miss Patience never talked down to him that way, as if he was a foolish bother. Now he knew for sure something was up.

Master Edgar appeared in the doorway. "Boy! What are you doing in here? Get your hide back where you belong."

"I called him, Edgar, to run an errand for me." Patience widened her blue eyes in Tandy's direction. "Go on now,

Tandy. Get me some headache powder from your mama, and be quick about it."

Grateful, Tandy slunk from the room to get the powder he knew she didn't need and returned to an empty parlor. When he moved to the piano to leave the pain remedy, he noticed something. The paper she'd been scribbling on was gone.

Heavy-hearted, he knew why she was nervous. She was meeting her beau again tonight with another love song.

He considered letting her walk alone this time, but his love was stronger than his disappointment. Miss Patience needed a man to keep her safe in the dark. If he couldn't marry her, he could be her guard. Wouldn't nobody object to that, not even the master.

Once outside, the night air nipped at him, much colder, and he shivered in his thin jacket, wishing he could run full out and work up a sweat. But if Patience found out he followed her, she'd laugh at him, or worse, realize how he felt about her. He'd die of humiliation. So, he ambled along in the nippy wind, pausing when she paused, walking when she walked but always careful to keep his distance.

After she entered the mill, he snuck into his hiding place and settled to wait. He was her secret protector. Even if she never knew, he'd make sure her travels to and fro were safely conducted. Not like her beau, who let her roam about the countryside alone and vulnerable.

Minutes later, a tall man entered the building and moved in the direction of the office. His footfalls echoed like ghost cries. The tales Old Hob had told Tandy about the devil and dead men rose up to grab him in the dark. He shivered again, but not from the cold.

The man extinguished his lantern, and the building was blacker than Lucifer's heart. Gooseflesh prickled Tandy's skin. He had a bad feeling but didn't know why.

Maybe the devil was coming to get him.

"Jack?" Patience's voice sounded uncertain and strange enough that Tandy peeked around the stairs.

He couldn't see well, not with only one lantern burning and that one as low as possible. But he watched the man put his hands on Patience and pull her close. He saw the kiss, saw her cloak slide to the floor.

He shouldn't watch, and in truth, he couldn't.

Sick inside worse than the grip, Tandy hustled out of the mill, moping to know his suspicions were true. Maybe soon she'd marry and leave Peach Orchard. The bleak thought liked to split his heart right in half.

He found his way down the steep incline to the area below the waterwheel and inches from the silvery black creek, a place he and Ben liked to play and where the air was warmed by the gears and pulleys of the mill. Head in his hands, he settled next to the giant, silent wheel to wait and mope.

A scream ripped the night. Tandy bounced to his feet.

"Miss Patience?" he yelled.

Another scream sent him scrambling up the incline. He fell, felt the dirt and rock dig into his knees but clawed the earth to rise again and race inside the mill.

Patience screamed a third time as Tandy rounded toward Edgar's office, his feet thundering on the wood as hard as his heart thundered in his chest. Patience and the man were on the floor, her dress bunched above her legs. She fought and scratched, begging him to stop. The man drew back and struck her.

Patience went silent.

Tandy knew what was happening. He'd been around the animals in heat season. He'd heard the talk in the quarters. Worse, he'd heard the same kinds of sounds coming from the slave cabins a time or two.

His knees shook, and he was more afraid than he'd ever been in his life, but he had to stop the man from hurting her any more. Patience was a maiden lady. No man had a right, but this man was big, much larger than Tandy. A boy would be an ant against a bull, the same as Miss Patience.

Desperate for a weapon, he scrambled the length of the building toward the back room where Master Edgar kept the tools. Behind him came the horrible grunts and groans and the sound of Miss Patience's pitiful cries.

Hands shaking, he stumbled inside the storeroom and frantically felt along the dark walls until he found something, anything to make the man stop. He had to make him stop. He had to. He was her protector. And there was nobody else around.

Pitchfork in hand, he raced back to the mill office. Wild with terror and fury, he screamed, "Stop!"

The man paid him no mind.

The grunts and noises sickened Tandy until he thought he might vomit.

"Stop! Stop it!" He raised the pitchfork and with all the strength gained from chopping wood and hauling tow sacks, Tandy plunged the sharp tines into the man's back.

The man stiffened, and for a frozen instance, time stood still. Then, with a quiver and a jerk, the stranger collapsed, tumbling to one side. A final gurgle escaped his lips, and evil lay still.

Crying now, his vision clouded by tears and his body quaking, Tandy hurried to Patience's side. Her torn clothes and bruised body shocked him. Even in the low light, the sight was pure awful. He reached down to straighten her skirt, but she cried out, shrank back and tried to crawl away.

"Miss Patience, I'm Tandy. Tandy. Don't worry. He won't hurt you no more. I'm gonna cover you up. That's all. Don't be scared no more. Please, Miss Patience." His voice broke on the last part. He hadn't kept her safe. He'd tried but he'd failed.

Wild, terrified eyes gazed out as if she didn't see him, but she didn't move away when, gently, he straightened the torn clothes and covered her battered, quaking body, his head turned away from her humiliation. Curled into a ball, she whimpered, keening the scariest sound he'd ever heard.

Tears dripped from his chin and clogged his nose. He swiped at them with his sleeve and stood for a long, lost minute, wondering what to do next. Patience's attacker didn't move. Tandy touched the inert form, afraid the man was dead. Afraid he wasn't.

And then he ran.

CHAPTER 31

1864. Peach Orchard Farm

Tandy no longer noticed the cold as he raced like a madman toward the quarters. Legs trembling, tears falling, he stopped once and lost his supper. Then he ran again, praying and begging sweet baby Jesus for help.

He'd get Mama. She'd know what to do. Mama would help Miss Patience.

As he broke into the clearing near the cabins, he slammed directly into a large, bulky form. A hand caught him by the scruff of the neck and yanked him up like an unwanted pup.

"Whoa there, boy, what are you up to?" A lantern lifted high overhead, and a man's fleshy face peered down.

Tandy raised his eyes to Master Edgar. He didn't wonder then what the master was doing in the quarters. And it didn't matter anyway. Master Edgar could be anywhere he wanted to be.

Too scared to lie and too breathless for detail, he blurted, "Miss Patience. She's hurt. A man..."

The enormity overwhelmed him, and he began to sob again. He didn't aim to. He was a man and men didn't cry, but the tears kept coming.

Edgar gave Tandy a hard shake.

"Speak clear, boy. What's happened? Where?" The master's tone was harsh and impatient.

Tandy shuddered in a breath. "The mill. A—a—man—forced her. On the floor. She's hurt. I think he's...dead."

The master spun toward the mill, then back toward Tandy. Voice grim and threatening, he shoved a finger in Tandy's face. "Not a word of this to anyone. You hear me, boy? Not one word."

The master had blood in his eyes. "Yes, sir. Please, sir, hurry. She's hurt."

As scared as he was of Master Edgar, the farm owner was Miss Patience's brother. He'd take care of his baby sister.

Edgar gave him a rough push in the mill's direction, and together they rushed across the fields and traversed the road. Though the master had a crippled foot, he moved fast. The limp barely slowed him down.

They reached the mill, and once inside, the pitiful sound of Miss Patience's whimpers brought a curse from Master Edgar. Handing the lantern to Tandy, he gave a dismissing glance at the inert stranger and knelt by Patience's side.

Tandy averted his gaze, not wanting to see the pitchfork poking up from the man's back.

"Edgar's here, baby sister. Don't you worry. I will take care of this."

Awkwardly, as if unsure how to show tenderness, the master patted Miss Patience's hair. Then he rose and moved toward the man, motioning to Tandy to follow. "Hold the light higher so I can see him."

Tandy knew better than to refuse, though he feared losing his supper again. He'd prayed he was in a nightmare and that he hadn't really thrust a pitchfork into someone's back, but there it was, sticking straight up.

Master Edgar held his hand over the man's mouth. "He's dead."

Tandy began to wail.

The master backhanded him. "Stop it! Stop that noise. We have work to do."

Tandy shuddered the cries back down his throat and watched in horror as the master shoved a boot against the man's side and yanked the pitchfork loose.

He jabbed the handle toward Tandy. "Take this to the creek and clean the tines good. Then get back in here."

Though he was loath to touch the pitchfork, especially the bloody tines, Tandy did as he was told. Miss Patience's piteous whimpers followed him out of the mill.

He'd killed a man. Killed him dead.

Scared as Tandy was, he was glad the sorry soul was in hell where he belonged.

Nobody could hurt Miss Patience and get by with it.

When he returned, the master had already managed to load the dead man onto a cart normally used to tote bags of corn and meal. Like the pitchfork, Tandy would never look at the cart the same again.

"What we gonna do with him, Master?"

"The only thing we can do." The master's face was grim. "If anyone finds out what happened here, my sister will be ruined…and you'll be hanged. Or worse."

Tandy's knees went out from under him. He collapsed on the floor. What Master Edgar said was true. He hadn't thought the situation all the way through. He'd killed a white man. No matter what the white man had done to Patience, Tandy was black and black didn't kill white.

"I didn't mean to. I only wanted him to stop hurting Miss Patience."

"Won't matter and you know it. Get up. Stop sniveling. You're a man now. Act like one."

"Did I do wrong?"

For once, the master paused to look at him. Almost with pride, he laid a hand on Tandy's shoulder. "No, boy. You did right. But you and Patience are both in danger. You must never tell a soul what happened here tonight. Not if you want to stay alive. You understand?"

Tandy swallowed thick regret and fear. He glanced again at Patience. At some point, Master Edgar had laid his coat over her.

He heard what the master was telling him. If word got out, he would be tortured and hanged, and Miss Patience would be ruined. No matter that she was innocent and Tandy had had no choice. They would both be judged guilty.

"Yes, sir. But what we gonna say about Miss Patience? She's hurt and her face be all bruised up."

"We'll tell everyone she took a bad fall. She'll rest in bed for a few days to convalesce. That's all anyone needs to know. She'll recover and forget all about this."

Tandy looked at the broken woman lying on the floor. Her white hair tangled and loose, her eyes were closed, and tears dampened the floor around her. Her body still quivered and shook. And she made that awful keening noise.

He didn't think Miss Patience would ever forget this night. How could she? He never would. But he knew better than to argue with the master.

"She's cold, Master. Shaking so bad."

"We have blankets in the office. Get them."

When Tandy returned with the covers, Edgar knelt once more by Patience. Stroking her hair, he said, "Rest now, baby sister. I will keep this ugly night a secret between the three of us. I promise you, no one but us will ever know. I will make certain of that." His jaw tightened. "And no one will hurt you ever again."

Tandy gently spread the blanket over her curled body, taking heart when she gripped the edge with shaking fingers, fingers that could make magic, fingers that came from Heaven.

How could anyone hurt Miss Patience?

Edgar patted her head again. "We're going to get rid of this filthy Yankee, and we'll be back for you. Rest now. We're close by. Tandy will come running if you call."

Though her eyes didn't open, silent, silver tears continued to stream across her cheeks and puddle on the floor. A crumpled sheet of music lay a few feet away.

Tandy's chest hurt so bad, he could hardly breathe.

"Let's get a move on, Tandy. To the basement with this piece of trash."

It was the first time in Tandy's life Master Edgar had called him by name.

Together he and the master carted the dead body to the lower stairs and pushed him over. He thumped and thudded and tumbled all the way into the basement.

Edgar stood at the top for a few seconds, catching his breath. "Get the lanterns and the shovels. We've got a long night ahead of us."

Tandy raced up the stairs, stopping to look at Miss Patience and whisper his concern before gathering the needed tools to bury a man. That's what they were about to do. Him and the master. They were gonna bury a man in the dirt floor basement.

When he returned, Master Edgar was shoving aside a rough-hewn table sometimes used for oiling gears or sharpening tools. A long swath of moist dirt spread out along one block wall.

Grim and silent, they each took up a shovel and began to

dig. After fifteen minutes both sweated, though the basement was chilly and smelled like rotted leaves. Master Edgar paused and leaned on his shovel, out of breath, his round belly heaving. Masters didn't do much shoveling.

"Want me to go get Pierce, Master Edgar, sir? He's a good digger and don't talk much." Pierce dug all the family graves and soldier graves, too.

The master panted like a dog, eyeing him with a look Tandy had never seen before. A look that scared Tandy even more.

When he finally spoke, his words were solemn, slow and certain. "No. Leave Pierce be. I don't want to have to sell him, too."

The cold fingers of fate squeezed Tandy's throat as realization set in. He'd killed a white man. He was doomed, one way or the other.

Master was gonna sell him.

CHAPTER 32

1875. Colorado

Tandy's story stunned Benjamin speechless for several seconds. The long-ago night's terrible events flickered through his mind, both shocking and revealing.

Birds twittered and fluttered through Colorado aspens whispering in the breeze, but the Tennessee scene in his head brewed dark and cold.

"I killed him." Tandy, now a man grown, gazed at his palms as if seeing that terrible night and the deadly encounter. "With all my weight and strength, I drove a pitchfork clean through his loathsome heart."

The thick knot of horror gripped Ben's chest.

"You saved her. Killed to protect her." He balled his hands into fists. "And for your heroism my father sold you."

"I do not wish to justify Edgar Portland or his reprehensible deeds, especially concerning my mother." Tandy offered Ben a sidelong glance. "At times, during those early weeks away, scared and lonely, I wished I had plunged the pitchfork into him as well. Does that shock you?"

Ben drew a hand over his face and squeezed at his cheeks.

Shocked? Perhaps. But where Edgar deserved no compassion, Tandy did.

"You should have been rewarded, not sent away."

"You're not seeing clear, Ben. You think a black boy wouldn't hang for murdering a white man?"

"It wasn't murder."

"We both know the law wouldn't see things that way. They'd see color. I would die, and Miss Patience would be dragged through a trial, humiliated and shamed when none of it was her fault." He wagged his head from side to side. "Do not mistake my meaning, Ben. Your father was every bit as vile as the Yankee, but secrets told can get a man, or in my case, a boy, killed. Edgar knew the best-kept secret was the one farthest away."

"I never guessed."

"That's the way we intended. Patience deserved no less."

"Nor did you." Ben turned saddened eyes on his half brother. "Yet the man's death drove you away."

Tandy's face went hard as granite. "He deserved to die. I do not regret being the instrument of his entry into hell."

Ben bent for a rock and turned it over in his hands, absently wondering if the sparkle was gold. Tandy had killed. He hadn't murdered.

"I recall when Patience fell from the wagon and wasn't herself for a time, but we all took my father's word for what happened." His mouth twisted. "He left us little choice."

Tandy removed the rock from Ben's hand.

"Fool's gold." Tandy scratched his thumb over the shiny yellow surface. "A rock that claims to be gold and yet is not entirely what it appears. Like some situations. Make no mistake, Benjamin, our father was not altruistic in his decision concerning me. He was livid at my mama and yours because of the secret letters, and he jumped at the fortuitous opportunity to send me away and kill two birds with one stone—preserving Patience's secret and punishing our mothers. Miss Charlotte and Mama would pay for their sin with my salvation."

Ben's nostrils flared. "Being sold like an animal is not salvation for anyone." Tandy didn't reply for a moment. Instead, he put a thumb on the rough edge of the rock and curled his index fingers along the bottom. Then he let it fly. The fool's gold skipped merrily for a few feet before the foamy current swallowed it up in one quick gulp.

As water covered over the scar, Tandy spoke again. "Being sold to Robert Wellston became the best thing that ever happened to me. Eventually."

Ben startled. His gaze flew to the brown face of his brother. "I don't understand. How could that be possible? You were forced to leave everything and everyone you knew. Even your mother."

"And don't think I didn't mourn all of you and despise your father with everything in me, but Wellston was a staunch abolitionist, a devout Methodist. Though I didn't know it at the time, he bought me to free me—after I'd learned a trade and how to take care of myself. I wasn't the first slave child he purchased, but I was the last and the most fortunate. He believed if he bought as many child slaves as he could, he could change their futures. And he did." A soft smile lit Tandy's eyes. "Remember that story your mama used to read to us? About Joseph in the Old Testament?"

Ben hiked an eyebrow, puzzled by the reference. "His own brothers sold him into slavery, away from everything he loved and knew."

"In the end, Joseph's life was better and lives were saved. Edgar, like those brothers, did not intend the sale for my benefit, and had he known Wellston for an abolitionist, he would have likely sent me elsewhere. Yet the hand of providence took his cruel actions and gave me a better life. A life I value."

Tandy clapped a hand on Ben's shoulders. "Now you understand why I can never return to Honey Ridge. Not even to see my mama."

"But years have passed. No one suspects."

Eyes wise with experiences Ben could only imagine gazed at him sadly. "A man is still buried under the mill."

"Did Papa know who he was?"

"A Union courier, according to the things we found in his pockets."

"But why was he in the mill that night? Was he courting Patience? A Union man?"

"She'd never seen him before. Her beau was a Reb, Jack someone. She'd begun meeting him when the Federals camped at the house to share messages in code about anything the captain or the men spoke of that might help the Confederacy. After the army moved out, she continued by sneaking information from Captain Will's letters to Miss Charlotte."

"The code. Was it written in her piano music? Her compositions?"

"Had to be. She always took the sheet music with her."

"Patience was a spy." Ben could barely take it in.

Tandy laughed lightly. "Last person you'd ever suspect, which is likely why the Rebs recruited her. That, and she was already sweet on Jack. Your father figured the dead man somehow discovered the subterfuge and waited for his chance to take revenge."

Ben noted Tandy's careful reference to their father and did not blame him for his reluctance to claim kinship. "My aunt was that Yankee's revenge against the South."

"A guess, but I'd say yes. I've given the circumstances a

great deal of thought over the years, praying that no one comes looking for a missing Union courier."

"Many men were lost or never identified during the war. That's what Mama and the captain said. I think your secret is safe."

Tandy stepped away, shaking his head. "Nine years isn't long enough to separate a black man from murder. I have come too far to die with a noose around my neck."

As sorry as the situation was, Ben heard the truth in Tandy's words. No matter the reason or the time, in the eyes of the law, Tandy was guilty because of his mother's race.

"Papa had a room built in the basement—a room with a wood floor—to hold all manner of machinery along with an old worn-out granite wheel that weighs a ton. Never knew why he kept the thing. I realize now it was to cover the grave." Tandy couldn't come home, but Ben had one more promise to give. "You can be sure when I take over as owner no one will ever take a shovel to the basement floor. Not as long as I live."

Tandy sighed as if a weight had lifted. "I'm obliged. I am also relieved you know the truth."

"Such a secret must be a heavy load."

His half brother made a soft, huffing noise. "For years, I had nightmares of a man coming at me from the pits of hell with a pitchfork sticking out of his back."

"And now? Does he still haunt you?"

Tandy's teeth flashed white. "Now I dream of the woman carrying my baby child. Even with my eyes open, I dream of her. I'm a happy man, Benjamin. Life here is good to me."

"You don't miss us? You wouldn't like to fish the creek again and walk the woods and eat your mama's fried chicken?"

Tandy chuckled. "Now you're tempting me."

"Then come home. Travel back with me at least for a while.

Bring your wife and surprise your mama. Make her happy as nothing else could. Surely, you would be safe for a short visit."

Tandy sobered, his voice going soft and nostalgic. "How I'd dearly love to see her. But I cannot go, Ben. Don't ask me to risk everything now that I have a wife and a baby on the way. I must stay for them and for their future as well as my own."

"All right. All right." Ben sighed, resigned. Tandy's well-being was far more important than his own selfish longing to have the man return to Tennessee. "I'll say no more except to remind you that Lizzy will want to see that baby."

Tandy's face brightened. "Do you suppose she'll come to Colorado? If I write a letter and send her fare? Do you think she'll come so far?"

"You'd steal Lizzy from us?"

Teeth flashed. "If I can."

Ben laughed. "Then, I suppose all that's left to do is ask her."

CHAPTER 33

1875. Peach Orchard Farm

The return trip to Tennessee was much shorter than the journey east and then west. Ben arrived in September when the bees buzzed in the gardens and an occasional whiff of wind promised that cooler days were coming.

The family greeted him with exuberant joy. Mama wept and wept, though when asked, she declared she was the happiest woman in the world. Lizzy killed a fat hen that she claimed hadn't laid an egg all summer, and they feasted as if Christmas had come early.

When he'd shown the housekeeper Tandy's letter and handed over the envelope of money, Lizzy had gone silent as the grave, her eyes so wide he thought they'd pop.

"I have never seen that much money in my life." Then, as if the notion struck her between the eyes, she gripped Ben's wrist. "Tell me true, Benjamin. Is he an outlaw? Where did he get so much money? I hear of outlaws in the West. Tell me my boy is not a highwayman."

So Ben told her of Tandy's success at the hands of an abolitionist, and though Lizzy was not one to cry, she sniffled with pride. "My boy is a hotel owner? A fine, upstanding businessman?"

"Yes, ma'am. He is. A successful one. And he's going to be a pappy soon. You must take his offer and go."

She tilted her head in proud wonder. "Must I?"

"Yes," he said gently. "I insist."

So it was decided that Lizzy and Abram would travel to Denver. Though he hoped they'd return, Ben doubted if they ever would. Family was everything.

Family. Like his Aunt Patience.

His mind seldom strayed from Tandy's story of that fateful Christmas that had changed all their lives. If Ben was especially solicitous toward Patience, it was understandable. At least to him. She carried the secret weight of a rape and a man's death inside her soul. Such a thing was too much for anyone to bear alone. But bear the burden Patience had. The seemingly fragile woman was as strong as an oak.

On this particular day, a week after he'd arrived home to Peach Orchard, he saw her gazing out a window in the dining room. Wondering if the past still haunted her as it did him, he stepped up beside her.

Through the window he saw what held her attention. Or rather, who. Johnny Atkins moved through the expansive garden beyond the back porch where he tugged dark red beets from the earth. A wheelbarrow half filled was parked at his side.

"Somebody's going to be making beet pickles soon," Ben said.

She lifted her beautiful face, her lips curving. "Johnny does favor my pickles."

Johnny. The way she said his name was almost musical.

The lamp of knowledge flickered on inside Benjamin's

head. Johnny wasn't the only one carrying a flame for someone he thought he couldn't have.

"Aunt Patience, may I tell you something?"

She studied him, those guileless blue eyes showing concern and curiosity. "What is it? You look so serious."

"Tandy told me everything."

She sucked in a breath, the joy in her expression turned to shame. She turned her head aside.

"Ben. No." Her voice sounded so small and lonely.

"No one knows but me, and I shall never tell another soul." He took her hands in his. "But I believe there is someone *you* must tell. Someone who will understand as no other ever could. Someone who loves you with all his soul."

He peered pointedly toward the garden patch.

Patience shook her head. "I couldn't."

"Do you love him?"

She hesitated not at all. "Yes. But I'm not worthy of such a fine man."

"Are you aware that Johnny thinks the same? That he is not worthy of you because of his blindness and disfigurement?"

"But that's nonsense. Johnny Atkins is good and decent and so very smart. He's not a bit lazy, and his laugh is like the sun coming out after a storm." Two spots of indignant color blazed on her porcelain cheeks. "His wounds don't matter one iota to me. Handsome is as handsome does."

"He thinks the same of you."

She ducked her head. "Because he doesn't know the truth."

"Nor does he know you love him." Hands in his pockets, he focused on the outdoor scene and the hardworking Johnny. "Don't you think a good, decent man like Johnny deserves love in his life? Especially when the woman of his dreams loves him, too? How can you deny him the joy of love when you possess the power to give it? Is love not a gift from God Himself?"

She stood for a long time, staring out the window at the blind man whose heart she held. Finally, she said, "Does he love me? You're sure of this?"

"He told me so himself. He fears you will never return the feelings. His heart pines for you."

"Oh." Her hands covered her mouth as she thought and considered. "Johnny. Dear, dear Johnny. The handsomest heart in Tennessee."

"He's waiting to hear those words from you. You don't have to tell him everything at first unless you want to, but give the man a chance to court you. Put him out of his misery." He smiled a little when he said that. "Then, if love grows fonder, tell him everything. I promise you nothing will change his feelings."

"What if he is ashamed of me?"

"Not Johnny. Never Johnny."

Hope and determination began to rise in her voice as a symphony rises to a crescendo. "You are right, and I am self-ish. Johnny deserves to know the truth, so he can decide for himself. I want no subterfuge between us."

"Like you, he has known sorrow and loss not of his own making. I assure you, Johnny will love you all the more for your courage. Go to him. Tell him."

"Johnny loves me," she said in wonder. "I think I always knew. How awful of me to make him miserable."

Ben said no more. He didn't need to. Patience could work out the rest for herself. She was not nearly as simple as some believed, and what she didn't know with her mind, she understood with her heart. At least the important things.

She drew up her shoulders, stiff and straight as an arrow the way she'd been taught, this gentle soul with an iron spirit.

Then, she patted Benjamin's chest and swept across the room to the door and stepped out. She turned back for his assurance, and he gave her a nod. She nodded, too, smiled a radiant smile and raced across the porch.

Ben watched as she descended the steps, her skirt held off the dust, and called out, "Johnny!"

Johnny dropped the beets and whirled toward the beloved voice, face already wreathed in pleasure at the mere sound of his name on her lips. Couldn't she see the love shining there? Ben was sure she could as she approached her true love and began to speak.

Johnny stood in listening form, head cocked to one side, nodding over and over again. Even from this distance, Benjamin saw the wonder come over the blind man.

After a bit, Patience reached up and slowly removed the dark glasses. When Johnny quickly turned his face away, she gently drew him back to her, touching the disfigurement with tender, loving fingertips, her mouth moving all the while.

Ben could well imagine her kind and loving words.

And when he thought she could display no greater love, Patience found Johnny's hands and lifted them to her face, inviting him to touch, to see with his gifted fingers.

As if in a daze of rapture, Johnny began to explore the beauty he'd only imagined, the beauty she now offered only to him.

Heart full, Benjamin closed the drapes and turned away, leaving them to their privacy and their newfound love. He reached in his pocket and withdrew the blue marble.

"All is well, my brother," he said softly. "All is well."

CHAPTER 34

Present Day. Honey Ridge

Grayson stared into the calm, unassuming creek as his mind replayed the events of that fateful night over a hundred fifty years ago. An ache centered in his chest.

"Tragic. In so many ways."

Here on the creek bank the hum of voices and clatter of construction carried on, but Grayson heard none of it. He heard, instead, the terrified cries of an innocent woman and felt the desperation of a young boy forced to take the only possible action to stop a heinous act.

Inside his head, the tumblers slowly clicked into place. The skeleton buried in the basement. The unusual musical scores. Even the odd mix of pathos and happiness in Patience's compositions.

He understood now.

Hands dangling between his knees, he swiveled toward Lem, eager to know the details so he could fit all the parts into one solid whole.

"Your grandfather told you this story?"

"He and my daddy. Passed it down, so to speak."

"Then Tandy must be your ancestor, your great-grandfather."

Lem hitched his chin toward Valery, mustache curled the slightest bit. "Figured that one out right quick, didn't he?"

She didn't look at Grayson, and for that small reprieve, Grayson was glad. He wasn't ready for the tidal wave of emotion she engendered in him, not here on the creek bank with the past swirling around them like foam from the waterfall. This was Patience and Tandy's moment, not theirs. He doubted they would have any more moments between them.

"Heartbreaking." Valery's voice was soft and sad. Like his heart.

He didn't know why she'd come to the mill. Surely, not to see him, not after the last episode when she'd returned home too drunk to make sense. Not after she'd been with someone else. He had gotten the message loud and clear. She liked him, but he wasn't the only man in her life.

The truth of that had burned in his mind like a forest fire, threatening to consume him.

Regardless, his foolish, foolish heart had leaped like a gazelle when he'd seen her slip-sliding on silver ballet flats down the incline toward him. When he thought they were over, she reappeared looking too beautiful and alive to ignore.

Something deep and dark troubled her. Something from the past. Like Patience, she held herself away.

Funny how things that happened long ago reverberated through the ages to affect today.

He could relate to that.

Valery could relate as well, though her silence frustrated him. The moment they'd met in the foyer of Peach Orchard Inn, they had connected on some elemental level. Past wounds. Past scars.

He wanted her to go away. He'd crumble if she did.

Desperate not to drink in her perfume or fall at her feet and grovel, he directed his remarks to Lem. "The baby Tandy's wife carried, was he your grandpa?"

"Yes, sir. He was. The first of five children."

Valery spoke again, and Grayson fought not to look at her. He lost the battle.

"Your great-grandfather lived on this property. Right here. He would have worked inside the mill and fished in that creek."

"Kinda nice to see how round the world is at times. Full circle, as they say." Lem smacked his lips together in a satis-fied sound. "I like thinking about my kin sitting right here on this rock to fish and ponder. Likely even took a swim now and then."

Lem was as rooted to this land as a river birch. No wonder he came and went as he pleased, unconcerned about trespassing.

"And right here in this creek was where Tandy washed bloodstains from the pitchfork." Valery shivered. "I can't get that picture out of my head. A boy so young forced to do such an unthinkable act."

"To protect Patience in a way he couldn't protect his mother." Grayson understood the sacrifice. Love made a man do crazy things, even when the man had been a boy. "He did his best for her. The death, the burial, even cleaning away the evidence, not knowing his devotion would send him far away."

"But to have to kill and then be forced to bury the body and clean the pitchfork. Edgar Portland was a horrible man." She shuddered again, her face stricken.

This tender heart, caring soul, who mourned for the lost babies of Peach Orchard, now mourned for Tandy. "No ar-gument there."

From the opposite creek bank Oats, the spaniel, plunged into the pool. Ripples worked wide rings in their direction as the happy dog paddled her way across the water.

Long ago, blood had washed from the pitchfork and ebbed from this creek out to the river and beyond. Blood and death.

"He was only a boy."

"Heartache don't know age, child." Lem speared Valery with his pale eyes. "But I suspect you understand that better than most."

Valery glanced away, pensive, silent.

Even Lem recognized her inner pain, and Grayson wouldn't be a bit surprised if the old geezer knew the reasons. Not that he'd let Grayson in on the secret. Like his forefather, his lips were sealed.

Whatever drove her, Valery didn't find him important enough to tell.

"Your roots are right here on this property." Grayson circled a finger around the setting. "You're a Portland."

"I guess that's about right. Edgar was Tandy's father, so the master, sorry as he was, would have been my great-great-grandpappy, and Miss Patience was Tandy's aunt." Lem chuckled. "I haven't wrangled out what kin she and I would be, but Mama said my blue eyes came from the Portlands even though one of my other grandmothers was as Irish as a potato. Figure all that out and win a prize at the county fair."

Grayson had never noticed Lem's color one way or the other. All he'd seen was an ancient, blue-eyed man deeply tanned and wrinkled by the sun. Now he saw a man with deep history running through his veins.

He did the mental calculations. The years and numbers added up. Through Tandy, Lem was a Portland. As stunning as the story, Lem was a direct descendant of the slave boy who'd killed a rapist and helped bury him beneath the mill. Grayson's mill. He was also the descendant of a ruthless slaveholder. Life was a tangle sometimes.

"Once upon a time, all things being equal, this property would have belonged to you."

Lem waved off the idea.

"All that's water over the wheel, son. I got no claim. Don't want none. Portlands sold out long ago and moved on. Tandy did all right without Portland money and so have I." He rubbed his whiskers, mustache twitching. "Surprises you, doesn't it?"

He had to admit it did, but then, Lem Tolly was full of surprises, and if he'd learned one thing from repurposing old buildings, it was not to judge a book by the cover.

"That said, I wouldn't mind having a thick steak now and then from that restaurant of yours when it opens up."

Grayson's mouth tipped. "Carte blanche." And then, "On the house."

"I know what it means, son. *Parley voo francay.*" Lem slapped his leg.

The trio chuckled at the gross mispronunciation.

"But the story's not finished, Mr. Tolly." Valery hooked a chestnut curl behind one ear. Silver bracelets caught the sunlight and glinted. "What about Patience? Did she tell Johnny about that night?"

"Eventually. As Ben predicted, Johnny was furious but not with Patience. You see, he loved her with all his soul. He only wanted her and what was good for her. With him and her strong faith, she was able to put that night behind her and grab hold of the good man right in front of her."

"They married?" Valery's eyes grew moist. Grayson looked away. She affected him too much.

"They married, had two young ones and lived good long lives together. Story goes that they doted on each other into old age and died only a few days apart."

"Neither wanted to be without the other."

"Appears so."

Valery put a hand to her heart. "How incredibly romantic. After the suffering they had both been through, they found happiness together. Now that we know her story, her music makes sense, doesn't it, Grayson?"

"Every emotion is there," he answered. "From darkest despair to sweetest joy."

"Love made all the difference." Her brown eyes held his. "Love and faith in herself and in him."

Grayson swallowed, unable to look away, his heart yearning toward her. "She trusted him to love her anyway."

"And he did," she murmured softly. "He loved her in spite of her past."

Something in her words made his heart throb. "It's what a real man would do."

She blinked and sat up straight, mouth slightly open. Suddenly, she leaped to her feet. "I have to go."

"Valery?" He put out a hand. Something had shifted. Something was happening. She couldn't leave now.

Valery shook her head, hair flying, bracelets shining. Then she scrambled up the incline and left him on the creek bank, bewildered again.

Valery drove back to the inn with revived hope singing in her heart. No wonder Patience's sheet music moved her so deeply. Patience knew heartache and loss far deeper than anything Valery had ever experienced. Yet she'd made a conscious decision to release the bitterness and choose faith, forgiveness and love as the watchwords in her life. Like Valery, she'd felt unworthy of a good man's love, but somehow she'd found the strength within to reach out anyway. Johnny had welcomed her with open arms.

If a nineteenth-century woman with few options could find such strength, so could Valery.

"Grayson loves me," she said to the windshield. "I know he does, and I love him."

But what if love wasn't enough? What if he rejected her?

Patience had borne the same worries. By telling Johnny, she risked the secret shame, risked her family's reputation, risked rejection and worse.

"Everything turned out for the best. They loved each other. They grew old together."

She wanted to grow old with Grayson Blake.

And what of Tandy? Wasn't he like Patience in many ways?

Even though the circumstances of that horrid night cost him a great deal, he'd not only escaped slavery, he'd become a free and successful man. He hadn't clung to bitterness against his father or the fate that had sent him far away from everything he loved. He'd chosen to embrace the opportunities life offered and thrived because of it.

Lem Tolly was living proof of that.

Just as Patience trusted Johnny with the truth about herself and the rape, Valery knew she could find the courage to tell Grayson.

She would, and she would hope and pray he hadn't already washed his hands of her.

But before she could ask his forgiveness, she first had to forgive her mother and herself. She had to take charge of her own life.

Instead of turning into the drive at Peach Orchard Inn, she aimed the Toyota toward Honey Ridge and her mother's house.

Her palms grew sweaty against the steering wheel, and she prayed all through town, past the bakery and Sassy Sister's Boutique, past the red light in the center of Main Street, and down Cedar Street to the handsome brick home where she'd grown up.

She drew in a deep breath to calm the swarm of butterflies in her belly and marched up to the front door.

"Mama!" She pushed the doorbell and turned the knob. "Mom! Where are you?"

Connie Carter appeared from the left hallway, a frown between her eyebrows. "What's wrong? Why are you yelling?"

She hadn't meant to. "Sorry. I need to say something."

Caution crossed her mother's face. "If this is about the other day—"

"It is. Please, listen this time."

"We've talked enough. The subject is closed."

Anger bubbled up inside Valery. The subject was always closed. Every painful topic was swept under the perfectly tidy rug.

She opened her mouth to argue and then clapped it shut again.

Patience and Tandy had chosen the high road. They'd forgiven and let go of the past.

With renewed courage, she walked the four steps that separated them and closed a sixteen-year gap as she wrapped her arms around her mother and whispered, "I forgive you. Will you forgive me, too?"

Connie burst into tears. "I've been thinking about you all week. My heart is broken for you, and I don't know what to do anymore."

"Just let me talk, Mama. Let me share my heart and my dreams and my desires. I *need* you to hear me…and I need your help."

Her mother nodded, sniffling as she pulled away to grab a tissue.

Valery found her own cheeks wet. "Make that two."

With a watery smile, Connie handed over the tissue. "I promise to listen this time."

She didn't understand the change in her mother, but she was not about to question it. So, as tears flowed, she talked. About her love for Grayson and how he'd given her the desire to dance again. About the child she'd given up for adoption. About her battle with alcohol.

"I want to go to counseling at the church. Will you go with me?"

Connie already shook her head. "Carters don't air their problems outside the family. You know how we are."

She'd expected that answer. Every problem in her life—the men, the booze, the mistakes—wrapped around that awful time when she'd gotten pregnant and given up her child. Nothing would ever be right again until she found peace with her past.

"I can't fix what's broken all by myself. I've tried. And even if he'd have me, I won't saddle Grayson with my issues. I want to be a woman he's proud of, a woman who stands tall beside him."

Connie's chin hitched a notch higher. "Any man worth his salt should appreciate you. If he doesn't, he's a fool."

A glimmer of a smile peeked out among Valery's tears. *Mama. Oh, Mama.* Defender and destroyer all in one well-groomed package.

"I love you."

"I love you, too, darling girl. If I made mistakes along the way, I never meant harm. All I ever wanted was your happiness." She glanced down, shoulders slumped. "For all my good intentions, I failed you."

The admission gave Valery the wings she'd clipped long ago. "I failed, too, but we can fix things. I'm going to counseling because I must. I'm sorry that upsets you, but alone or with you, I'm going."

Her mother nodded, silent for a long, painful moment. Then, lips trembling, she said, "I understand."

With a final hug, Valery left her mother standing in the doorway, face stained with tears and a Kleenex clutched in one hand. She waved as Valery drove away.

First to the church to make a counseling appointment with Pastor Ramsey and to sign up for the next AA meeting. Then to the inn to await Grayson. They had a lot to talk about.

She prayed Grayson would give her another chance, like Johnny had given to Patience and she to him. She prayed that he would understand and forgive.

But there was only one way to find out.

Grayson believed in making up time when he could. He'd wasted too much of it sitting on the creek bank listening to Lem. Not that he regretted the hour spent. But after Valery and Lem had left, he remained at the mill long after the contractors packed up their tools and headed home for the night. Devlin stayed until his belly growled and then abandoned him with a laugh and a wave and the word, "Sucker."

Grayson had waved him away. He was a workaholic, but why not? Nothing else to do around here, not now that he'd decided Valery was not the woman for him.

He still didn't understand why she had come to the creek, but the way she'd bolted told him plenty.

A pain jabbed him under the rib cage. He'd thought she was the one. Had wanted her to be since he was fifteen years old. But he clearly wasn't as important to her as he'd believed.

While he worked, he ruminated about Valery and also on Lem's story about Patience and Tandy. By the time he returned to the inn, night lay over the lawn, and bright rectangles of yellow light beckoned him to rest. The house, like a motherly presence, waited for her children to come home.

He'd no more than taken off his boots when he noticed an envelope on the floor inside his door. Curious, he opened it. Valery's exotic scent lifted from the folded vellum card. In black cursive filled with loops and curlicues, she had written:

You are cordially invited to a picnic in the dark. We need to talk. Call me if you are willing. Text me if the answer is no. I'm waiting. Love, V.

A picnic in the dark. His lips curved. Leave it to Valery to be creative.

He read the note again, pondering. Should he? Or should he let this thing go before they both got hurt worse than they already were?

With a shake of his head, he knew the answer before he asked the question. Valery was worth the effort. One more chance. One more try.

She wanted to talk. That had to mean something.

He reached for his cell phone and dialed her number.

Forty-five minutes later, he followed her instructions out the back door and into the peach orchard. The powerful scent of budding peaches sweetened the journey toward a twinkle of lights.

"Impressive," he said as he entered the small clearing.

Strings of tiny white lights draped from tree limbs and a glowing lantern dangled above a small table set with crisp white linen and gleaming china. A squat candle flickered between small pots of flowers. Lilacs, he thought, from the fragrance.

Valery stood beside the table, hands clasped in front of her like a nervous child in a Christmas play.

"If the mosquitoes don't eat us. But the candle is citronella."

"That should help." He wanted to ease her nerves, though he suffered a few of his own.

"Are you hungry?"

"Starved. No lunch. Lem took up too much of my day."

"I wondered why you were so late." From an insulated bag, she withdrew two plates, set them on the table and removed the lids. The smell of fried chicken made his mouth water.

"You've been waiting long?"

She waved away the notion. "No big deal. Come on. Sit down and eat. The food is still warm and the drinks are cold."

He pulled out her chair and then took his own. "You smell as good as the chicken."

Her smile flashed. "So do you."

A shower worked wonders. "It's beautiful out here. I've never been on a night picnic."

"Me either." Honeyed eyes glanced at him and then back to the liquid gurgling into stemmed glasses as she poured their drinks. "Peach tea. I hope that's all right."

"Perfect." He touched the lavender flowers. "My grand-mother loved these." And because of her, he loved them, too.

"Actually, these are hers. I cut them at the farm. I didn't think anyone would mind."

Something tilted in his chest. She'd driven all the way to the farm to choose flowers she knew he would appreciate. Sentimental flowers. Meaningful flowers.

He put his hand over hers. "Thank you. Grandma would be pleased. Tickled pink, she'd say."

Valery gave a breathy laugh and withdrew her hand.

He tucked into the meal, contemplating. A strange tension hung in the air. He couldn't quite put his finger on the cause, but Valery was anxious. So was he.

She'd chosen the cover of darkness on purpose. Awful truths were easier to confess in the intimate confines of night. A full belly and a romantic setting with nature's night music around them gave her courage.

She hadn't been this uncertain since she'd signed the papers giving away her daughter.

She watched him eat and picked at her own meal. Hunger evaded her. She was too full of the secret bursting to be released.

Somehow she managed a cordial conversation. They talked of Lem Tolly's heartrending tale and of the skeleton his crew had discovered. Of Patience and Johnny and Tandy. When he told her he'd figured out the key to the cryptograms, she wasn't surprised. His incredible intellect was part of his attraction.

"Lem's story filled in the blanks. When I knew I was reading a war message and not a love note, everything fell into place."

"What do the notes say?"

"She shared the movement of Union troops toward Nashville. Places and dates, troops and generals."

Fascinated, Valery asked, "Where would she have learned those things?"

"As Lem said, she must have begun when the Union troops used the house as a hospital. After their departure, William Gadsden wrote to Charlotte. Patience read those letters and passed along any information she could glean that might help the Confederacy."

"Amazing." She dabbed greasy fingers on a napkin. "And, though she didn't know at the time, none of her messages made any difference at all."

"No. They didn't."

"Had she known the war's outcome, she could have been spared a great deal. A man wouldn't have died, and a boy would not have been exiled."

"But she didn't know, and that's a lesson for us, I suppose." He gestured with a chicken leg. "We can't look into the future. We only have now. Even when something we've done turns out badly, we have to believe we did the right thing in that moment."

Would he still believe that when she told him?

Troubled and mulling, Patience's past forgotten and her own looming large, Valery picked at her food while Grayson finished his.

Finally, he folded his napkin and leaned toward her across the narrow table. The candle flickered, bathing his face in gold shadow. "Thank you for this. After the other night I thought…"

He let the words fall away, unnecessary. They both knew what had happened. Now, he was giving her an opening to explain, to make things right between them.

Anxiety slithered down Valery's spine in gooseflesh. It was now or never. As much as she'd prefer to run, she was not leaving this orchard until he knew everything. If afterward he walked away, her heart would break, but she would survive.

She cleared her throat and gripped the linen napkin. "I owe you a huge apology. Grayson, I am so very sorry."

"No apology needed, though one is appreciated. I just want you to be okay."

"Nothing happened that night." She rolled her eyes, self-deprecating. "Except me getting toasted. What I mean is, I wasn't with another man."

Blue eyes lit with candle gold held hers. Was that hurt she detected? Had he believed the worst of her?

"This is no excuse, but I was upset about something. Stupid, I know, to run to a bar to soothe my anger, but I intended to have only one drink." She looked down at the wadded napkin.

"And things got out of hand." His words coaxed, understanding without judgment. Or at least they sounded that way to Valery.

"Things always get out of hand. I can't seem to control myself even when I want to."

"My mother was the same. She couldn't handle the situation alone. She needed help. Maybe you do, too."

Her sigh whispered on the night air. "I finally faced that truth. Because of you. I don't want to hurt you."

"I don't want you to hurt yourself."

"That's why, today, when I left the mill, I made a counseling appointment with my pastor and signed up for AA meetings at the church."

His fingers twined with hers. "Want me to go with you?"

Her heart stuttered and then flooded with love. "You would, wouldn't you?"

"Whatever you need to get well." His soft smile was warm and tender. "You don't need alcohol to be incredible. You already are. That's the woman I want."

He couldn't have said anything that encouraged her more. Her battered self-esteem rose a notch like a flag testing the wind and hoping for calm.

Maybe, just maybe, he'd be as understanding about the rest.

More nervous than when she'd auditioned for Nashville, Valery rose and moved slightly away from the lantern light. Arms tight over her chest, she couldn't look into his face and say the words. The truth was too hard, too dangerous. All the what-ifs and insecurities crowded in to choke her.

Grayson stayed where he was, but she could feel his gaze against her back.

"There's something else I have to tell you, and if you hate me afterward, I'll understand."

"Nothing you say will make me hate you." She heard the

scooted chair and felt him move in her direction. When his long, pianist's hands lightly touched her shoulders, she shivered.

"I'm crazy about you, Valery. I have been since I was a gangly teenager."

She took a step forward into the darkness and felt his hands fall away. "Hear me out. You may change your mind."

"I don't think so. Not if you care for me, too."

Her eyes dropped shut. Care for him? The phrase was too mild. She'd begun to breathe again when he was near. She'd begun to see colors and feel hope and believe in the future.

"I do," she whispered. "Oh, I do."

He touched her again. His fingers wrapped around her upper arms and pulled her back against him. She longed to lean into his strength and absorb his steadiness. Grayson was rock solid and secure, steady as the rising sun. She wanted to have that, too.

"Does this have to do with why you refuse to dance?"

She nodded, throat thick. "Dance was my life. I wanted it more than anything."

"Ambition isn't wrong."

"Mine was. I was willing to give up anything and every-thing for a dance career." She hung her head, contemplating the dark ground and the darker place in her soul. "And I did. I gave up the greatest gift of all."

He remained quiet, holding her against him as if his lion's heart could beat through to hers and give her courage.

She shuddered and sucked in a long, long breath, feeling the rhythm of his heart against her back, drawing strength from him.

"When I was sixteen, I didn't go to New York to study dance, even though that was the story Mama told everyone."

"Where were you?"

"Savannah." She gripped her fingers together in a knot. "In a maternity home. I had a baby, Grayson."

He flinched but didn't back away. Instead, his arms came around her, and he kissed the top of her ear. "Boy or girl?"

Tears welled in her eyes. "Girl. She was beautiful."

"How can she be anything else?" Slowly, he swiveled her around to face him, expression so tender that tears began to slide down her cheeks. "You were a kid, Valery. It happens."

"You don't know everything."

"Then tell me."

So he could know the worst. So he could see what an awful person she really was. He'd run then. Or ridicule and abuse her. She'd been down that road before.

As if her thoughts winged across time, a melody began to play. Perhaps the song was in her head, perhaps not, but the music reminded her of Patience. She had faced her greatest fears and come out the victor.

Grayson cupped her chin and kissed her forehead, quietly encouraging.

"Mama convinced me to give her up. She said I would never realize my potential as a dancer with a child clinging to my hip. My career would be over."

"A tough call all the way around. You were sixteen. Your mother was probably scared and worried. There were no easy answers."

"I know. I know. I was far too young to make such a life-changing decision alone. So I let Mama make it for me. We chose our family's reputation and my dance future over my precious baby girl."

"And you've never forgiven yourself."

"I'm so ashamed. Not of her, but of myself for giving her away. After Mikey was abducted the guilt nearly ate me alive—" She dropped her head again. "Life makes no sense sometimes."

"You thought this would make a difference to me? That I would judge you or hate you for a choice you made when you were a teenager?" He tilted her chin upward, searching her face with his gaze. "I could never hate you. Quite the opposite. You've held my heart for a long time. All I ask is that you keep it safe."

A smile spread over her face and through her being. "And you have mine." She placed her hand on his chest, scarcely believing her good fortune in finding this incredible man. "Thank you for understanding, for caring."

"You didn't make it easy." But his gentle smile forgave her.

"I know, I know, and I'm sorry. I still have a lot of junk to work through before I can be the person I want to be. You deserve my best."

"We'll work through the junk together."

Did he really mean those words?

She took the plunge. "Will you go to counseling with me? At least a couple of times? I'm really scared to go alone."

He touched his lips to her forehead. "I'll go as many times as you want me. Whatever you need."

She needed to find her daughter. She needed permission to dance again. But kicking the booze came first. Her daughter deserved to meet a sober, dependable birth mother. She wanted her child to be proud.

"I love you, Grayson."

His smile rivaled the lantern light, and they kissed, melting into one another with passion and relief.

The music in her heart grew louder. Grayson pulled away, head tilted as if he listened, too. "Hear that?"

She nodded. Patience's music, a beautiful waltz, lilted on the wind. "I thought I was imagining."

"Then we're imagining together." He swung her into waltz position and began to move across the grass.

She gave herself up to the music, to him. He held her close so that their hearts beat as one and his breath mingled with hers. He kissed her neck and cheeks and lips a hundred times, and she responded in kind as they swirled and twirled and dipped.

The golden glow of the lantern pushed back the darkness while overhead silver stars twinkled and the moon smiled down at the pair, giving its blessing, giving permission.

And they danced on into the night.

EPILOGUE

Eight months later. Honey Ridge, Tennessee

Opening night took on a whole new meaning.

Valery slipped a diamond stud into her ear and stepped back to observe the woman in the mirror. She ran a hand down the side of the sleek red cocktail dress.

Behind her, having come into her room to see if she was ready, Grayson looked on, a soft smile on his handsome, handsome face.

Valery's heart squeezed with love for this good man who'd opened her eyes to so much.

"You're gorgeous." The glow in his expression was bright enough to light her inside and out.

She straightened his tie, though the silk Hermes didn't need adjusting. She simply wanted an excuse to touch him, though she needed none.

"I had to spiff up since I'm *almost* officially engaged to the brilliant, incredibly handsome and suave owner of Blake Brothers Old Mill Restaurant." In black tux and red bow tie, he made her heart sing. And dance.

Tonight the elegantly rustic restaurant held its grand opening and, in the private dining room upstairs, an engagement party. They'd intentionally waited for the grand opening to officially announce their engagement, though no one in Honey Ridge would be surprised.

She'd never dreamed she could be this happy and fulfilled. Through pastoral counseling and AA she'd learned to accept her past and move forward without the need of alcohol. She'd learned to like Valery Carter again.

Grayson held her by the upper arms. "I'm proud of you."

She glanced to the side, proud, too, but humbled by his love and confidence. "Clean and sober for eight months. I couldn't have gotten here without you."

He'd attended every AA meeting, sometimes driving from Nashville to be with her.

"Yes, you could have."

He was right, of course. Her brainy man usually was. She was strong now. Maybe she had always been strong and hadn't known it. But Grayson's support had given her wings, in more ways than one.

He'd flown with her to Savannah and held her shaky hand while she'd submitted a written request to the Georgia Adoption Reunion Registry. At age eighteen, if her daughter chose, she could inquire about her birth mother. Valery didn't want to disrupt her child's life, but she wanted her to know that she was loved and the reunion door was wide open. Someday she would meet her child. Until then, she'd wonder and wait, praying for that phone call. For now, she'd done all in her power and could leave the rest to God, a lesson from AA that had brought her great peace.

Grayson's hand slid down her arm to grasp her fingers. "Come up on the balcony with me."

"I thought we needed to go soon."

"Humor me. I have a present for you, and I'm trying to be romantic."

"Ooh, I'm all about romance." She laughed. "And gifts!"

"Grab your shawl."

She also grabbed an envelope from her vanity and followed Grayson up the stairs and out onto the upper gallery. She barely noticed the chilly weather. Not when the stars sparkled and across the way the glow of lights illuminated the sky above the Old Mill Restaurant.

Cars motored on the road in between, dozens of them, heading to the grand opening. He and Devlin had done it. They'd repurposed the derelict building into an elegantly rustic eatery. She couldn't be prouder for him.

Tonight was special in so many ways.

Turning slightly to face her, Grayson reached inside his jacket. "I want to give this to you now when we're alone."

He held a thick manila envelope.

Valery laughed, feeling soft and tender. "I have a gift for you, too."

From behind her back, she withdrew a letter-sized envelope.

His smile was tender.

"You first." She handed over the envelope, eager to see his reaction. She wasn't disappointed. His eyes widened with wonder as he read.

"Uncle Chuck agreed to sell the farm?"

"It took a little wheedling and a call from Mama, but this is his official acceptance of the down payment."

"Your mom? What? How?"

"My mother is a powerful woman." She chuckled at the expression on his face. "It turns out, your uncle and my mother went to high school together and at one time were a thing." She put the word "thing" into quotes.

"He still carries a torch for her?"

"I didn't ask. I simply let her work her magic. She was thrilled, Grayson, to do this for you. For me." As if her mother needed to make up for past mistakes, she'd gone out of her way to secure Chuck's promise to sell. "When he found out his nephew was engaged to Mama's daughter, he capitulated."

"Does this mean you've changed your mind about living in Nashville? Because if it does, you may not like *my* present."

"We've already talked that one over and agreed on Nashville as home base. That's where your business is, and I love the city. All that shopping!" She laughed at his grimace. "The farm at Honey Ridge will be our weekend getaway where you can relax and escape the pressures." She gave the top of his shoulders a quick massage. "No more tech neck and antacids for my future husband. I want you around for a long, long time."

Julia and Eli had the inn under control. She was no longer needed here, and wherever Grayson went, that's where she wanted to be; but Honey Ridge was good for him, and she wouldn't let him go back to his former driven, uptight lifestyle.

"I don't even know what to say. I hated seeing Pappy's farm abandoned."

"Maybe one day we'll retire there, and the grandkids can come visit the way you and Devlin did."

"No wonder I'm marrying you. You're brilliant." He pushed a bigger, thicker envelope toward her. "Open yours. We seem to be on the same wavelength."

Excited, she flipped the clasp and took out a sheaf of legal-looking papers.

"What is this...? Oh!" Valery gasped. "Oh, Grayson."

She could barely breathe from the thrill. To slow the pounding of her heart, she clutched the papers to her chest. "My studio. You bought the building for my studio."

"The day we were in Nashville and you went wild over this place, I saw the possibilities."

She whacked him on the chest with the papers. "You never let on! I thought you didn't like the place."

"I didn't want to get your hopes up until I was certain we could make the deal."

"I can't believe it. My own dance studio." She flung her arms around his neck, tears starting. "Oh, now I'm ruining my makeup."

Chuckling softly, he pushed her back enough to kiss away the happy tears. "I love you, future Mrs. Blake. Only happy tears from now on."

"I love you, piano man." She tossed her hair back, feeling beautiful and happy enough to fly away like a hot air balloon.

"Ready?" He held out a hand, mouth curved. "For the rest of your life?"

Nodding, heart singing, Valery placed her hand in his. "More than ready."

As they rounded the bottom of the stairs, from somewhere came the sound of lively, happy piano music, a testament to their joy.

Together as one, they paused, exchanged secret smiles, and then ran out into the night.

Behind them, Peach Orchard Inn sighed and the music played on.

★ ★ ★ ★ ★

AUTHOR'S NOTE

In my research for *The Innkeeper's Sister* I was surprised to learn that emancipated slaves dominated a number of businesses after the Civil War including catering, barbering, hospitality, and hairdressing. For example, in 1873 an elegant, successful hotel, The Inter Ocean Hotel, was built in Denver, Colorado, by Barney Ford, a former slave. Ford became Denver's most prominent black businessman. He and his hotel were the inspiration for Tandy's Wellston Hotel.

Cryptography. For millennia, governments, soldiers, diplomats and others have devised methods of sending encrypted messages to protect confidential information. One famous cryptogram, the Caesar Cipher, is attributed to Julius Caesar's military genius. Musicians such as Bach—and my fictional Patience—sometimes created ciphers within their compositions. One simple method was to give notes letter names that ultimately spelled out a message. A key or a very clever codebreaker was needed to decipher the code.

Depression of 1873. The years following the American Civil War were a time of worldwide prosperity, although the American South continued to suffer. Railroads especially prospered and expanded until the industry collapsed in 1873, beginning what is sometimes called the Long Depression. The New York

Stock Exchange shut down for ten days, factories closed, banks closed, many fortunes were lost, and the number of destitute overwhelmed the country. Effects of the 1873 Panic lasted for decades, stirring tensions between labor and management.

Gristmills. During the early days of America, farmers needed a means of grinding their home-grown corn and wheat into flour and meal, so gristmills dotted the landscape. Run by water power, most were built on creeks or rivers with a giant waterwheel used to turn grinding stones that weighed nearly a ton each. Because most everyone required their services, mills became popular places for social gatherings, including parties and picnics.

Bottle Trees. The superstition of creating a "bottle tree" to ward off ghosts and evil spirits is believed to have come to the American South with slaves captured from the Congo. According to Appalachian lore, several bottles, often cobalt blue, are hung upside down on a bush or tree, traditionally crepe myrtle. At night, the "haints," attracted by the color, enter the bottles. Sunlight the next day destroys them or the bottles can be corked and tossed into the river. Today, bottle trees serve primarily as novelty lawn decorations.

Many of you have asked if Mikey, Julia's abducted son, will ever be found. While I would truly love for him to come home, I felt a sudden reappearance would be contrived and not realistic to the story. The child who first inspired *The Memory House* has now been gone for twenty years. As her family says, "love always hopes," and I'm leaving Julia with that promise. Perhaps someday…